I'M ADDICTED TO HIS LOVE

Taniece

To my loving parents, Valerie & James McDaniel & beautiful sister, Sharon Rest In Paradise.

Disclaimer: This is a re-release of Addicted: Street Love Is Everything. If you've already read it, then please skip. If you haven't or would like to read it again, I truly hope you enjoy!

CONTENTS

SANAA LOVE

I pushed the glass door open and flipped the light switch. I stood there at the door observing as the lights slowly turned on from dim to bright. Even after six months, my chest still ached as if it happened yesterday. Tears welled up in my eyes threatening to fall.

The *Glitz* drawn out in silver cursive inscription bounced off the white back wall at me. I tiptoed over to it, tracing my fingertips across the word, sensing tension in my limbs.

"Ma, why did you have to leave me the way you did? You know I can't survive this world without you," I whispered, and the tears finally escaped, pouring down my warm cheeks. I could no longer hold them in.

It's been six months since she's been gone. Six long months since I found her sitting in her pearl white Maserati Ghibli with a bullet between her eyes and a cigarette dangling from her fingertips.

I was supposed to be in the car alongside her, but she sent me back inside the shop to grab her purse she left sitting on her desk. If I didn't know any better, I'd think she knew something was about to happen and didn't want me in harm's way.

My mother, Yonnie was my lifeline. The air that filled my lungs. The only thing I had in this world. Shit, she made up my entire existence and someone had snatched it away from me. Left me pulseless. Trying to figure out how I was going to survive this cruel earth without her.

My eyes danced around the nail shop. It's been shut down ever since my mother was killed. People were out of work for months. In order for me not to lose everything she worked so hard for, I swallowed my sorrow and get up off my ass. This place was my mother's pride and joy and I couldn't let it all go down the drain. Someone needed to step in and run this place. That someone was *me*.

I moved across the white marble floors passing the white nail stations on my right and the silver-studded throne chairs at the pedicure stations on my left. A huge silver chandelier hung over my head. I flipped the open sign on and slipped my tan cardigan off my tense shoulders, tossing it on the arm of one of the chairs.

The door chimed, alerting me someone just entered it. I turned around and was greeted by Mia's bright smile.

"I'm so glad you called and told me last night you were opening this place back up. I hated working for those fools over there at *Glam Nails*," she pulled me in for an embrace. Shortly after, the rest of the girls were filing inside.

"Come on girls, we got a lot of work to get done before clients begin showing up."

"Are you sure they are going to come? We have been shut down for months. *Glam Nails* stole most of Yonnie's clients," Mia replied with her face twisted up.

"All we can do is hope they are loyal enough to my mother to come back." I sighed, taking a deep breath, grabbed my cardigan, and went to the back where her office was located. I needed some time to talk myself into believing this was the right idea.

I pushed the door open to the office that had the same color scheme as the rest of the place; silver and white. I plopped down in the chair behind her desk, resting my face in my palms. I used to come and work at the shop for my mother, but I knew nothing about running this place.

The thought of disappointing her kept seeping into my mind.

"Ma, what am I going to do? I know nothing about keeping this place afloat." I cried.

My brow wrinkled, and I leaned back in her white rolling chair. The tears were coming down nonstop, then I heard my mother's voice creep up into the back of my mind.

"Wipe those got damn tears Sanaa! You got this shit. You can do whatever you put your fucking mind to. We hustlers out here, baby."

I wiped the tears from my eyes with a smile on my face. I swear I missed my mother and her crazy mouth.

Knock! Knock!

I positioned myself upright in the chair, "Come in!"

"Uh, I hate to bother you Sanaa but there's a guy out here for you," Layla, the receptionist announced glancing over her shoulder.

"A guy?" My brow rose.

"Yes, a guy. It's not an average guy either. It's one of the Maserati's."

"You can send him in."

I grabbed the vanity mirror off the desk and checked my face to make sure I didn't have any snot dripping from my nose or dried up tear stains on my cheeks. I rubbed my red nose and stood up from the chair, straightening out the invisible wrinkles in my white floral romper.

I've heard about the Maserati's, but I've never really encountered any of them in person. The things I've heard weren't anything nice either. I don't see how people could get mixed up with those sorts of people. It only intrigued me to know what he was doing here.

My mother dealt with them once a long time ago, so she could pay her mortgage off on the shop. *I know that's not why he was here.*

Layla pushed the door all the way open. "Mr. Maserati."

The most gorgeous specimen adorned my presence. Goosebumps quickly took over my entire body as I gawked up into his face. I felt like a shrimp to a giant. His tall frame towered over my 5'4" physique and I was wearing thigh high boots, so he had to be tall as hell.

Layla was still standing in the doorway being nosey as hell. He pushed it closed in her face then turned his attention back to me. *Rude muhfucka.*

"Ahem," I cleared my throat. It was dry as fuck, possibly from me being thirsty over him. I'd never lusted over a man as much as I was lusting over him. Who could blame me though? He was a good-looking man. "What can I do for you, Mr. Maserati?"

"Mr. Maserati is my father and last time I checked I wasn't him. You can call me Soul."

"*Soul,*" I corrected myself.

"I came to talk to you about the shop." He unbuttoned the buttons on his navy suit jacket and took a seat in the chair that was in front of the desk. I stood still, getting the perfect view of his jet-black 360 waves that were spiraling out of control. "Are you going to sit or just stand there?" he asked, gesturing his vanilla-colored tattooed hand across the desk at my chair.

"Sorry, yes."

I got an empty feeling in the pit of my stomach and wanted to flee out of there, but I stayed to see what he had to say.

"You may or may not know this, but this shop is in our shopping center and it belongs to us..."

"Okay, and?" I cut him off.

"Don't interrupt me while I'm speaking to you."

Who the hell does he think he is?

"Since it's in this area, we will be cleaning our money in here. Someone from the Mafia will drop the cash off to you and you deposit it into the bank. Don't try to steal from me because I know how much will be in those duffels, plus I got eyes and ears everywhere. Just do as you are told, and we shouldn't have any problems." He got up from his seat, buttoning his jacket back up.

"Wait, what!" I jolted up, peering into his dark, almost black eyes.

"You heard everything I said. I'm not repeating myself."

"I'm trying to understand what makes you think I'm going to just agree to this mess? You can't just stroll in here and tell me what I'm going to do and expect me to submit in return."

"I can, and I just did. You don't have much of a choice but to do as I say. Do your job and do it right. I'd hate to put a bullet in that pretty ass face of yours, but I'll do it." He pulled the office door open and disappeared.

GABRIEL "SOUL" MASERATI

Those freckles...

Those beautiful freckles that went from her cheeks and across the bridge of her narrow nose. The tiny specs that moved with every wrinkle of her pierced nose. They were one of her best assets.

Her lips weren't too big nor were they too small. They were just perfect for me.

Her eyes...

My grandmother always told me; the eyes were the windows to the soul. Hers must be the windows to this *Soul*. Slightly slanted, and darker around the outer rim of the pupil but hazel brown in the middle. They drew me in the moment I stepped foot in that office.

Her beautiful gaze was intimidating, but somewhere deep down there was a little girl yearning to be loved. Not by just anyone but by someone like *me*.

She was by far not the average woman I chased. I was used to the women who were extremely curvaceous and wore long hair down their backs.

But Sanaa kept tucking her short blonde hair back behind her pointy-pierced ear. Her entire ear was pierced from the bottom to the top with stud diamond earrings. When I told her not to interrupt me while I was talking, her tawny-beige skin turned beet red. I was certain she wanted to curse me out but held her tongue.

Her right wrist was adorned with a very detailed rose drawn out with Yonnie's name intertwined in it. I wasn't used to women having tattoos but hers was sexy as shit. It made me wonder if she had any more tattoos elsewhere.

"Soul..."

I drifted back from my thoughts of Sanaa. My mind been on her ever since I left out of the shop just hours prior.

"How did it go?" my father, Gabriel questioned me leaning forward onto his massive dark mahogany desk.

"Everything's cool."

"Good, I'd hate to have to put a bullet in her." He picked up the box of Cuban cigars out his desk drawer and tried to hand me one.

"I'm good." I got up from the desk, brushing my hand across my waves. "I'm sure you won't have to worry about any of that with Sanaa."

6

"Better hope not, because I won't hesitate."

"Just stay away from Sanaa. I'll look after her and make sure she stays on the straight and narrow."

"You better," he agreed.

I shook my head, buttoning up my suit jacket then left out of his office.

My father wasn't a big part of the family businesses anymore, so he handled most of his work from home. Whenever there was a meeting with him, it was right there in the comfort of his compound. If he ever stepped foot into one of our establishments, something huge was about to go down or something was wrong.

I made a stop in the kitchen on my way to the front door to say goodbye to my mother. She'd have a fit if I was to leave the house and not say anything to her.

My mother, Vanessa was my beautiful black queen. We were mixed with Italian and African American decent. That's one of the many reasons why women were always falling at our feet.

I stepped into the kitchen, fixing my gold cufflinks on my suit. My mother was busying herself around the kitchen, barking out orders to Alfonso, the family chef and sipping on her a glass of red wine.

When her and my father first got together, she wasn't in love with the idea of having a chef prepare meals for her. Growing up in the hood, she was used to cooking her own food. Might as well say my father was her knight in street king armor. He took her away from the horrible lifestyle she was accustomed to and tossed her into this massive mansion. They been happily together ever since.

"Ma, you have to slave over that man like that? Will you just let him cook?"

"I just want to make sure he's doing it right. I be wanting my food with some flavor. Sometimes he doesn't put enough spices into the food," she responded on her tippy toes, looking over Alfonso's shoulder while he was stirring something in a pot on her stainless-steel stove.

I gripped her by her wrist and pulled her small frame into my body, wrapping my arms around her neck. I kissed her on the top of her head.

"Don't be handling me like that before you make me waste my wine," she fussed, wrinkling her narrow nose.

"If you do then I'll buy you a ton more. I came in here to let you know I was about to leave. I have to get to the house; Sofia is waiting for me."

"Okay, baby I'll see you later." She wrapped her arms around my midsection then I let her go.

I left out the house, hitting the key fob to unlock the doors on my black Lamborghini Aventador and climbed inside. I whipped out the U-shaped driveway onto the streets of St. Louis zigzagging in and out of traffic. I was supposed to been home. Sofia was going to go in on my ass soon I stepped through the door.

I got tired of her thinking there was another girl every time I couldn't answer the phone when she called. Or whenever I was out late handling business. I was a busy man and she knew the moment she got with me.

I loved Sofia, but I wasn't in love with her, that was my only issue. The reason we got together in the first place was off the strength she was full blooded Italian and my father loved her. We were something that had gone completely too far. We'd been together two years, so I had no choice but to love her. She been throwing out little hints here and there about marriage but that damn sure wasn't about to happen. I just played stupid whenever she did it.

I pressed the garage button on my pad which was hooked to the sun visor when I turned onto my street. My house was a little while outside of St. Louis, sitting on acres of land. My neighbors were miles away, just the way I liked them. I didn't really like foreign people all up in my personal space.

I pulled into my ten-car garage and parked. The garage door came down soon as I climbed out the car. I used the entrance in the garage that brought me into the house near the kitchen.

"You're late as usual, Soul. Where have you been?" Sofia quizzed me, popping up out of nowhere. I almost knocked her over when I stepped into the door. She probably was sitting, waiting for me to arrive and jumped up when she heard the garage lift up.

"I had to take care of some business. Let me run in there and shower, then we can go to dinner."

I immediately began undressing, making my way to the staircase that was in the back of the house.

"The least you could have done was called to let me know you were going to be late," she fussed, following closely behind me.

I tossed my jacket onto the bed and tugged at the lower half of my shirt, pulling it out my pants. I unbuttoned my shirt and turned to her. Sofia gazed up at me with her huge chocolate brown eyes. I cupped her beige face.

"I lost track of time. I had a meeting with my father. I'm here now so stop stressing the shit." I let her face go then went into the bathroom, sliding the shower door back and turned on the water. "Bae, grab my black Armani suit out the closet for me!" I yelled out to her over the running water.

Sofia appeared in the doorway with a mug on her face. "Which one? Because, I mean you have like a million of them."

"Just grab one and a black shirt, too." I shut the shower door then stepped underneath the waterfall showerhead. Hopefully, my thoughts of Sanaa would wash down the drain with all the dirt I accumulated from the day. I washed up with my Tom Ford body wash and got out the shower, wrapping a towel around my waist.

My clothes were lying on my California King bed when I stepped out of the bathroom. Sofia sat on the edge of the bed. Her lips pursed together, then she rose.

"What is it Sof?"

As I was getting dressed, I glanced up and saw her pacing, making slight movements with her hands like she was trying to figure out exactly what she wanted to say.

"See, I was wondering if you would change your rules just for one night and allow me to stay the night. I get tired of driving all the way home after nights like this."

"That's a negative. You already know how I feel about that shit Sof."

Not only did I not like foreign people in my personal space, I didn't too much like people in my space at all. I didn't allow Sofia to touch me unless I touched her first. Out of the two years we have been together, she's never spent the night with me. That's probably another reason why she thought I had another woman elsewhere. Which was far from the truth.

"I just don't understand why you're always doing me like this," she whined and plopped back down on the bed, resting her face in her palms. Her long, off-black hair fell into her face.

"It's nothing personal Sofia, you know that."

"But I just want to stay one night, Soul. Just one night," her voice cracked as she spoke.

"No."

I pulled my suit jacket on and stepped in front of her, placing my grandfather's gold links on. Sofia lifted her head and her gaze met mine.

"Will you dry your eyes and fix your makeup? I don't want you going out of the house looking like that. I'll be waiting for you in the car." I pecked her softly on the lips and left out the room.

NAOMI COPELAND

Sanaa was more than my best friend. More along the lines of my sister. We been in each other's lives ever since Pre-K, and I didn't have any plans of going anywhere any time soon. Some people find their soulmates in relationships. Well, she was my soulmate, sort of. Best friend soulmate, that is.

We had this strong connection with each other, almost twin-like in a sense. Whenever something was wrong with her, I could feel it. Like at the very moment. Sadness washed over my body out of nowhere. I got this urge to be near Sanaa and that's exactly what I did. I got up out the middle of my Psychology class and rushed over to *Glitz*.

"Everyone stop what you're doing, the bestie has arrived!" I sang when I pushed the door open with my arms in the air. All eyes fell on me, some even rolled, but I just waved it off. I didn't want to end up whooping someone's ass then they be ready to sue Sanaa. She already had too much on her plate as it is.

My eyes roamed around the salon, hoping to land on Sanaa but I didn't see her anywhere. "Where's Sanaa?" I asked Layla, who was at the receptionist desk on the computer.

"She's in the office. Has been for most of the day." She looked over her shoulder to make sure no one was listening on before she continued. "Ever since one of the Maserati's stopped by here. I don't know what was said but she's been in there about to pull her hair out."

"I'll go see what's going on. Thanks."

Just as I thought, something was bothering my bestie and I needed to cheer her up.

Sanaa and I spent most of our days in the nail salon with Yonnie, so I already knew where the office was. I knew where a lot of things were located here as a matter of fact.

I pulled my Sony digital camera out my bag when I reached her office door and turned it on. Videoing was a hobby of mine. Actually, it was my passion. I loved recording the simple interactions people shared with each other on a day to day basis, then watching them later.

"Who's that beautiful girl sitting behind that desk?" A bright smile appeared on Sanaa's face.

"What are you doing here?" she questioned, tucking her hair back behind her ear. She always had a habit of doing that, especially when she was nervous. Her hair was cut in a pixie cut but she been letting it grow out.

"I came to check on you. I know this was your first day as head bitch in charge and I just wanted to make sure you were alright." I shut the camera, placing it back into my bag. "What's this I hear about one of the Maserati's coming up here? Was it Berlin?"

"No, it was *Soul*." She added emphasis on his name. He must had her feeling some type of way.

I was hoping it would have been Berlin. I've never seen any of the Maserati's in person but the way the streets were talking about Berlin, I wouldn't mind meeting him just to see if he was actually the way they described him to be.

"But what did he want?"

She sighed a deep breath, then rested her elbows on the desk, holding her tiny head up. "He told me I have to clean money here for him. When I asked what made him think I was going to agree to it, he told me I didn't have much of a choice and he was serious as hell too. I don't know what I'm going to do."

"You going to clean the money. The fuck you thought you were going to do? Might need some excitement in your life to take your mind off you know..."

I didn't want to say her mother's name because she was still kind of down behind her death. I couldn't imagine what she was going through. I was hurting but not as bad as she was. Yonnie was like a second mother to me with as much as I was around.

"I just don't want to mess up and end up losing Ma's salon. I'd never forgive myself if anything was to ever happen to this place." She sighed again, and her eyes danced around the office.

"You won't. I got your back. If you have to do it then I'll be right here helping you. I promise you; we'll do whatever it takes to keep this place." I gripped her arm, gently squeezing it to assure her everything was all right. "Sit in here and take all the time you need to get yourself together. I'll go out there and see what I can do."

"You're not going back to class?"

"No, they weren't talking about shit anyway. They were putting me to sleep in that muhfucka." I hooked her chin when I got up from the chair and flashed her a smile.

"Naomi..." she called out when I reached the door.

"Yeah?"

"Thanks for always being there for me. I don't know what I'd do without you."

"No problem boo."

11

I stayed at the salon for the remainder of the day with Sanaa, just helping out wherever I could so she wouldn't have much stress on her. The shop finally come to closing time. All the girls cleaned their stations and dipped.

Sanaa was at the desk, cleaning the cash register out as I swept the floor.

"You did alright today, babes. Do you really think you won't be able to do this?"

She touched the base of her neck. "I mean, I really don't know."

I stopped sweeping the floor and briefly glanced over at her, resting my chin on the top of my hand. "I think you'll be a kick-ass boss though, Sanaa. You just have to see the shit yourself."

"Maybe you're right. I'm just beating myself up for no reason."

"There isn't a *maybe*. I know I'm right."

I rested the broom up against one of the stations and Sanaa shut the register. I climbed into one of the pedicure chairs and watched as she counted the earnings she made for the day. It wasn't a huge day, but I was certain once everyone found out the shop was back up and running, they'd come flying back.

"What do you have to do now?"

"Nothing, just lock this money up in the safe, then lock up the shop."

"Do you want me to do it for you?" She looked exhausted and could barely keep her eyes open.

"No, it's fine. I got it."

"Well, call me as soon as you make it home, so I'll know you made it safely." I got up from my chair, hugged her then left out the door.

BERLIN MASERATI

"That's the shit I'm talking about."

I was sitting in the Jacuzzi relaxing out on the balcony of my condo. I took a swig of my Louis Xiii while watching the two bad bitches I picked up earlier from the strip club wind their hips to Drake's *"Nice for What"* playing loudly in the background. Both were topless with their perky breasts on full display in nothing but a thong.

My dick stood at full attention watching the twins feel all over each other. Their hands were slowly roaming across each other's body, not sparing a single crook or curve. I grabbed my blunt out the ashtray, firing up the tip of it. I took a couple tokes, letting the smoke invade my lungs then blew it out.

"Bring y'all fine asses over here," I demanded, guzzling down some more of the liquor.

They both flashed me their beautiful smiles and climbed over into the hot tub with me. One sat on either side of me. The one on the right took the bottle out my hand. I took another pull from the L and the one on the left pulled my face to hers, locking lips with me. I blew the smoke into her mouth and she blew it out.

I kissed the other, shoving my tongue into her mouth. I explored every inch of her mouth I could reach. Twin number two's hand went underneath the water, gripping my dick inside my Versace briefs.

"Él está trabajando con un monstruo (He's working with a monster)!"

"English baby girl. I don't speak that el Taco Bell shit."

"She only said she likes the size of your dick," twin number one responded and the other nodded with a grin on her face.

"What's your names again, shorty?"

"I'm Camelia and that's Jimena. How many times do we have to tell you our names?"

"What I'm about to do to you, names ain't even going to be important shorty. Show me something sexy," I ordered, then put the blunt out in the ashtray relaxing back against the hot tub.

They both moved in front of me. Camelia cupped Jimena's face and shoved her tongue down her throat.

"Give me a little more action."

Jimena pecked Camelia softly on the lips, then left a trail of sweet kisses down to her caramel candy drop nipple before slipping it into her mouth. I gripped my dick listening to the tender moans escaping from Camelia's mouth. I was about to fuck the shit out of both of them. They were going to be so sprung on the dick that they were going to be begging me to drop the dick off in their pussy again by the time I was done.

"The hell is going on here!" Megan yelled from the doorway.

I was so wrapped up in the twins I didn't even hear her come in.

"What does it look like? You got two eyes; I'm sure you can see." I asked her, easing up from the water. The twins stopped making out and gave their attention to Megan. "Don't pay her no mind. Keep going."

"I been calling your fucking phone and now I see why you weren't answering."

"No, I wasn't answering because I didn't want to talk to your ass," I corrected her and climbed out the Jacuzzi. "How the hell you even get in here anyway?"

"I used the key I made the other day while you were sleeping." She dangled the key in front of my face, and I snatched it from her. Gripping her roughly by the arm, I drug her into the house.

"That better be the only one you had, too."

Megan wasn't my girl, just someone I messed around with from time to time. She seemed to not know her fucking place. If the pussy wasn't so good, I would have been kicked her to the curve. She did too much in my book.

Midway to the door, she pulled her arm away from me and stopped. "I thought we had something good going but I find you in here with two bitches," she cried, and I could see the tears forming in her eyes.

"Megan," I sighed pinching the bridge of my nose, "you know things weren't that serious between us."

"I know but I caught feelings for you. Thought they were obvious. I was cooking dinner for you every other night of the week. Supplying you the pussy on demand with no questions asked. Shit, I was even washing your dirty drawers like I was your mama."

My jaw clenched, and my eyes squinted. "Megan, we can talk about this later? Don't you see I'm busy right now?" I clutched her arm again and she snatched away.

"No! We're going to talk about this now, Berlin!"

She stormed back onto the balcony where the twins were. I wish I was out there with them. Megan needed to take her ass back to wherever she come from.

She picked their clothes up off the floor and tossed them to them.

14

"Y'all have to get the hell out, now!" she shouted, and they got out the hot tub.

I shook my head and pinched the bridge of my nose. The twins rushed into the house with water dripping from them onto my hardwood floors.

"Where y'all going?" I asked them.

"We're leaving. Obviously, you have too much going on. Give us a call whenever you're free," Camelia said, then they both left out the door without even bothering to put their clothes back on.

"See what the hell you did!" I scrubbed my hand down my face. "Fuck Megan!" She jumped from my loud bark.

"It's okay babe. They didn't know what to do with you anyway." She rubbed her tiny hands up my abs to my chest and I caught her wrists, roughly shoving her up against the wall by the hallway. "Are you mad at me?" she asked me, gazing up into my eyes with her light brown ones.

"You feel that shit?" I pressed my rock-hard dick up against her midsection and she nodded her head. "The bitches you just ran off was about to handle that shit for me."

"I can do it for you, daddy."

I let her arms go and she dropped down to her knees, releasing my monster. She put him into her mouth and I roughly fucked it, not caring she wasn't prepared. She gagged, causing more saliva to form in her mouth.

"Do that shit just how I like it," I demanded, pressing my palm up against the wall, leaning my head back. "Yeah, right there," I groaned. Her tongue twirled around my dick and she tickled my balls as the tip pounded the back of her throat.

A few more pumps and I was releasing my seeds down the back of her throat. I snatched her up by the arm and drug her to the front door before she could even register what was going on and tossed her on the other side of it.

"Berlin wait!" she cried out rushing toward me, but I shut the door in her face.

It was time I ended shit with her because she was catching feelings and I definitely didn't feel the same way about her. Later, I'll let them know downstairs she isn't allowed back in the building.

My phone chimed as I made my way down the hallway to my bedroom. It was in there on the charger. I didn't see any need in having it when I was entertaining company. I picked it up off the nightstand and a text stared back at me.

Ivy: *I miss you. I just got off work and wanted to let you know I made it home safe like I always do. Goodnight.*

I swiped the message off the screen and tossed the phone onto the bed.

SANAA

"Ah fuck Q!" I moaned, holding on to the headboard of my queen-sized sleigh bed. My eyes rolled to the back of my head and mouth formed a huge 'O' as I felt my fourth climax take over my body.

Quentin glared up at me with a half-smirk on his face. He wiped my juices off his mouth then tossed himself on the bed beside me.

"Got damn," was the only thing I could manage to say when I smiled over at him. Sweat rolled down my bare chest as it heaved up and down. We been in my bedroom having sex for what seemed like hours.

I called him the night before stressing over all this shop mess. He couldn't come then but showed up on my doorstep this morning ready to supply me with his dick. I called and told Layla I was going to be late coming in this morning, already knowing what was about to go down.

Quentin was far from my man but the closest thing I had to one. Whenever I needed to release, he came running, no hesitations. We did other things like Netflix and chilled or grabbed a quick bite to eat but that was as far as our relationship went.

Being in a relationship has crossed my mind multiple times but I didn't want to ruin things between us. We had a good thing going with the way things were. Why put a label on something and ruin it?

"Do you really think I'll be good at running the shop?"

He picked up his blunt off my nightstand that he sat there when he first got into my bedroom and tucked it between his purple lips that poked out from underneath his neatly trimmed mustache. Quentin was fine to a certain degree. His skin was a rich-sepia and didn't have any marking on it.

He brushed his waves with his hand. "No doubt about it, Sanaa. Why are you stressing yourself about that shit in the first place?"

I sighed a deep breath. "I don't know. I'm just not used to being a boss. I'd rather mellow out in the background. You know that Q."

He tucked my hair back behind my ear and grazed his thumb against the side of my face. It was the simple things like that which made me like him so much. Quentin could have smashed then dipped on me every single time, but he always showed me some sort of affection to let me know he cared. That I was more than just a booty call.

"It's time for you to show everyone what you can do, babe. Running that place is in your blood. Unleash the monster I know is in there." He poked me in my chest with his index finger.

The entire time he was talking all I could think about was my mother. How much I missed her. How much I wanted to spend time with her. See her face one final time. Reach out and touch it. Not stare at a frozen smile or mug on a picture.

I gazed off into the distance, feeling my eyes began to water.

"What's wrong bae? Did I say something wrong?"

"It's not you," I rubbed my index finger underneath my nose and sniffled, "I was thinking about my mama."

He took one final drag from his blunt then put it out, tossing his arm around my shoulder. His soft lips pressed against the side of my forehead; his beard tickled a little bit. He was the first person I ran to when I found my mother dead. It took me months to stop having nightmares about her. It's going to take me even longer to stop getting upset whenever I think about her or someone brings up her name.

"Yonnie is up there in heaven screaming at you this very moment for you kicking your own ass about running her shop. I can hear mouth now." We both laughed at the same time. "Sanaa, I ain't raise no bitch! Better get up off your ass and make them hos bow down to you."

"Whaaaaaaaaattttttttt!" I shot straight up in the bed and eyed him funny. He damn near sounded like her to a degree. I couldn't help but laugh at him.

"What? You know it's the truth."

Everyone knew how Yonnie got down. She especially didn't play any games when it came to me. She was one of the realest females you would ever encounter. Her name rung bells in the streets of St. Louis. That woman been a hustler ever since she was younger than me, trying to pave a way for herself. That was the main reason why I couldn't let all her blood, sweat, and tears go down the drain.

"Thanks for the laugh, I needed it."

"Any time."

I glanced over at the alarm clock on the nightstand. It was going on ten and I was still at the house.

"I need to get up and take a shower, so I can get to the shop."

"So, you kicking me out already?" He frowned.

I climbed out the bed, grabbing my panties and t-shirt off the floor from beside it to put in the dirty clothes hamper.

"You know it's nothing like that. I'd love to stay in bed with you all day, but I got *responsibilities* now."

"It's cool. I understand bae. I was only joking." He walked around the bed to where I stood and gripped me by my tiny waist, pulling me into his frame. "But I wouldn't mind going another round with you before you go." He softly kissed me in the crook of my neck.

My body shivered from the tickling feeling of his beard grazing against my skin. I tilted my head, so he could get better access. My neck was my spot and he knew it, that's why he was trying to use it against me.

"No Quentin," I whined.

The clothes dropped to the floor from my grasp. I wrapped my arms around his midsection and eased my hands up his back, pinning my body closer to his. Heat radiated off both of our bodies.

He gently bit down on my neck and my matte black stiletto nails dug deep into his skin. I tugged on my lower lip, feeling my pussy drench. He knew exactly where to touch me to turn me on. There was no way I would be able to go to work like this. I had no other choice than to give in and let him have his way with me again.

"Q," I moaned.

"Un-uh?"

His kisses moved in a line down to my left breast.

"Don't..."

My breasts were sitting up perfectly. My dark nipples poked almost as hard as my nails. He had me turned all the way on at the moment and there wasn't any turning back.

He traced the circle of my nipple with the tip of his tongue before slipping it into his mouth.

"Q," I whimpered.

"Yeah?" he mumbled with his mouth filled with my breast.

"Fuck me," I replied not even thinking twice.

The only thing that was on my mind was him filling up my walls and making me cum. He cupped my ass, lifting me up off the floor and I wrapped my legs around his waist.

"Oh, I'ma fuck you aight."

SOUL

That crater which appeared in her cheeks every single time she laughed was sexy as fuck to me. Her pearly white smile came in a close second to the freckles I loved so much. She brushed her hair back behind her ear and giggled some more.

I wanted to be the reason for her grin, not him. And, what the fuck was he doing there in the first place?

That nigga didn't get his nails done nor did he have any business being in there. Not wanting to cause a scene in front of Sanaa, I stayed posted up against my car in front of the shop and watched them interact. I hated that nigga but only put up with him off the strength of my sister. I wanted to put a bullet in his ass numerous times but didn't want to cause pain to her.

He finally brought his ass toward the exit and I couldn't wait to hear what lie he was about to tell.

"You getting your nails done now, nigga? I knew you were a fuck nigga." I shook my head at his pathetic ass existence as he jumped at the sound of my voice.

"What are you doing here, Soul?" he questioned me then his eyes fell on the gold Glock, which was resting in my hand, leaning against the crotch of my pants.

"Better question is what the fuck you doing here? I don't see A'Karri with you."

I stood, straightening my posture, sizing him up so he knew I wasn't playing any games with him. Everyone knew how I was when it came to my little sister. I'd go to war with God, the Devil, the entire fucking world over her. He was no exception. If I even got the slightest inkling of a feeling, he was trying to fuck her over, I was going to serve his parents his head on a silver platter and force them to eat his organs like he was Sunday dinner.

"I was getting my dick waxed. You want to see?" He began unbuckling his pants, but I stopped him.

I closed the gap between us and eyed him down. My gun went up to his chin, not even caring it was broad daylight outside. This was my family shopping center, and no one was stupid enough to call the police on me.

I never really got my hands dirty, that was Berlin's job, but I would if I had to. I was so close to pulling the trigger. My finger itched like a muhfucka.

"If you do anything to hurt A'Karri, I won't hesitate to put a bullet in your ass. Now get the hell out of here," I warned, then took a couple steps back away from him. He been in my personal space for a little too long. "And, stay the hell away from Sanaa."

"Whatever," he mumbled and stepped down off the curb. I stood there watching him until he climbed into his car and pulled out of there.

I turned around, tucking the gun back into my waistline and pushed the door open to the salon. Sanaa's smile disappeared when her eyes landed on me. It kind of made me feel a certain type of way but I pushed it to the back of my mind.

Thoughts of the things my father said the day before seeped into my mind. That was the reason why I stopped by there to make sure she was all right. I didn't want him to try and go after her. For some odd purpose, I felt like protecting her and didn't even know why.

Honestly, I didn't even know Yonnie had a child, let alone daughter until we showed up to the funeral to show our respects. It was then that I first laid eyes on her. I could see why she never spoke of her. Her daughter was stunning.

Sanaa tugged on the bottom of her white ripped jean shorts. I liked them. They gave me the perfect view of her gorgeous long legs. They were toned but not too toned where she looked like a man. They were just right. The teal crop top she wore crisscrossed over her stomach and I could see the butterfly belly button-ring hanging.

"What are you doing here Soul?" she asked, walking off and giving me a flawless view of her round ass. It bounced with every step she took.

"I came to check in on you, to make sure you were aight," I answered.

She led me to her office and held the door open for me to enter. I stood while she rounded the desk and took her seat.

"Check on me for what? I did as you told me to."

"I just wanted to make sure you were comfortable doing your job or else we would have to retire you the same as we did the last guy."

She crossed her arms and uncrossed them. I could tell she got uncomfortable with what I said from the way she shifted in her seat.

"I'm fine, you don't have to worry about me. Is there anything else I can help you with? I was busy before you walked in here."

I gawked at her and for a brief second, she stared back then trained her eyes elsewhere. That still didn't stop me from looking. Instead of her stud earrings, she had a silver wing earring that connected from the top of her ear to the lower part. Everything about her was sexy as hell. My dick was trying to go stiff from looking at her too long. That's never happened before.

I got the sudden urge to be close to her. Reach out and touch her. That's never happened before either. I knew it was time for me to get out of there.

"Why are you looking at me like that?"

"No reason. Let me see your phone."

"For what?" she asked me, brow raised.

I couldn't believe the shit I just said but I was about to come up with an excuse for me storing my number in her phone. I wasn't sure if she was going to use it, but I hoped she would.

"Just give me your phone." She placed her iPhone on the middle of the desk, and I picked it up, punching my name and number into it. "Call me if you need me or run into some sort of problems," I said, placing it back down on the desk. Her hand grazed mine as she reached out to grab her phone.

"I can handle myself." She got up from the chair. "I have to get back to work now."

"Yeah, me too." She followed me to the office door. I got one more glance from her before I left out the shop. If I was going to have my way, and I normally do, Sanaa was going to be mine.

A'KARRI MASERATI

I paced back and forth at the front door angry as hell. Not too long ago, I had gotten off the phone with Soul and he told me he seen Quentin at a nail salon being all cozy with a bitch. I tried to get him to tell me which one it was, so I could go and question the hoe about it.

Okay, so maybe I was lying. He knew I was going to whoop her ass and that's the reason why he wouldn't tell me which one it was.

Soul could have easily been telling me a lie because he never liked Quentin in the first place. I wanted to believe my brother, but I was conflicted. On one hand, I had the man I loved so much and been with for the last two years, who I thought could do no wrong. Then on the other, I had my brother who I knew would do anything to protect me including lie.

I hated feeling this way.

Soul only added fuel to the fire. I been blowing Quentin's phone up all morning and he wasn't answering. I loathed whenever he did me like that. I always jumped to conclusions and he'd blame it on him working. Sometimes it was true but others I felt like he was lying.

The front door finally pushed open and he stepped through it with a smile on his face like nothing was wrong.

"Where the hell have you been Quentin! Huh! I have been blowing your phone up and you can't answer!" I mushed him in the forehead.

"It ain't even nothing like that bae. Will you just calm down?"

I took a couple steps back from him and he shut the door.

"What were you doing at that nail shop? You were with another bitch, Quentin? And don't fucking lie to me either." I stood there with my hand propped up on my hip.

"Now, bae, why would I be with another bitch when I got all this right here in front of my face?" He clutched my waist smirking and I shoved him back away from me.

"What the hell were you doing there then?"

My breathing grew louder, and I shot him an icy glare, fighting back my tears.

"Bae, I don't know what Soul told you, but I dropped Quenby off to get her nails done. That's it."

"You sure that's it, Quentin? It sure as hell doesn't seem like that's *it* to me."

Soul could have easily mixed his facts up. I wanted to believe him, but Quentin would never hurt me, not intentionally anyway. Things between us been going great lately. We even begun talking about marriage, so I know he wouldn't do anything to mess that up between us.

He gripped my waist again and that time I didn't push him away.

"I promise you that's it, babe," he assured me, gazing directly into my eyes. I didn't see any hesitation in his, so I was going to let the shit go for now. At least until I saw otherwise.

"Okay, I believe you."

"Good, I was thinking I was going to have to take this back to the store."

He smirked and reached into his pocket, pulling out a long Tiffany box. He popped it open and staring back at me was a silver tennis bracket. He took it out the box and placed it around my right wrist.

"What's this for?" I queried not taking my eyes off the glistening bracket.

It was beautiful. Quentin rarely bought me gifts but when he did they were amazing. I cherished those moments.

"For you being the best girlfriend in the world." He pecked me on the lips.

"I love you so much." I threw my arms around his neck and kissed him deeply.

QUENTIN PEARSON

I should have known Soul was going to try and put his nose in my business with A'Karri. Then he got the nerve to tell me to stay away from Sanaa like that's his girl or some shit. Too bad the little bullshit he tried to feed A'Karri didn't work. She was too in love with me to even think I would cheat on her.

Sometimes when I wasn't reachable, she would assume I was cheating on her or another chick held my attention, but I'd show her she was the only girl for me. A'Karri's and my bond was unbreakable and no matter what Soul tried to do to pull us apart, it only brought us closer.

I knew I was going to have to do better at giving her more affection and attention, so she wouldn't get to assuming things again. I had to play my moves correctly, so I wouldn't get caught slipping by Soul, or anyone else for that matter, yet again. There were going to be only so many times I could talk myself out of a situation before she actually started to believe the shit.

My eyes shifted to A'Karri who was sleeping peacefully in my arms. She was beautiful as hell with her big pouty lips that were almost bigger than her face. She was a little darker than her brothers with a golden fawn complexion. Her silky black hair was pulled back in a tight ponytail and even after the sex session we just had, her baby hairs were still in place.

I eased over, letting A'Karri's head fall softly onto the pillow and gently climbed out the bed. Just hours prior I made love to her to assure her she didn't have anything to worry about.

Really, the bracelet I stopped by the store and bought was an apology gift. I already knew Soul got to her before me and I wanted to butter her up in case she didn't believe the lie I told her. Lucky for me she did.

I been lying in bed trying to figure out what I was going to say to Sanaa when I saw her. I don't know if Soul told her about me and A'Karri or what. Just in case he did, then I was going to have to deal with that mess when I got there; come up with a believable lie to tell her. Sanaa was smarter than that, she'd catch me in my lie and probably toss me out on my ass before I even got mid-sentence. But at least I can say I tried.

I went into the bathroom and took a quick shower. I didn't want to go over to Sanaa's smelling like sex.

We weren't exclusive or anything, but I liked Sanaa a lot and would hate to lose her, especially to Soul. I had to get to her before he did.

I quickly got dressed and snuck out the door before A'Karri woke and asked me where I was going. Normally, after a night like that, I'd stay with her but if she was to call or something, I'd just tell her I went home to get some rest for an early day in the morning.

I stepped off the elevator in Sanaa's building and went up to her door.

Knock! Knock!

I stood there fidgeting, waiting for her to answer the door. I prayed she didn't have a scowl on her face when she did.

Sanaa greeted me with a huge smile and dimples sunken into her cheeks. *Good, he hadn't told her.* I eased into the door wrapping my arms around her.

"What's that for?"

"Missed you; that's all, baby girl." I softly kissed her on the cheek then let her go. She shut the door behind me. The scent of pasta attacked my nostrils. "Were you eating?"

"Yeah, I just finished."

She headed into the kitchen that was just off her living room. Here condo wasn't huge or anything, it was more on the line of cozy. Just big enough for her. It consisted of one bedroom and two and a half baths.

"Were you hungry? Do you want me to fix you a plate?"

"Nah, I'm good."

I took a seat on her gray sectional and just watched as she made her way around the kitchen cleaning up her mess. She had on these red and white biker shorts with a white sports bra. Sanaa was sexy as fuck to me. She was slimmer than A'Karri, but she still had curves, nonetheless.

"What made you stop by without calling first?" she asked, and I could hear dishes clacking together.

"Come here." I patted the empty space next to me on the couch. "I want to talk to you about something."

She stepped into the living room. "What is it?" Her head tilted to the side and a smile slowly crept up onto her face.

"Come sit."

"You're making me nervous Quentin."

I could tell she was since she called me by my entire name.

She sat down beside me with one of her legs resting underneath her.

"Earlier when I left the shop, I saw Soul going in. What was he doing there?"

"Don't tell me you're jealous?" Her smile reappeared.

"I'm being serious Sanaa. What was he doing there?"

Her whole mood changed, and her arms crossed over her chest. "It was nothing. We talked about some things and that was it."

I could tell she wasn't telling me the entire truth, but I wasn't going to pressure her. I had a strong feeling I already knew what he was doing there anyway.

"He ain't a good guy. You need to stay away from him."

"You don't have to worry about me, Quentin. I can handle myself. I'm sure you already know that." She got up from the couch, but I caught her wrist, pulling her back down into my lap.

"I know you can handle yourself Sanaa. Just promise me you'll stay away from Soul and the rest of the Maserati's."

"How am I supposed to do that when they own the shopping center?" She scrunched her face up at me.

"Don't be looking at me like that. Just promise me you'll stay away from them. They aren't good people, Sanaa."

"Yeah, yeah whatever I'll stay away."

"That's all I asked." I pecked her gently on the lips.

Smack!

I hit her on the thigh.

"Ouch, that hurt!" she whined and got up from my lap rubbing her thigh.

"I'll make it feel better later after you finish up in the kitchen." I stood up from the couch, pulling my shirt over my head. I already decided I was going to stay the night with her. "I'll be in the bedroom when you're done."

NAOMI

S anaa been stressing a lot about everything lately, so I wanted to take her mind off things. I talked her into going to *Limitz* with me. She was against the idea at first, but as always, I got my way when it came to her.

I moved through the club pulling Sanaa along behind me by the hand, winding my hips to the song that was playing. I wasn't sure who the rapper was, but it had a nice beat to it.

I took Sanaa straight up to the bar, so we could have a couple drinks before we went out to the dance floor. We arrived in an Uber, so we didn't have to worry about getting so drunk that we couldn't make it home later.

I squeezed between some guy and chick who were cuddled up at the bar. I could feel the guy eye fucking me, but the girl wasn't too pleased with my presence.

"Excuse you! We were having a conversation before you came over here!" she yelled.

I sized her up then rolled my eyes. The bitch didn't look like much of a threat to me. She was like one of those nerdy hos who was trying their best to fit in. If anything, I posed a risk to her.

"And you can finish when I leave." I took my attention to the bartender who was at the other end of the bar. "Aye!" I shouted, waving my hand in the air to grab her attention. She smirked at me putting her index finger up in the air, then finished helping the guy who was sitting at the other end of the bar.

I couldn't help but lock eyes with him. He was sexy as fuck, probably the best-looking nigga I seen in a long time. I wouldn't mind drinking an entire tub of his bath water.

My throat grew thick and body temperature rose. I desperately wanted to be near him.

I could tell he was your average playboy from the way he stroked his neatly trimmed beard as his bushy brows rose while looking at the bartender's juicy ass. She was up on her tippy toes trying to get a bottle of Louis Xiii off the top shelf. That still didn't stop me from wanting to be in his presence.

He had low black eyes and his lips pursed underneath his thin mustache. A stud diamond earring danced in his left ear. He brushed his hand across his jet-black, thick hair. I could tell he was mixed with something from the texture of his hair. The top part of his fade was wavy and thick. Not your average nigga hair.

I tugged on the corner of my lower lip keeping my eyes trained on him. He flexed his vanilla, sleeve-tattooed arm as he picked up the bottle, she'd just handed him and took a swig from it. By how tight his white shirt was, I could tell he was solid and packing abs underneath. His eyes shifted in my direction once again and he winked, immediately making me soak my panties. I quickly turned away from him.

The bartender stopped in front of me. "What can I get you, boo?"

"You can get me two shots of Remy and my friend wants two shots of Patron." I was a dark drinker, but the only thing Sanaa drunk was white. She set the glasses down in front of me and I handed Sanaa hers. We tossed our drinks back then rushed out to the dance floor.

Sanaa wasn't in the dancing mood, so she just stood there while I danced. I got this sudden feeling someone was watching me. I glanced back over at the bar but didn't see him anymore. My eyes roamed around the club in hopes they would fall on him, but I couldn't locate him.

Knowing he was somewhere near watching me, I turned around propping my body up against Sanaa's and began winding.

"What are you doing?" she asked loudly over the music.

"Trying to grab someone's attention. Just go along with it."

It wasn't the first time we danced on each other like that. Sanaa was always with my shit, so I knew she wouldn't have a problem going along.

"Whose attention?"

My eyes finally landed on him and he was sitting up there in a VIP section with this other guy who looked just like him. They both were fine as fuck but the one I'd just had my eyes set on not too long ago seemed like he was more my type.

"Don't stare too hard or long. But do you see the guy up there in the section with the white shirt on staring down at us to the left?"

Sanaa sneak looked over then I heard her gasped.

"What? What's wrong?"

"That's Soul up there," she replied freezing up behind me.

So, that's what Soul and Berlin look like? If that was Soul, then the other man with him had to be Berlin which fascinated me even more. I been wanting to set my eyes on him ever since I first heard his name pop up in a conversation at the shop back when Yonnie was alive.

Sanaa's hands clutched my sides as I bent over twerking my ass on her. My long-sleeve, red sequin dress was riding up my ass, but I didn't care. I kept on dancing.

A few moments later some intoxicating cologne attacked my nostrils and a hard body pressed up against my ass. I lifted straight up, and a pair of strong arms wrapped around my body. I didn't even have to look back to know who it was. He was right where I wanted him.

"You got my attention. Question is what are you going to do with it?" his cocky ass whispered into my ear. I kept winding my hips to the song.

"I'm going to fuck you. That's what I'm going to do. Question is, are you going to let me?" I mimicked him and felt his dick rising and it felt like a third leg.

"No, you not. You're just talking shit."

"How much you wanna bet?" I turned straight around and came face to chest with his sexy ass. When he was sitting down, I hadn't realized he was that tall. But now that he was standing just mere inches from me, he was tall like a giant.

"If you serious then meet me out front." He didn't utter another word, just left heading toward the exit.

I quickly went to look for Sanaa not wanting to miss my opportunity to have sex with Berlin. I been dying for this moment for as long as I could remember. I found her sitting at the bar drinking on a fruity drink.

"I'm going home with Berlin. Are you going to be alright?"

"Naomi!" she shrieked.

"What?" I half-smirked.

I had the chance to fuck a living walking God. Did she really think I was going to give up that opportunity? I didn't give a damn if I never saw him again, I would have accomplished what I was aiming for the longest to do.

"You heard me right. He's waiting on me right outside. I feel bad just leaving you alone when it was my idea to come out in the first place."

"It's cool girl. I'll just finish up my drink and catch an Uber home. You know they always waiting outside the club anyway."

"Okay." I pulled Sanaa in for a hug then rushed toward the exit before he got to thinking I wasn't going to come.

BERLIN

y eyes been glued to shorty ever since I first caught a glimpse of her ass while she was eye fucking me at the bar. I wasn't going to say anything to her, but her body was calling my name. That fat, firm ass poking from underneath that dress, Lord have mercy on my soul. Those thick juicy golden-brown legs of hers were screaming for me to plant kisses all over them.

She was the perfect shape, almost like a coke bottle. Then what really drew me to her more was the fact she was natural. Baby girl's hair was thick and curly, stopping in the middle of her back. I knew I could grip that shit hella tight while pounding in her pussy from behind and the shit wouldn't come out.

When she told me, she wanted to fuck me it threw me for a loop but I wasn't about to question her motives. If shorty wanted to give me the pussy, then I wasn't going to stop her.

I went out to my red Ferrari 488 GTB that was parked out front at the curb. Every time I came out, valet knew to keep my car close in case I had to make a quick exit. Tonight, was no different.

Even though I liked Ivy a lot, that still didn't stop me from wanting to see what shorty was about. Ivy and I weren't that serious, but we were getting there.

I sat in the car for five minutes waiting for her to come out the door. I thought she was fucking playing, so I pulled off from the curb. Just when I was about to take off out the parking lot, I saw her step out the door and quickly threw the car in reverse.

"You were just going to leave me like that?"

"Thought your ass was bullshitting. Time is money and I don't like to waste either. You getting in the car or no?"

"Yeah."

Without hesitation, she opened the passenger's side door and slipped into the seat. I pulled away from the curb before the door was even closed all the way.

Since I didn't know much about shorty, I took her to the Marriott St. Louis Grand. It was a hotel I frequented whenever I wanted to smash a chick. I didn't want to take her back to my place anyway and risk Ivy popping up on us. I told her she could come over tonight when she got off work and I was sure she was going to be angry when she got there, and I wasn't home. That was better than her finding me in bed with another chick.

Shorty stood to the side while I talked to the girl at the desk to get a room. It didn't take us long to get up to the suite. I pushed the door open and she immediately attacked my lips with her glossy purple ones. My hands went up to her head, gripping her soft hair. She kicked the door closed with her foot.

I scooped her up into my arms by the ass and carried her into the bedroom part of the suite, tossing her down on the bed. She half-smirked up at me, then ran her tongue across her upper lip.

"What's your name anyway?" I asked, her pulling my shirt over my head and tossing it to the floor.

"Why does it really matter? It's not like we're going to see each other again after tonight." She reminded me of someone... myself.

I gripped her by the ankles, tugging her to the edge of the bed. "You not going to tell me what your name is?"

"Nope." She pressed her lips together not breaking my gaze. I ripped her dress straight down the front and she let out a gasp. Her juicy breasts sprung to life. "Why you rip my dress? You could have just unzipped me."

My eyes glued to her beautiful body. I rubbed my hands up her thick thighs squeezing them. They felt like cotton underneath my fingertips. Even though she didn't want to see me after this, I knew this wasn't going to be a one-time thing.

"Since you don't want to tell me what your name is then I guess I have no other choice than to fuck it out of you." I jerked on the thin fabric of her thong and it ripped right off.

"I don't know what you think I'm going to wear out of here later to get home."

I reached into my pants pocket, pulling a Magnum out then pushed my pants to the floor. I ripped the condom open and slid it down my dick and spread her legs as wide as they would go.

Smack!

I slapped her on her neatly trimmed pussy before positioning my dick at her opening. Her shit was already soaking wet, dripping from her pussy to her asshole.

"Mmmhmm," she groaned feeling my dick flood her insides.

I held her legs back, pounding my dick inside her.

"You still not going to tell me what your name is?"

"No," she moaned. I held onto her thighs tighter, giving her deep hard strokes. "Fuck Berlin!" she whimpered.

"What's your fucking name!" I barked, feeling sweat beads form on my forehead. She was still being as stubborn as ever.

Her legs shook like an earthquake and I knew she was close to climaxing, so I pulled out. Her eyes popped open, bulging up at me. Chest heaving up and down.

"What you do that for?"

Without warning, I plummeted my dick deep off in her and she shrieked at the top of her lungs.

"Name!"

I lifted my leg placing my left foot flat on the bed and smashed my dick into her. I was trying to touch the bottom of her muhfucking soul.

"Oh fuck! It's Naomi!"

"It's what? I don't hear you."

"It's Naomi, Ber-liiiiinnnnnnn!"

My lips curved into a grin now that I got what I wanted to know out of her.

I dropped my leg back to the floor and wrapped my hand tightly around her throat, leaning down by her ear, I whispered, "You going to submit to me, Naomi?"

"Fuck, if you keep giving me dick like that, I'll do whatever the hell you want."

"That's the shit I want to hear. Now, get your ass up here and bless this muhfuckin' throne."

I let go of her neck and laid down on the bed on my back. Naomi did just as I told her to and climbed between my legs, positioning herself to give me some of that sloppy toppy, I knew was in her.

After sex, we fell asleep. I was awakened by my phone vibrating like crazy on the nightstand. The sun peeked through the window. I picked the phone up and saw it was going on 7:00 in the morning. I had several missed calls from Ivy which only meant she was pissed the fuck off with me.

I turned over and Naomi was no longer beside me. I looked around the room but didn't spot her anywhere. I got up from the bed and went into the bathroom to take a leak then saw she left me a message on the mirror in pink lipstick.

I had to get home, so I could get ready for class. Here's my number, don't be afraid to use it. Oh, by the way, I took your shirt. -Naomi

I chuckled at her little message then got dressed so I could make it home to shower. Lucky for me, I always kept a spare shirt in the car for times like this.

SANAA

I been running the shop for a week now and surprisingly, I was doing a better job than I thought I would have been. Things were running smoothly and most of *Glitz's* clients found their way back to the shop along with some new potential ones.

"Did you figure out what style nail you wanted?" I asked the girl who sat across from me. She came in not too long ago wanting to get her nails done but wasn't sure what style she wanted.

"I want almond. Do them all white with this glitter except do my ring finger a powder pink." She handed me the glitter she wanted to use, and I nodded my head.

I started the process to do her nails.

"I swear I need to get rid of this sorry ass nigga," one of my mother's most loyal customers, Ebony announced.

She been coming here for what seemed like forever. She was sitting in the pedicure chair getting her toes done. She always came in here complaining about her boyfriend, yet she was still with his sorry ass. Mia rolled her eyes and kept scrubbing her feet.

"What he do now?" Mia asked her as if she really cared.

"That nigga still ain't found him a job. I'm tired of taking care of his ass. Then I think he cheating anyway."

The door chimed, and my eyes lifted from the nails I was working on to it. Soul walked in wearing a black Armani suit with gold links. His white button-up shirt had the top buttons undone and I could see his tattoos peeking from underneath.

That man was too fine for his own fucking good. My eyes weren't the only ones that had fell upon him. It seemed like everyone in the shop was eye fucking him, but his eyes were locked on me.

I squeezed my thighs together to stop my pussy from gushing. If I kept staring at him any longer, I was going to have a tsunami between my thighs. Every time I saw him, he always had that effect on me. Sitting in his hand was a duffel bag so I already knew why he was here.

"Tip, can you take over for me? I need to take care of something right quick." I rose to my feet.

Without saying anything to him, I walked toward my office and he followed suit. I pushed the door open, letting him enter first. He dropped the duffel on the white chaise lounge. I tucked my hair back behind my ear when his eyes landed on me again. This man always made me nervous; his gaze was so intimidating.

"Why do you keep showing up at the shop? Don't you have workers to take care of this for you?" I quizzed him.

"Don't fucking question me. Get in here and shut the door."

I rolled my eyes and stepped into the office, pulling the door up behind me.

"What is this about?"

"Didn't I just tell you not to fucking question me?" This nigga was really feeling himself and I was 2.5 seconds away from shoving my size 6 red bottom up his ass if he kept talking to me like he was crazy.

"What's going on with you and Quentin? I saw him in here the other day and don't lie to me about it either."

"Why you all in my personal business like you're my man or something?" I screwed my face up at him.

I didn't have to answer his question. The only thing I was supposed to do was clean that stupid ass money for him. My personal life had nothing to do with him. In fact, it was off limits.

"Just answer the question Sanaa."

I sighed deeply then took a seat behind the desk. I wasn't certain what he needed to know all this for but if it was going to get him to shut up then I'd tell him. Part of me wanted to linger on the question just to keep him in my personal space for a little longer but I could tell he'd get impatient with me soon or later.

"If you must know, Quentin and I have a thing going on."

"What kind of *thing*?"

He was making me kind of uncomfortable going into details about my relationship with Q. From the stern expression on his face, I could tell he wasn't playing about me answering his questions either.

"You know... we have sex from time to time. Why you need to know all this anyway?"

"When was the last time y'all had sex?"

My face immediately turned beet red. "A couple nights ago."

Soul's fist balled up and his teeth clenched. He turned around, snatching the door open and walked out.

"Soul!" I called out behind him, but he kept walking.

I rushed from behind my desk to go after him but by the time I made it out into the shop he was peeling out the parking lot.

"What was all that about?" Layla appeared at my side and asked.

"I really don't know."

I pulled my phone out the back pocket of my white jeans and dialed Quentin's number, but he sent me to voicemail. Soul was tripping asking me all those questions then just left without saying anything.

"I can finish them," I told Tip and she got up letting me have my seat again.

The entire time I was doing the girl's nails I couldn't help but think about Soul. He was a little too worried about my sex life. Then he kept popping up at the shop when he really didn't have to. *Does he have a thing for me?* I blushed just pondering that crazy idea.

SOUL

Hearing about Quentin sleeping with Sanaa pissed me the fuck off for more than one reason. I was angry because he was trying to play my sister like a fool. Then I was on ten about the fact he been touching Sanaa. His fingers been feeling her in places I craved to touch.

She was probably angry with me for the way I walked out on her. I didn't do it intentionally, but I had to find Quentin and give him a piece of my fucking mind.

As much as I told A'Karri not to fuck with that nigga she still did the shit anyway. She didn't even believe me when I called and told her about him being at the nail shop. He tried to feed me some bullshit about getting his dick waxed. I knew better than that shit when it came out his mouth, but I didn't speak too much on it.

Quentin thought I was playing about the things I told him was going to happen if he ever fucked over my sister. My word was bond and I was going to show him I didn't play when it came to my family.

Berlin might have been the hothead out of the three, but I'd do what's essential when necessary. And, right now, I was about to shove my Glock so far down Quentin's throat that the fucking bullet was going to come flying out his asshole when I pulled the trigger.

I parked my car in front of Quentin's building downtown. With what time of day it was, I was positive he was at work. The nigga did so terrible at the street life that he had to go find him a nine to five. That should have told A'Karri something then, but she was too blinded by the shit.

I didn't give a damn who was in the building, I was about to rock that muhfucka and anyone else in there who might get in my way.

I hopped out of my car with it still running. I wasn't worried about anyone being stupid enough to jump behind the wheel and snatch my shit. Especially if they valued their fucking life.

I took the elevator up to the floor his office was on. When it dinged, I stepped off and like always, all eyes fell upon me. I tread through the office with my fists balled up, heat coursing through my veins. I was about to rearrange Quentin's face until the muhfucka was unrecognizable then put a bullet in his ass right there in that very fucking office.

"Excuse me but you can't go in—" I shot the little white bitch an icy glare and she shut up immediately.

I pushed the double doors open to Quentin's office. He was in a meeting from the looks of it. His gaze met mine and he already knew I was about business.

"Both of y'all got to the count of one to get the hell out before your fucking brain matter is splattered right along with this nigga's." The two men took one glance at me and knew I was serious as a heart attack. They both jolted from their seats and rushed past me out the door. I shut the doors locking them, so we wouldn't be disturbed.

"What the hell you doing here?" he quizzed rising from behind his desk.

"Don't play stupid Quentin. You already know what I'm doing here."

I pulled my Glock from my waistline placing it on the desk. His eyes shifted from the gun to me and sweat beads formed on his forehead. He stumbled back away from the desk.

"What the fuck did I tell you?"

If I recall, I remembered telling him to not fuck my sister over and to stay the hell away from Sanaa. Somehow, he managed to not do either. Now it was time for him to reap the consequences.

"I don't know what you're talking about," he quickly lied.

"Oh, you don't do you?"

Pulling my suit jacket off, I placed it on the back of the chair in front of his desk. I rolled up the sleeves on my shirt not once breaking his gaze.

"Man, I ain't been fucking with no Sanaa."

"Sanaa says otherwise."

Quentin backed up against the glass window. I picked my Glock up and shot three times.

Pow! Pow! Pow!

He jumped hard as hell as the glass shattered behind him. I missed him on purpose. I rushed behind the desk, gripping him by his shirt, leaning his body out the window.

"I don't fucking play about my got damn sister, Quentin." I pushed him a little further where the entire upper half of his body was out the window. "Give me one good reason to not let you plummet to your fucking death."

"I'll leave Sanaa alone if that's what you want!" he yelled trying to save face.

"That's not what I wanted to hear." I lifted him a little then slammed his body on the window seal. I was sure the glass probably dug into his back. I had even gotten cut a little bit on my arm.

"I'll leave A'Karri and Sanaa alone! Happy now!"

Boom! Boom! Boom!

Someone was beating at his office door. They probably called security or the police when they heard the gunshots and him hollering like a little bitch. I had a right mind to shove his ass on out the window and watch him fall to his death, but I knew A'Karri would probably hate me for the rest of her life if I had.

"Good, I'm going to hold you to that." I let him go and tucked my gun into my waistline just as his office door was forced in. The rental cops stood there with their stun guns drawn like they were really going to do something to a real one.

"It's cool," he quickly dismissed them.

I grabbed my jacket, tossing it over my shoulder.

"If I have to come back to find you about either one of them, I'm going to kill you the next time. I don't give a damn if A'Karri tries to beg you to come back to her, your ass better break her fucking heart or I'm going to break your mama's when I deliver her the news that I killed you and send her your fucking big ass head."

Quentin could play with me if he fucking wanted to. Just as Berlin, I'm quick to buss my gun if not quicker. I wouldn't hesitate to rock his ass to fucking sleep then go home and sleep like a fucking baby. I been wanting to do that shit for the longest and I just hope he gave me the chance to make my dreams come true.

NAOMI

I sat there in the middle of my bed Indian style with my camera glued to my eye. Berlin had his head resting against my diamond studded headboard with his eyes closed blowing smoke rings. That man was so sexy to me.

When I first met him, I thought we were going to just have a one-night stand but that turned into two and now this was my third time spending time with him. It wasn't anything serious. The only thing we were doing was having sex. That's what we just got done doing then he rolled a blunt.

While he was relaxing and basking in the amazing sex we just encountered, I slipped his shirt on and grabbed my camera. I wanted to capture him in the moment.

"The hell you doing?" he asked me, peeking from his left eye. I was surprised he could barely keep them open.

I snatched the blunt from him and took a couple puffs from it. "Get your panties out a bunch. No one's going to see it. Don't want your girl to go ballistic on your ass." I snickered, shutting the camera and placing it on the nightstand.

The second time we got together, he told me all about his girl, Ivy. Well, technically he said she wasn't his girl just some chick he liked but they were working up to that level. I didn't understand how he liked her when he was fucking me and probably several other girls behind her back. It was none of my business, so I didn't get all into it.

His phone buzzed, and he swiped it from the nightstand.

"Who is that? Your *boothang*?" I teased, leaning up trying to see what the message read.

He turned the screen, so I could see what she said. I felt some type of way seeing her name saved as *Babe,* but I didn't speak on my feelings. She wanted to know if he wanted to get together with her later.

"Are you?" I questioned him, falling back onto the pillow beside him. I grabbed the lighter off the bed and lit the tip of the spliff since it had gone out.

"I don't know... Maybe."

I watched him as his fingers swiftly moved across his keyboard. I took a couple tokes from the blunt then placed it between his lips.

"What you got my number saved as?" I was just being curious. I was sure it wasn't anything special. "Pretty Pussy?" I laughed looking at the name he had my number saved under. "Aren't you worried she'll see that in your phone?"

"She doesn't go through my phone or nothing when we're together. That's one of the things I like about her. She trusts me."

"Why do you cheat on her the way you do?"

"I wouldn't call it cheating, just keeping my options open. We're not officially together. When we get exclusive, things might change. I don't know. I haven't found the *woman* to make me want to be faithful."

"Maybe you're just looking in the *wrong* places."

He shrugged his shoulders then leaned over putting the blunt out in the ashtray.

"Enough with all this serious shit." He gripped me by my waist and pulled me into his lap. I gazed into his low red eyes and a smirk crept up on his face.

"What you smirking for—" before I could even finish my sentence, Berlin had lifted me up and slid me down on his dick. "Mmmhmm," I moaned, shutting my eyes.

It was like his dick was the perfect size for me. He filled me up just right. My pussy expanded to fit his dick like a glove. He lifted his shirt up over my head and tossed it to the side.

"You got the most beautiful breasts I've ever seen." His eyes fixated on my melons. "And I've seen plenty breasts." Using both of his hands, he caressed them so tenderly as I slowly bounced up and down on his dick.

"Ooohh," I hissed, tucking the corner of my lower lip between my teeth. My pussy unleashed a waterfall on his dick.

His hands eased up from my breasts and wrapped around my throat. Holding my neck, he fucked me roughly from underneath. The strokes sped up and seemed to go deeper, hitting my spot at the perfect angle.

"Got damn Berlin!" I whimpered, body trembling.

"Look at me while you take this dick."

I slowly peeled my eyes open and met his gaze. His face was tensed up, eyes glossed over. It was turning me on, even more to know he wanted me to watch him cum. I felt myself connecting deeper with him at that moment.

"Oooh, I'm about to cum," I cried, digging my nails deep into his biceps.

"Open them eyes back up. I wanna watch you cum."

I stared at him, feeling my orgasm take over my body. It was like he had intensified it somehow.

He laid me back on the bed and pounded into my pussy. He hit every angle and corner his dick could reach. Suddenly, he snatched his dick out of me and released his warm seeds onto my stomach.

As if I couldn't bask in the moment after having the most amazing sex with him, his phone began ringing. I thought it was Ivy calling him until he answered the phone.

"What's going on bruh?"

I laid there on the bed with his seeds spread on my stomach looking like a toaster strudel.

"You lying bruh," he gritted into the phone, climbed out of bed, and went into the bathroom turning on the faucet at the sink. To be nosey, I got up and went behind him. Not wanting him to know I was listening in on his conversation, I grabbed a rag wetting it, so I could clean his nut off my stomach.

"Where you at? I'm on my fucking way." A few moments later, he ended the call, placing the phone on the counter.

"Who was that?"

"Soul. I gotta go take care of something right quick."

He quickly washed his dick and balls then went back into the bedroom to get dressed. I wasn't ready for him to leave just yet. I wanted him to stay in bed with me and we cuddle up and watch movies for the rest of the day or something. I couldn't tell him that because I didn't want to run him off, so I just let him leave.

He slipped on his last Jimmy Choo sneaker and laced it up. I stood there fidgeting with my fingertips, trying to decide what I was going to say to him.

Smack!

He slapped me on the ass then grabbed his keys off the dresser. "I'll hit you up later if you're not busy, Ms. Pretty Pussy." He shot me a half-smirk and I couldn't help but return it.

"Okay, just be careful," was the only thing I could muster up to say.

He eyed me suspiciously, then left out the bedroom. Seconds later, I heard the front door shut.

"Be careful?" I palmed my forehead. I sounded like a lovestruck teen.

BERLIN

Naomi was acting strange before I left. I wasn't sure what was going on with her, but I'd ask her about that later. I had to go and see what was going on with Soul. That nigga just called and told me he almost killed Quentin but wouldn't tell me what for.

I didn't want to leave Naomi right that second, but I had to go see what the hell was going on. If Soul was to kill Quentin, A'Karri was going to raise hell. She'd never forgive either one of us and I didn't have anything to do with the shit.

I popped up at the warehouse on 19th Street where he most likely was going to be. Knowing him, he was going to need to clear his mind after what had gone down and he wouldn't be able to do so going home to Sofia's nagging ass.

I went inside the warehouse passing the guys who were packaging up some cocaine in the main room and headed straight to the back to where the offices were located. I pushed his office door open without even knocking.

Soul shot me daggers soon as his eyes landed on me. I was pissed off as well, just as he was. Quentin was hurting our little sister and we didn't play when it came to our family. That nigga already knew I don't give two fucks about his ass. My mother had to stop me from putting a bullet in him before. This time, there won't be anyone around to stop me. I was going to put his ass six feet under for breaking my little sister's heart.

"Close the door," Soul ordered then rested his elbows on the desk, rubbing his temples. From where I was standing, I saw blood trickling down from his arm.

"You need to get that shit cleaned ASAP."

I shut the door and took a seat in the black leather chair in front of his desk.

"That shit ain't nothing but a scratch."

"Why the fuck you ain't call me though? You know I would have handled that nigga for doing sis like that." That's what the fuck I did—took care of shit.

He pissed me the fuck off. I thought I would be the first one to know about something like that. Soul knew how I was when it came to A'Karri. She hated I was so overprotective of her, but I had the right to be especially when it came to fuck boys like Quentin. Now she was going to be sitting at home crying her fucking eyes out over this bitch ass nigga.

Quentin was never good enough for my sister. I knew that the day I found out he had stolen from her, yet she ran right back to the nigga like nothing had fucking happened. Her trust should have been fucked up behind that, but she still loved on the nigga like no tomorrow. *Fuck, I should have just put that bullet in his ass then we wouldn't be worried about all this shit.*

"I was handling the shit," he calmly replied.

I jolted up from the chair rocking the desk. "You was handling it! That nigga supposed to be fucking dead. How the hell were you handling it when you walked out of there leaving that nigga still breathing!" I barked, nostrils flaring.

My breathing sped up and my hands balled into fists. I was ready to knock the fucking wind out of someone. That someone in particular was Quentin.

"Calm the fuck down Berlin before I knock your ass out," he warned, relaxing back into his chair.

"How am I supposed to calm down? That nigga still walking this got damn earth after he fucked over A'Karri. Other niggas get word that we let him live after some shit like that and they'll be lined up and down the street ready to pull some shit on one of us." I spun around on my heels and headed for the door.

"Where you going?" he questioned me rising from his chair.

"To go take care of what you couldn't do."

Before I could even have my hand all the way on the doorknob, Soul had me pinned up against the door applying pressure to the back of my neck with his arm and my arm bent behind my back.

"No, that's what you're not going to do. That's not your place Berlin and you're going to leave the shit alone. A'Karri is a big girl and she can handle it."

"Get the fuck off me Soul."

"I'm not letting you go until you promise me, you're going to leave the situation alone. We got bigger fish to fry. Quentin's punk ass ain't even worth our fucking time nor energy."

I couldn't believe he just wanted me to leave the shit alone. Soul already knew how I was and how I got down. That was like mission impossible to me. My trigger finger was itching, and I don't know if I could promise him something like that then end up going back on my word. Just as his, my word was bond that's why he was trying to get me to agree to it.

"I don't know about that Soul."

He shoved my body harder into the door. "Promise me Berlin. I know you don't want A'Karri to be pissed off at you for the rest of your life. You love her too much."

I sighed a deep breath. "Aight." He let my arm go and took a few steps back away from me. I rubbed the back of my neck. "I promise you I'm going to leave it alone but what I'm not going to promise is that a bullet won't find a way into his skull if I run into his ass."

"Sounds fair enough," he said then went back behind his desk.

This nigga really had me leave Naomi's good pussy ass to come here for this shit. I actually thought he was going to be down to rock that nigga to sleep with me.

"I'm out of here, bruh because you tripping," I announced and snatched the door open.

A'KARRI

I was mad. No, mad wasn't a strong enough word to describe how I was feeling at the moment. I was angry as hell staring at the text message Soul sent me just moments ago.

I told you Quentin was no good but don't worry I took care of it.

I tried calling his phone to see what he was talking about, but he wouldn't answer. *Took care of what? Was Quentin dead?* There were so many questions flowing through my head. That message could mean several things all in one.

I sat there on my couch about to pull my hair out, trying to figure out what was going on. I tried calling Quentin to make sure he was all right, but he couldn't seem to answer either. I called his cell and office with no response. Even though I was sure he done something fucked up for Soul to step in, I was still worried about his well-being. That's just the effect he had on me.

I worried about him more than I worried about my damn self. That's what was wrong with me.

"Fuck it," I mumbled, rising from the couch, heading into my bedroom. I slipped my feet into my burgundy Versace slides and scooped up my keys off the dresser. Soul was going to have to deal with me one way or another. He couldn't just drop something like that on me then give me the silent treatment.

Whatever he did, he should have come to me first about it. I thought we were better than that. I could have handled whatever was going on with Quentin. I was tired of them all treating me like I was a baby. I was twenty-two-years-old for crying out loud, far from a child. Just because I was the youngest, they thought that whatever they did or said goes but things didn't work that way. I lived my life the way I wanted to live it, not for them.

I snatched my silver Rolls Royce truck door open and slid into the butter seats. I shut my eyes and took a deep breath before starting the truck.

Since Soul didn't want to answer the phone, I called around until I found someone who knew where he was. The entire ride to the warehouse, I was thinking of the things I was going to say to him. It wasn't easy trying to figure out my words when I didn't really know what the situation was.

"Lord, please don't let him been done killed Quentin. At least not until I'm able to talk to him first," I prayed and whipped the truck into the first parking spot I saw at the warehouse.

Boom! Boom! Boom!

I banged on the door, waiting for someone to come to it. I was so angry I wasn't thinking straight. I had a key to the place along with all the others and they were hanging in my hand, but I forgot all about them until Mason finally answered the door.

"Where is he?" I quizzed him.

"In his office getting ready to go."

I shoved straight past him, storming to Soul's office. He wasn't about to step foot out of this warehouse until I gave him a piece of my mind.

"Soul!" I roared before I even made it to his office. I pushed his door open with so much force it flew back into the wall making a loud thud.

"What you doing all that for A'Karri?"

"What was that shit you sent me?"

"I know you can read A'Karri with all that money Pops spent on private schools so don't ask me that stupid ass question," he coolly responded, pissing me off even more.

My lip curled as I stormed over to his desk. I roughly gripped him by his bleeding arm.

"The hell happened to you right here, huh Soul?" He wasn't bleeding for nothing so that only confirmed he done something to Quentin.

"I cut myself. Is that a problem with you?" He jerked his arm back away from me.

"Will you stop playing these fucking childish ass games with me and just tell me what the hell is going on Soul?"

"Quentin was cheating on you. I found out because the girl told me she been fucking him."

"You're lying." I laughed, feeling tears well up in my eyes. I didn't want to believe Quentin did something like that. I wasn't going to believe it.

"I'm not lying, A'Karri. When have I ever lied to you?"

Boom!

I pounded my fist down onto his desk.

"Stop fucking lying to me, Soul!" The tears that were threatening to fall had begun falling. They cascaded down my cheeks and dripped onto my breasts that were peeking out the top of my blouse.

Soul got up from his chair and rounded his desk. His hands cupped my face and gazed deeply into my watery eyes.

"I'm sorry, Karri." I tried to blink back the tears. "You don't need that fuck nigga no way."

I snatched my face away from him and stumbled back. "You don't know what the fuck I need! What did you do to him, Soul?"

"Nothing his bitch ass couldn't handle." He fumbled with his cufflinks to avoid eye contact.

"Did you kill him?"

"Does it really matter?"

"Who was she?" I questioned him. I didn't know if I really wanted to know who the girl was, but I asked him anyway.

"Yonnie's daughter," he replied.

"How come you didn't come to me first about it? I could have handled it."

I was hurting deeply inside finding out Quentin had cheated on me. My heart shattered into tiny million pieces. My chest was ablaze. My throat closed in on me and my lungs felt empty. Part of me wanted to go and confront the ho but didn't want to look stupid doing so.

"I don't think she knows about you. So, just stay away from the shop aight," Soul stated like he read my mind or something.

Just because he told me to do so doesn't mean I was going to do it. I pulled my phone out my back pants pocket and tried calling Quentin again. He had some explaining to do with his doggish ass. Well, more like saving face because I was certain he was going to have a lie buried somewhere deep down to justify what he did.

Once again, my call got sent to voicemail.

"You might as well stop calling that nigga because he's not going to answer."

"What's that supposed to mean?"

"I told him to leave you the fuck alone and I'm pretty sure that nigga values his life." Soul shot me a half-smirk and I rolled my eyes.

"I just wish all of you would stay out of my fucking love life!"

"We are only trying to do what's best for you Karri."

"WHAT'S BEST FOR ME!" I laughed, then shoved him in the chest. "You don't even know what's best for your fucking self. Why don't all of you do me a favor and stay the fuck out of my life!" I headed for the door but stopped in my tracks. "Does Berlin know?"

From the stupid blank expression on his face, I already knew the answer to my question. "Great, just fucking great!"

I stormed out of there with only one thing on my mind. I had to find Quentin and give him a fucking piece of my mind.

Out of all the things we conquered together he just had to go out and destroy our relationship like it was nothing to him. I been fighting and fighting since day one to keep and hold this relationship together and now I see it was all for nothing. He threw our love away for some bitch whose pussy probably wasn't even hitting on shit.

I hopped back into my truck and pulled out the parking lot heading for Quentin's house. If Soul got a hold of him then that's the only place he could be at the moment. His ass better be there too, or we were going to have a bigger problem than we already do.

QUENTIN

After my little run-in with Soul earlier, I had to go to the hospital to get my back checked out. There were tiny shards of glass stuck in there that they had to pull out, but he didn't do any real damage, not how he would have liked.

Soul and all the Maserati's pissed me the fuck off. I was tired of them thinking they ran everyone and everything in St. Louis. Because of him, I had lost the love of my fucking life.

Someone had to stop them and that someone was me. I'm not putting up with their bullshit any fucking more.

Boom! Boom! Boom!

Someone was banging on my front door like they were crazy. I left out of my bedroom and rushed to it to see who it was. Peeking out the blinds, I saw A'Karri on the other side of the door. Both of her hands were balled up into tiny fists. She had a mean mug on her face, so I knew she was pissed. Soul probably got to her before I could.

"Quentin, open this fucking door! I know your ass in there because your Porsche is parked out front!"

I didn't want to let her inside. Not because Soul told me to stay away from her but for the fact she was angry as hell about me cheating on her and there was no telling what she was going to do. A'Karri was destructive when she's mad and is capable of anything. I just got home from the hospital; I wasn't trying to make another trip back there.

She walked away from the door and I thought she was leaving that was until I heard...

Crash!

I quickly snatched the front door open and rushed outside seeing A'Karri throwing bricks into the windshield of my car.

"What the hell are you doing!" I shouted at her. My hands gripped the sides of my head. I couldn't believe she threw not one but two bricks into my damn window.

"I told you to open the fucking door!" she charged toward me and I didn't know if I should be terrified or not since she had another brick in her hand. I didn't want her to go upside my head with it. "You been fucking cheating on me?" her chest heaved up and down.

"Babe, just let me explain."

"There's nothing to fucking explain. What you going to explain? The way you fucked her? All the positions y'all did and where you fucked her at?"

She was right, there wasn't anything I could explain. I cheated on her several times and liked doing it. I couldn't tell her that though or else she would most definitely beat me to death with that brick, so I had to result to a different approach.

"I'm sorry, babe." I went to touch her, but she stumbled back away from me. Her eyes grew wet with tears and the shit killed me. I loved A'Karri, I really did but that got damn Sanaa kept bringing me back with that fire ass pussy between her thighs.

"You're sorry? That's all you have to offer me is your weak ass apology?"

I glanced around, and the neighbors had begun coming out of their houses. Guess they heard all the arguing and shit A'Karri and I were doing and wanted to be nosey.

"Just come in the house so we can talk about this," I suggested, not wanting all those people to be in my damn business.

"We don't have nothing to talk about, Quentin." She went to leave but spun around on her heels. "Was she worth it?"

"No, she wasn't worth it bae. Nothing's worth me losing you. If I could go back in time, I swear I wouldn't have done it."

I was lying but she didn't need to know all that. If I had to tell her the grass was blue to gain her forgiveness and we move on with our relationship, then I would. I wasn't prepared to lose her, I'd damn sure try my best to fight for her.

"Why did you do it?" she asked, and tears flowed down her cheeks. I felt like shit knowing I was the cause of her heartache. Soul had to pay for this shit.

"Babe, I honestly don't even know. I'll do whatever it takes for you to forgive me."

"Forgive you?" She laughed that crazy ass laugh of hers. She wasn't laughing because I said something funny. She was aching and trying to mask the agony.

"Muhfucka, I forgave you when you stole from me. I forgave your bitch ass when got my fucking house shot up and I had to blame it on someone else. I forgave you when you cheated on me the first time and gifted me with gonorrhea. I can't forgive you no fucking more.

You've broken my heart too many fucking times to count Quentin and I can't stick around and keep letting you crush my soul. I deserve better than this. Than you... Out there is someone who's going to love me the way I'm supposed to be loved. Treat me the way I'm supposed to be treated. Your time with me has fucking expired and it's time you get out my fucking life, for good this time."

Her hand rose, and the brick lunged toward me, so I ducked, and it flew into the house hitting the painting that hung on the wall knocking it to the floor.

"So, we really over A'Karri?"

She's told me she was done numerous times before but always came back. For some reason, this time actually felt like it was final. She was really tired of me and my shit.

"How about we let my ass walking back to my truck answer that fucking question for you."

She made it to her truck and gripped the door handle. I rushed over to her clutching her wrist. "You're really going to leave me, Karri?"

I heard a clicking noise just as she turned to face me, and the barrel of a gun shoved into my ribcage. "Get your fucking hands off me, Quentin. We're over."

I gazed into her eyes and saw no hesitation within them. We were officially over and there was nothing I could do about it, so I let go of her wrist and took a couple steps back away from her. I stood there watching as she climbed into her truck then backed out of my driveway. Mark my words, Soul was going to pay for what the fuck he did if that's the last thing I do.

SANAA

It was another successful day at the shop, and everyone had gone home leaving me to clean and lock up. The girls always wiped down their stations before they left but I was a neat freak and wanted to make sure nothing was out of place before I headed home.

Ella Mai's *"Ready"* album played through the Bluetooth speaker and I sung along with the lyrics even though I wasn't the best singer in the world. I was alone so there wasn't any shame in my game.

The door chimed, and the scent of his expensive cologne took over the shop halting me in my steps. I turned the music down, slipping my phone into my back pocket while still giving him my back.

He asked me all those questions about my sex life with Quentin earlier then dipped on me without uttering another word. What was he doing here now? I know damn well he didn't show up just to make sure I dropped that money off earlier.

"What are you doing here?"

I turned to him and saw his arm was bleeding. "Oh, my God what happened to you!"

"It's nothing but a scratch."

"It looks like more than a scratch, Soul. Come here and let me take a look at it."

He still stood there with his feet planted in place. I gripped him by his hand, and it felt like electricity shot through my fingertips. He must have felt it as well because he pulled away or it could have been the fact he didn't want me to touch him.

"Just let me take a look at your arm. I promise I won't bite."

I grabbed his hand again and that time he didn't pull back. I took him over to one of the chairs and gestured for him to sit down.

"Let me go get a wet rag. I'll be right back." I hurried to the back closet and grabbed a rag and the first aid kit then wet it in the sink.

I don't know what I wanted to help him for when all he's ever done was be rude to me. I kneeled down in front of him and dabbed his tattooed arm with the rag. The cut wasn't deep as I thought it was, so he didn't need stitches or anything.

"I'm sorry about leaving like that earlier. I had to come back and let you know that."

I looked up from his arm and was drawn straight into his eyes.

"It's fine."

"It's just when you told me about Quentin, I had to talk to my sister about it. Quentin is... *was* her boyfriend and I couldn't let her keep going with the relationship, knowing that fuck nigga was out here cheating on her and shit."

"I'm not surprised. I mean, I didn't know he had a girlfriend, but it doesn't catch me by surprise that he does. Like I told you earlier, our relationship was mainly sex. He took care of my needs. That's it." I shrugged, then wrapped his arm up with a gauze. "I liked having him around, but I guess it's time we ended whatever this is."

Soul's hand cupped my face and grazed my cheek with his thumb.

"All better." I hurried up and got up from in front of him. I put everything back where I got it from then grabbed my purse out the office. When I came back Soul was still sitting in the same spot. "Shop's closing now," I announced, hitting the light switch and he stood.

"Since you're locking up how about I take you out for a quick bite to eat? You know to apologize for leaving you the way I did earlier."

My stomach grumbled letting me know I better not pass up on that opportunity. I didn't think it was ideal to be going out with Soul, but I wasn't about to pass up on a free meal.

"Sure, why not?"

He held the door open for me then I locked up. I headed toward my candy apple red Maserati, but he grabbed my arm pulling me toward his car.

"What about my car?" I questioned him pointing my thumb in the direction of my car.

"I'll bring you back to it. No one's crazy enough to mess with it while it's in the parking lot anyway."

He lifted the door up on his Lambo and I slid into the seat. His car even smelled like his cologne. I took a huge whiff before he made it around and got in alongside me.

As he whipped in and out of traffic my eyes kept shifting over to him. His face held a stern expression the entire time he drove. *Did he have to be so serious?*

We pulled into the parking lot and he took me up to Kemoll's, an Italian restaurant. He opened every door for me being such a gentleman. I couldn't help but wonder if he was just putting on or if this was actually the way he was.

The hostess sat us down at our table near the window per his request. The view outside the windows was amazing. All you could see was the St. Louis skyline.

This was my first time ever coming here and if the food was as incredible as the view, I'd definitely be coming back.

"Can I start you off with something to drink?" she asked with a bright smile.

"Uh, yeah, bring me a bottle of your most expensive wine."

"No, you don't really have to do that," I interrupted him.

Soul shot me a look and I quickly shut up. I wasn't the one paying for it and if he wanted to cash out on this dinner then that was his business.

"Your waiter will be right over with your wine," she stated then pranced off.

"You know you really didn't have to do that. I would have been fine with something cheaper."

"I don't do cheap."

"Excuse me then, Mr. Maserati." I picked the menu up and looked over it. The food was expensive as well, so it only made me wonder exactly how much that wine was going to cost him. I eased the menu down eyeing him over the top of it. He stroked his low trimmed goatee.

Soul's face was smooth and basically hairless. He had a thin mustache which only meant he probably didn't like all that hair on his face. I didn't mind though; it was sexy as hell to me.

"Aren't you supposed to be looking at the menu?" his eyes shifted from his menu to mine and I blushed. I hadn't realized I had been staring that long for him to notice I was looking.

"I can't figure out what I want."

"Do you just want me to order for you?"

"You might get something I don't eat." I sat the menu down on the table giving him my undivided attention.

"Everyone likes steak. You like steak, don't you? Unless you're vegan or some shit."

"No, I love meat." My face turned beet red after I realized how I sounded when I said that. My chest tightened, and I wanted to slide underneath the table and stay there for the remainder of our date.

The waiter finally came to the table with our wine. He poured my glass then Soul's before placing the bottle on the table.

"Do you know what you want to order?"

Soul's lips began moving but I zoned out. My lips parted feeling slightly parched staring at his chiseled face. *Wonder if the rest of his body was molded like that.* My eyes moved from his face down to his neck where I saw his tattoos peeking from underneath his unbuttoned shirt. I pressed my legs together in hopes to stop my pussy from doing what it does best—leaking like a faucet.

I stroked my neck wondering just what he was working with between his legs. *Hopefully, I'll get a chance to brush up against him and I could find out.*

Dinner went by like a breeze. Spending time with Soul was like a breath of fresh air that I so desperately needed. He made me forget everything that was going on at the shop even if it was for a brief second. The food was divine, and I'd definitely be coming back there whenever I had the cash to spare.

My cheeks were sore from smiling too much. I don't think I've grinned that much in my entire life. He complimented my smile telling me just how much he loved it with my deep sunken dimples.

When we were getting ready to leave, Soul stood and dug down into his pocket pulling out a wad of cash. He dropped a couple bills on the table not even counting them. Guess you could do that when you were making more money than you really knew what to do with.

He placed his hand on the lower half of my back and guided me toward the exit.

SOUL

When I invited Sanaa out to dinner, I didn't think I was going to have that much of a good time. She kept me intrigued the entire time we were at the table. I didn't want to end dinner, but I didn't want to keep her out too late either. I knew she would have to get back to her car, so she could go home and get some rest.

As we made our way to the exit, I kept glancing at the side of her beautiful face. The smell of her perfume wasn't too strong, but it was just right. I kept getting a whiff of it with the smallest gestures she made like tucking her hair back behind her ear. It definitely was making my dick try to brick up.

Her being this close to me, I wanted to spin her around and kiss her on the lips, but I kept fighting the urge. That's all I wanted to do when she was sitting across the table from me.

A woman stepped out of her chair almost bumping right into Sanaa. I was about to go in on her ass until I locked eyes with who it was... Sofia. She stood with her arms folded underneath her breasts and her face scrunched up and eyes wide. Out of all the places in St. Louis she just had to be in the same establishment as me.

"Soul, I've been calling your phone because we had plans tonight and now, I see how come you weren't answering because you were out with *her*." Sofia eyed Sanaa up and down who was still standing close to me with my hand on her lower back.

"Technically, we didn't have any plans. You asked me earlier to come to dinner with you and your parents, I told you I was busy."

I didn't want to go out to dinner with her parents for more than one reason. The main purpose was they never liked me in the first place. Honestly, I wasn't too fond of them either. Sofia should have known better to ask me that shit. I wasn't about to sit down with them at a table and pretend to like them. I wasn't fake, and I never would be.

"Busy doing what? On a date with this bitch?"

"Bitch! Oh, I got your bitch!" Sanaa eased away from my side, stepping directly into Sofia's personal space. For a second, I thought she was going to hit her.

"Sofia, watch your fucking mouth," I intervened, pulling Sanaa back to my side.

I know the way it probably looked to Sofia. Like I was taking Sanaa's side in the matter. On the outside looking in, people maybe thought Sanaa was my girlfriend and not Sofia with the way I was becoming protective of her.

"Are you serious right now? You blow off dinner with my parents, so you can be with another ho! And why she standing so fucking close to you anyway!"

I could tell she was feeling some type of way. Sofia out of all people knew how I didn't like people in my personal space. Yet, Sanaa was standing here with ease.

"I don't know what's going on but you're getting the wrong impression. There's nothing going on between Soul and I, so you can just pump your brakes and quit with all the name calling before my foot finds its way up your ass," Sanaa warned then turned to me. "I'm just going to go."

"But I'm the one that drove here."

I brought her here, so I was going to take her back to her car. It was only right.

"It's cool. I'll just catch an Uber back to my car. It's obvious you have something to take care of. Thanks for dinner though."

Sanaa eased away from my side and I wanted to run behind her but with the way Sofia was eyeing me at the moment, I decided against it.

"You doing too fucking much Sofia." I went to walk off, but she came behind me.

"What you mean I am doing too much? How am I supposed to react when I find my *man* with another bitch?"

I stopped, turned to her and gripped her by both of her forearms. "Didn't I just tell you to watch your fucking mouth? You better not let the word bitch slip from your mouth again when it comes to her."

Sofia's eyes grew wet with tears. She was in her feelings with how I was reacting to her calling Sanaa a bitch. It actually shocked me. The only person I been this protective over was A'Karri.

"You like her, don't you?"

"Does it really fucking matter?"

I let go of her and plucked the lint off the wrist of my jacket to avoid eye contact with her. If I was to stare at her now, I was sure it would be obvious just how much I liked Sanaa.

It was never my intention to hurt Sofia, but I kept feeling this connection to Sanaa. I don't know if I should act on that feeling or just push it to the back of my mind. Sofia been with me for the last two years holding me down, so I owed her my loyalty. But how could I put my heart through that? Staying with her only because of loyalty. She deserved better than to be led on for no apparent reason and I damn sure did.

"I'm about to go."

"You're not going to stay for dinner with my parents?" she questioned me.

"Did you really think I was playing when I told you I wasn't having dinner with them?" My brows snapped to my hairline when I asked her that.

"Well, dinner shouldn't last long." She closed the space between us, gripping me by the collar of my shirt. "I can just come by your place when I leave here."

I gripped her by the wrists and lightly shoved her away from me. Her entire face turned beet red and she froze in place.

"Don't bother. I don't feel up for company tonight," I said and walked off leaving her standing there.

She ruined my perfectly good date with Sanaa and thought she was going to come over there and get the dick? She had life fucked up. She could stay her ass right there with them stupid ass parents of hers. I was good on that.

NAOMI

I been stressing with the Psychology test I had coming up in a couple of hours. I tried to do everything to take my mind off things. Even trying to read a book I knew I wasn't going to be able to get into. I wasn't much of a reader but if it took my mind off that test then I'd be happy.

I studied some more sitting on the bench outside on the campus of the University of Missouri. That just made me want to pull my hair out even more.

I called Berlin's phone in hopes he would take my mind off things, but he didn't pick up. I just figured he was busy and didn't really worry about it. I don't want to blow his phone up like crazy and he think I'm becoming clingy or something.

I don't know why I was stressing in the first place. I had been studying hard for the last couple days to ensure I passed that test. In my heart, I had it down pact but in my mind, I kept doubting myself.

My phone began vibrating while I was scrolling down my Snapchat. Berlin's name and picture—that I snuck and took while he was sleeping the other day— popped up on my screen. The corners of my mouth curved up and my heartbeat skipped in my chest.

"Hey Berlin," I sang when I answered the phone. It was quiet in his background so there was no telling where he was at.

"What's going on? I saw you called me earlier, but I was in a meeting."

"I just wanted to talk to you for a while to take my mind off this test I got coming up."

"Man, don't tell me you're still stressing yourself out about that damn test. You got that shit Naomi and you know it." I heard a beeping sound coming from his background, so he must was in the car.

"Where are you anyway?"

I tried to not ask him too many questions, so he wouldn't think I was overstepping my boundaries. I loved whatever this was we had going on and didn't want to mess things up with him.

"At the store. I stopped to grab me a swisher. What you must want something?"

I started to say *you*, but I opted out of saying it.

"Yup, I want a pineapple Fanta and a bag of sour cream and onion chips. Make my dreams come true." My cheeks burned from the gigantic smile that adorned my face.

"You want me to come all the way over there just to bring you a soda and a bag of chips?"

I snickered just imagining his face at the moment. He was always contorting his face into these ugly ass expressions that were sexy as hell to me.

"Yeah, sure do."

"You got life fucked up. I ain't coming that way."

"Whatever Berlin it's not like you have something else to do in the first place."

I didn't know what he had to do. He could have easily been about to go and see another chick... well, his girlfriend to be specific. Whatever he wanted to call her ass. I always got jealous whenever she would call, and he'd be around me and answer the phone. Even though I didn't really want to admit it, I wanted him all to myself.

"You don't know what I got to do. I could be about to slide up into something slippery." He chuckled but I didn't find a damn thing funny. I heard his car beeping again, so he must was back in it.

"No, you not because that something slippery is attached to me and I don't see you nowhere near here." He burst out laughing at me, but little did he know I was dead serious.

"Aye, my line beeping so I'm just going to have to hit you up later. Good luck on your test though." Before I could even say thank you, he had disconnected the call.

I slipped my phone into my bag then pulled my camera out and just began recording. This couple was sitting on the grass across from me and they looked so happy. The guy's hand palmed her face and she smiled brightly at him while gazing into his eyes.

I zoomed in just to catch the moment then moved the camera around campus. Someone who felt familiar was walking my way. I zoomed in even further and saw it was Berlin. His eyes were somehow fixated on me. Girls were falling at his feet, but he paid them no attention. It was like I was the only thing on his mind.

I quickly shut the camera then stood to my feet smoothing out the wrinkles in my olive dress. I didn't actually think he would have shown up here. When I told him what I wanted, I was joking but he stopped directly in front of me with a half-smirk on his face and the items I asked for were dangling in his hand.

"Thought you said you weren't coming?"

"I know what I said. Here."

I took the soda and chips from his grasp and placed them down on the bench behind me.

"What time is your test?"

I glanced down at my phone checking the time. "I got like maybe another hour. Why you ask?"

Berlin reached behind me grabbing all my things. "You're about to take a walk with me. You said you were stressing so I'm about to take your mind off shit for a moment." He placed my belongings into my bag and handed it over to me.

"Where we walking to?"

"Does it really matter? Stop thinking so much and just do." He gripped me by the hand and led me away from the bench.

We had been walking for what seemed like forever. We walked and talked for so long that we wandered away from the campus.

This guy stood on the side of the road with a cardboard sign in his hand that read *"I'm hungry"*.

"Wait," I told Berlin then dug into my purse to find my wallet. I wasn't sure if I had any cash in there because I rarely carried it around, but I wanted to check.

Before I could even get my wallet out, Berlin jogged across the street where the guy was standing and dug into his pocket. He pulled out a wad of cash and handed half of it over to the guy. I was in total awe. I never thought Berlin would do something like that.

He shook the guy's hand then jogged back over to me.

"That was really nice of you." Maybe he wasn't the bad guy everyone tried to make him out to be.

"I try to help out whenever I can. I know I can't save everyone in the world but if I can reach a few people then I'm fine with that. Come on and let's get you back to campus so you won't be late for your test."

When we got back to campus, Berlin walked me to my building. I wasn't ready to end things between us, but I knew I had to if I wanted to make it to class on time. What happened just moments ago, had me looking at Berlin in a new light.

"Thanks for taking my mind off things."

"You're welcome now take your ass in there and ace that shit." He gripped me by the wrist pulling my frame into his and his lips fell atop of mine. The way he kissed me didn't feel the same as he always did when we hung out together. This time... things felt more connected. I felt connected deeper to him the more our tongues brushed against each other.

He pulled back and my heart skipped plenty of beats for him.

"I gotta bounce but you got this shit, Naomi." He turned around leaving me standing on the steps feeling like he had taken a piece of my heart along with him.

BERLIN

"Bae, do you want something to drink!" Ivy yelled from the kitchen.

On my way to see Naomi, Ivy called wanting me to come over. I thought it was really what I wanted but the entire time I was there the only thing I could think about was Naomi and the kiss we shared before I left.

That kiss...

It was deeper than any other kiss we ever shared. I was being drawn to her more than I'd like to admit. It's crazy because I actually thought this was going to be only a smash and quit it but spending time with her turned things into more.

I loved how we could just chill back and spend time together, just smoking and forget about the outside world. Naomi was different from all the rest of the women I was used to dealing with. She didn't look at me from the money in my pockets like most chicks did. She saw me for *me*. I loved how I could let my guard down around her and show the real me.

It got tiring being a hard ass every day all day. I had to be ruthless for the streets to respect me. But being with Naomi, I could be *me*.

"Berlin, did you not hear me?" Ivy brought me back from my thoughts. I was so lost thinking about Naomi I hadn't even realized Ivy standing in front of me.

My eyes roamed from her flat midsection up to her perky breasts that were heaving to her beautiful rich terra-cotta face. Her long black hair was tucked behind both of her ears and her thick brow was raised. From the twisted expression she gave me, there was no telling how long she had been standing there.

"What is wrong with you? Do you not hear me talking to you?"

"I'm sorry bae, my mind just all over the place." I clutched her by the waist and pulled her between my legs, gazing up into her face.

"What's going on?" she asked, rubbing her hand across my hair and resting her chin on my head. I could tell she was concerned about me. If she really knew what was going on, then she had the right to be. I was 2.5 seconds away from walking out on her and going to find Naomi.

I liked Ivy a lot but things between us didn't feel the same ever since Naomi walked into my life. She was a great woman, but I was just confused. I had been trying to figure out if this thing, whatever we were trying to build, was really what I wanted. And after today, things became even more complicated for me.

"Nothing, it's just work."

"You sure?"

"Yeah."

"Well, I'm about to pour me a glass of wine. Do you want anything?" She pulled my arms from around her and headed into the kitchen.

"You got something stronger than that?" I questioned her, leaning back, pulling my vibrating phone out my front pants pocket.

"Uh, just some Cîroc. You know I don't do much heavy drinking."

"Nah, I don't want anything." I swiped the screen just as she came back into the living room. Naomi was calling me, and I couldn't answer the phone while I was there. I'd just have to call her back when I leave.

"Who was that?" She plopped down on the couch beside me, taking a sip from her wine glass.

"Just Soul. I'm sure he doesn't want shit. I'll call him back later." I set my phone down in my lap then grabbed my blunt from behind my ear, placing it between my lips. My phone vibrated again but before I could grab it and see who it was Ivy had reached into my lap and snatched it up.

"Soul, huh?" She jumped up from the couch with my phone in her hand. "Who the fuck is this, Berlin!" She turned the phone and showed me a picture of Naomi flashing on my screen making the kissy face. Even if I was to lie about it there was no point. It was nothing I could tell her to justify who Naomi was.

"A friend," I honestly told her then lit the tip of my blunt.

"This doesn't look like a normal friend to me. How about I just answer the phone and ask her who the hell she is then."

"Don't answer my got damn phone, Ivy," I warned not even bothering to move. She wasn't stupid enough to answer my shit.

"Who the fuck is she Berlin?" Tears filled her eyes and she held onto my phone for dear life. "Can you please just answer me?" The tears cascaded down her cheeks and snot dripped from her nose. She was hurting but I don't see how she was hurting that bad when we were only dealing with each other for the last couple of months.

"I did answer you."

"Are you sleeping with her?"

"What do you need to know all that for?"

"JUST ANSWER MY FUCKING QUESTION!"

I didn't have to put up with this bullshit, so I got up from the couch and approached her. She stumbled back until she fell into the wall behind her.

"I suggest you take all that bass out your voice before you make me angry." I snatched my phone from her grip and slipped it into my pocket.

"It's over! Get out!" Her chest heaved up and down and she pointed to the front door. I hope she didn't think she was hurting my feelings by putting me out her little one-bedroom apartment. Shit was about big as my got damn closet.

"Bet," was all I said then turned around, placing my blunt back between my lips and relighting it.

I snatched the front door open and slammed it behind me. It was probably for the best we ended things right then.

Pulling my phone from my pocket, I dialed Naomi back and listened as the phone rang in my ear.

"Berlin!" she shrieked when she answered the phone and I couldn't help but smile knowing she was cheesing from ear to ear.

"What's going on? I saw you called me twice, but I was taking care of something."

I climbed over into my car shutting the door behind me and relaxed back into the seat.

"I'm sorry I called you back to back like that, but I just wanted to let you know I passed my test with flying colors!"

"I told you that you had that shit. I don't even know why you were stressing about it in the first place. Maybe you can swing by my place a little later and we can celebrate."

I realized this was going to be her first time coming there. Normally, I went to her place but that was only, so we wouldn't get caught up with Ivy.

"Your place? You sure about that? But, what about Ivy?"

"Don't worry about her. I'll text you the address." I ended the call and immediately sent her my address then started the ignition and pulled away from the curb.

SANAA

I been running the shop for a month now. I was proud of what I accomplished so far. Once I put all my fears to the side, I was able to run the shop how my mother would have wanted me to.

"To one month of success!" I clinked shot glasses with Naomi and tossed my shot back.

"Bih, can you hurry up and get dressed now? We were supposed to be gone already."

I let time slip away from me. When Naomi first brought up the idea of going out to club *Crisis*, I wasn't down for it but of course, she talked me into it. It was only right I celebrated my success the right way.

My bedroom looked like a tornado hit it from me tearing up my closet trying to find the perfect dress to wear. I didn't want to go out and buy anything when I had all those clothes. Naomi, on the other hand, didn't mind wasting time going to the mall and getting her something to wear.

The powder pink velvet mini dress with a split up her right thigh and matching choker was gorgeous. It showed off her beautiful rich thick legs.

I opted for a navy-blue satin dress that had my breasts sitting up exceptionally perky. I let Naomi beat my face. It was rare I wore makeup but tonight, I figured I should just let my hair down and go out and have fun.

"Have you seen my silver Christian Louboutin's?" I asked her, getting down on my knees looking underneath my bed. I wrecked my bedroom and wasn't able to find anything.

"You mean these?" She held up a pair of shoes dangling them in my face.

"Yeah, where were they?"

"Right there on the bed where you left them. Now, can you hurry the hell up before we aren't even able to get inside?"

I slipped one shoe onto my foot and hopped around trying to slide the other on. I grabbed my silver clutch and keys off the dresser and left out my bedroom, hitting the light switch.

It didn't take us long to make it to club *Crisis*. If we had been even a few moments later, we probably wouldn't have gotten in. That's just how packed the place was.

It had a nice vibe going on. Women were out on the dance floor twerking their asses screaming for attention. I followed Naomi up to the second floor. We were stopped at a rope.

"They good!" a deep voice called out. I looked over and saw Berlin sitting on a couch with a bottle of Louis Xiii in his hand and Soul sitting across from him. All I could see was the back of his head and those deep-set waves, but I had a feeling that's who it was. My heart always skipped a few beats whenever he was near.

He came by the shop a couple times after that little incident with his girlfriend, but I tried my hardest to avoid him. I didn't need any of that drama in my life. I already had enough going on.

"Tell me you didn't Naomi." I roughly gripped her by the forearm and my eyes damn near popped from my head.

"Come on and stop overthinking things."

She gripped me by the hand and led me into the VIP section. Berlin eyed Naomi like she was a juicy piece of steak. He licked his pink lips and stroked his chin. I admired the way he was gawking at her. It was like she was the only person in there. If only someone would look at me that way.

It was then I knew the little fuck sessions they claimed they were having were more than just that.

"Berlin, this is my best friend, Sanaa and you two already know each other." She shoved me toward Soul and I lost my balance falling into his lap. Our eyes locked for a brief second, turning my face beet red. I slid from his lap over onto the couch beside him brushing my hair back behind my ear. Naomi giggled then plopped down in Berlin's lap.

"What you up here drinking?" She snatched the bottle away from him and took a sip from it. "Damn Sanaa, you need to try this shit."

"No, I'm good."

"No, *you're* not."

She gave me this look and her hand went across the table that was in the middle of the two couches. I knew she wasn't going to give up until I took a drink, so I seized the bottle from her taking a couple gulps.

"Happy now?"

"Not until you take these two shots."

She moved so fast that the shots were already poured and sitting down on the table in front of me.

"Let me find out you're trying to get me drunk."

"You need to let loose Sanaa. We're celebrating remember? So just take your shots."

I tossed back both of the shots then leaned back on the couch. The effects of the liquor was slowly trying to take over my body. My eyes shifted over to Soul who was beside me sipping from a cup and bobbing his head to whatever song they were playing. He looked weird to me. This was the first time I had seen him dressed down. His look showed more of a thuggish side to him and it was kind of intriguing.

He had on a simple pair of Balmain jeans with a red Versace t-shirt and red and black Balmain sneakers.

"You just going to stare me down but not say shit to me?"

My feet shuffled, and my ears felt like they were on fire. I hadn't realized he saw me gazing at him.

"Ahem," I cleared my throat. "Hi, Soul." I leaned down pouring myself a cup of Patron and orange juice.

"That shit sounded dry as hell." He turned in his seat facing me. His eyes were low and red. Ain't no telling how long he had been drinking. "I want a better greeting than that." He leaned the side of his face by mine and tapped his cheek. The craters in my face appeared when I realized what he wanted—a kiss. I quickly pecked him on the cheek and he moved back. "That's better."

Fucking around with Naomi, I had gotten wasted. I was so drunk I begun dancing in front of Soul feeling myself up. I could tell he was enjoying the view because his eyes had to yet leave me since I stood in front of him.

"You're drunk. You know that?" He grinned up at me.

"I'm not drunk. You don't know what you're talking about." I went to take another sip from my cup, but he snatched it away from me almost spilling it on my dress, but I stumbled back so it hit the floor.

"You're drunk Sanaa. I think it's time you get home."

"How are you going to tell me?"

I went to walk off, but I tripped over my own feet and almost hit the floor. I would have if it wasn't for Soul catching me.

"Aye, Sanaa's drunk I'm about to take her home," he told Naomi and Berlin, but they were too busy feeling each other up with their tongues down each other's throats.

"No, you're not. I came here with Naomi and that's who I'm leaving with."

"You sure about that?"

I stood there with my arms folded underneath my breasts. He scooped me up lying me over his shoulder and left out the section. His arm covered my ass, so no one could see my panties. I couldn't believe he was taking me out of the club like that. It was so embarrassing!

SOUL

When Berlin told me he was meeting Naomi and her girl at the club, I didn't want to go but I did anyway just to get out for a little while. Sanaa walked into the section and my entire mood changed. I tried to talk to her about Sofia for the longest, but she didn't want to hear what I had to say. I was going to use this as my chance to let her know what was up.

She got wasted as fuck and I knew it was time for her to go home before she did something she'd later regret. I didn't want anything to happen to her that's why I volunteered to take her home. I knew she wasn't going to agree to it, but I was going to show her what I say goes. Plus, it would give me an opportunity to talk to her in private not having to yell over the music.

She sat on the passenger's side of my Rolls Royce Wraith with her arms folded underneath her breasts. She was in her feelings because I made her leave early. We were parked in front of her building, but she had yet to get out the car. It wasn't like I wanted her to leave. At least not at that moment.

"Sanaa," I called out to her, shifting in my seat.

"What Soul?" she cut her eyes at me but wouldn't fully look at me.

"Look at me." She let out a heavy breath and turned to me. "I just wanted to let you know I was sorry about what happened that night I took you out to dinner. I should have told you I had a girl, but I didn't think that really mattered. It was only dinner."

"It's fine." Her face relaxed then she gazed out the window.

"Is there something bothering you?"

"I wasn't trying to drink that much tonight. I'm sorry if I overstepped my boundaries."

"Why did you get drunk like that? It wasn't only to celebrate either." I could tell something else was bothering her, but I didn't really know what it was.

"I miss my mama. She was everything to me. I just wish I could have had more time with her, you know?"

Silence lingered over the car. I hooked her chin and turned her face to me.

"I'm sorry about your mother, Sanaa. Yonnie was a good woman."

That was all I could offer her. Her eyes grew wet with tears and I felt like shit. It was our fault her mother was dead and now here I was sitting here with

Sanaa and withholding that from her because I didn't want her to hate me. If I was to tell her, she'd probably never talk to me again and that's something I just couldn't chance.

"Thank you." I wiped her tears away with my fingertips. "Quentin called me the other day, but I didn't answer and put him on the blocklist."

"Why did you begin messing with him in the first place? You're a beautiful woman Sanaa and you could have any man in the world that you want. Quentin is nowhere near on your level."

"Quentin was the closest thing I had to a boyfriend in a while. I guess I enjoyed not being attached to anyone for a while. I didn't have to worry about getting my heart broken. That's what William did."

"William?"

She pulled her shoes off and crossed her legs in the seat. Normally, I would have gone off if someone else done that shit but with her, I just let it slide.

"Yeah, William. He was my last boyfriend who I found in the bed with another girl. We were together for four years and he just broke my heart like that. I didn't want to experience the heartache again."

"How could someone cheat on you?"

Sanaa was beautiful and within the short time we spent together since I met her, I knew she was smart and sweet. That night she wrapped my arm up, she didn't have to do it, but she did.

"I don't know. I guess I attract the wrong men. None of my relationships ever end well."

"Maybe you have just been looking in the wrong places."

"And, what's the right place? You?" She laughed that sexy laugh of hers, displaying those deep dimples. It took everything in me not to grab her by the face and kiss her luscious lips.

"Why does that have to be so funny?"

"Because you have a girl..."

"You don't have to remind me of that."

"Seems like it." She stared straight out the windshield before continuing, "I just wish I could find a good man, you know? One that's going to treat me the way I'm supposed to be treated."

"Like a queen?"

"Exactly. Why is it so hard to find him?" Her eyes shifted back to me and this time they were glossy again.

"Maybe you already have met him and you're just overlooking him. Or it could be the wrong timing. You just have to be patient." I wasn't sure if she caught on to the fact I was talking about myself.

"Maybe you're right." She took a deep breath and leaned her seat back as far as it would go.

"I hope you're not about to go to sleep."

"No, I'm just thinking. Tell me about your girlfriend. Are you happy with her?"

Her eyes closed, and I brushed the stray strands of hair back out of her face. She wore makeup on her eyes, brows, and lashes but that was it. Her freckles were still evident on her face. I wanted to kiss every inch of her face, from where they started to where they ended.

"She's been there for me for the last couple of years."

"That's not what I asked you. Are you happy though?" Her eyes peeled opened and stared into mine.

"No." There was no point in me lying when I already knew I wasn't happy. Things between Sofia and I had been bad ever since... well, before they even began.

"Why don't you leave?"

"Loyalty," was the only reason I could give her.

"Maybe you should reconsider that then. Loyalty is always good but what's loyalty without love? You may act all tough and shit but I'm sure you want to be loved just as much as I do."

"You're just drunk that's all Sanaa."

"That may be true but I'm still in my right mind. I'm getting sleepy so I'm going to go up and go to bed. It was nice being able to talk to you."

She leaned over hugging me tightly. I didn't even want to let go of her. She climbed out the car shutting the door behind her.

I knew from the moment I meet her she was going to be something special. Our little talk put a lot of things into perspective for me. I sat there watching as she entered her building before pulling away from the curb.

NAOMI

I had scheduled an appointment with Sanaa to get my nails done. I needed it. The new growth on my nails was getting outrageous. I kept putting off getting a fill in for a while now. I wasn't even going to worry about it until Berlin brought it up when I was sucking his dick. I felt so embarrassed that he went as far as giving me the cash to get them done.

I walked into the shop and Sanaa was finishing up another girl's nails. I took a seat in one of the empty chairs waiting for her to get done. I wasn't in a rush. I didn't have anything to do for the day. My entire day was dedicated to my nails.

My mind drifted off to Berlin again. We were spending a lot of time with each other lately. I think I was getting more emotionally attached to him but didn't want to admit that truth. I guess I was afraid if I was to say it out loud, things would take a drastic turn for the worst. The one thing I didn't want to do was set myself up for despair. Just because I felt a certain way about him didn't mean he felt the same way about me.

"You ready?" Sanaa asked bringing me back from my thoughts.

I was so caught up in a daze I hadn't even realized she was finished doing the other girl's nails and was wiping down her station.

"Yeah," I got up from the chair and sat down in front of her.

"You good? Seems like something is bothering you. You came in quiet and that's not you. What's wrong?"

"I just was thinking about some things," I replied not really wanting to get all into it.

Sanaa grabbed my hands looking down at my fingernails. She cut her eyes up at me. "Since when did you start letting your nails look like this Naomi?"

"I've been busy." I smiled, thinking about Berlin yet again. *I wish he would just get out of my mind for a second.*

"Busy doing what? Fucking Berlin?" She snickered, seeing me scrunch my face up at her. "What? You have been spending a lot of time with him lately. Keep on your ass is going to end up pregnant."

"I know it's just..."

"Just what, Naomi? Please don't tell me you're already pregnant."

71

Taniece

I was preparing myself for what she was going to say once I told her this. I glanced around the shop to make sure no one was listening in on our conversation. I didn't know who all Berlin knew and didn't need them running back telling him what they overheard.

"I think I'm falling for him, Sanaa." I scratched behind my ear avoiding eye contact with her as I admitted the truth.

I never thought this day would come. I was the type of person who really never wanted to be in a relationship. I skated through life with nothing but un-relationships and cuddy buddies which was perfectly fine with me.

Honestly, I thought that's all I was going to ever need. That is until I met Berlin. He had me looking at things differently and possibly wanting to be in a relationship for the first time. I was yearning for more and that wasn't me.

Had I known he was going to change my life; I wouldn't have ever gone looking for him in the first place. Things were complicated now, and I loathe difficult relationships.

"Are you serious?" All I could do was nod. "Does he know?"

"I don't really want to tell him, Sanaa. I don't know how he feels about me and I don't want to ruin the good thing we have going right now."

She dropped my hand and brought her attention directly to my eyes. "Naomi, you're crazy if you think he doesn't feel the same way. I saw the way he looked at you that night at *Crisis*. It was like you were the only person in the room for him. I'd kill to have someone look at me like that."

My face grew warm after she said that. I don't know how I missed it. *What if she was right and he was just waiting for me to shoot my shot first?*

"Still, I don't know. Maybe I'll just keep riding the wave and see where it takes us. But enough about me and Berlin. Tell me what happened when you left with Soul."

She playfully rolled her eyes then a smile crept up on her face. I'm not even sure if she knew it was there.

"Soul's cool and all but he has a girlfriend and I'm not trying to put myself in a predicament to get hurt. I'd rather just stay away from him."

"But it's obvious he likes you, Sanaa. Apparently, you like him as well. Maybe you need to act on your feelings."

If anyone deserved to be happy in a relationship it was Sanaa. She had been through so much lately and I just wanted her to find happiness. I was afraid if she didn't find it soon, she'd never do it.

"Doesn't matter. I'm not about to be a homewrecker."

"You better go wreck the shit out of that nigga's home if you know what's best for you. You might fuck around and miss out on a good man because you're too stuck in your old ways."

"You're the one to talk. Didn't you just tell me you think you're falling for Berlin but don't even want to tell him? So, who's really stuck in their old ways?" She screwed her face up at me. I hated she was actually right. Most times she was. "Go dry your nails."

We talked so long; I hadn't even realized she was done. I got up and went behind her then sat down at the table. She turned on the drier and I stuck my hands underneath the blower.

I was going to think about telling Berlin how I really felt but I wasn't sure if I'd actually go through with it.

BERLIN

This chick Melissa I had met the other night called me up wanting me to come get her and shit. She had a boyfriend, so I couldn't chill at her house. We were on our way to the Hilton downtown when my phone began ringing. It was sitting in the cup holder on the charger. I pulled up to a red light and grabbed it. My father's name flashed on the screen.

"Yeah, Pops?" I answered not wanting the phone to ring too long or else he'd be ready to go in on my ass.

"Where you at?"

"Downtown, what's up? Something wrong?"

I cut my eyes at Melissa to make sure she wasn't eavesdropping and shit.

"We have a problem with Logan. You're supposed to have a handle on that shit. He hasn't coughed up his money and he took product. The hell you out there doing? Let me find out you can't handle your fucking job and I'll give that shit to someone else who can." He disconnected the call before I could respond.

"Fuck!" I growled, dropping my phone back in the cup holder. I busted a quick left running the red light.

"Where we going?" Melissa questioned me.

"Just sit back and ride."

Xplicit wasn't that far away from me so I could make a quick stop there, handle my business, and go on about my day. It shouldn't take long if things went accordingly.

I pulled up into the parking lot and threw the car in park. I turned to Melissa who was staring out the window at the club.

"I have to go in there and take care of some business right quick. Stay your ass in the fucking car."

I reached over taking my Nine out the glove compartment. I checked the clip to make sure it was full before slipping it down into the front of my pants. Then, I got out of the car and went into the club.

It was empty because it wasn't time for them to open yet. Just like a lot of other places, *Xplicit* was owned by the Maserati's but someone else rented it out. The owner, Logan bought product from us from time to time and we'd never had a problem with him before. That is until now. There's always someone that got greedy and thought they could bite the hand that fed them. Just because I had been chilling lately, they thought I wouldn't show my ass.

My mind was so wrapped up in Naomi, I been neglecting my duties and now the shit was beginning to show. If my father was getting on my ass, then I really was slipping. He wouldn't hesitate to snatch my stripes away from me and give everything I'd worked so hard for to someone else.

I went up to the bar where the bartender was stocking the shelf. "Where the hell is Logan?" I placed my piece down on the countertop and her eyes expanded.

"Uh, he's in his office."

"Would you be kind enough to go back there and get him for me? Then you can go home for the day."

I leaned across the bar, picking up the bottle of Remy and took the top off. She looked like she wanted to say something to me but didn't. She backed away until there were a few feet in between us then rushed off to go grab Logan.

Not long after they both showed up. Logan stopped in his tracks when his eyes landed on me. This muhfucka thought just because he was white, I wouldn't fuck his ass up. My hands didn't discriminate when it came to an ass whooping and my bullets damn sure didn't know race when they left the chamber.

"The hell you still standing there for? Didn't I tell your ass to go home?" She looked over at Logan like she needed permission to leave when I just told her to. He nodded and she zoomed out of there. The door slammed behind her.

"What are you doing here Berlin?"

"You got something that belongs to me." I took another swig of the liquor.

It wasn't as good as the Louis, but it'll do for now. I needed something to calm my nerves before I put a bullet in Logan's ass, then I'd be fucked up. I would have come there for nothing and my father damn sure would put his foot up my ass.

"I made an agreement with Mason. I didn't have the money that time so he said I could get the product off first then pay for it later."

Crash!

I lunged the Remy bottle at the liquor shelf, and it shattered right along with the bottle it encountered.

"Does Mason have Maserati attached to his fucking name?"

"No, but—"

"You damn right. No, the fuck he doesn't." I jolted from the barstool with my strap in my hand and rushed Logan.

Wham!

I struck him straight across the face with the gun knocking him to the floor.

"How the fuck you think you can just make a deal with him like he run some shit?" I yelled as I cocked the gun back and shoved it into his mouth. "Where the fuck is my shit Logan? I either want my fucking product or my money. You got

2.5 seconds to answer me or else I'm pulling this got damn trigger." I clenched my teeth and stared him directly in the eyes.

The door to the club opened and I turned my attention toward it. Melissa stood there with her mouth ajar.

"Thought I told your stupid ass to stay in the fucking car!"

Logan got bold and tried to fight me for my gun. He hit me in the throat, and I fell back onto my ass grabbing it. If she didn't bring her dumbass in here, then I wouldn't have to deal with this shit. He quickly grabbed the gun and turned it on me with a half-smirk on his face.

Situations like this were the reason why I didn't want to have a girl. They didn't fucking listen and she damn sure wasn't any help at the moment.

Finally catching my breath, I spat, "You going to shoot me, muhfucka? Shoot me then but once they get word, I'm dead, you and your entire family fucking dead including that pretty ass little newborn of yours."

"You touch my family and I'll..."

"You going to what?" I laughed in his face and pressed my forehead on into the gun. "Pull the trigger and you'll find out. Pops already knows where I went because he sent me here. Shoot me, nigga." I smiled up at him, knowing he wasn't going to go through with it. "That's what the fuck I thought."

Wham!

I punched him right in the dick bringing him to his knees. The gun fell from his grip and I picked it up.

Pow!

"Ahhh!" he yelled, gripping his thigh.

I shot him in the thigh and Melissa shrieked.

"Next time you got a gun aimed at someone I suggest you pull the trigger. Now, where the hell is my fucking money?"

"Upstairs in the safe. The code is 112234."

Pow!

I shot him right between the eyes. Hope he didn't think he was going to still live after pulling a gun on me. I turned to Melissa.

"No, please don't," she cried out, but it was too late.

Pow!

The bullet went crashing through her skull sending brain matter and blood everywhere. She was a witness and I knew better than to send her out into the world when she saw me kill someone. If she just stayed in the car like I told her to then she'd still be alive.

Pulling my phone out, I texted the clean-up crew. Someone new would be running *Xplicit* by the end of the week. That's what happened whenever we retired someone who worked for us.

I jogged upstairs and grabbed all the cash out the safe he owed for the product he took. I had to stop slipping before I was the one lying on the floor with a bullet between my eyes.

SANAA

I was working nonstop and felt like I needed a break. I took the day off leaving Layla in charge. I told her not to call me unless it was absolutely necessary. I decided to go to the mall and get a little shopping done. I wasn't splurging or no shit, but I was buying a few things.

I walked around St. Louis Galleria all by myself with a couple of bags. It was rare I went shopping but when I did, I bought some things I thought were to die for. I never really saw the point in going broke on buying clothes and shoes when you already had a closet full at home.

I was inside at Bath & Body Works stocking up on more lotion when my stomach growled. I knew it was time for my mini shopping spree to come to a close. I paid for the items I had and left out of the store. There was nothing in the food court I wanted to eat so I was going to stop by somewhere to grab something on my way home.

As soon as I stepped out the door, I bumped right into someone and my Bath & Body Works bag dropped to the floor.

"I'm sorry." I bent down to grab my bag, but they beat me to it.

"No, it was my fault."

I'd recognize that raspy, deep baritone voice from anywhere. My lips turned up into a smile as my eyes traveled from his tattooed hand up to his crisp light gray suit sleeve, white button-up shirt, and then landed on his handsome ass face. I ran straight into Soul and felt like he had snatched every bit of mine right out my body. That was one of the effects he always had on me whenever I was near him.

I hadn't seen or talked to him since the night he took me home from the club. I kind of regretted some of the things I had told him, but I couldn't take them back, so I might as well face him head-on.

"What are you doing here?"

"Came to pick up my new suit." He held up the Brooks Brothers dress bag. "I see you've been doing a lot of shopping."

"I wouldn't say a lot."

I only had about five bags in my hands. Out of my entire trip, I spent no more than two thousand dollars. That was a lot in my opinion. Way less than what he probably spent on that one suit though.

78

My stomach growled again and this time it was loud as hell. I tugged on the lower part of my charcoal t-shirt and lowered my head. I know Soul heard my stomach; everyone within a two feet radius probably heard it. That's just how loud it was.

"You hungry?" He shot me a half-smirk.

I wanted to tuck my tail and run out of there. He probably thought I was some pig of an eater. I was always thinking about food in his presence. *I hope he didn't think I wasn't eating at home or something.*

"A little," I shyly responded, tugging on my earlobe and pressing my lips together.

"Sounds like more than a little. Come on let's put something on your stomach."

"I don't think that's a good idea."

He had a girlfriend and I wasn't trying to get in the way. We already had spent too much time together.

"It's just a bite to eat Sanaa. Stop overthinking things." He took my bags from my grasp and walked off. I stood there for a moment and realized I didn't have much of a choice, so I caught up to him.

"Where are we going? I don't want anything from the food court. I was going to stop by somewhere on my way home and get something."

"I don't eat that mess anyway. But I don't know. What you feel like eating?"

"I think I want some fried chicken and I don't mean that Popeyes or Churches type of chicken either."

"I know just the place to take you."

We stepped outside, and the sun rays beamed down onto my skin. It was hot as hell and I was glad I talked myself out of wearing jeans this morning and put on a pair of shorts.

"I'm driving this time. You know what happened the last time I went to eat with you." I giggled to mask the awkwardness.

It was funny now but when it happened, I was pissed the fuck off. I didn't even want to see his stupid face again but had to remember he wasn't my man and had done nothing wrong.

"You don't have to worry about Sofia. She wouldn't be caught dead in a place like that. You can drive though, just follow me."

I hit my key fob, popping my trunk and he placed my bags into it.

"That's fine by me."

He shut my trunk and pulled the driver's side door open for me. I climbed into the car.

"I'll pull around behind your car, so you can follow me."

I nodded my head and he shut the door and disappeared.

Part of me knew it was wrong to be agreeing to go out to lunch with him. He was basically my boss and he had a girlfriend. None of this was right but I still craved to be near him. Desired to feel his touch. Anticipated the feel of his lips. Soul always drew me to him like a magnet and whenever I was close to him, I couldn't find it in myself to resist him.

His Lambo pulled up behind me, so I put my car in reverse. I followed him all the way to Gourmet Soul Restaurant and Catering. I loved that place. It was where I always went when I had a taste for soul food. Especially after my mother got killed.

I climbed out of the car and followed him inside.

We ate lunch and talked about our pasts and childhoods. I really enjoyed Soul's company. He was so easy for me to talk to. By the end of lunch, I felt closer to him. I didn't want to get too close because I didn't want to get attached. The only thing that could come out of that attachment is heartache. My heart couldn't bear that shit at the moment.

After we left lunch, we ended up going to catch a movie. It was nice because it had been a minute since I've been to the theater.

Soul and I had spent the entire day together. We had such an amazing time that we lost track of time. It was nice not having to worry about all our problems for the day.

As we were heading out of the theater together, I kept glancing over at Soul. Like always my heart skipped a few beats for him. I don't know what it was about him that was so alluring to me.

I lightly bumped him brushing my hair back behind my ear.

"I had a good time today."

"I'm glad that you did. Maybe we can do it again sometime."

"Yeah, we'll see about that."

I didn't want to make any future plans with him. He needed to get rid of that girlfriend of his, then maybe we could talk. I stopped in my tracks and turned to him.

"I think you should get going. I've kept you out long enough."

"You could keep me out longer if you wanted to." He shot me that sexy ass half-smirk of his that was to die for. I creamed a little bit in my panties.

"You and I both know that's not a good idea." Then I turned and left.

If I had stayed a moment longer things probably would have turned for the worst. By the end of the night I undoubtedly would have been bouncing up and down on his dick. I wanted Soul in the worst way, and I knew I had to fight the urge to keep my sanity.

SOUL

I had fun spending time with Sanaa. I ended up telling her things that Sofia didn't even know about me. I found it so easy to talk to her. Our time together had expired, and I wasn't ready for her to leave just yet, but I didn't want to seem clingy asking her to stay with me a little longer.

After she left, I drove home. My entire ride there the only thing on my mind was her. I had to figure out exactly what I wanted to do. On one hand, I had Sofia who was amazing in her own way, but she and I didn't connect the way I wanted us to. On the other, I had this remarkable ass woman Sanaa who I was keeping a secret from that could end whatever we had before it even began.

I had this connection with Sanaa that I've never had with anyone else including Sofia. Every time I was near her, I always got this sudden urge to touch her. It scared the shit out of me because I've never wanted someone in my personal space like that. But with Sanaa, all I craved was to keep her close to me.

I hit the button on my pad to open my garage when I pulled onto my street. Soon as I pulled into the long driveway, I saw Sofia's white Porsche parked. I already knew it was about to be some shit if she was over my house this time of night. It was going on 10:00 pm and she hadn't even told me she was coming over.

I parked in the garage and prepared myself to go inside. When I got in the house it was dark as hell, so I assumed she had fallen asleep waiting for me to get there. I searched the first floor looking for her. Sofia knew she wasn't allowed to spend the night there, so I was going to send her home before it got too late.

I found her sitting on the sectional in the living room scrolling through her phone. When she felt my presence, she glanced up and locked eyes with mine.

"Where have you been all day Soul?" Her face held a stern expression when she asked that. Her foot tapped lightly against the floor and her arms folded underneath her breasts. "We were supposed to have gone to a dinner party at Kacee's. Do you not know how it feels for me to be there alone watching everyone else with their significant others? I had to go there alone, Soul!"

She pounded her fist down on the couch beside her and rose from her seat. I had forgotten all about that shit. That was the reason why I had gone and picked up that suit in the first place. When I got with Sanaa, I had lost track of time and forgot what my priorities were.

"I was with Sanaa."

Her nostrils flared and her eyes went to slits.

"You were with Sanaa? As in the same bitch you were with when I ran into you at Kemoll's?"

"Yeah, and what I tell you about calling her a bitch, Sofia?"

I tread upstairs to my bedroom and she came behind me.

"You fucking left me alone, so you could be with another woman, Soul!"

I stopped in my tracks pinching the bridge of my nose. I was not up to argue with her tonight. The only thing I wanted to do was climb in bed, but I knew she wasn't going to leave there without getting her point across.

"I'm sorry I forgot about the dinner party. It honestly had slipped my mind but I'm not about to do this shit with you right now. Will you just go home, and we talk about this later?"

"You're trying to put me out the house, so you can invite that bitch over!"

"What the fuck did I just tell you about calling her a bitch!" I roared.

Sofia was truly pissing me the fuck off now. She knew what she was doing. She wanted me to get angry and if she kept pushing my buttons, I was going to end up doing something I'd regret.

She closed the gap between us. "That's right, I called her a fucking *bitch*. What are you going to do about it?" Her chest heaved as she glared up into my eyes.

"I suggest you take your ass home and forget this shit before you piss me the fuck off."

"And if I piss you off exactly what are you going to do?"

She rested her hand on her hip, waiting for me to respond. I just prayed she took her ass on about her business before I ended up hurting her feelings. I said I forgot about the party and she should have just left the shit at that. I get she's angry with me for spending the day with Sanaa, but the shit was harmless. She was acting like I had been fucking her or something.

I lightly shoved her to the side and went on into my bedroom. I took my suit jacket off, pulled my shirt out my pants, and began unbuttoning it.

"Did you fuck her, Soul?" her voice cracked as she asked.

I didn't have to turn around to know she was on the brink of crying. Sofia was making a big deal out of nothing.

"No, I didn't fuck her."

"I want you to stay away from her, Soul. Promise me that you'll stay away from her."

"I can't promise you something like that when she works for me. I'll have to deal with her one way or another."

"You have other people that can handle that Soul. You don't have to deal with her you just choose to."

"So, what?"

I went into the bathroom and started the shower. I was over this conversation with Sofia and was about to put her out of my house.

"So, what? Stay the hell away from the bitch or lose me. It's your choice."

"You know how I feel about ultimatums." I gripped her by her forearm and took her downstairs to the front door. "It's time for you to go. I'll talk to you tomorrow when you're not so angry because right now you're not thinking straight. Call me and let me know you made it home safe."

I shoved her clutch into her chest and pushed her across the threshold, shutting the door in her face before she could object. I think it was best we both got a good night's rest and start fresh in the morning. She may have been mad at me then, but I was sure she'd probably forget all about why she was pissed in the first place by the morning.

NAOMI

I had an exam earlier and been stressing over it the same as I did with every other test. I needed something to take the edge off, so I invited Sanaa to come out with me to *Armon*, a bar downtown to have a couple drinks with me. I decided on a bar and not a club because I didn't want to be around too many people. I was still wearing the azure blue romper I had worn to class just hours prior.

I had no plans on staying too long so that's why I didn't go and change. My outfit was fine for the bar anyway. A pair of heels would have really set it off but the Giuseppe sandals I had on were just fine.

I sat in my yellow Audi Q3 waiting for Sanaa to pull in the parking lot. I was surprised when she agreed to come out with me when I asked the first time. Usually, I would have to damn near beg her to go somewhere but I guess she was in a good mood.

I spotted Sanaa's candy apple red Maserati pulling into the parking lot. Yonnie had brought one for Sanaa when she'd purchased one for herself. She always wanted Sanaa to match her fly. Yonnie did whatever for that girl to make her life easier.

Some people toss their kids out on their ass when they turned eighteen. But, Yonnie worked her ass off to ensure Sanaa would have a better life. By the time Sanaa graduated from high school, she had an eight hundred credit score, a brand-new condo and was pushing a got damn Maserati just like her mother's.

She still had Yonnie's Maserati, but it was parked in the garage at her condo. I told her she was crazy for not pushing them both, but she said she couldn't bring herself to get back in the car after finding Yonnie dead in it.

Sanaa climbed out of her car and walked up to my driver's side door. I let the window down and her face was just glowing.

"What you so damn happy about?" I pushed the door open and got out.

"What you mean? I always look like this."

"You a lie. Your natural face is a mean mug. I watched you get out your car with those deep dimples showing." I pinched her cheeks and she slapped my hand down. "You smiling for a reason, so spill the tea ho."

"Wellllll, I just spent the day with Soul."

"I should have known it was something. You agreed to come out with me too quick. Hope I didn't pull you away from him."

I held the bar door open for her to enter then I went in behind her. We found a table in the far back corner, so we could be to ourselves and talk about Soul. She was going to tell me everything that happened.

"No, I was already heading home when you called me."

"You mean to tell me you didn't try to get the dick? You're long overdue." I snickered, and she playfully slapped my arm.

"Not everyone is getting dicked down on a regular basis like your freaky ass."

"I damn sure am. But tell me what happened and don't leave out any details."

I made myself comfortable in the chair and waited for her to tell me about her date with Soul. She may not call it a date but if she spent the entire day with him, then it was a *date*.

"Well, I bumped into him in the mall. We had gone to lunch then to see a movie. We talked about everything under the sun."

"Including you getting the dick, right?"

"No," she laughed. "I honestly don't think that we are going to have sex."

"Now, you're just talking nonsense. You are spending time with that fine ass man who's probably carrying a third leg around in his pants just like Berlin. You better jump on that shit."

"I don't want to hear what Berlin has between his legs." She scrunched her face up at me.

"That thang is big, juicy, thick, and long. Mmmhmm." I nibbled on my lower lip just thinking about the muhfucka. "As a matter of fact, let me see where he at because I think I need that shit."

"While you do that, I'm going to go to the bar and get us something to drink."

I slipped my phone out my purse and shot Berlin a text. I stared at the screen waiting for him to reply. When I looked up, I saw a chick bump into Sanaa making her drop our drinks on the floor and they spilled all over her.

"Ah hell nah!" I jumped up from my seat and rushed over there. "Excuse you bitch, but I know you saw her walking there with those big ass eyes!"

"Naomi, meet Sofia, Soul's girl." Sanaa rolled her eyes then grabbed a napkin and went to dab her shirt.

"I don't give a damn who the hell she is, she owes you a fucking apology because I know she did the shit on purpose!"

I folded my arms underneath my breasts, waiting for her to apologize to Sanaa. If she knew what was best for her then she'd do it.

"I'm not apologizing for shit! This bitch needs to stay the hell away from my man!" Sofia yelled, grabbing the attention of several bystanders.

"You need to chill out Sofia. No one wants Soul."

It was crazy how calm Sanaa was in the situation. I would have been bucking on that bitch and quick.

"That's a fucking lie! You spend a little too much time with my man and I know you can't resist him. I mean look at him. He's handsome and wealthy as fuck. No one can resist him." She closed the gap between her and Sanaa and glared down at her. The bitch was tall as hell for her to be a woman. "Stay the fuck away from my man or I promise you'll fucking regret it." She walked off like it wasn't shit. I stood there with my mouth agape.

"You just going to let the bitch walk off like that after she disrespected you?" I questioned Sanaa.

"I'm not worried about her. Let's go back to our seats."

"Hell nah! I'm about to show you what you do to disrespectful bitches like her!"

I ran behind her, gripping her by her hair and clocked her upside her head. Before I could get her good, Sanaa grabbed me, pulling me in the opposite direction.

"Just let me whoop her ass one time and I promise you she won't be a problem anymore!"

"I told you it's fine Naomi."

"No, the hell it's not. Sometimes you're too fucking nice because you know that bitch needs an ass whooping! She fucked up my mood. I don't even want to have drinks anymore. I think we should just go because if I see that ho again, I'm going to rip her a new asshole."

BERLIN

I stared down at the message that had just come through from Naomi. I hadn't seen her in a couple days and that was only because I was forcing myself to stay away from her. Things between us were becoming complicated. She was driving me to feel things I've never felt before and the shit was scary as hell.

At this point, I really didn't know what to do. I tried fucking with other girls to take my mind off of her, but it seemed hopeless, thinking about her was inevitable. It was like she was embedded in my mind and that's never happened to me before.

She wanted to see me, and I was debating if I wanted to leave and go over there. She didn't really flat out and say it, but I already knew what *"What you doing big head"* meant. Naomi was fiending for the dick.

She had texted me the night before late as hell, but I didn't respond to her. I know if I kept ignoring her, she'd only get frustrated and probably think I was fucking with another bitch. I didn't want her to go off and fuck someone else. I was confused trying to figure out what I should do.

Should I put aside my pride and just allow what I knew was coming to happen? I never thought the day would occur that I could say Berlin had fallen for a chick. I tried to keep them all at a distance, so I wouldn't get caught up but somehow, Naomi snuck up on my ass.

I couldn't even enjoy myself now because my mind was on her. Closing out the text message I had been staring at, I went to the video I had of her in my phone. She didn't even know I had taken it of her the other day when she was at my house.

She had come over to Netflix, chill, and smoke with me. We had been drinking but of course, she went a little harder than me. She was tripping off the Kush and liquor and I filmed her dancing around my living room. I think that's the first time I realized I was actually falling for her.

A smile crept up on my face. I was so lost in the video that I hadn't noticed Soul sit down beside me.

"The hell you smirking for?" He snatched my phone away from me and looked at the video of Naomi.

"Man, I don't really know what to do."

"What you mean?" he asked me, handing my phone back.

I hit the home screen and dropped the phone down in my lap. We were at this stupid ass dinner party that my parents had thrown. I dipped off and sat down on the couch to get away from all those people in there.

They never really wanted me around in the first place. I was like the black sheep of our family. Everyone worshiped the ground Soul walked on. They wanted me to be more like him, but I could only be me. I wasn't about to change myself for anyone. That's the reason why Pops was always on my ass.

"I think I'm falling for shorty and I don't know what the hell to do. My heart tells me to go on and let go. Just let the shit happen but my mind is telling me I'm fucking up and to stay the hell away from her. I have never been in love before bruh and the shit is scaring the hell out of me."

"Look, I'm going to give you some advice. Love comes around maybe once in a lifetime if you're lucky enough to get that. If you feel like she's the one, then just go with the flow. Every man needs that one woman behind him. His backbone, rib, heart, to hold him down when no one else can."

"I really think Naomi might be that for you. I got that vibe when she was with you that night at the club. She's changing you and it's for the better. You used to be wilder than this. You might as well say she's the calm to your storm. It's rare to find that shit. So, the best advice I can give you is that you better get your girl before you lose her."

The shit he was saying was making hella sense. I already had peeped all that shit out.

"You sitting in here being big bruh and shit, but I haven't been looking out for you like I'm supposed to. It's time I play big bruh. You need to let that ho Sofia go and stop tryna please Pops. Your ass ain't happy. You're at your happiest when you're around Sanaa. Take your own advice."

I jumped up from the couch not even giving him time to object to the things I had said. I never really liked Sofia in the first place. She was a gold digger to me, and I was certain he already knew that shit. Things between them weren't going anywhere and I was sick of seeing him put his happiness on the back burner to satisfy someone else. He better get like me, say fuck Pops, and go for what he wanted.

I rushed out the front door and jogged down the steps to my car and hit the key fob. My mind was all over the place, but I knew exactly where I was going. I drove to her condo without thinking twice. I parked in front of the building and jumped out the car rushing inside.

I stepped off the elevator on her floor and went up to her door.

Knock! Knock! Knock!

I didn't know if she was there, but I was hoping she was. *Maybe I should have texted her back before I came over there to make sure she was.* I had been standing outside for five minutes and she had yet to come to the door.

Boom! Boom! Boom!

I was growing impatient. My head tilted back, and I stared up at the ceiling, running my hand down my face. Finally, I heard the locks click and Naomi pulled the door open with a bewildered expression on her face.

"Berlin?"

I rushed her, palming both sides of her face, meshing our lips. We kissed long and hard. Our tongues intertwined with each other and my heart thumped rapidly in my chest.

"What was that for?" she asked after I broke the kiss.

I shut the door behind me and pulled my suit jacket off, tossing it on the arm of her chaise lounge.

"Sorry, I just been hella busy lately." It was late as hell and it looked like I disturbed her from her sleep.

Her hair was pulled up in a messy bun and she was in an oversized t-shirt and panties. I gripped her by the hand and took her to her bedroom.

I pulled my shirt out my pants and unbuttoned it, tossing it to the floor then pulled my slacks off. The only thing I had on was my Versace briefs.

"You want to have sex?" she shot me a half-smirk and pulled her shirt over her head. I stopped her, tugging it back down.

"Not tonight bae. I just want to hold you."

I took her over to the bed and climbed into it. She eyed me strangely but snuggled close to me as I wrapped my big arms around her frame. I laid there thinking of things I could do for her, to show her how I feel about her. It wasn't long before I heard her light snores and I drifted off to sleep right behind her.

SANAA

I was angry about the shit that had happened the other night with Sofia. I was never one who liked drama that's why I always tried my best to avoid it, but she was taking things a little too far. Even though it was obvious that there was nothing going on between us, I still posed a threat to her. She should have been checking his ass instead of stepping to me. Soul needed to do something with his girl before she ended up bringing me out of my character and getting her ass beat.

Since I didn't really know how to find Soul, I got Naomi to talk Berlin into giving me his address. It was quite easy actually. All it took was one phone call and he agreed. I thought I would have had to beg him, but he gave it to me with no hesitation.

If I had known he stayed so far, then I probably would have thought twice about this. I went on to his house anyway to avoid a dramatic situation that I knew would occur if we didn't have this conversation.

I pulled into his driveway and wasn't sure if he was there with what time of day it was and then there were no cars parked outside. I would have turned around and gone back to the city, but I hadn't come this far for nothing. I got out of the car and knocked on the door.

I stood there fidgeting with my fingernails waiting to see if someone would answer. I wasn't sure how this conversation was going to go. I hoped I was able to tell him what I needed to say and walk away from there.

The heavy green door finally pulled open and Soul stood on the other side in a pair of black basketball shorts that showed off the top of his Versace briefs, as well as the thin hairline that led from his sunken belly button down to his dick. He was shirtless, and every single tattoo was on display. I licked my chapped lips but that didn't even quench my thirst.

Just as I thought, he was chiseled all over. I could wash my clothes on his abs. Better yet, I had something else I wanted to run across them.

"What are you doing here, Sanaa?"

"I got your address from Berlin because I needed to talk to you."

"Of course."

He stepped to the side and I walked in. His house was huge with tall ceilings and marble floors, looking like a scene out of that old ass show MTV Cribs. A staircase with a catwalk stared back at me. A gold chandelier hung from the ceiling. It only made me wonder what the rest of his house looked like.

I don't know why I was standing there in awe. I didn't expect anything less coming from a man like Soul.

"Have a seat in the living room and I'll go grab a shirt." He gestured to the left and I stepped into the all-white living room.

I couldn't have a room like that in my house. I'd be too afraid that I'd spill something and never get it out.

I sat down on the edge of his sectional, clasping my hands together on my knees, waiting for him to return. When I was driving up here, I just thought I was going to give him a piece of my mind at the door. Not come in.

Soul came back downstairs pulling a white t-shirt down over his head. I pouted a little on the inside because I was enjoying the beautiful view.

"What did you need to talk to me about?"

"Ahem," I cleared my throat attempting to wipe the dirty thoughts I was having of him from my mind. "I bumped into Sofia the other night. You need to check your girlfriend because if she steps to me again, I'm going to whoop her ass. I tried to tell her don't nobody want you." I scrunched my face up.

I was only putting on for him. I didn't want him to know how I felt about him. How much I yearned to be close to him. Lick my tongue across those ripples in his stomach. Rub against him to only get the scent of his cologne on my clothes so I could smell him all day long. How I craved to throw my ass back on his dick. The many times I thought about how soft his lips would feel against mine.

"Is that so?" A smile passed his lips and approached me.

My heart dropped to the pit of my stomach and I shot straight up from the couch, moving around the glass coffee table to put space between us, but he didn't stop there. Soul kept walking toward me until he had me cornered against the wall, his mini bar, and him.

"What you running for?"

"I'm not running."

I unbuttoned the top of my blouse. Suddenly, it felt like a hundred degrees in his house. I fanned myself with my shirt hoping it would calm me down, but it was impossible with Soul standing this close to me. His lovely scent tickled my nostrils. I wanted to grab him by the shirt and pull his body into me, but I fought the urge.

"What do you call it then?" His brow rose when he asked.

He planted both of his hands against the wall on either side of me. I swallowed hard not knowing what he was going to do next.

"You know you want me, Sanaa. Just admit it. You've wanted me from the day I walked into your office."

"Okay, so what? And?"

Soul shook his head and took a couple steps back away from me. He was confusing the shit out of me. I wasn't expecting him to react like that once I did admit that I wanted him. I felt like he tricked me and like a dumb ass I had fallen into his trap.

"Don't act like you don't want me either Soul."

"I'm not good for you. You're better off without me."

"I'm better off without you? You don't know me well enough to tell me some shit like that!"

My pulse was speeding. Soul had pissed me off just that fast.

"Calm down Sanaa. I was only speaking the truth. You don't need a man like me. You deserve better."

"You know what? Fuck you, Soul!"

I shoved straight past him and rushed out the door, slamming it behind me. How the hell was he going to tell me what I deserved?

Soul dangled himself in front of me like a piece of meat and when I fell for the bait he snatched it right away from me. I wasn't up for the games he was playing. I'm over the bullshit. If I never saw his face again it'll be too soon.

SOUL

I know Sanaa was angry as hell with me by the way she had just stormed out of there, but it was all for the best. She didn't want nor need me in her life, especially if she was to find out the truth about her mother. I was only trying to save her heartache. Protect her from me. Maybe one day she would understand.

When she told me about Sofia, the shit pissed me the fuck off. I told her ass to stay the hell away from Sanaa, but she took her ass out there and approached her like she was my side piece or some shit. I told her there was nothing going on between us and she couldn't even take my word for it. I didn't need someone so insecure in my life.

Immediately after Sanaa left, I called her over. I didn't tell her what I wanted her to come over for. She got all excited thinking I wanted to spend time with her and shit, but little did she know I was about to break my foot off in her fucking ass. That was another reason why Sofia and I wouldn't survive. She just doesn't fucking listen.

Knock! Knock!

The knock on the front door brought me back from my thoughts. I got up from the couch and swallowed the last of the Remy that was in my cup then put it on the mini bar. I rubbed my hand down my face and pulled the front door open.

Sofia was standing on the other side with a trench coat on. I already knew what was underneath it—nothing. Sadly, for her, we weren't even going to make it to that point.

"Get your ass in here." I grabbed her by the forearm and snatched her into the house, shutting the door behind her.

"Damn, what's your problem?"

"What the hell did you say to Sanaa the other night?"

"Really, that's what you called me over here for?"

She stormed into the living room and flopped down on the sectional with her arms folded underneath her breasts and her lips twisted up.

"I told you to stay away from that girl. I told your ass that we didn't have shit going on, but you didn't fucking listen."

"Did you really think I was going to just sit back while you run around town with that ho? News flash Soul, you're my man, not hers."

She rolled her eyes at me. I wanted to smack them into the back of her fucking head, but I didn't put my hands on women. I might jerk her ass around a little bit or choke her while having sex but that was about as far as I would take things.

"I know that I'm your man. I'm also a grown ass man and can have whatever type of company that I choose. If I was out there chilling with a got damn stripper or prostitute and told your ass wasn't shit going on you were supposed to believe me. How are we going to have a relationship when you don't even trust me? That's the number one thing in a relationship... trust, Sofia."

"I do trust you, Soul. I just don't trust *her*..."

"Which means that you're insecure as hell."

My head was starting to hurt dealing with her ass. I was beginning to regret calling her over there.

She jumped up from the couch and hurried over to me. "Babe, I'm not insecure. I just love you so much and don't want to lose you to anyone else. Is that such a bad thing?"

She rubbed her hands from my stomach up to my chest. I gripped her by the wrists and shoved her away from me.

"Stay the fuck away from Sanaa. This my last time telling you."

"Oh my God, you like her, don't you?" Tears came to her eyes and dripped from the corners.

"Sofia, I'm not going there with you right now."

It was time that things between us came to an end. Just as Berlin said, things aren't going anywhere, and I truly wasn't happy being with her. The one person I wanted to be with I couldn't. I don't know if I'd be able to keep that secret from her much longer and if she was to find out...

"Okay, if that's really what you want, Soul, then I'll stay away from her." She went to touch me again and I took a couple steps back away from her.

I shook my head, "No, Sofia, what I really want is for you to get out my house. We're done."

"You're really breaking up with me all because I told that bitch to stay away from you? What type of shit is that!"

"Bring your fucking tone down."

"I'm not doing shit! Tell your bitch she better watch her fucking back because I'm coming for her," she warned and went toward the front door but I snatched her by the wrist, shoving her up against it.

Sofia's chest heaved as she stared back at me with glossy eyes. She was probably terrified that I might do something to her. And she was right to be. If she did anything to Sanaa, she was going to be the one that's going to have to watch her back.

"If you harm even one little hair on Sanaa's head. If she even breaks a fucking nail dealing with you, I'm coming for your ass. So, you better be the one to watch your own fucking back," I said through gritted teeth and released her.

She eyed me for a few moments not uttering a word. "If that's really how you feel." She shoved me away from her then snatched the front door open, slamming it behind her.

I knew she was angry, but it was best we ended things right then and there and I stop stringing her along. But one thing was for sure, she better had stayed the hell away from Sanaa or I was going to be paying her a visit and it wasn't going to be a friendly one either.

NAOMI

C lass seemed like nothing but a drag today. The only thing I wanted to do was go home and climb over into my bathtub and soak for hours.

Berlin had been on my mind for most of the day. He had been acting strange lately. I'm not sure what it was but I kind of liked it, so I wasn't complaining one bit. Especially, when he came by the other night and just wanted to hold me. He's never done anything like that before, but it was amazing for him to do it even if it was just that one night.

I stepped off the elevator on my floor and was met by white and pink rose petals scattered everywhere. It was sweet whoever had gone out of their way to do something like that for their significant other. No one has ever done anything like that for me before.

The rose petals led around the corner and straight up to my front door. I was confused, to say the least because I knew Berlin hadn't done anything like that for me. Not when our situation was supposed to be only sex. I wanted it to be more than that, but I wasn't going to get my hopes up.

I learned when I first started messing with Berlin that he wasn't the relationship type of guy. He dealt with too many females and I knew he wasn't going to want to settle down any time soon. I couldn't force him into doing something that I wasn't ready to do myself. Neither one of us was out looking for a relationship but with the way things had been going lately, it might just be a good idea.

I put my key into the door and unlocked it. I pushed the door open and was met by at least twenty-four dozen white and pink roses sitting all over my living room. There were so many of them in there that I could barely see my furniture. It looked like a flower shop had vomited in there.

A smile crept up on my face and I shut the door. Berlin had gone overboard with all the flowers. He could have just gotten me a single rose and I'd be happy. I could tell he wasn't used to doing things like this. It was sweet though.

What I wanted to know was how the hell he had got into my apartment in the first place. I never gave him a key and there was no sign of him breaking in.

I moved around the roses and headed into my bedroom. When I got in there, I saw an Alexander McQueen dress bag lying on the bed along with a Christian Louboutin shoe box and a rectangular Tiffany box.

There wasn't a note attached or anything to tell me what the hell was going on. The least he could have done was told me what he wanted me to do but I guess it was obvious that he wanted to take me somewhere. Even though I wasn't up for it, I was going to go along with his plan anyway. He'd gone through so much trouble to bring it together and that's the least I could do.

I pulled my black floral dress over my head and tossed it into the corner of the room then went into the bathroom. When I got in there, my bath water was already drawn with what smelt like lavender bubbles inside. There were candles lit on the sides of the tub along with a bottle of Armand de Brignac Ace of Spades Rose and a champagne flute.

My cheeks burned from the wide smile that adorned my face. I swiped my hand across the water, and it was still hot so that only meant he had to have left just moments before I got there. I unclasped my bra dropping it to the floor then slipped my black lace panties off. Climbing over into the tub, I rested my back up against it then poured me a glass of wine.

I was only going to drink one glass because I didn't want to get too carried away not knowing where he was going to take me. I sat in the tub for a good forty minutes before I got out. I got dressed and by the time I picked up the Tiffany box there was a knock at my front door.

Opening the door up, Berlin stood on the other side in an all-black suit that perfectly complimented with the red floor length dress he had gotten me. When I took the dress out of the bag, I immediately fell in love with it. It flowed freely with one split that went up to my left thigh.

"You look beautiful."

He gently took the Tiffany box from my clutches and popped it open. Resting within it was a diamond necklace. It sparkled so brightly with all the tiny diamonds that made up the necklace.

"You really didn't have to do all this." I stood there in awe.

"Yeah, I did. Turn around."

I did as I was told and lifted my hair up, so he could place the necklace around my neck.

"Let's go, ma'am, your chariot awaits."

I couldn't help but snicker at him. He was really outdoing himself at the moment.

"Berlin," I softly called out, staring into his eyes.

"Yeah, Naomi?"

"What are we doing?"

I was just going to go along with his plan, but I had to know what was going on here. Not once had Berlin ever uttered the words date to me and now, he had planned out an entire night for us. Even went as far as drawing my bath water.

I wasn't used to things like this. In fact, I've never really gone on a date in my life. Sure, I've gotten a bite to eat here and there with a guy, but I wouldn't really call it a date. This would be my first real date and I wanted to make sure that it was a date and not just a stunt he was pulling. I had to be certain he was trying to take us to the next level, so I wouldn't just be assuming things and run him off.

"I'm falling for you, Naomi."

Butterflies swarmed my stomach at the sound of him saying that. I thought I'd never see the day that Berlin Maserati would be smitten over me.

I closed the space between us and palmed both sides of his face. "I fell for you a long time ago, Berlin Maserati."

"How come you didn't say anything?"

"I didn't want to mess up what we had going. I knew the type of guy you were when I first started messing around with you and I didn't want to try to force you to fall for me. If we never took things to the next level, I was happy with the way things were."

I kissed him softly on the lips. He may be falling for me but that still didn't mean he was going to change his ways for me. If he wanted to take things to the next level, then he had to prove to me he was going to let all those bitches he was fucking with go and be with me and only me.

"What does this mean for us now?" I questioned him to see if we were on the same page.

"I want you to be my girl, Naomi."

"You sure you're ready for all that?"

"I was ready that night I showed up at your door. I'm ready to give this thing a try if you are."

I nodded my head and he pushed me up against the wall planting his lips back on top of mine.

BERLIN

Being in a relationship wasn't going to be easy but for Naomi, I sure was going to try. After having that talk with Soul, I figured I might as well stop trying to hold myself back from feeling what being in love felt like. Naomi was the one for me and I could sense the shit.

I had put together a concrete plan to take her out to dinner and just woo her for the night. When I saw her in that dress, I had to let her know exactly how I felt about her. It wasn't guaranteed she felt the same way but at this point, I didn't give a damn.

My hands roamed up and down her sides as her lips attacked mine right there in the hallway by her front door. I had already made up my mind we weren't even going to make it to dinner. I wanted her and in the worst way possible.

She peeled her body from the wall and gripped me by the collar of my shirt, pulling me into the house with her. I kicked the door closed with my foot; my lips still locked with hers.

For a brief second, we broke our kiss and she eased her hands from my stomach up to my shoulders, pushing my jacket off. It cascaded to the floor and she tugged on the lower half of my shirt until it was out of my pants.

Gripping the middle of my shirt she snatched it back, ripping it open and just stared at my chiseled abs and chest.

"Did I ever tell you just how much I love your body?"

She planted soft kisses from my abs up my chest, then my neck. Finally, she landed on my lips again. Scooping her up into my arms, I carried her into the bedroom then dropped her down on the bed. From where her dress split, I ripped it right open and her breasts sprung to life.

"I wanted to keep that dress." She pouted.

"I'll buy you another one."

I slipped her panties off, dropping them to the floor. Pulling my shirt and pants off, I kicked them to the side.

Naomi got up from the bed pushing me down on it. My dick stood at full attention when she climbed between my legs, wrapping both her hands around my dick. I already knew what she was about to do when she smirked up at me.

She slipped one of my balls into her mouth and gently sucked on it then licked up my shaft with the tip of her tongue. Still holding onto my dick with both her hands, she slipped it into her warm mouth and her eyes crossed as she sucked up and down.

As she sucked, she stroked my dick in a circular motion. I heard her gag on the dick and it caused my toes to curl in my socks. She kept slurping, licking, sucking, and deep throating my shit until I felt myself getting ready to cum.

I gripped her by the back of her head, fucking her mouth roughly until I released my seeds down the back of her throat.

I stood flipping her over onto all fours. She had the perfect arch in her back. That was one of the things I loved about her. She knew everything to do in the bedroom that turned me the fuck on.

I spread her cheeks, positioning myself at her opening. Her pussy was soaking wet. So wet that her juices were oozing from her hole. I slapped my dick against her clit and eased it on inside her. Soon as I entered she let out a moan.

"Mmmhmm."

I slowly eased into her and she matched my rhythm lightly bouncing her fat ass back on my dick. I watched it jiggle every time she came back on it.

"Oooh, it feels so good," she whined.

"I ain't did shit yet. You doing all the work." I chuckled and gripped her by her waist. I was done playing with that pussy and I was about to fuck her ass to sleep.

I forcefully pounded inside her from behind. With every stroke, I gave her I was trying to touch her fucking soul. Naomi's screams grew louder, and she gripped one of the pillows dropping her face into it. I reached around her snatching it from her, tossing it to the floor.

"I want to hear all that shit. Quit fucking playing with me, Naomi."

Smack!

I slapped her hard on the ass and pulled my dick out. Popping her on the pussy again, I plummeted deep into her and she screamed out in pleasure and pain.

"Fuck Berlin!"

"That's right. That's my muhfuckin' name. Say that shit again."

I pulled out of her again and rammed my shit back into her.

"Berlin! Fuck I'm about to cum!" she whimpered.

I reached down underneath her and rubbed her clit to intensify her orgasm that was about to take over her body.

"Fuuuccckkkk I'm cumming!" Her entire body shivered like an earthquake was forming between her thighs.

"Bounce that ass back on this dick, Naomi."

"I'm fucking bouncing!"

Smack! Smack!

"Bounce that shit harder. I want to feel like you about to break my shit."

"Ugh! Fuck!"

"Flip that ass over."

She turned over and I slipped her right back down onto my dick then lifted her up in the air. My biceps flexed as I held her in place bouncing her up and down on my dick. I watched as it repeatedly smashed into her stomach.

"You-you-you going to make me cum again."

"Don't just talk, fucking cum."

Her body trembled again letting me know she was close to her peak. For the first time since we been messing around, I made her squirt. She skeeted all over my lower abs.

I dropped her back onto the bed bending her legs back and dropped my dick straight into her. Her nails dug deep into my biceps and I held her legs back and pounded into her.

"Fuck, this pussy good as fuck."

I kept stroking, feeling myself close to my own peek. I felt accomplished making her cum twice, so I dumped my seeds deep off inside her then eased my dick out. Cum was still oozing from the tip. I fell down on the bed beside her.

Both of our chest's heaved, and we panted trying to catch our breath.

"That-that shit was... fucking amazing."

"I love you," I told her, gripping her pulling her close to me. She laid her head down on my chest and tickled it with her fingertips.

"I love you too."

SANAA

Buzzzzzzz

I peeled my eyelids open at the sound of my phone going off. I peeked over at the alarm clock on the nightstand and it was going on six in the morning. I wasn't supposed to get up for another couple of hours. *Who the hell is disturbing my sleep?*

Grabbing my phone off the nightstand, I stared at the unknown number flashing across the screen. I debated on answering it for a brief second but did anyway. If someone was trying to reach me this time of morning, then it was a possibility that it may have been important.

"Hello?" my groggy voice spoke into the phone.

"Hello is this Sanaa Love?" the male's voice asked on the other end of the line.

I sat straight up in bed wondering exactly who I was speaking with.

"Yes, and may I ask who this is?"

"This is officer Michael with the St. Louis police department. I just responded to your alarm going off at your shop. Can you get down here as soon as possible?"

I quickly jolted from bed rushing over to the closet to grab something to throw on.

"What's going on at my shop?"

"I think that it's best we talk about this in person. Can you come to the shop right now?"

"Yes, I'm on my way." I disconnected the call and quickly threw on a pair of jeans and a t-shirt.

The only thing I could think was that something horrible had happened. If the police were at the shop and the alarm was going off, then something was wrong. Someone had to have tried to break in and I could only hope they hadn't taken anything. Lucky for me, I had already deposited the money into the bank that Soul had sent by earlier or else I would have been fucked.

There was no way I would be able to explain to him it wasn't my fault his money had come up missing. He'd probably think I had something to do with it then it'll be off with my head.

Out of the entire time I had been running the shop, nothing has happened. They just had to come playing around there now but why?

After I slipped my feet into my silver sandals, I grabbed my keys and was out the door. I sped all the way to the shop praying that it wasn't anything too bad going on there.

I whipped into the parking lot parking right by the squad car. I couldn't even pick my mouth up off the ground when my eyes landed on the *Glitz*. It was destroyed. The glass was broken out of all the windows including the door.

I fumbled trying to open the car door, so I could get out. I walked up to the building with watery eyes. All the hard work my mother had done was completely gone. I had failed her as a successor and a daughter. I let someone come in and shatter every dream she's ever had. They ripped the last thing I had of my mother away from me and the shit burned in my chest.

Chairs were thrown all over the place. All the nail polish bottles were tossed over the floor. Most of them broken others poured out. Everything in there was flipped. I stepped over the threshold. Glass cracked with every step that I took.

The word *bitch* was spray painted in red over *Glitz*. Every mirror in there was busted just as the windows. I went to the back to the office and the door was kicked in. They flipped everything upside down in there as well.

Tears cascaded down my cheeks. The safe behind the desk along with the chandelier were the only things untouched. That let me know that this had to have been a personal attack. But, I didn't have any enemies. I tried my hardest to stay out of drama. Who the hell could have done this?

I dropped to the floor in the middle of the shop and cried my heart out. I cried for my mother. I cried for failing her. I cried because I didn't know what the hell to do next.

My stomach hardened. I had this tightness in my throat like my lungs were about to cave in on me.

"Do you know who could have done this?" Officer Michael asked me.

I shot daggers at him. "Do you think if I really knew who did this that I'd be in here crying about the shit? Can you just get out my fucking shop!" I screamed out at him. I didn't mean to take my anger out on him, but he was the closest thing that was in here.

"If you can think of anyone that could have done this please don't hesitate to give me a call."

He gently placed his card on the floor and slipped it over to me.

"GET THE FUCK OUT! NOW!"

I was no longer upset. I was angry. No, I was more than angry. I was mad as fuck and someone was going to fucking pay for doing this shit.

I slipped my phone from my pocket and called Soul. I didn't want to deal with him, but he was the only person I could think of who could help me now.

He answered the phone on the first ring.

"Hello?" he spoke sounding like he was wide awake over there.

"Can you get down to the shop. Someone broke in and destroyed everything," I whined into the phone.

"I'm on my way."

I ended the call and placed my phone back into my pocket. Pulling myself up off the floor, I went to get the broom, so I could start cleaning up.

The only thing I had managed to get up was all the broken glass in the doorway before Soul came rushing in. The sun was now beaming bright outside and I could get a better look at all the damage.

His nostrils flared, and he bared his teeth. I knew something was wrong when he walked through the door. Well, open space now since they broke it.

"I'm sorry Sanaa. I'm going to fix this and take care of who did it."

"What you mean? You don't even know who did it."

"Actually, I do."

He pulled his phone out and pressed play on the screen. I stood there watching as Sofia and someone else destroyed my mother's shop.

"How the hell you get that?"

"I got security cameras installed in all of our places."

"So, it's your fault that my mother's place is gone to shit!"

I shoved him hard and he stumbled back a little bit.

"If you want to blame it on me then that's fine."

He closed the gap between us, and I pounded my fists into his chest. I hated him right now. This place was everything to my mother which only meant it was everything to me. Now, look at the place.

"You can take all your anger out on me. I'm going to fix this Sanaa, I swear."

"You better because this was all I had left of my mother and now it's barely hanging on by a thread."

The tears seeped back into my eyes. I didn't want him to see me cry but I couldn't help it. I was hurting and the only way I was going to get over this anger was if I hunted Sofia down and whoever else helped her and make those bitches pay for what they did.

SOUL

I felt bad as fuck after I found out A'Karri and Sofia vandalized Sanaa's shop. When she first called me, I didn't hesitate to pull up the security cameras to find out who had done it. I lied to her when I said we had cameras in all our establishments. People had their own but *Glitz*, in particular, had *our* cameras because money had begun coming up missing about a year ago. And I mean huge amounts of cash. That's how I found out that Yonnie had been taking shit from us.

She started out with small amounts off the top that we wouldn't too much notice. Then she began getting greedy taking larger sums. That's how we caught her stealing. The rest was history.

Sanaa was fucked up in the head behind this shit and I knew I had to do something to take her mind off things. I hated seeing her with that frown on her face and tears in her eyes.

"Come on we're leaving." I took the broom from her and leaned it up against the wall.

"I can't go anywhere with this place looking like this."

"No one can do any more damage to this place that's already done." She side eyed me, taking what I had said totally out of context. "You know what I meant. Just come on."

I grabbed her hand and led her out to my Ferrari. I opened the passenger's side door for her and she slid into the seat.

"You good?" I stood outside the car and asked her. She nodded, so I shut the door and jogged around the car. As I climbed inside, I pulled my phone out and dialed my assistant Emily's number.

"Yes, Soul?"

"I need you to tell them to get the Jet running and meet me at my house with a few things. I need some feminine products along with a couple outfits to fit a size..." I briefly glanced over at Sanaa then took my eyes back to the road. "a size eight. Oh, and I need a swimsuit as well. I'm getting on the interstate now, so you need to meet me there."

"Wait, where are we going?" Sanaa interrupted me.

"Yes, Soul," Emily responded.

I ended the call and dropped my phone into my lap.

"We're taking a little trip to take your mind off things. Don't stress it because I'm sure you'll love it." At least I hoped she would.

It didn't take me long to make it out to the house. When we walked inside all the items I had asked for were sitting on the couch. I grabbed the bags handing them over to Sanaa.

"Follow me so you can take a shower."

I led her upstairs to my bedroom and showed her where everything was then grabbed a few items out my drawers packing a light bag for myself as well as sticking the other things that she wasn't going to use in there.

I was surprised she was complying with my little plan. Usually, she would have given me lip. Maybe things were worse than I thought they were.

By the time Sanaa had returned from the bathroom, I had changed into something a little more comfortable than the suit I was wearing. I had on a pair of khaki chinos with a white Burberry polo shirt.

Sanaa stood before me in a burgundy long tub dress that showed off her figure perfectly.

"You ready to go? The jet is waiting for us."

"I honestly don't think any of this is necessary."

"I didn't ask you what was necessary. I want to do something nice for you. Will you just let me?"

"Fine, but it doesn't mean that it's going to take my mind off of things. What should I do with these?" she asked, holding up her dirty clothes.

I took them from her and dropped them into my hamper without even thinking twice about it. It's crazy because no other woman has ever left anything over my house before yet here I was keeping her dirty underwear. I grabbed our bag and took her downstairs to the Lincoln Town Car that was sitting in front of the house waiting for us.

* * *

Almost three hours later we were standing on the beach in Miami with the water ripping against our bare feet. Sanaa stood off to herself in her sexy yellow bikini that complimented her skin tone extremely well. I observed her from where I was standing, not wanting to get too much into her personal space. I had already kidnapped her and taken her to another state not even knowing how she felt about it.

I could tell her mind was heavy. She stood there with her arms folded underneath her breasts, staring out into the clear blue water. I watched as she took a deep breath then exhaled. I brought her out here to take her mind off things not for her to think about it even more.

I slowly strolled over to her and could hear her sighing heavily. Scooping her up into my arms, I carried her out to the water.

"Soul!" she shrieked squirming in my arms. "Put me down!"

"Stop stressing about things. I told you I was going to take care of it."

The water crashed against our bodies. I sat her down on her feet in the ocean and the water almost took her away. She dipped down underneath the water and came back up brushing her hair back. The way the sun was beaming down on her, I got lost in her beauty.

Sanaa was on a whole other level of gorgeous. I could spot every freckle that lined her face. Just how beautiful her hazel eyes were. My heartbeat quickened with every moment my eyes stayed trained on her.

Water splashed up in my face and it was then that I realized she had done it. She grinned up at me and I gripped her underneath her arms, picking her up into the air. She smiled down at me and I couldn't help but return the smirk.

I gently eased her down and she draped her arms around my neck. We were lost in each other's eyes for a moment. I knew I shouldn't be doing this, but I did it anyway. She cupped my face and my lips locked with hers. She slightly parted her lips and I slipped my tongue into her mouth. I explored every depth of it I could reach.

"I want you," she said when she pulled back.

"You sure about this?"

"I've never been surer about anything."

I carried her up to our six-bedroom home that sat right there on the beach. I took her through the sliding back doors that led into the kitchen. We didn't even make it to the living room let alone one of the bedrooms.

I had been wanting Sanaa for the longest but was fighting the urge.

I sat her down on the kitchen table and she gazed up into my eyes. I intertwined my fingers in her wet hair and pulled her face to mine again. With my free hand, I untied her bikini top and her beautiful pierced dark nipples came into view. Just the sight of that already had my dick bricking up.

I cupped her breast and licked around her nipple with the tip of my tongue. When I pulled back, I left a trail of my saliva dripping from my mouth to her nipple. I planted soft kisses from her breasts up to her neck. I noticed when I made it to her neck, she titled her head to the side, letting me know that was probably her spot.

"You want me to kiss you here?"

I lightly brushed my fingertip across her skin and goosebumps appeared over her body.

"Please?"

Licking the tip of my tongue across her neck, her body shuddered.

"That's your spot?"

"Yes," was all she could muster up.

I gently sucked on her neck and light moans seeped from her lips.

"Mmmhmm."

I eased my hand down to her pussy, slipping it down the front of her bikini, grazing her bald pussy. I didn't stop until my hand reached her clit and tenderly rubbed it.

Sanaa's legs opened up like the pearly gates of heaven.

"I want you to cum for me. You think you can do that?"

She nodded.

"I want to hear you say it."

"I'll cum for you, Soul."

Tugging on either side of her bikini bottoms until they were off, I tossed them to the floor. I got down on my knees in front of her gently pushing her straight back onto the table. I softly kissed her on the pussy. Her legs shivered again.

My lips latched onto her pussy and the moan that escaped her lips was so sexy to me.

"Mmmhmm, Soul."

I loved the way my name rolled off her tongue. She could just say my name and it'll probably make my dick stiffen.

I licked her pussy in a circular motion. She tried to run from me, so I gripped her and pulled her back down to the edge of the table. I squeezed her breast and sped up my licks. Her hand gripped me by the back of my head rubbing my waves.

"Fuck, Soul," she whimpered.

I kept my eyes locked on her when I felt her back form an arch. Her face contorted into beautiful expressions as she sensed her climax take over her body.

"Oh, my fucking God!" she screamed at the top of her lungs.

She tried to run again, and I pinned her down on the table and wouldn't let up until she was done climaxing.

"Stop fucking running from me, Sanaa."

"I can-can't help iiiittttttt!"

I finally let go of her pussy and stood straight up. My dick was hanging on the side of my leg stiff as a brick, ready to plunge into something wet.

I wiped her juices from my face with the back of my hand.

"Take me, Soul."

"I'm about to fucking feed your soul."

I roughly snatched her all the way to the edge of the table. I dropped my pants to the floor and Sanaa's eyes protruded as she stared at my dick.

"Don't worry I'll be gentle with you."

I rubbed my dick up and down her slit, getting it nice and wet before positioning myself at her opening. I amazed my damn self because I was about to go inside her raw, something I've never done before. I've always used protection even with Sofia.

I eased my dick inside her.

"Ungh!" she cried out tossing her head back.

I leaned my body down on top of hers, kissing her lips softly. My hand gently gripped her neck as I slowly deep stroked her. She dug her nails deep into my back holding on for dear life.

"I want to be yours, Soul," she whispered meeting my gaze.

"I keep telling you I'm no good for you, Sanaa."

I planted a sweet kiss on her chin.

"I don't care, I want you."

I stood straight back up, holding on tightly to her waist as I pounded my dick in and out of her. Her hands tightly gripped the sides of the rocking table to hold on. She just needed something to grip.

"Fuuuccckkkk Soul I'm cumming again!" her voice cracked a little as she spoke.

"Cum all over that dick, bae."

I felt a gush of fluid rushing my dick. I tossed my head back in ecstasy. Sanaa had some of the best pussy I've ever encountered. The shit was so fucking wet and tight that I wanted to crawl in the muhfucka and live in it.

"Fuck I'm about to cum."

I was so used to wearing a condom that I wasn't even thinking straight. I held her in place by her waist as I released my seeds. By the time I realized what I had done, it was already too late.

NAOMI

I had been blowing up Sanaa's phone for the last couple of days. I found out that someone had destroyed the shop and I wanted to make sure she was all right. I knew how she felt about that place and also knew she had to have been taking things hard. It must have been worse than I thought because she wasn't even responding to me.

I was about to go hunt her down when there was a knock at my front door. Pulling the door open, Sanaa stood on the other side with a bright smile on her face.

"You look a little too happy for someone who just found out that her mother's shop was vandalized. Let me find out you were the one who did it." I gripped her by the forearm and snatched her into the house. "The hell have you been anyway ho? I have been blowing your phone up to make sure you were alright. I was this close to filing a missing person's report on you." I held my index finger and thumb an inch apart. I wouldn't even say it was an inch because they were almost touching.

"I just had the most amazing couple of days."

"What were you doing?"

She plopped down on my couch and that stupid ass smirk was still on her face, but she wasn't spilling any tea. She was really pissing me the fuck off. How is she going to come in here smiling and shit but won't tell me what's going on?

"If you don't get to talking, I'm going to put your ass on the other side of that door." I pointed at it to let her know I was not playing with her ass. She already had me stressed out over nothing.

"I spent the last couple of days in Miami with Soul."

"You didn't bitch?" my mouth fell ajar. I sat down on the coffee table in front of her. "Did y'all have sex?" She smiled harder and the dimples in her cheeks sunk in even deeper. A quick nod confirmed it. "That's what I'm talking about." We slapped hands with each other.

I was wondering exactly when she was going to let her guard down and fuck that man. I was proud of my bitch like she had just walked across the stage or something.

"How was it?"

"Naomi," her gaze met mine, "it was amazing. He's the best I've ever had."

"I'm so happy for you." I pulled her in for a hug.

It was nice of him to take her away for a while to get her mind off things. Now that she was back, it was time for us to address the situation at hand.

"What are you going to do about the shop?"

The smile that once graced her face faded.

"That bitch Sofia and Soul's sister did it."

My face contorted into a frown. I understand why Sofia would do it but Soul's sister?

"What does Soul's sister have to do with anything?"

"Oh, I forgot to tell you that she was Quentin's girlfriend," she shrugged her shoulders.

"I told you that you needed to handle that bitch Sofia. Bet you listen to me the next time. So, what are we going to do about them hos?"

I was ready to whoop some ass whether she was down to help or not. Them bitches were not about to get away with what they did.

"I don't know. I don't know anything about either one of them for real."

"But you got the last name though." I jumped up from the coffee table and rushed into my bedroom grabbing my phone off the bed. "What's Soul's sister's first name?"

I didn't know it. Berlin told me he had a sister but never told me what her name was. It was like they kept her a secret or some shit.

"A'Karri."

I searched her name in Instagram and she popped up. That ho had thousands of followers. She was cute, looked just like them. I scrolled her feed until I came to a club flyer.

"And now we got a location. That bitch going to be at *Xplicit* tonight." I turned the phone showing Sanaa the picture of the club flyer. A'Karri was hosting a black and white party at *Xplicit* and we were going to be there.

"You really think that's going to be a good idea? Don't you think that she'll have some sort of security with her?"

"And if she does, I'm going to whoop their ass as well. Just say the word Sanaa."

I clasped my hands together like I was praying.

"Guess we're going to *Xplicit* tonight."

"That's what the fuck I'm talking about. That bitch is going to wish she never stepped foot in your shop when I'm done with that ass."

BERLIN

When Soul called and told me what A'Karri had done I couldn't believe the shit. I never thought our sister could be so stupid over a nigga. I know she wasn't the mastermind behind that dumbass plan. Sofia came up with that shit and dragged her along with her. Because they were friends she jumped on the bandwagon like a fool.

A'Karri needs to get over the shit that fuck nigga did to her and move on with her life. I promise that's the best thing she could do right now.

When Soul had told me he was going to go over and have a talk with A'Karri, I told him I'd meet him there. It was only to ensure he didn't end up killing her for what she had done.

I knew how he felt about Sanaa. It was kind of almost how I felt about Naomi. When Soul loved, he loved hard and would do anything to protect his loved ones. I didn't think he would do anything to actually harm our little sister, but I knew he would come close to it.

Knock! Knock!

I knocked on her condo door and leaned up against the wall, waiting for her to come to it. I loved my little sister to death but sometimes she took things a little too far. She was smart as hell but could be vulnerable as fuck sometimes. I hated whenever she allowed people to talk her into doing dumb shit.

The door finally pulled open and I was greeted by her warm smile. That only told me that Soul hadn't made it there yet. If he had then she would've surely had a scowl on her face by now.

"What are you doing here, Berlin?"

"I can't come and check on my little sister? I haven't heard from you. I'm starting to feel like you love Soul more than you love me."

I brushed right past her into the condo and plopped down on the couch.

"I love you both the same, Berlin."

"You sure don't act like it. I always have to be the one to come looking for you," I fake pouted and pulled a blunt from behind my ear placing it between my lips.

"Un-uh, you know you can't smoke in here."

"I smoke where I want to smoke."

"Except in here."

I struck my lighter and she snatched my blunt away then broke it in half. I scrunched my face up at her.

"You owe me a fucking blunt."

"Whatever," she waved me off and bounced into the kitchen then came back with a glass of wine. "You coming to the black and white party tonight?"

"You know I'm going to be there and support you."

"Good because I'm really nervous. This is the first party that I've hosted by myself and I just want everything to be perfect."

She took a sip from her wine glass and there was a knock at the door. A'Karri didn't budge. I exhaled and got up from the couch.

"Guess I'll answer the door."

"Un-huh."

I shook my head and went over to the front door. Soul was standing on the other side.

"What's up bruh?" I dapped him up as he stepped into the condo.

"Wow both of my brothers standing here before me. Wonder who died," A'Karri sarcastically said then turned back around to sit on her love seat. I'm sure she already knew what the visit was all about.

"A'Karri, I need to holler at you for a sec."

"No, you don't." She rolled her eyes and took another sip from her wine glass.

That just confirmed my accusations.

"A'Karri, I'm not playing with your ass." Soul was getting frustrated with her. He snatched the glass from her lips and sat it down on the coffee table.

"Do I need to remind you that you're standing in my shit?" She relaxed back on the couch folding her arms underneath her breasts and glared up at Soul who was towering over her.

"I don't give a damn who shit I'm in. When I tell you that I need to holler at you, you gon' fucking listen."

"I already know why you're here."

"Why the hell would you do something so stupid coming after Sanaa like that? That shop meant everything to her, and you and Sofia destroyed it like it wasn't shit. Sanaa hasn't done a damn thing to you, A'Karri. When she found out Quentin and you had a thing, she called it off. She had no clue that you existed. What you did was wrong as hell and you know it."

"Why you over here scolding me like I was the only one who did the shit." She shifted in her seat, turning away from Soul.

"Don't worry, I got a few choice words for Sofia's ass as well." Soul gripped A'Karri by the face forcing her to look him in the eyes. "I like Sanaa. I like her a lot and I want to see where things can go between us. I can't do that with you and Sofia harassing the shit out of her. You need to stay in your fucking place and get over that shit Quentin did. I told you that nigga wasn't good for you, but you chose not to fucking listen. Stay the fuck away from Sanaa, A'Karri. This my last time telling you."

"I have to agree with Soul on this one Sis. That shit was wrong as hell. What if someone had come and done that shit to you? Put yourself in her shoes."

"I can't believe the both of you are ganging up on me like this." Tears ed her eyes. She knew she was wrong for the shit she did.

"I gotta go," Soul announced and headed for the front door.

I waited until he was gone before I spoke again. "Soul really likes this chick, A'Karri. I've never seen him happier than when he's with her or speaking of her. Just give her a chance. If not for yourself, do it for him. He deserves to be happy just like the next person." I leaned down kissing her on top of the head. "I'll see you tonight and I'm sure you gon' kill it."

SANAA

I couldn't believe I had let Naomi talk me into this mess. Here I was walking through the doors of *Xplicit* with Naomi hot on my heels. Everyone, there was wearing black and white except us.

We weren't there to party, so we weren't dressed the part at all. People eyed us strangely as we passed. Both Naomi and I wore a pair of shorts and a simple t-shirt. Her hair was balled up on top of her head. She was ready to whoop some ass. She even went as far as bringing a small container of Vaseline with her.

That was one of the things I loved about my girl. She was always down with the shenanigans and was going to look out for me whether I wanted her to or not.

"Do you see that bitch!" she yelled over the loud music.

My eyes danced around the club looking for A'Karri. They finally landed on her in one of the VIP sections.

"Yup, and guess who's up there with her."

"Who?"

"Sofia." I smirked, rubbing my hands together.

"Whoop two bitches at one time; let's go."

Naomi shoved her way through the club. We made it up to their section and the bouncer stopped us at the rope.

"You're not allowed back there."

"The hell I ain't. Do I need to call Berlin and let him know you won't let me gain entrance?" Naomi asked him with her hand propped on her hip and her phone resting in the other.

He quickly removed the rope giving us access.

"That's what I fucking thought," she spat and stepped into the section.

We walked up to where A'Karri and Sofia were both sitting down, sipping on some fruity mixed drinks.

"Well, look what we have here." Sofia giggled when her eyes finally landed on us.

"I see y'all like to be sneaky as fuck and attack people when they aren't looking. She's here now and I bet not neither one of you will bust a fucking move."

My eyes shifted from A'Karri to Sofia. They both sat there like they weren't fazed which only angered me even more. On my way there I was debating with myself, trying to figure out if this was the right thing to do. Now that they were sitting in front of my face, I was certain. They both had to pay for destroying my mother's shop. And they were going to pay in muhfucking blood, the same thing she bled to build that place.

"You go left, and I'll go right," I told Naomi. I wanted Sofia more than I wanted A'Karri. I was about to wipe that fucking smirk off her got damn face.

"Wait what?" A'Karri asked not catching on to what I was alluding to.

I picked up a cup off the table and tossed it right into Sofia's face. It wasn't satisfying enough so I lunged across the table at Sofia the same time that Naomi went for A'Karri. The love seat they were occupying turned over and all four of us were on the floor. Sofia was lying on her back as my fist went straight across her face.

Wham!

"You fucking destroyed everything my mother built you, stupid bitch!"
Wham!

I punched her across the other side of her face. I had hit her so hard that spit and blood flew from her mouth.

"This shit for my fucking mama!"
Wham! Wham!

I picked her head up and hit it on the floor. It made a thud when it came into contact with it. Before I could get another hit in, someone grabbed me off her from behind. I looked back and it was the bouncer.

"Let me fucking go I wasn't done with that ho!" I yelled. I still had more fight in me and I didn't want to stop until her face was unrecognizable.

"Y'all gotta go." He carried me toward the exit of the VIP section.
Crash!

My body slipped from his clutches and I turned around as he was dropping to his knees. Naomi stood behind him with a broken Patron bottle in her hand and her eyes wide.

"We aren't leaving until these bitches know not to fucking play with you again."

I couldn't believe she had actually done that shit. Okay... I could.

Sofia pulled herself up from the floor. I rushed over to the table picking up the Remy bottle that was on it and hit it against the edge of the table.
Crash!

"Where the fuck did you think you were going? You destroyed my shit so now I'm going to destroy yours."

Her eyes darted to the broken bottle that was in my hand.

"W-what are you going to do with that?"

"What?" I lifted the bottle and smirked at it. "Oh, this little thing?... I'm going to rearrange your fucking face with it."

"You're fucking psycho!"

She stumbled back away from me. I ran toward her and was scooped up from behind again. That time I didn't even have to look to know who it was. His cologne rushed up my nose soon as he picked me up.

Soul...

A sudden ease washed over my body and I dropped the bottle.

SOUL

I wasn't even going to show up at that stupid ass black and white party. A'Karri had pissed me the fuck off and normally, I'd support anything she was doing but this time I had to show her that I wasn't playing with her.

I got a call saying I needed to get my ass to the club. A fight had broken out and it pertained my sister and Sofia. I was walking in there ready to fuck some shit up until my eyes landed on Sanaa. I slipped my gun back in my waistline and scooped her little ass up before that bottle in her hand went across Sofia's face.

Berlin grabbed Naomi tossing her feisty ass over his shoulder. She was still kicking and screaming wanting to get a hold of my sister who was pulling herself up off the floor. I couldn't lie, Naomi had gotten the best of her and she was pissed.

Mason grabbed A'Karri and one of the bouncers got Sofia. We carried all the girls to first floor and out the club, so we could see what the hell was going on. I thought after I had that little talk with A'Karri earlier I wouldn't have to worry about some shit like this but guess I was wrong.

I needed to sit all of them down and talk to them like they were children since that's what they were acting like. The shit was straight embarrassing as fuck to know my sister, ex, my girl, and her best friend was in there tearing up my shit like that.

"A'Karri, don't think that just because Soul is here now that I'm not going to get in that ass too!" Sanaa yelled, squirming in my arms. I had a death grip on her, so I wasn't worried about her going anywhere.

"Bitch, that's why my brother killed your mama!" A'Karri shot back.

My heart dropped to the pit of my stomach. My worst fear had just come to life and I wasn't sure how I was going to get out of this mess.

"She's lying, right?" Sanaa asked as I sat her down on the ground beside my Escalade. Tears formed in her eyes as she gazed up at me. "Tell me it's not true, Soul. Did you kill my mother?"

"Sanaa, just let me explain."

"You son of a bitch!"

Wham!

Her hand connected with my face. Tears streamed down her cheeks.

"How could you!"

Her tiny fists landed on my face and chest wherever they could hit. I felt like shit that she had to find out about that like this.

"Bae, calm down and just let me explain."

"Fuck you, Soul! I fucking trusted you!"

I just wanted to reach out and grab her, but I knew she wasn't going to let me since I was the cause of her pain. I attempted to touch her, but she slapped my hand away.

"Don't fucking touch me!"

"Sanaa, babe..."

Smack!

Her hand went across my face again.

"Just give me time to ex—"

Pow! Pow! Pow!

Gunfire rang out and I shoved her into my truck, snatching my piece from my waistline. I looked up and saw Quentin's car speeding away from the club and Berlin was hopping into his car to go behind him. My eyes scanned the parking lot to land on A'Karri but the only person I saw standing there was Sofia. Mason was lying on the ground bleeding as well as an innocent bystander who was probably on their way into the club.

"The hell just happened?" Sanaa peeked her head out the truck.

I rushed over to Sofia gripping her by the forearms. "Where the hell is A'Karri, Sof?"

Her lips trembled as she glared back at me. Her shivering arm pointed in the same direction Berlin and Quentin had gone in.

"He-he-he took her!"

It only took a split second for me to realize Quentin's bitch ass shot Mason and kidnapped A'Karri. That had to be the reason why Berlin went behind him the way he did. Along with the fact he already wanted to rock him to sleep for hurting our little sister.

"What's going on?" Sanaa questioned me as I bent down to check on Mason.

"You good?"

"Yeah, I'm alright. I can make it to the hospital just go make sure Karri is straight."

"I'll take him to the hospital," Sofia intervened.

That was the only thing I needed to hear. I rushed back over to my truck and jumped in the driver's seat.

"Shut the door," I ordered Sanaa.

"For what? Tell me what's going on!"

I leaned over and closed the door for her since she seemed not to be able to do it. I started the truck and pulled away from the curb heading in the same direction Berlin went. I didn't think I would be able to catch up to them since they left way before me but I was going to try.

"Wait, where's Naomi!" Sanaa panicked looking out the back window. Her body trembled, probably terrified from the gunshots that happened a moment ago.

"Calm down, she's safe with Berlin wherever they may be."

I leaned back, pulling my phone out my front pants pocket and tried calling Berlin's number but he sent me to voicemail. My pulse raced at the thought of something bad happening to A'Karri. This was one of my worst fears. I tried so hard to do whatever I could to protect her, but I should have known that with the lifestyle we lived, something was bound to happen soon or later.

My eyes shifted over to Sanaa who was shaking her legs. I could tell something was on her mind, I was just patiently waiting for her to let me know exactly what it was.

"Fuck it, I can't take it anymore!" she shouted, and her eyes poured into mine. There were tears in her eyes and I waited for her to say what was on her mind. "Why did you kill my mother, Soul? Better yet, why did you kill her and not say anything to me about it? Out of all this time I've been getting close to you, yet you said nothing. If A'Karri hadn't said anything then I would have never known; you weren't going to tell me."

Tears flowed down her cheeks and I felt like shit but there was nothing that could be done to change the past. She thought that she was ready for the truth but that's far from actuality. I like Sanaa... a lot and didn't really want to hurt her but what did I expect was going to happen when the truth finally came out?

"Can we talk about this later? You see I'm busy right now trying to find my sister."

"No, Soul! We are going to talk about this now! Please just tell me the truth for once," her voice cracked as she spoke.

Skkkkrrrrrttttttt!

Her body jerked forward as I slammed down hard on the brakes.

"Fine, you want the truth Sanaa, then here's the fucking truth. Yonnie was a got damn scam artist. She worked for us for years and shit was going well until she thought she deserved more. She started taking small amounts off the top of the cash we were giving her to deposit. We didn't notice it at first until she got greedy and began taking larger sums.

I had to kill her, Sanaa. If I didn't get to her before my parents did, then she would have died a gruesome death. They probably would have gotten you as well so you should thank me."

"Thank you! Thank you!" She laughed hysterically.

Smack!

Her hand quickly connected with my cheek before I even realized what was about to happen. I gritted my teeth to stop myself from knocking the shit out of her. Quite frankly, I was tired of her putting her hands on me.

"My mother wasn't a scam artist she just did what was necessary to fucking survive out here in these streets. She took care of me on her own with nobody's help. Nobody! It doesn't fucking matter what the hell she did, she didn't fucking deserve to die the way she did. You could have handled the shit a different way."

Sanaa shifted in her seat to where she was all the way facing me. Tears were still pouring down her cheeks.

"Y'all left my mama sitting in her fucking car with a bullet between her eyes. Put yourself in my shoes. What if it was your mama? You found her dead like I found mine. Just because she did wrong doesn't justify what the fuck y'all did."

"I know Sanaa and I'm truly sorry. There's nothing I can say to make it right, but can we please talk about this later after I find my sister?"

Beeeepppppp!

Car horns honked behind me grabbing my attention. We were sitting in the middle of the road for some time now and a long line of cars had gathered behind us.

"No, we cannot."

Sanaa gripped the door handle and pushed the door open.

"I'm not staying in this truck with you. You can go and find your sister on your own, Soul. I'm done."

She jumped down out the truck slamming the door behind her. I slung the truck in park and got out.

"Move this fucking truck!" some guy yelled behind me still honking his horn, but I ignored him. I had bigger things to worry about than his raggedy ass Toyota Camry.

"Where are you going?"

"As far away from you as possible!" she shouted over her shoulder steadily walking away from me.

"Sanaa, will you just get back in the truck and I'll take you home?"

She spun around on her heels facing me while walking backward.

"I'm not getting back in that truck with you. Goodbye Soul."

"Sanaa!" I shouted. She flipped me the bird and gave me her back as she made her way down the street and bent the corner.

I knew things were going to be bad between us when she found out the truth, but I didn't think they would get this horrible. The only thing I could do at this moment was give her some time to cool off then try to talk to her later. But right now, the only thing I could worry about was finding A'Karri safely and putting a bullet in Quentin's skull.

SANAA

If Soul actually thought I was going to stay in that truck with him after finding out he killed my mother, then he was a damn fool. I felt betrayed for letting my guard down with him and he did the exact thing I was terrified of—broke my heart. My shit was fragile, and he knew that. I sat there in his Wraith and basically poured my heart out to him. I told him why I was so guarded. I feel like a complete idiot for being so trusting of him.

Most of this was my fault. He warned me numerous times he wasn't good for me. How come I didn't listen? Why did my body go against my better wishes and yearn for his touch? I should have gone with my first mind and just stayed away from him, but then I felt like the universe was trying to bring us together. He was always there everywhere I turned. Flaunting his handsomeness in front of me. I couldn't help but fall for the bait.

I hugged my body and kept walking down the sidewalk. My mind was clouded, and I needed to clear it. To think with a clear head, I had to get away from Soul.

Soul's Escalade sped past me and my eyes stayed trained on it until it was no longer in view. I hated his very existence. I felt like shit for still wanting to be with him after I found out the truth. That's the real reason why I jumped out the truck. I couldn't betray myself let alone my mother any longer.

The one person I wanted to give myself to was the cause of all my heartache in the first place. Maybe that was the reason why he slowly began to open up to me. He felt sorry for what he did. Being nice to me wasn't going to gain my forgiveness. He did the unthinkable and I don't think he could ever be forgiven for something like that.

Walking home was not an option seeing how I stayed on the other side of town. I pulled my phone from my back pants pocket and went to the Uber app to get a ride.

"Just get back in the truck Sanaa and I'll take you home." I looked up over the top of my phone and Soul was sitting on the side of the street with his window down.

"Soul, just go on about your business and leave me the hell alone."

I crossed the street and he followed riding slowly alongside me. I rolled my eyes. He needed to catch the hint that I wanted nothing to do with his ass and go on about his business.

"Sanaa, come on. I'm damn near pleading for you to get back into the truck. I promise I'll take you straight home and won't utter another word to you. I just don't want to leave you out here like that."

I continued to give him the silent treatment, thinking maybe he'd finally catch the hint. I wanted to stop and scream at him, but I held my composure. I couldn't make any promises if he didn't leave soon that I'd stay that way.

From my peripheral, I saw the truck jerk then heard the door fly open. Soul stepped in front of me gripping me by the forearms. I gazed deeply into his dark eyes, feeling myself gradually slipping into his daze. I shook my head to bring myself back to consciousness.

"Sanaa, I'm sorry. I should have told you the truth, but I didn't know how. I don't expect you to forgive me or anything just get back in the truck, please."

My tears were now coming back down full force. I was standing there, staring the man I was slowly beginning to love—who happened to be my mother's killer—right in the face. I swallowed hard not being able to find the words I wanted to say to him. They were getting caught in my throat.

A car pulled up right behind Soul's truck.

"My ride's here. Can you let me go so I can leave?"

His grip on my arms loosened and he stepped back away from me. I wiped my eyes and rubbed my nose taking one final look at Soul.

"Goodbye Soul."

I turned away from him heading to the car, sobbing like a muhfucka. The tears seemed to not be able to stop from flowing. My heart was heavy, and I was conflicted. Even if I wanted to, I don't think I'd be able to look past what he did and still be with him.

We hadn't talked about it but I thought that after we made love back in Miami that we were going to work toward something. Something we both craved to have with one another. Now whatever that spark was we had; it was slowly withering away.

QUENTIN

"LET ME FUCKING GO QUENTIN!" A'Karri yelled, squirming in my arms. I was holding on to her tightly in the back seat while Luca whipped in and out of traffic in hopes we wouldn't get caught. I was terrified if I let her go, she'd jump her crazy ass out the moving car. Or better yet, snatch the gun I was holding in my free hand away from me and shoot me with the muhfucka.

I was surprised I was even able to get away with taking her. It wasn't my motive to begin with. When I pulled up in front of the club and saw Soul and Berlin out there along with Sanaa, I was aiming to riddle them with a couple bullets, but I didn't want her to get in harm's way. Since I had her, I was going to force her to listen to me whether she wanted to or not.

"Will you just calm down? You're acting like I'm trying to hurt or kill you."

"You can't hurt me any more than you already have," she shot back at me, tugging at my heart a little bit. I let out a heavy sigh, I hated myself for causing harm to her. Maybe I should have just left Sanaa alone. Then I wouldn't be going through this mess.

I tried to fight the urge to stay away from Sanaa, but it seemed inevitable. Her pussy was always calling me to dive between her thighs even when I was with A'Karri. I don't know what it was about her that kept pulling me back like a magnet.

"I never wanted to hurt you, Karri. You should know better than that."

A'Karri was everything to me. My love for her ran deeper than the deepest ocean. She and I fought with her family since day one so we could stay together. She rocked with me when I didn't have shit to my name. Loved me when no one else could or would.

I planned on marrying her one day but now that her brothers planted seeds in her fucking head, all of that was ruined. I couldn't really say it was all because of them, I played a huge part in it as well. She put her heart in my hands and in return, I crushed it like it wasn't shit.

"Stop this fucking car and let me out, Quentin! I'm not playing with your ass!" She still squirmed, trying to get loose. I felt her heart racing in her chest and couldn't tell if she was afraid of me at the moment or what.

"The car will stop when we know for sure Berlin and them aren't following us anymore," I replied, looking out the back window to make sure I didn't see either of them. Today was not the day I was trying to meet my maker.

She burst out laughing like I said something comical. "You're crazier than I thought if you think they aren't going to hunt your ass down for kidnapping me."

"They can try all they want but they aren't going to find us."

I instructed Luca to take us to my parents' old warehouse off North Florissant. No one knew of the place because my parents kept it under wraps. They were using it to supply drugs out of back in the day. When my father got sick, he handed it down to me but of course, with the Maserati's in the way, everything went to shit. That was another reason why I loathed their existence. I needed to get rid of all of them and fast so I can take back what's rightfully mine—my streets and my girl.

I hadn't been back to the place since I shut down shop. It only reminded me of what a failure I'd become. I was sure my parents were probably turning over in their graves because of me.

The place probably was crawling with homeless people among other things. I should have tried to keep up the appearance for their sake, but I was being lazy and angry all at the same time. After I handled Soul and them, then I might come in and clean the place up.

Luca pulled up in front of the building and I pushed the back door open then slid out still holding onto A'Karri. I didn't want her to try and run away from me before I could get my point across to her. She was a feisty little thing, that was one of the things that drew me to her in the first place.

"What the hell is this place?"

"Don't worry about all that." I carried her into the dusty building. Cobwebs and roaches were everywhere.

"If you don't take me back where the hell you got me from right now, Quentin!"

I sat her down on top of a dusty table that sat in the corner of the building. I knew she was going to get angry with me because she was wearing white and it was going to stain her clothes.

"I just want to talk to you, that's all. Just give me a few minutes of your time. That's all I'm asking of you."

"I know damn well you didn't kidnap me just to get a few moments of my time. You could have got that shit without shooting at my brothers and snatching me up."

"You wouldn't listen to me otherwise." I scrubbed my hand down my face and slipped my gun down the front of my waistline.

She folded her arms underneath her breasts. "Why would I want to listen to your lying cheating ass? You were probably only going to tell me another lie again. If you told me the truth in the beginning, then maybe we could have worked through the shit like a couple of adults. We don't have anything to talk about at this point, Quentin. Our relationship is gone to shits because *you* keep fucking it up."

She broke eye contact with me and stroked the back of her neck. She was getting frustrated with me and I could tell.

"I know and I just want to fix things, babe." I reached out to stroke her face, but she whacked my hand away. "I don't want to lose you. As a matter of fact, I can't lose you, Karri." My eyes glossed over. I was really in my feelings about her not wanting to be with me anymore. Can't she see I was trying?

A'KARRI

"Look, Quentin, I love you so much but putting my life in danger the way you did isn't the way to get me back." This crazy muhfucka just pulled up in front of the club and started spraying bullets not paying attention to what he was doing. Anyone of them could have easily hit and killed me.

"I wasn't trying to put you in harm's way. That's the reason why I grabbed you in the first place. I'm not holding you here against your will or anything Karri. I only wanted to talk to you, that's it."

I jumped down off the table and wiped the dust from the back of my dress. "Since you're not holding me here then I guess I can leave, right?"

"Karri, wait." He gripped my wrist and I snatched away from him. My eyes met his gaze and my upper lip curled up.

"No, Quentin, I won't *wait*. I never want to see your face again." I felt my eyes getting misty with tears and I knew I had to hurry up and get the hell out of there. He didn't deserve to see me waste any more tears on him. Not the way he treated me. I told myself I wasn't going to waste any more time or energy on Quentin, and I planned to keep that energy now.

I rushed toward the exit where the guy who drove us there was standing blocking it.

"Get the hell out my way." He quickly stepped to the side without uttering a word.

"Karri!" Quentin called out behind me, but I kept walking, wiping tears from my eyes. They seemed to flow nonstop as my heart caved in my chest. This was the exact reason why I didn't want to see his face again.

Whenever I saw him, I always second guessed myself and wondered if I was making the right decision by leaving him. Quentin knew how I felt about him. That was the reason why he kept trying to get close to me; sooner or later, I would give in to him. That was something I really didn't want to do.

I stepped outside and it seemed as if I was in the middle of nowhere. I didn't have my phone or my purse on me, I left it back at *Xplicit* after the fight. I walked until I came across a cab that was driving down the street and flagged it down. When it pulled over, I rushed to it hopping in the back and gave him my parents' address.

That was the first place I could think to go to let them know I was all right. I could have easily gone into a store or borrowed someone's phone but knowing Soul and Berlin, they wouldn't believe I was all right until they laid eyes on me. I also wanted them to promise me they will leave Quentin alone. Because he shot at them first, they were going to hunt him down and put him six feet under. Even though he hurt me to my core several times, I didn't want that for him. I loved him too much.

The cab pulled up to the gate of my parents' house. I used the speaker at the fence to contact them. I could have easily gotten out the car, but I didn't have the cash to pay him for my ride. Niggas get hostile about they shit. I know I would if someone owed me some money. I was just trying to avoid a situation going left.

"Daddy," I spoke into the speaker.

"Is that you, A'Karri?" Soul's voice spoke back.

"Yeah, come out here to the gate and bring some money with you." I let go of the button and relaxed back in the seat. A few moments later, I heard the gate buzz and my eyes landed on Soul. He handed the driver a hundred-dollar bill and I climbed out of the car.

"How did you get away from Quentin?"

"He let me go." I shrugged my shoulders and headed up to the front door where my parents and Berlin were waiting for me. They were excited I made it back home safely.

Never did I once think Quentin was going to harm me in any way. He may have fucked up a lot but I knew he genuinely cared about me.

"I'm so happy you're okay!" my mother beamed, pulling me into her warm embrace.

"Ma, you're killing me." I mumbled and she let me go then took a few steps back away from me.

"Sorry."

"You know I'm going to kill Quentin, right? He had me riding all over this fucking city looking for his ass," Berlin chimed in.

"Well, I'm fine." I tugged on my lower lip, trying to figure out just how I was going to say this. None of them were going to be happy once the words seeped from my lips.

"What's on your mind, baby girl?" my father asked me.

I brushed straight past them into the house and began pacing across the living room floor. "Okay, I know you guys might be mad at Quentin and whatnot but I really don't think it's necessary for you to go after him. Neither one of us got hurt and he was only trying to prove a point."

Taniece

"Karri, please tell me you're not that stupid to believe the shit that just came out of your mouth."

"Berlin!" my mother shrieked.

"What, Ma? She actually going to stand here and tell me what she *thinks* I shouldn't do. That nigga came for me first so I'm going to finish the shit."

"Berlin's right, Karri. Ain't no letting go of that shit so you might as well get that one out of your head," Soul agreed with him.

"Daddy!" I whined, feeling the tears forming at the rim of my eyes.

"What baby girl? I'm not in that. I see you're fine and that's all I was worried about. I don't have anything to do with what your brothers choose to do with Quentin's ass," my father spoke his peace then walked off with my mother right on his heels.

"You might as well stop looking like that because them ugly ass faces ain't going to stop us from putting a bullet in his ass." Berlin made me fucking sick with his ugly ass. I wish he would get a girl or something then he'd stay the hell out of my life.

"For your sake lil' sis, we'll kill him quickly and make it as painless as possible."

"Speak for yourself Soul, because I plan on torturing the nigga for all the bullshit he put her through."

"Ugh! I can't stand neither one of you!"

I stormed out the front door slamming it behind me. I wanted to get as far away from them as possible. I don't know why I thought they were going to listen to me. They always claimed to be doing what's best for me even if the shit caused me pain in the end.

"Fuck!" I yelled. I came out the door forgetting I didn't drive there or have any cash so I wouldn't be able to go anywhere.

I pushed the door back open and Berlin and Soul strolled toward me.

"Can one of y'all give me a ride?" I pouted, poking my lower lip out.

"Better call and ask Quentin since you want to be Captain Save A Nigga so badly." Berlin walked straight past me out the door and hopped into his car speeding out the driveway.

"Yeah, I'll drop you off. I got your shit in my truck too," Soul answered, opening the passenger's side door for me.

"Thanks."

"You was wrong as hell for blurting that shit out to Sanaa like that too. That wasn't the way to handle that situation. I'm starting to think you want me to be alone forever." He shut the door on me, and I felt like shit. But what was done, was done and there wasn't anything I could do about it.

130

NAOMI

I heard the bullshit A'Karri screamed at Sanaa as we were being carried out of the club. There was so much going on I couldn't get to her and check on her to make sure she was all right. I know she had to be hurting after finding something out someting devastating like that. I know I would be.

She and Soul were becoming close and I was actually rooting for his ugly ass but after that shit, she needed to kick him to the curb. ASAP! It took everything in me not to go over to his place and whoop his ass for crushing my best friend's heart. I wanted happiness for my friend, but I didn't want it like that. There were plenty more fish in the sea and I was sure she'd be able to find her one.

I stood outside Sanaa's front door waiting for her to answer. I knocked on her door ten minutes ago and she still hadn't come to it. After Berlin dropped me off at home, this was the first place I came.

I pulled my phone out and tried calling her, but her phone was going straight to voicemail. When I was about to call her again and leave a message, she rounded the corner with a scowl on her face.

"Where the hell you been at? I have been out here for the longest waiting on you." I propped my hands up on my hips and rolled my neck. She should have been had her ass home which made me wonder exactly where she'd been.

"I caught an Uber home. There was no way I was going to stay in that truck with Soul." She stuck her key in the door and unlocked it, then pushed it open.

"Hell nah, I would have made that nigga bring me home. You tripping." I pushed the door closed behind me and Sanaa went straight into the kitchen then came out with a bottle of Patron. She didn't even have a cup or a chaser which only meant she was about to drink it straight. *Yeah, things were bad.*

I sat down on the couch and watched as she chugged some of the liquor down like it was water. She finally was moving on from her mother's death and they just dragged her right back down.

"I'm so fucking done with Soul. I swear!" she blurted then flopped down beside me.

That's what her mouth said but her body and face said otherwise. Just as I craved Berlin like a crack fiend, she yearned for Soul. It was easy to say one thing but complicated to actually put forth the effort to do it.

"You really are done with him or are you just saying that?"

Her forehead wrinkled as she gazed off into space. "It wouldn't be hard, Naomi. It's not like we were anything major. We made love one time and that's it. Yeah, I had a strong connection to him and liked him a lot but it was nothing more to us. I won't die if I cut his ass off."

I couldn't believe Berlin hadn't said anything to me about them killing Yonnie. It angered me he kept something like that away from me. I wanted to ask him about it but he dropped me off so fast and pulled away from the curb I couldn't even ask.

"You were actually happy, and I thought the both of you would have been good together. I hate that happened and he was wrong as hell to keep something like that from you. If he wanted to build something with you no matter how huge or small it was then that should have been one of the first things he told you."

"Then he had the nerves to try and make her out to be the bad person to justify what they did to her. That shit really pissed me the fuck off." She took another gulp from the liquor shaking her head.

"Don't you think you need to slow down a little on that?"

"For what?" She scrunched her face up at me. "It's not like I'm going anywhere. Might as well drown myself in my sorrows."

"But you don't need to get too drunk, Sanaa. I know how you get when you get drunk." Soul would be calling me telling me to come get her from outside his house before the night was over with. Liquor and her emotions didn't mix well whatsoever.

"The only thing I'm going to do is crawl my ass into the bed and go to sleep then wake up tomorrow praying this entire night was only a fucking nightmare."

I hooked her by the chin, tilting her face toward me. She stared back at me with glossy eyes and I could tell she was on the brink of tears. I hated my friend was feeling this way and if I could take the pain from her and carry it then I would.

"I'm sorry baby girl but this shit is reality. Getting drunk with that liquor isn't going to fix anything. You need to get you a good night's rest and start fresh in the morning."

I pulled the bottle from her hand and placed it on the coffee table. I got up from the couch, gripping her by the hand and led her down the hallway to her bedroom. It was pitch black in there but I could see the bed and that's all mattered. I pulled the covers back and she climbed into it with tears pouring down her cheeks. I knew eventually they were going to come.

"My heart hurts, Naomi," she sobbed, and I covered her up with the sheets.

"I know babe. It'll get better with time." I leaned down kissing her on the center of her forehead. "Get some rest and I'll call and check on you in the morning."

I left out of her bedroom and the front door, making sure it locked behind me. I was about to head straight home, but I wanted to go to Berlin's and give him a piece of my mind. Hopefully, by the time I make it there he'd be home. And since I wasn't going to call him to let him know I was coming, I prayed I didn't see something I didn't want to when I got there.

I got into my truck and headed to Berlin's. I wasn't sure how this conversation was going to go once I got there. Just like Sanaa, I was angry as hell as well. She and Soul may not have been that close but Berlin and I damn sure was. *How could he not tell me something like that?* He knew Sanaa was my best friend and he should have known I was going to get pissed the same as her once I found out.

When I got to his condo, I went up to his floor. My nerves were all over the place. I thought about turning around and getting the hell out of there before things went left. I had this eerie feeling in the pit of my stomach that they would.

I fidgeted with my fingers as I stood in front of his door, waiting for him to answer it. My heart thumped in my chest and it felt like I was losing air in my lungs. I brushed my hair back out of my face with my hands just as the front door pulled open.

Berlin stood there in front of me in nothing but a pair of white Versace boxer briefs. If my mind wasn't heavy at the moment, I would have jumped into his large arms and begged him to take me right then and there.

"Naomi, what are you doing here this time of night?"

BERLIN

I should have known something was up when I opened the door and saw Naomi standing on the other side of it. What she wanted this time of night beats the hell out of me, but I was about to find out. I was just about to climb in bed when she knocked on my front door. Lucky for me, I wasn't doing shit I didn't have any business doing or else I would have been shit out of luck.

She stood there, gazing at me with tears in her eyes. I gripped her by the hand and pulled her into the condo, shutting the door behind her.

"What's wrong, bae?" I cupped her face and gazed into her glossy eyes. She shifted her eyes away from me not even wanting to look me into mine. "Bae, will you just talk to me?"

Naomi slapped my hands down then took a couple steps forward and hugged herself. I pressed my frame up against her from behind. Brushing my fingertips against her shoulder blade, her body shuddered.

"How come you didn't tell me, Berlin?"

"Tell you what?"

She had me confused thinking I did something wrong. I stood there trying to figure out exactly what I could have done. Played out every situation in my head but came up empty-handed.

She slowly turned to face me, and I noticed the tears dripping from the corners of her eyes. "About Yonnie..."

Fuck! I'd completely forgotten about the shit A'Karri blurted earlier when we were leaving the club. Was she really in her feelings about that when it wasn't even her mother? I get she was close to Sanaa, but that situation wasn't hers to be stressing over.

"I didn't think it was important."

"How is it not when Sanaa's my best friend? Do you not think I deserve to know something like that?" She let me touch her long enough to wipe the tears from her eyes then whacked my hand down.

"I honestly didn't think the shit was important. What you want me to do? Tell you about every person we murked?"

I hope she wasn't about to make a big deal out of this shit. It was best she just let it go and we go on with our night.

"No, I don't expect you to tell me all that, but I did expect you to tell me about Yonnie. She was like a second mother to me. Now, I'm not even sure what to do..."

"Do about what?"

"Us..."

"What you mean about us?" I had a feeling in the pit of my stomach that I already knew what she was alluding to, but I wanted to hear it out of her mouth.

"After the things I found out today, I'm not sure if we should be together."

Boom!

My fist went straight through the nearest wall and she jumped. I pulled it back out and my gaze met hers. What she was saying had to be a fucking joke. She couldn't be serious.

"The hell you mean you're not sure if we should be together?"

I felt my temper rising. Both of my fists balled up and I had to keep them hanging at my sides so I wouldn't do something I would regret. She had me feeling things I've never felt before. Doing the impossible for me and here she was telling me she no longer wanted to be with me over some shit which happened before I even knew she existed. That shit was nowhere near fair. She didn't have the right to hold something like that over my head.

"It's only right that we end things here, Berlin."

Boom!

I punched the wall directly beside her head and she jumped again. Her chest heaved as she gazed up at me. I knew that look all too well she was giving me. She was terrified of me.

"This shit between us ain't ending until I say it is. You might as well get that shit out of your skull." I tapped her on the side of her head to get my point across.

Tears poured down her cheeks. I took a couple steps back away from her because her being scared of me isn't something I wanted. All I wanted to do was love on Naomi. Show her how much I care for her. This relationship thing was all new to me but I'll be damned if I was just going to let her walk away from me that easily.

"You can't just tell me what I'm going to do, Berlin. This between us will never work. I owe that much to Yonnie."

"Fine, you want to walk out of here then take your ass on." I stepped out the way and she eyed me then glanced at the front door. She hesitated for a moment then went for it but I gripped her by the wrist.

I hated seeing the tears cascading down her cheeks. The shit tugged at my heart and soul knowing I was the cause of that shit.

"I ain't never begged for shit in my life," I palmed her face, "don't walk out that door on me, Naomi. I love you and I've never loved anyone other than my family before. Please don't go."

"Why do you have to do me like this, Berlin?" She was now crying hard as hell.

"I'm not doing you like anything. All I want is to be with you and you're acting like it's a fucking crime."

"In my book it is. I'll feel like I'm betraying Sanaa and Yonnie if I stay with you." She gently pulled my hand down from her face and got on her tippy toes and kissed me softly on the lips.

My chest caved in as she pulled back from me. That's something I've never experienced before. I felt like a little bitch feeling my heart break in two. She was really trying to leave me over that bullshit.

"Goodbye Berlin." She glanced me one final time with tears in her eyes and pulled the front door open.

"Naomi..."

The door shut and it was then I knew things between us was over. I picked up the lamp off the end table and slung it into the wall.

Crash!

I flipped the table right along with the sectional and everything else in the living room. My anger was getting the best of me and by the time I was done in there, my living room looked as if a tornado ran through the muhfucka. My eyes were glossed over and I needed to do something to take my mind off things. Normally, I would have called a chick over, but I didn't want to not knowing if Naomi and I would be able to fix things, so I just settled for a fat ass blunt and a bottle of Louis Xiii. I sat there alone in the darkness of my bedroom and smoked and drank myself to sleep.

SOUL

I couldn't sleep after that shit went down with Sanaa. I tossed and turned all night long trying to find out what I was going to do to get her back. I didn't expect her to understand where I was coming from. Well, part of me did with Yonnie for a mother. I looked at it as all the dirt she done in her day finally caught up to her.

Sanaa didn't know all the things her mother did. She thought she was some heavenly woman when she was far from that. I wasn't trying to justify what was done as right but it was what needed to be done.

Tossing the covers back, I climbed out of bed, heading straight into the bathroom. I handled my hygiene then scrolled through my phone to check my calendar to see what I had to do for the day. My entire day was free, so I dialed Berlin's number to see where he was.

"What bruh?" He sounded like he was still asleep when he answered the phone. That wasn't like him. Even when he gone out the night before, he'd still be up bright and early. That's just the way he was.

"Don't tell me your ass still fucking sleep over there. You need a fucking wakeup call or something?"

"And if I am?"

I heard shuffling noises in the background.

"I'm about to come over there. We need to talk." I disconnected the call then grabbed a pair of gray sweatpants and a black t-shirt. I didn't even feel like putting on a suit. Guess both Maserati boys were off their toes for the day.

After I got dressed, I went downstairs and grabbed my Escalade keys and left out the door. It didn't take me long to get to Berlin's condo. When he let me in the door, I thought I was in the wrong place. I had to look at the muhfucka twice. That nigga's shit looked like hell. His furniture was thrown all over the place. He had two big ass holes in his wall.

"The fuck you did last night? Fought Floyd Mayweather?" My brow rose when I asked. I got done observing the apartment and began flipping his furniture back over. He was in there trying to clean up the mess he caused.

"Man, Naomi broke up with my ass last night. I don't even know how to feel about that shit."

"Aw, don't tell me my little brother over there experiencing his first heartbreak and shit," I joked and he gave me the finger. He was really in his fucking feelings.

"I'm glad you find this shit funny as hell. I don't know what the hell to do."

"I came over here to talk to you about my damn problems and you're going through your own shit." Never did I ever think I'd see the day when both of us were fucked up over a chick. Especially not Berlin anyway with all the women he went through. I think that nigga saw more pussy in one month than I've ever seen in my whole lifetime.

"What happened?"

"Sanaa walked out on me yesterday and don't want to have shit else to do with me."

"Damn, I'm sorry to hear about that bruh." He sat down on his couch and pulled out a pre-rolled blunt, sticking it between his lips. I plopped down on the other end of the couch. He took a couple tokes from the blunt then tried to hand it over to me.

"Nah, I'm good." I hadn't smoked weed since I was back in high school. I been gave up on that nonsense. Smoking Kush wasn't for me. I'd rather sell the shit and end our relationship there.

"So, what are you going to do to get your girl back? I know you're not just going to give up on her. I can tell you care about her, Soul. You can't just let her get away from you like that."

"It's not like I want her to get away, but I don't think I'd ever be able to get her back after she found out we were the reason for her mother's death."

"I'm sorry, bruh."

"It's not your fault." I relaxed back rubbing my hand across my waves. "Do you really think she'll be able to find it in herself to forgive me?"

"Everyone deserves a second chance. You just have to figure out a way to get her to see how much you care about her. Do something she wouldn't expect you to then try to sit her down and talk to her about it."

"Maybe you're right about that. I'll give it a try but I'm not sure if it's really going to work. You need to take your own advice and try to get your girl back. Tell her it was my fault and you had nothing to do with the shit."

Berlin chuckled, placing the blunt back between his lips and lit the tip again since it gone out. He took a few pulls from it then blew the smoke out. He glanced over at me with his low, red eyes. "You know me better than that, Soul. I ain't no snitch. I'll figure out a way to get her back."

"Do you want me to try and talk to her about it?"

"Nah," he coughed then cleared his throat. "I can handle it myself. You got your own problems and shit to take care of."

"Aight. I'm about to bounce. I got a few things I need to handle." I dapped him up then stood from the couch. "You need to clean this shit up in here. Shit look awful." I shook my head and left out the front door.

As I made my way down to my truck, I pulled my phone out and dialed Emily's number.

"Yes Soul?" she asked when she answered the phone.

"I need you to do something for me. Get one of the best designers in St. Louis and an architect and meet me at the office in an hour. We have some business to take care of."

"Yes, Sir," she quickly complied.

I disconnected the call and slipped the phone into my pocket as I climbed into my truck. I sure as hell hoped this shit worked because if it didn't then I don't know what I was going to do.

SANAA

I rolled over in bed and glanced at the alarm clock. It was 7:21 am and I had to be at the shop in an hour to meet with the guys I hired to help me get it back in shape. I didn't feel like pulling myself out of bed. My mind weighed heavy after the things I found out a couple days ago.

I kept wanting to reach out to Soul but fought the urge. After what he put me through, he didn't deserve another second of my time let alone my tears. I still couldn't believe I gave away a piece of my heart to a man who snatched my entire world, shattered my very existence.

Sighing a deep breath, I tossed the covers back on my bed. I pulled my legs to the side and climbed out, dragging my feet to the bathroom. Lord knows I didn't feel like doing anything except for staying in bed all day long but if I didn't get up now, I'd never get up. It wasn't like I had someone who would do everything I needed them to do for me. I was on my own in this mess.

I hurried up and handled my hygiene then went into my walk-in closet to figure out what I wanted to wear for the day. I wasn't in the mood to dress up or anything, so I just settled on a simple yellow tube dress and a pair of gold Jimmy Choo sandals.

By the time I got dressed, my stomach growled like clockwork. I went into the kitchen and popped an Eggo waffle in the microwave and poured me a cup of coffee. Drinking coffee wasn't a regular thing for me, I only did it whenever I needed a pick me up like I did at the moment. My body was exhausted and hoped it would wake me up.

I dripped a little syrup on the waffle and shoved it into my mouth then grabbed my coffee mug, purse, and keys off the countertop and headed for the door. Hopefully, by the time I made it to the shop, I'd have a little more energy. If I didn't, I'd only be grouchy as hell for the remainder of the day.

I pulled up in front of the shop and finished off my coffee then stepped out of the car. My mouth fell to the ground when I looked up at the door and saw it was replaced right along with the windows. The guys I was supposed to meet weren't due there for at least another forty-five minutes so I'm sure they weren't the ones who did it.

I unlocked the door and pushed it open then stepped inside. I stood there in total awe. Everything in there was completely replaced with newer model furniture. It still had the same color scheme as before—silver and white, but this time it had a splash of purple; my favorite color.

"Who could have done this?"

Was it Naomi? She was my first thought but then I knew it couldn't be her. Her parents paid for her school tuition and for her to live rent-free until she graduated. It wasn't possible she had the money lying around to pull something off like that.

I moved through the shop just looking at everything. The pedicure throne chairs stood taller than before and looked even more comfortable. The bowls lined up in front of them were stainless steel. I brushed my fingertips across the tables as I made my way to the back where the office was.

On the office door in silver inscription, it read *"Sanaa's"*. A smile crept up on my face and there was no telling how long it been there. I pushed the door open and the most beautiful office awaited me.

A silver and white marble desk sat on top of a white fur rug with a purple chair behind it. White lilies sat in a purple glass vase on top of the desk. The walls were white except one purple wall adjacent to the desk. A large picture of Yonnie when she was younger hung on the back wall.

Moisture filled my eyes. Someone had gone out of their way to do something so nice for me and I wasn't sure how to feel. I couldn't wait to tell Naomi about the shop. Whoever did this for me, I was truly grateful for it.

"Do you like it?"

His voice sent chills down my spine and made the hairs on the back of my neck stand straight up. I should have known he was the one behind this. I slowly turned around to face him.

"I love it but why did you go out of your way to do this for me?"

At this point, it didn't even matter about him seeing me cry. Those tears were tears of joy not from the sadness of him breaking my heart. I appreciate him going out of his way to make up for something that was his fault to begin with, but it still doesn't change the way I felt about him. I was still angry with him and I was going to let it be known.

"I wanted to do something nice for you. I felt bad after finding out Sofia and A'Karri were the ones who trashed the shop. I wanted to make things right with you and thought this would be the perfect start."

I wiped the tears from my eyes and rubbed my index finger across my nose. "Well, you shouldn't have done it. I'm thankful you took the time out to do something like this for me but it doesn't change the fact I'm still mad as hell with you."

He went to touch me, and I stumbled back away from him.

"I know you're angry Sanaa and I don't expect anything less from you right now. If I could go back and change things now that I know you, I'd make sure Yonnie was still alive. I can't change the past and I regret taking her from you, but it's in the past Sanaa. All I ask is that we be able to move on from this. I really want to see where things can go between us."

As much as I might want to be with Soul, I knew things between us would never work out for the sake of my mother. He could have done anything else in the world but taking mine away from me ended whatever we were attempting to share.

"I'll keep cleaning the cash for you because like you said I don't have much of a choice but that's as far as this relationship thing between us will go. Can you leave now because I have a lot I have to do today, starting with canceling a meeting I had this morning." I went behind my desk and picked up the phone off the receiver. He still stood there with a somber expression on his face. I eyed him, lifting my brow.

He scrubbed his hand down his face then backed out of the doorway. When I heard the door chime, I exhaled, placed the phone back on the receiver and flopped down in the chair, dropping my face in my hands.

NAOMI

I kept second guessing myself about leaving Berlin. He's the only thing I could think about for the last couple of days. I tried so hard to not pick my phone up and call him. He kind of scared me the other night when I told him we needed to end things. For a second, I actually thought he was going to hit me.

I didn't think he felt that deep for me until I saw his eyes glossed over before I walked out on him. I kind of felt awful for doing him the way I had. It wasn't his fault, and I tried to put the entire thing on him. I was making him pay for something that happened before we even got together. Some may say I'm selfish, but I felt like I owed that much to my best friend to stop seeing him.

I got out of bed and went to the bathroom. Every month like clockwork my period came on and for the last week, I checked myself to see if there were any signs of it. I prayed like hell it would pop on some time or another. It had me terrified because if it didn't then it only meant all the sex Berlin and I had without protection finally caught up to me.

It scared me shitless to think I might be pregnant. I wasn't sure if I was ready to have a child just yet. I still had school to think about then it was the fact Berlin would be the father. I don't even think he wanted kids. He's never mentioned anything to me about it.

I finished up peeing and wiped then checked the tissue to see if my period had come on and still nothing.

"Period, where the fuck are you? You come on when a bitch doesn't want to see you but now that I do, you want to take a vacation and shit."

I sighed a heavy breath and got up from the toilet. The only thing I could do was face my fears and run to the store to get a pregnancy test. Might as well go on and find out if I was pregnant or not—rip the band-aid right off.

I rushed to the Walgreens down the street and grabbed the first pregnancy test I saw on the shelf. I wasn't sure what brand it was and really it didn't matter. They all worked the same and I'm positive this one would serve its purpose.

When I got back home, I went straight to the bathroom and peed on the stick. I placed it on the countertop and stayed glued to the toilet, waiting for the three minutes to be up so I could check it. The entire time I sat there, my heart thumped in my chest. My palms became clammy and I kept wiping them on my pants. Sweat beads formed on my forehead. My alarm went off alerting me that the three minutes were up.

I sat there for another three minutes, anticipating picking the test up.

"Please don't be positive. Please don't be positive," I kept reciting over and over as I picked it up off the counter and gazed down at it. "YES!" I screamed and jumped up from the toilet. I did a little happy dance as I looked at the negative sign. Lord knows he was with me then.

I tossed the test into the trashcan then went into my bedroom. Throwing myself onto the bed, I dialed Sanaa's number. I knew she was probably at the shop with what time of day it was.

"Bitch, what are you doing?" I asked her soon as she answered the phone.

"Getting ready to open the shop back up. You sound like you're in a good mood."

"Wait, you got the shop fixed that quick?" I thought she would have let me know when she was going to work on the shop so I could come over and help her out. I didn't want her to have the burden of doing everything on her own.

"Actually, Soul was the one who surprised me this morning. Everything is just beautiful, Naomi. I wish you could see it," her voice cracked a little bit as she spoke, and I could tell she either been crying or was on the brink of it.

"That's so nice of him. I still hate his fucking guts though." I sat up straight in the bed.

"Yeah, tell me about it." She sighed deeply into the phone.

"Look, we're going out to *Crisis* tonight. I feel like celebrating."

"Celebrating what?" she questioned me.

"My un-pregnancy, ho."

"Did I miss something?"

"I thought I was pregnant for a minute, but my period is just late."

"I don't really feel up to going to the club, Naomi. Maybe we can just do a dinner instead," she suggested but I wasn't feeling that. I wanted to go out and twerk my ass so that's exactly what I was going to do.

"We're going out and I'm not taking no for an answer. Be ready by twelve and I'll be by your place so we can catch an Uber together." I disconnected the call before she could object to the idea.

* * *

I twerked my ass on the dance floor at club *Crisis*. Sanaa was really being a party pooper, so I left her sitting at the bar with a mug on her face. If I knew she was going to be this down about coming out with me then I would have left her ass at home.

I tossed my third drink back and it had me feeling amazing. My mind was free, and I wanted it to stay that way. Even if I was only forgetting about Berlin for a couple of hours that was fine by me. I already knew by the time I left to head home, he was going to creep right on back into my mind.

Some guy came up behind me while I was dancing, pressing his frame up against me. I didn't mind; it was only a dance, so I twerked and popped my ass on him until the song ended. He spun me around where I was facing him.

"What's your name, shorty?"

I smiled up into his face. He was a decent looking guy and could probably take my mind off of Berlin for the night so I wouldn't mind going home with him. I didn't plan on seeing him again after tonight, so I decided to give him a fake name.

"Kelly and what's yours?"

"Luca. So, Kelly, tell me what it will take for a nigga like me to get your number."

"Hhmp, it depends." My eyes shifted away from him up to the VIP section.

I don't know why but something was drawing me to it. My eyes landed on Berlin who was up there with some chick in his lap. If I was being honest about it, it rubbed me the wrong way. He seemed all happy and shit now that we weren't together and I'm not sure if I wanted to accept the shit.

I stormed off, heading up to the VIP section with a mug on my face. I completely forgot I was standing there talking to Luca, but he'd just have to wait until I gave Berlin quite a bit of my mind. Surprisingly, the bouncer let me in with no hesitations. I stopped and stood directly in front of them and cleared my throat.

"Ahem."

BERLIN

When my eyes landed on Naomi standing in front of me, I quickly tossed shorty out my lap onto the couch beside me. I didn't expect to see her there and it was just my first reaction. I grabbed old girl, placing her back into my lap when I came to the realization I hadn't done shit wrong.

She was the one who walked out on me. If I wanted to enjoy the company of a chick I just met at the club then I was doing no wrong.

She stood in front of me with her face contorted into a frown and her hand resting on her hip. Naomi acted like she'd just caught me cheating or some shit. I couldn't lie and say I wasn't enjoying the mug on her face because I was. At least she knew she fucked up by leaving me.

"What the hell is this, Berlin?" she quizzed me.

"What does it look like?" My brow rose, touching my hairline.

"So, you're just going to sit up here and disrespect me like this in front of my face?"

"Tell me how I'm disrespecting you, Naomi?"

"BY HAVING THIS BITCH IN YOUR FUCKING LAP! That's how!" She glared at me and her golden face turned fire red. She was angry and it was a good thing. It let me know she still cared.

Pissing her off wasn't my motive but it sure as hell was a plus. Shorty who was in my lap had come up into my section on some groupie type shit not too long ago. At first, I was just kicking it by myself drinking from the bottle of Louis Xiii. I didn't have anything else to do so I told the bouncer he could let her inside.

By the way Naomi was looking at the moment, I was starting to believe it was the wrong thing to do. But then, she couldn't make me feel bad for trying to take my mind off of her. Everything else I tried didn't seem to work.

"Naomi, you need to chill." I lifted the girl from my lap and sat her down on the couch then stood in front of Naomi. "Do you not remember you broke up with me?"

"Do I need to go?" the girl asked. I couldn't even remember what her name was.

"Yes!" Naomi shouted, leaning her head to the side so she could eye the chick.

"No!" I barked over my shoulder.

Naomi side eyed me, but I just brushed it off. She had to know she couldn't have her cake and eat it too.

"So, it's really like that Berlin?"

"You damn right. What do you mean? How is it supposed to be?" I sensed hesitation in her eyes as she glared back at me. The night she broke up with me she seemed like it was what she really wanted but now she wasn't so sure.

Tears streamed down her cheeks and her chin trembled. "I didn't think you would move on so fast. It doesn't even seem like you actually gave a damn about me."

I didn't really want to take it there with Naomi. Not in front of this chick that I was just vibing with before she showed up. I loved Naomi, something I didn't even think I was capable of but I wasn't about to sit there and let her play with my emotions and shit. At the end of the day, I was still Berlin Maserati and I'd forever live up to my name.

"Shit ain't even like that Naomi and you know it."

"Well, if it's not then send that ho on about her way."

I glanced back and old girl was sipping from a cup and bobbing her head to the music like she wasn't even fazed by the conversation I was having with Naomi. It shocked me because any other chick would have gone crazy right about now.

Naomi was really tripping if she thought I was going to get rid of shorty for her to only go on about her business afterward. She didn't want to be with me and didn't want anyone else to be. Shit didn't work like that. Since she wanted to walk out of my life then I was going to move on with the muhfucka.

"Nah, I'm good on that." I sat back down pulling the chick right on back into my lap. Naomi stood there in my face with her mouth ajar and tears still evident in her eyes.

"Get this bitch out of here Berlin, I'm not fucking playing with you!" she barked, and I just chuckled in her face. That only made her get even angrier because her eyes grew wide and her chest heaved. "I'm glad you think this shit is funny but if you don't get this ho out of here and fast, I'm not going to have any other choice but to whoop her ass and yours too," she warned.

Naomi wasn't crazy enough to put her hands on me so that was the least of my worries. She lunged toward me and I hopped up dropping the girl to the floor.

"Got damn Berlin," she cried out, pulling herself up off the floor rubbing her ass.

I slung Naomi over my shoulder and carried her downstairs toward the exit. I stepped out the door placing her down on her feet. The door pushed back open and Sanaa stepped out with a mug on her face.

"What you manhandling my girl like that for?"

"Your girl wilding. Y'all need to take your ass home."

"I'm not going anywhere until you get that bitch out your section. I don't know why you're trying to take me as a fucking joke, Berlin," Naomi replied, closing the space between us.

"Take your ass home, Naomi."

I pulled my pants up some and headed back to the door. The bouncer pulled the door open for me.

"You see those two right over there?" He briefly glanced Naomi and Sanaa then nodded. "They aren't allowed back in here tonight."

"Berlin, you're fucking full of shit!" Naomi shouted, lunging toward me but the bouncer grabbed her. I flashed her a smirk and shut the door behind me. Since she wanted to play games, I was going to show her I could play them better.

QUENTIN

After that mess had gone down when I shot at Soul and Berlin then took A'Karri, I been staying away from everyone and everything lying low. I was pretty sure they would come after me sooner or later on some revenge type shit.

Since things between A'Karri and I were officially over, my mind has been going to Sanaa. I tried to stay away from her, but I couldn't seem to do it. I found myself sitting outside her shop waiting on the last nail tech to leave so I could go in there and talk to her. She probably was going to go upside my head when she saw me.

I hated that Soul got to her and caused her to break things off with me in the first place. We really had a good thing going on and she couldn't deny it.

The last girl left out the shop and climbed into her car a couple cars down from mine. I watched Sanaa through the window moving around the shop, straightening up things.

I was sure her nipples were poking through the red tube top she wore because I could tell she wasn't wearing a bra underneath. The white jeans showed off her perfect round ass. I licked my lips and climbed out of the car as she made her way to the back of the shop.

I slowly eased the door open and it chimed.

"Sorry, we're closed!" she shouted from the back then appeared. Her mouth fell open and posture stiffened when her eyes landed on me.

"Hi, Sanaa."

"What are you doing here?"

"Wanted to see you."

"Well, you did now you can go." She brushed past me to the door and pulled it open. "Goodbye, Quentin."

"You know you don't really want me to go anywhere. I don't know why you're tripping like that." I stepped directly in front of her and heard her swallow hard as she gazed up into my eyes. I brought my hand up to the side of her face cupping it. "I just want things to go back to the way they were."

149

"You know we can't do that. You got a girl anyway."

"No, I don't. A'Karri and I broke up." I ran my free hand down her back and pulled her body into my frame. She gasped.

"It's not safe for you here. I'm sure they're out there right now looking for you."

"This would be the last place they'd think I'd be."

I tilted her face to the side and planted a kiss on her neck.

"We can't do this, Q."

When she called me Q, I knew I had her exactly where I wanted her. Her hand let go of the door and it closed. I reached over, turning the lock.

"Why not? Because you're fucking with that nigga, Soul?"

I was about to show that nigga exactly how it felt when he snatched A'Karri away from me. Honestly, I think the only reason I showed up to her spot in the first place was to hurt his ass. I prayed after I fucked the shit out of her that he'd find out somehow and get even more pissed the fuck off. I was about to take every fucking thing away from that nigga he loved including the fucking empire he tried to protect so fucking much. Everything that was owed to me was going to be mine again by the time I was done.

I reached down unbuttoning her jeans and was surprised she didn't bother to stop me either. I pushed them down and she stepped out of them. I lifted her up, pinning her body against the door. I was sure people walking by would be able to see what we were doing but I didn't give a damn.

Unzipping my pants, I pulled my dick out and eased him into her soaking, wet pussy.

"Mhm," she moaned out, digging her sharp nails into my back.

I gently bit down on her neck and she moaned out even louder.

"You like that shit?" I asked as I gave her long deep strokes.

"Y-yes," she whimpered.

I stared her into the eyes and she nibbled on the corner of her lower lip. I slipped her lip into my mouth and shoved my tongue between her lips. She brushed her tongue against mine and I felt her releasing a gush of fluids on my dick. Her teeth sunk down into my lower lip, letting me know her climax was taking over her body.

"Fuuuccckkkk," she mumbled.

Her pussy sounded like macaroni as I dug into her guts. The shit gripped the hell out my dick like it always did when I went up in it. That's the reason why I could never stay away from her. That tight, warm, dripping wet pussy was always drawing me back.

"Got damn, I missed this pussy."

I eased out her pussy a little bit and she pulled me right back in. Her shit was just that on point.

"I want you to cum again before I do. You think you can do that for me?"

"Un-huh."

I pulled her off the wall and held her by her waist as I pounded in her pussy from the bottom. She leaned her head back, planting both of her hands on the wall.

"Oooh, fuck Soul!" she cried out. She probably didn't realize she just called me that nigga's name. It almost made my dick go limp, thinking she was fantasying about that nigga while I was in her but I kept going. I was about to get my nut off. I'd just say something to her about it when I'm done.

"I'm about to cum!"

I kept smacking her spot repeatedly until I felt her body shivering underneath my fingertips. When I knew she was done cumming, I released my seeds inside her then dropped her to her feet.

I went and grabbed a washcloth out the closet and wet it in the sink then cleaned my dick off. The entire time, Sanaa stood off by the door in silence. I turned to her, stuffing my dick back down in my pants.

"What's wrong with you?"

She let out a heavy sigh. "This was a mistake Q."

"How? That shit was good as fuck. You and I both know you wanted that shit."

"I thought I did..."

"Don't tell me this all because of that nigga Soul." I released a heavy sigh.

"This has nothing to do with Soul."

"You're a liar because you called me that fuck nigga's name while I was fucking you." I shook my head at her.

"Things between Soul and I are... complicated."

"Well, they just got even more *complicated*. Try explaining to that nigga that you just let me fuck." I laughed at her stupid ass.

If she wanted to be with Soul then that was her business. I wasn't about to try and prove to her that nigga wasn't shit. I was sure he'd do that all on his on before it was over with.

"This can't happen again."

"Whatever Sanaa." I pushed the door open and left out the shop. Because of Soul, both of my women wanted nothing else to do with me. I was over this nigga destroying my fucking life. It was time I came up with a plan to destroy the entire family once and for all.

SOUL

My mind was still messed up all over Sanaa. It was so fucked up that I didn't even know what to do. I tried talking to her, even went as far as getting the shop remodeled for her and nothing seemed to be working out in my favor. She still wanted nothing to do with me. Shitted on me like I wasn't shit. Like the connection we had with each other meant nothing to her.

We connected on a deeper level than I've ever connected with anyone and I think that's really what was messing with me. I came to the realization I was feeling Sanaa way deeper than I thought I was. I was beginning to love her.

The shit was driving me so fucking insane, I went by *Armon* and had a few drinks to take my mind off things. I only planned to have a couple but that turned into an entire bottle with a few shots on the side. By the time I decided to leave, everything seemed a little hazy for me. I wasn't sure how I even made it to *Glitz* safely but I did.

When I pulled into the parking lot, I saw what looked like Quentin's car speeding out of there. I glanced over and Sanaa's Maserati was parked in front of the salon. I could have gone behind him and handled his ass for the shit he pulled the other night. I was too worried to see what he was doing with Sanaa this time of night to even think about chasing him down. The salon was closed and that's the reason why I waited to pop up then because I knew no one else was supposed to be there.

I got out my car and headed up to the door. When I approached it, I saw Sanaa wiggling into her jeans. My fists balled up and I stumbled inside. Her gaze met mine when she heard the door chime.

Her posture stiffened, so she knew she had done something wrong. I couldn't believe the shit I was staring at. She wasted no fucking time getting with that nigga. We had been together just days prior and I was going in her pussy raw with no hesitations and now she was fucking this nigga. It made me regret doing the things I did with her.

"Was that Quentin leaving out the parking lot? And why the hell you ain't got-got n-no pants on?" I slurred my words. Guess I was drunker than I actually thought I was. I hadn't been this drunk since back when Berlin and I used to club hard as fuck and were flashy about our money.

She cut her eyes at me then buttoned her pants. "Does it really matter?"

I rushed her roughly gripping her by the forearm. "The hell you mean does it really matter? That nigga doesn't have any reason being up in here. Are you fucking around with that nigga again? You gotta be if your ho ass in here pulling your got damn pants up and shit. Let me find out you had something to do with that nigga shooting at us that night."

"Soul, let go of my arm you're hurting me," she whined. I let her go and she stumbled back a little bit.

"I told you that we couldn't be together so it shouldn't matter who the hell I'm fucking. And you know damn well I didn't have anything to do with him shooting at you. This was the first time I saw him since I broke things off. You can believe me or you don't, that's your problem."

I shut my eyes and rubbed my temples. I was really letting Sanaa get the best of me right now.

"I'm trying to fix things between us and you're out here fucking the next nigga."

"IF YOU WOULDN'T HAVE NEVER SHOT MY MOTHER THEN YOU WOULDN'T HAVE SHIT TO FUCKING FIX, NIGGA!" she screamed at me.

Without thinking, I gripped her by the neck and shoved her body up against the wall.

"Bring your fucking tone down when you're talking to me," I warned.

Tears came to the rim of her eyes as she stared back at me. Her breathing got heavier and I realized what I had done. I didn't mean to put my hands on her in that way. I was losing my fucking mind over a chick. *The hell was happening to me?*

"Get your fucking hands off me, Soul!" she threatened through clenched teeth.

I slowly eased my hand down from her neck and stepped back away from her.

"I'm sorry. I'm sorry for everything, Sanaa. Just let me fix things. I'll buy you whatever you want. Do whatever you tell me to, just stop pushing me away."

"I don't want your money, Soul. You can't just fucking buy me to fix shit. That's not how shit work."

"It was with Sofia."

Whenever I fucked up royally, the only thing I had to do was buy her an expensive gift and nine times out of ten all else was forgiven. I keep forgetting Sanaa was completely different from Sofia.

"I'm not Sofia. And don't you ever put your fucking hands on me again." She rubbed her neck where my hand once was.

I felt bad as fuck for touching her like that. All I wanted to do was love on Sanaa. Show her she was the only woman for me. I felt disgusted knowing Quentin was just in her pussy moments ago. It angered me all over again just thinking about the shit.

"I know because Sofia wouldn't fuck the next nigga behind my back like you just did."

"Let's be clear Soul. I didn't do anything behind your back. Like I've been trying to explain to you for what seems like forever, we don't have shit going on anymore. Never really did in the first place, you was just a good fuck. That's all you'll ever be to me; a good fuck." She moved her finger between her and me and I followed it almost tilting over. "You and I are done and there's nothing you can do to fix the shit." She hesitated for a moment then her lips parted again. "In fact, Quentin and I are getting back together. For real this time. We're going to officially become a thing now so you can just take yourself on out of my shop and don't come back. You're no longer welcome here. From now on, just send someone else to drop the cash off for you."

She went over yanking the door open. I felt like I had completely lost her but part of me was telling me she was lying. Sanaa didn't want Quentin. I remembered her telling me she wanted me and only me. Her mouth was telling me one thing, but I knew her heart felt a different way.

I stepped in front of her and she took her gaze elsewhere trying her best not to look me in the eyes. It felt as if time stopped. I lowered my head knowing I was defeated and stumbled right on out of there. If she wanted me to stay away from her then that's what I was going to do. As much as I didn't really want to, I would for her. I climbed back into my car and peeled out of there.

SANAA

Having sex with Quentin was completely a mistake. I was still angry with Soul and wanted to take my anger out on something or better yet, someone. Quentin knew what to do to get me to submit to him and I loved it when we were messing around but now, I hated the shit.

I didn't want Soul to find out about me having sex with Quentin but he walked in and caught me with my pants down, literally. Out of anger, I lied and told him Quentin and me was going to get together when that was far from the case. Just as he, I never wanted to see Quentin again but I wasn't about to tell him that. I wanted to make him jealous and from the way he left, I knew my plan worked.

The way Soul looked at me before he walked out the shop broke my heart into a million tiny pieces. Our situation must was getting the best of him if he showed up here drunk as hell. That's the first time I've ever seen him off his square. Normally, he would have his shit together but tonight, he seemed like a broken man. I realized what I did and rushed out the door to stop him from leaving but he peeled out the parking lot before I could get to him.

He was so drunk and he didn't need to be driving. I may have loathed him at the moment but I didn't want anything bad to happen to him. The only thing I could do was pray he made it home safely and possibly call and check on him later.

I finished cleaning up the shop so I could go home and shower to wash away any trace of Quentin that might have been on my body. I grabbed my purse out the office and hit the light switch then pushed the door open. I sighed a deep breath as I made my way to my car. Thoughts of Soul took over my mind.

Buuuuzzzzzz

My phone began ringing in my purse. I pulled it out and saw Berlin was calling me. Thinking it may have been Naomi calling from his phone, I picked up.

"Yeah, Naomi?"

"Sanaa, this Berlin. Soul was just in a car accident..." he continued to talk but I tuned everything he said from that point out. My heart dropped to the pit of my fucking stomach and my knees grew weak as noodles. I slumped into the side of my car to hold myself up.

If I hadn't turned him away like I did then I wouldn't be receiving this phone call. I felt as if everything was my fault and I had the right to feel that way because, in all actuality, it was.

"Sanaa, did you hear me?"

"No, I'm sorry what did you say?" I cleared my throat and straightened my posture then opened my car door.

"They rushed him to Kindred Hospital in case you want to go up there. I know you two aren't on the best of terms but at the same time, I also know you two care about each other. I'm not sure how bad it is so if I was you, I'd go and see him." He disconnected the call and I dropped my phone into my lap.

I sat there staring out the windshield playing Berlin's words over in my head. My eyes glossed over and my pulse raced. *What if he wasn't going to make it?* I could lose him and as much as I kept saying I didn't want anything else to do with him, I wasn't certain at this point.

My heart ached for him. It cried out to be loved by him but my mind kept telling me to stay away from him; he's no good for me. I had a battle between what my heart wanted and what my mind told me I needed.

I sniffled and wiped the tears from my eyes and finally threw the car in reverse. I headed toward Kindred Hospital not knowing what was going to happen when I got there.

"Lord, please don't let Soul die," I prayed, pulling into the parking lot.

I parked in the first empty space I saw and jumped out of the car. I sped walked up to the emergency entrance then my strides decreased the closer I got to the door and halted altogether when I reached it.

My heart thumped so loudly in my chest I could hear it in my ears. I brushed my hair back with my hands, pacing in front of the door then shook them in an attempt to calm my nerves.

"He's going to be just fine Sanaa. Stop stressing yourself."

I took a couple of deep breaths and Berlin appeared at my side. He slung his arm over my shoulder and snuggly pulled my body into his frame.

"That nigga gon' be aight. I know you care about my brother that's why I don't get why you're putting him through that bullshit. Come on and let's go see what they have to say."

We entered the hospital and I stood off to the side while he talked to one of the nurses at the desk. My nerves were still all over the place and I just wished they'd calm down.

I looked over and Berlin's facial expression grew stronger. His jaws clenched and fists balled up. *Please don't let him knock this woman out in front of my face.* I didn't want to have to call Naomi and tell her Berlin got locked up for hitting a nurse. He must didn't like the things they were telling him. His hands loosened and he scrubbed his hand down his face then strolled toward where I was standing.

"What did they say?" I quickly asked him. The anticipation was killing me at the moment and I needed to know something before I went completely insane.

"Said they just brought him in not too long ago and will let me know something as soon as they hear anything. I asked them if I could go back there with him but she told me I had to wait out here in the waiting area. Stupid bitch," he huffed then went over and plopped down in one of the chairs.

I rubbed my hand up and down the back of my neck. I was really hoping they would be able to tell us something but I guess we were now playing the waiting game. I went over into the back corner by myself and sat down in the chair resting my face in my hands.

NAOMI

I felt stupid as fuck after embarrassing myself in front of Berlin the way I had the other night. I let the shit get the best of me when I should have just gone on home with Luca like I was thinking. Instead, I took my ass up there and completely showed all of it in front of him and the bitch he was entertaining. The ho probably had plenty laughs thanks to my stupid ass after he carried me out like a rag doll.

It just did something to my soul to see him with another chick. I know I was the one who broke things off in the first place, but I didn't expect him to move on so quickly. It was like he didn't even really give a damn I left. Maybe he was straight putting on when I was at his condo. Who knows?

I grabbed my popcorn out the microwave, poured it into a bowl and went into my bedroom. I didn't have any plans for the night, so I decided to just stay in the house and find a show to binge watch on Netflix. My bed was completely filled with nothing but junk food and sodas. I always said, *"junk food was the way to the soul"* and tonight I was about to feed my soul every bit of junk that was in a two feet radius.

I settled down in bed with my popcorn and grabbed my firestick remote. Soon as I turned it on, my phone began vibrating on my nightstand. I glanced over and saw it was Sanaa which was perfect because she could come over and help me eat all this mess.

"Hey boo," I said into the phone, popping a hand full of popcorn into my mouth.

"Were you busy?" she questioned me not sounding like herself.

Usually, when something was wrong with her, I could sense it but tonight I couldn't. Maybe it was because I already was in my own feelings about Berlin and it was blocking her.

"No, just scrolling through Netflix trying to find me a show to binge watch. Do you think this show 'Glow' is any good?"

"Naomi…"

The way she called out my name I knew something was wrong. I dropped the bowl of popcorn down on the bed and slung my legs to the side climbing out of bed.

"Where are you? I'm on my way."

I went over to my dresser and grabbed a pair of black tights and slipped them on.

"Kindred Hospital," she replied and sniffled.

"What you doing up there?"

I scooped my keys and wallet up off the dresser and headed for the front door. It didn't matter why she was there because I was coming regardless. But I did want to make sure she was all right to know if I should run red lights getting there or not.

"Soul was in an accident. I don't know if he's alright and I'm scared. It's all my fault, Naomi. If I didn't—"

"No, what you're not going to do is blame yourself for something you didn't do. I'm on my way, Sanaa."

I ended the call and wiped the tears from my eyes that were threatening to fall. Hearing her talk about Soul had me on the brink of tears right along with her. That was my best friend and when she hurts, I hurt. When she cries, I cry. When she's happy, I'm fucking great. Our bond was just that strong.

I made it to the hospital and rushed inside. My eyes danced around the waiting area until they landed on her sitting in the corner all by her lonesome. She had her elbows resting on her thighs and her tiny head lying in her hands. I rushed over to her kneeling down in front of her.

"I'm here and I'm sure everything's going to be alright." I gently rubbed her on her lower back. I could tell she was crying because I could see the teardrops on her thighs. "Did they say anything about him?"

"No, Berlin keeps trying to find something out but they won't let him know anything." She finally lifted her head up and her gaze met mine. Her eyes were red and puffy.

"Berlin's here?"

My heart thumped rapidly in my chest. He was the last person I wanted to see but what did I expect? Soul was his brother so of course, he was going to be there. I just hoped I didn't run into him while I was there. I didn't remember seeing him when I came in so maybe he'd stay away until I left.

"Yeah, he's right over there." She pointed over by the nurses' station and sure enough, he was there leaned up against the wall talking to his ex-girlfriend, Ivy. I knew it was her because he showed me a picture of her when we first started messing around.

She was wearing a pair of scrubs so this must be the hospital she worked at. Heat rushed over my body. They looked all cozy standing there talking to each other. He had that half-smirk on his face that he got whenever he was around me and I immediately felt jealous.

Ivy was a beautiful chick and I could see why he wanted her in the first place. She was thick in all the right places. You could see her perfect shape through her scrubs. She looked like a black Barbie with her weave flowing down her back. What really ticked me off was when he palmed her face and grazed his thumb across her cheek.

My heart broke in two just watching them interact. I was terrified she might try to take my place and he let her. We only been broken up for a short time and he'd been with two different women so far that I know of. It could easily be more knowing him.

"Are you alright?" Sanaa asked me bringing me back from my thoughts.

I hadn't noticed tears were pouring down my cheeks until I felt them drip onto my thighs. No, I wasn't *all right*. I was watching the man I loved interact with another woman and she was holding the hell out of his fucking attention. So much that he didn't even notice me in there. How was I supposed to feel about that?

I wiped my eyes and turned back to face her. "I just wanted to make sure you were okay. Don't mind me, I'll be fine," I lied. I felt like I was dying inside but Sanaa needed me more so I just put my emotions on the back burner.

"You're not okay; you're crying Naomi. I thought everything between you and Berlin was fine until that night at *Crisis*. What happened between you two?"

"I broke up with him. I couldn't be with him anymore knowing they were the reason Yonnie's dead," I answered her truthfully. Now, I was feeling like it was a mistake.

"You didn't have to break up with him for that, Naomi. Berlin wasn't the one who killed mama, it was Soul. You don't have to punish him for something someone else did. You were happy with him. You finally let go and started falling in love. Don't mess it up because of us, Naomi."

I glanced back over where Berlin was and saw Ivy grip him by the hand then lead him away.

"I got to go." I jolted up from in front of her and rushed out the door with tears pouring down my cheeks. I couldn't sit in there any longer and watch the two. I already messed up things between us. It was too late to try and fix anything. Berlin was moving on and I probably was going to have to as well.

BERLIN

My parents were gone to Paris for their wedding anniversary and had been blowing my phone up nonstop to see what was going on after I called and told them the news about Soul. I was pretty sure they were on a flight home right about now.

These nurses in this hospital were pissing me the fuck off. Wouldn't no one tell me what the hell was going on with Soul. How long I been up there, they should have found something out by now. I was getting ready to put my foot up their ass when Ivy appeared out of nowhere. I forgot she worked at this hospital.

She told me she got word Soul was in there and wanted to check and make sure I was all right. I was doing as good as I'll ever be until I finally was able to lay eyes on my brother. She talked to me to keep me calm. She already knew the temper I had on me and was certain things were going to escalate quickly if I didn't get the answers I needed.

The entire time I stood there talking to her, the only thing on my mind was Naomi. She was supposed to be there with me, not Ivy. I wanted her to sit there and tell me everything was going to be all right while I rested my head on her breasts and she stroked my hair. Even though I wanted to so badly, I fought the urge to call her phone and ask her to come up there with me. My pride stood in the way.

Ivy gripped me by the hand and led me to one of the closets we used to have sex in all the time when we were talking. It was always empty so we knew no one was going to be in there. If she was pulling me in there then I already knew what she had up her sleeve. If it was going to take my mind off everything for a moment, then I was going to let her.

She closed the door behind us and glared up at me.

"Don't just stand there looking at me. You brought me in here for a reason so go on handle that shit."

She tucked her lower lip between her teeth and it bounced when she let it go. She gripped me by my Gucci belt and unbuckled it then unzipped my pants. For the first time, my dick wasn't already stiff so she was going to have to put in the work to wake the muhfucka up.

She dropped down to her knees in front of me and gazed up into my face as she wrapped her hand around my dick. She placed him into her mouth and began sucking but it wasn't doing anything to me. A nigga was still limp as he was when she pulled him out my boxers.

I shut my eyes and an image of Naomi popped up in my head. I immediately felt my dick stiffening. A moan escaped Ivy's mouth as she slurped and licked on my shit.

He got all the way hard and I pulled it from her mouth. "Turn that ass around," I ordered, taking a condom from my pants pocket and ripping it open with my teeth. I was not about to go up in her without a glove.

She dropped her pants and turned around grabbing a hold of one of the shelves. I slipped my middle finger into her slippery pussy and fingered it a little bit to make sure it was ready to take this dick.

Smack!

I slapped her on the ass and watched it jiggle as I eased my dick inside her.

"Mhmm, Berlin," she groaned. "I been missing this dick like crazy."

"Can you shut the fuck up and let me concentrate?" I didn't want to hear shit coming from her mouth to fuck up the vision I had of Naomi in my mind.

I nibbled on my lower lip as I pounded my dick inside her from behind. Ivy was moaning all out of control and the shelf she held on to, began rocking. Shit was crashing to the floor but I didn't care. Then how loud she was I was certain people passing the door could hear her. I didn't care about that either.

"Yes, Berlin!" she shouted and I reached around covering her mouth with my hand.

"Didn't I tell you to shut the fuck up?"

"Un-huh," she mumbled, nodding.

"Then, shut the hell up."

I let go of her mouth and gripped her tightly around the throat not giving a damn if I was cutting off her circulation. She threw her pussy back on the dick, squeezing it with every thrust she took.

From the whining she was doing, I could tell she was about to cum. "Oh, fuuuucckkkkk, I can't hold it in anymore."

"Go on and cum," I ordered her. If she didn't then she would have been shit out of luck because I was about to release my seeds my damn self.

I felt her gushing on my dick so I released my seeds into my condom then pulled out of her. I snatched the condom off my dick and slapped it down into her hand.

"Get rid of that shit," I told her then stuffed my dick back down into my pants. The way I was talking to her was rude as hell, but she served her purpose—to take my mind off things and that was it. I wasn't thinking about taking things with her any further than they already gone.

"It's like that, Berlin?" I saw her on the brink of tears which only meant I needed to get the hell out of there with her. My brother was in there fighting for his life, I wasn't about to babysit a grown woman's fucking feelings and shit.

"Yeah, it's like that." I pulled the door open and stepped out into the hallway shutting it behind me.

I went back into the waiting area and Sanaa was still sitting in the same spot. "Did they say anything?"

She shook her head then I sensed hesitation in her eyes before her lips parted. "Naomi saw you... you know with that girl."

"So?" I sat down in a chair a couple chairs down from hers so I could think. Had I known Naomi was there then I would have talked to her instead of gone with Ivy. It wasn't anything I could do now about it. Naomi chose the route she wanted to take, and I couldn't do shit but stay in my own fucking lane.

SOUL

My eyes slowly peeled open. I glanced around and noticed I was inside a hospital room. The only thing I could remember was getting into it with Sanaa and leaving. I went to get up from the bed but my body was sore as hell. The nurse pulled the curtain back and stepped inside.

"You're finally awake. How are you feeling?" she questioned me, slowly walking over to my side.

"Sore as hell. What am I doing here?"

"You were in a car accident. You don't remember?"

Suddenly, after she said that, all my thoughts of the accident came rushing back to me. I was so angry with Sanaa about her having sex with Quentin and not wanting to deal with me anymore, I rushed off. I wasn't paying attention where I was going and ran a red light. A car hit me from the side pinning me up against a pole.

I rubbed my hands up and down my body to make sure I hadn't caused any real damage to myself.

"You're fine. You have a few lesions here and there but God must was with you for you to walk away with only scrapes and bruises." She flashed me a smile then headed for the curtain. "I'm right outside if you need me." She slid the curtain back.

Wonder if anyone knows that I'm here? I wanted to call Sanaa but for one, I didn't have my phone and two, I was still pissed with her ass. Pops going to kill me if he found out I was drunk driving and that's the true reason why I was in that accident. If Berlin knew I was here then I was pretty sure they were on their way home to check on me.

The curtain pulled back again and this time I was greeted by Sanaa's face. Her eyes were puffy and red like she'd been crying. I don't know what she was upset for, this was basically her fault.

"Hi," she softly spoke and slid the curtain back so we could have privacy.

"What you doing here?"

She rubbed her hand down the back of her neck avoiding eye contact with me. She was still wearing the clothes from earlier when I caught her after she had sex with Quentin. Apparently, she hadn't been home yet.

"Berlin called me and told me what happened. I've been here this entire time to make sure you were alright."

"You see I'm just fine. What's your excuse for still being here, now?"

"If you want me to leave then I'll go."

I just laid there not uttering a word. Her presence alone was ticking me the fuck off.

"Look," she paused for a moment and her gaze met mine. "I'm sorry about earlier. I feel like all this is my fault—"

"You should because it is."

"That didn't mean for you to agree with me." She sighed a deep breath then eased a little closer to the bed. "I didn't mean for you to walk in and see that. What I said about Quentin and me—"

"I don't want to hear shit about you and that bitch Quentin. If you want to be with that nigga then that's your fucking business."

"Will you just let me explain and quit cutting me off?"

"I'll let you explain when you go and wash your ass. Come up in here still wearing that shit after you fucked that nigga. I don't even want to look at your ass right now. Just go home, Sanaa."

Tears cascaded down her cheeks and if it was any other time, I would have felt bad and wanted to be her personal Superman but with the way I was feeling at the moment, I could care less.

"Fuck you, Soul!" She snatched the curtain back and stormed out of there. I exhaled once I knew she was gone then slung my legs over the side of the bed.

My body ached but I could endure it for the time being. I wasn't about to stay in that hospital knowing the cops would come snooping around soon or later ready to ask me twenty-one questions and shit. I didn't deal with the muhfuckas and I wasn't about to deal with them now.

Just as I grabbed my shirt and slipped it back over my head, Berlin walked into the room. "The hell you said to Sanaa?"

"Just told her the fucking truth."

"You don't have to do that girl like that, bruh. She has been sitting out there worried sick about your ass the entire time you were back here. In fact, she beat me to the fucking hospital when I called and told her what happened," he tried to explain but I wasn't feeling that shit.

"So?"

"The fuck you mean so? Obviously, she gives a damn about your stubborn ass and we all know you give a fuck about her. Might even be love there from the looks of it so stop trying to push that girl away."

"Push her away? She the one ended shit between us, not me." It was crazy how he was trying to make it seem like I was the one to blame here.

I stepped out of the room and the nurse which was in there just moments prior locked eyes with me. Berlin fell in stride alongside me.

"Did they release you?"

"No, but I'm not about to stay up here."

"Mr. Maserati, where are you going?" the nurse ran up to me and asked.

"Home."

"You can't go home yet; we haven't released you."

"Watch me."

I headed toward the double doors that lead out to the waiting area of the emergency room. If I wanted to leave there then I had the right to. They couldn't hold me there, not even if they had a gun to my fucking head.

"Where you headed?" Berlin quizzed me when we got outside. I spotted his Ferrari parked so I went for it.

"You about to drop me off at the house."

"No, the hell I ain't. Your ass better call you an Uber or some shit because I'm not about to drive all the way out there. Ain't nobody told your ass to move out there."

"Nigga, the drive ain't that fucking far. Give me your keys, I'll drive there and you can drive back. Crying like a little bitch and shit."

"Fuck you and don't wreck my shit like you did yours."

He tossed me the keys and I hit the key fob then slid into the seat. My mind briefly went to Sanaa but I quickly shook her from my head. If things between us were meant to be then, they'd be. I wasn't about to put any more stress on the shit. I was done chasing her ass.

SANAA

"You're pregnant."

"Say what now?" I asked the doctor to be sure I heard her right. She couldn't be looking at my results. She had to be looking at someone else's because Sanaa Love wasn't fucking pregnant.

"You're pregnant Sanaa," she repeated.

I sat there staring off into space trying my best to register what she just told me. How the hell had I been so careless? I was so wrapped up in Soul that I fucked around and gotten pregnant on the first time we had sex.

For the last week and a half, I been feeling like shit so I decided to come to the doctor to see what was going on with me. When she mentioned me taking a pregnancy test, I laughed in her face. I laughed so hard tears came to my eyes. Now that I was sitting here staring at my results, I didn't think anything was funny.

"And, you're sure this is right? Do I need to take the test again?"

"You can take it again all you want to but it's not going to change the fact that you're pregnant Sanaa."

Pregnant?

I fucked around and gotten pregnant by a man I didn't even want to see again. Soul hurt my feelings the last time we encountered each other, and I hadn't seen him since. Not once did I check on him after his accident and I didn't care if he was doing fine or not. I sat in that hospital waiting room worried sick about his wellbeing and that's how he fucking treated me.

I jolted from my seat and headed for the door. There was too much on my mind at the moment and I felt like my throat was collapsing on me. If I didn't get outside soon, I'd probably pass out in there.

I ignored Dr. Lee calling out for me and rushed out the exit. When I stepped outside, I took deep breaths to try and catch my breath.

The first person that came to mind to talk to was Naomi so I climbed into my car and sped all the way to her condo. I was sure she'd set me straight even if it was something I didn't really want to hear. It's funny how I was just ready to dig in her ass when I thought she was pregnant but turned out, she needed to dig in mine for being so stupid.

Boom! Boom! Boom!

I banged on Naomi's front door. I was impatient at the moment and couldn't wait for her to come to it. I needed to get this off my chest and I needed to do it now.

"Naomi!" I called out for her still beating on her door.

She swung the door open with a scowl on her face. Her purse was in one hand and her cell phone and keys in the other. If I didn't know any better, I'd think she was about to leave out the door before I got there.

"Why are you banging on my got damn door like you're the police, Sanaa?"

I brushed straight past her into the house. "I need to talk to you about something. Were you on your way out?"

"Uh, yeah you do see my purse and keys, don't you? I have class in an hour."

I sighed deeply and plopped down on her couch. "I need to talk to you about something."

"Can this *something* wait because if I don't leave now, then I'll be late with all this traffic." She scrunched her face up at me with her hand resting on her hip.

I squeezed my eyes shut, "I'm pregnant!" I blurted. I held my breath to try and stop my heart from thumping.

"You're what?" She pushed the door until it closed then came over to me. "Because I know you didn't just say what the fuck I think you said."

"Naomi, I'm fucking pregnant." Tears filled my eyes. The more I said it out loud, the more I realized this was my fucking reality. I was about to have a child. "I don't know what I'm going to do."

She dropped her purse on the coffee table and sat down on the couch beside me. She draped her arm around my neck and pulled me into her.

"What do you think you should do? I'm with you one hundred percent with whatever you want to do. You know I'm your biggest supporter."

"I don't even know if I want to tell Soul about the baby let alone keep it." There were so many thoughts running through my mind. If Soul and I weren't on such bad terms, then I'd think it was the universe trying to bring us closer together. With the way I was feeling, my first thought was I was being punished for falling for my mother's killer.

"Are you saying you want an abortion? Because there are other ways you can go about this..."

"Abortion might be my best option right now, Naomi. I won't be able to carry that baby for nine months then give it up. I don't want to keep this baby and fall in love with it the same as I did its father."

Her eyes grew wide as saucers. "You're in love with Soul?"

"I-I don't know. I think I am. How am I supposed to know if I am or not?" I knew what it felt like to love someone because I was in love with William once upon a time. Look how things turned out for me then. After that heartbreak, I told myself I didn't want to fall for anyone else again but Soul slowly captured my heart.

"You know whether or not if you're in love, Sanaa. Don't try to pull that shit on me because it's not going to work."

"Okay, fine I am but I don't want to be in love with him. Not after what he's done."

"The heart wants what the heart wants, Sanaa. I'm not trying to tell you what to do but I think you should let Soul know about his baby."

"Sounds like to me you are." I rolled my eyes at her and got up from the couch then went into the kitchen. I needed something to take the edge off. I know I wasn't supposed to be drinking while pregnant but I didn't have any intentions of keeping this baby so it really shouldn't matter.

I went into her cabinet and grabbed a bottle of Patron then popped the top off it. Just as soon as I placed it up to my lips, Naomi slapped it down and it went crashing to the floor.

"The hell are you doing, Sanaa? You know you're not supposed to be drinking while pregnant," she fussed, then went over to the pantry and grabbed the broom.

"Didn't think it really mattered when I don't plan on keeping the baby." I rolled my eyes at her then hopped up on the counter. She swept the shattered glass up into the dustpan.

"I think you should really think about it. Just take some time and sleep on things."

"I'll think about it if it makes you happy but that still doesn't mean I'm going to change my mind. What you got to eat in here because I'm hungry."

"I don't have shit for you, Sanaa. Better go home and eat your own food. Or better yet, call that baby daddy of yours and tell him to bring you something." She laughed at her own joke but I didn't see shit funny about what she said.

I had a baby growing inside me. This shit was very much real and I didn't know what I was going to do.

QUENTIN

I couldn't get my mind off of A'Karri. I tried calling her and she had gotten her number changed. Guess it was safe to say, she actually didn't want anything else to do with me.

Heat coursed through my veins. I plopped down on the couch and quickly rolled me a blunt to try and calm my nerves. As I puffed on it, I sat there contemplating ways I could hurt her the exact way she hurt me or worse. I know I was acting like a bitch ass nigga but love made you do crazy things. Even the unthinkable.

"All those muhfuckas are going to feel my fucking pain by the time I'm done with them," I spoke to myself.

I leaned back pulling my phone out my front pants pocket and dialed Luca's number. For what I was about to do, I was going to need his help.

"What, Q I was in the middle of something," he panted through the phone.

"Nigga, hurry up and catch that two-minute nut and get your ass over here to my house. Make sure you bring your strap with you too."

"You know I don't go anywhere without it and I'm not a minute man. Fuck off my phone." He disconnected the call and I dropped my phone into my lap then placed the blunt back between my lips.

I loved the shit out of A'Karri and couldn't believe she was willing to end things between us because I fucked up a few times. No one on this God's green earth was perfect. Neither was she but she tried to make it seem like I was the only one doing wrong here. She did some foul shit in our relationship but you don't see me crying about it.

We started talking about marriage a while ago. I told her how much I loved her and just how badly I wanted to marry her. I meant every word and if what I was about to do was going to bring us closer together then I was going to do it even if it brings her pain. She was going to come crawling back to me one way or another.

My phone vibrated and I picked it up from my lap.

Luca: *I'm outside.*

I put out the second blunt I started smoking after I finished off the first one and got up from the couch, grabbing my strap off the coffee table. Pulling the clip out, I checked it to make sure there were some bullets in it. Since I stopped dealing with the streets, I didn't really too much carry a gun around on me anymore but after I shot at Soul and them, I had no choice but to keep it glued to my side. That muthafucka went everywhere I went including the bathroom. I had to be cautious.

I left out the door and Luca was sitting at the curb in his white Tahoe. I jumped into the passenger's seat and dapped him up then told him an address to take me to. He didn't ask any questions, he just did it and that's one of the things I loved about him.

Luca and I been friends ever since middle school. I stayed dragging him into some shit and he didn't seem to mind. If you were to look up the word loyalty, I'm sure you'd find his face beside it. That's how loyal to me he was.

Luca pulled up in front of the house. It was pitch black outside right along with the house which only meant they were probably sleeping. I punched the gate code in and the fence opened. The only reason I knew the code was from when I was dating A'Karri.

"Shut the lights off and we're leaving the truck here. Don't want anyone to see it," I told Luca and hopped down out the truck. He followed suit. We both pulled our pieces out and eased around to the back of the house, not trying to make too much noise.

My heart pounded in my chest as I slowly picked the lock on the back door. I knew the alarm was going to sound soon as I opened the door that's the reason why I brought Luca along. He was good at things like that.

Beep, Beep, Beep, Beep

He rushed to the front of the house by the front door and snatched the alarm system off the wall and a few seconds later after cutting one wire, it was silent. My eyes roamed around the house to make sure no one heard the alarm going off. When all I heard was silence, I crept up the stairs toward the bedroom.

"You sure this what you want to do? If A'Karri finds out you were the one who did this, she'd never forgive you," Luca whispered.

"Yes, I'm sure. Now will you shut the hell up and let me do what I came here to do?"

I stopped in front of the master's bedroom door. It was cracked so I gently pushed it on open. One stiletto was in the bed. *Where the hell is the other one?* I didn't have time to stand there and question myself. I stepped to the foot of the bed and screwed the silencer onto my gun then lifted it.

My pulse raced and for a second I thought about not doing it, then I remembered it was the only way I could get her back to me. I had no other choice than to pull the trigger.

Pew! Pew!

Two bullets flew her way and I was sure they killed Vanessa instantly. I knew it was her lying in the bed and not Gabriel because the figure was way smaller than him. He probably was in his office or something anyway this time of night.

"Come on, we have to go find Gabriel so we can get the hell out of here."

I pushed Luca out of the room and we went back downstairs heading for Gabriel's study. When I got close to the door, I heard groaning noises coming from it. Gripping the doorknob, I slowly pushed the door open.

Gabriel sat behind his desk with his head thrown back biting down on his lower lip.

"Does your wife know you're in here cheating?" I asked him, grabbing his attention.

His eyes shot open and zeroed in directly on me. My gun pointed at him and he pulled the woman up from underneath his desk. The housekeeper was in here giving his ass head while his wife was upstairs in bed sleeping. That nigga was bold as fuck. I give him that.

"Oh my God!" she shrieked.

Pew!

I immediately sent a bullet crashing through her skull and her body slumped to the floor. I didn't need her drawing any unnecessary attention to us with all that screaming and shit.

"Quentin, what are you doing here?"

He stuffed his dick back down into his pants then brought his attention back up to me.

"I came here to kill you," I calmly replied.

"And what purpose do you think that's going to serve?"

"Oh, it's going to serve plenty of purposes because it's going to send your baby girl flying back into my arms once she finds out that not just one, but both of her parents got murdered."

"What you mean?" He shot straight up from his desk so fast that his chair fell down behind him. "You better not have done anything to Vanessa!" he barked.

"Oh, but I did. She's up there in your bed right now dead with two bullets in her." I shot him a half-smirk as I watched his jaws tighten.

He charged straight for me. "You son of a—" I dropped Gabriel right there in his tracks by sending a bullet through his heart.

I stepped over him and stared down into his eyes with my gun pointing at his forehead. "I'm about to take what's rightfully mine."

Pew!

NAOMI

The things Sanaa told me the night at the hospital weighed heavily on my mind for the last couple of weeks. Maybe she was right. I shouldn't have tried to punish Berlin for something Soul did. I had the right to be angry with him for him not telling me about it, but I think the both of us suffered enough not being together.

Every night my heart ached for him. I could barely sleep, wishing I was up under him. I'm not sure how he was taking us not being together but it was the complete worse for me.

I sat in my car for what seemed like forever, contemplating if I was going to go up to his condo and talk to him about things. I wasn't sure if he wanted to speak to me or if he was even alone in there. With the way our interactions had been going lately, I was pretty sure our conversation was going to end up going left.

After taking a deep breath, I finally climbed out of the car and headed up to the condo. I knocked lightly on his door and hoped he heard me. Part of me wasn't prepared to have this conversation with him but I knew it needed to be done in order for me to keep my sanity. I've been all out of my character lately over Berlin which wasn't like me.

"What are you doing here, Naomi?"

"I came to talk to you. Can we talk?"

He pulled the door all the way open so I took that as a yes and brushed past him inside. I stood fidgeting with my fingers trying to figure out exactly what I was going to say.

He sat down on the couch and pulled a blunt from behind his ear then placed it between his lips lighting it. My eyes wandered up and down his frame. Berlin was always sexy to me and this time was no different. He was walking around with no shirt on showing off that sexy molded body of his, wearing only a pair of white basketball shorts—which hung off his hips, displaying the top of his Versace boxers.

"You wanted to talk, so talk," he said, blowing smoke from his lips.

"I just want to say I'm sorry. I shouldn't have broken things off with you and I really regret it." Tears filled my eyes and I couldn't believe I was on the brink of crying. I really wanted to fix things but from the nonchalant expression on his face, I could tell it was probably over at this point.

"Come sit down right here." He patted the empty space on the sofa next to him. I slowly eased toward him, not taking my wet eyes off of him for a split second. "I told your ass not to go anywhere in the first place but you wanted to be hardheaded as shit so I had to prove a point to you."

"What you mean prove a point?"

"You're the only woman for me, Naomi. I told you I love you and that shit is real." He placed the blunt between his lips then reached over wiping the tears from my eyes.

"But what about Ivy? I saw you with her and I'm pretty sure you two did something. Or what about the girl who was with you at *Crisis* that night?" How could I be the only girl for him when he was spreading his love around St. Louis?

"Neither one of them meant shit to me. I'm not going to lie, I fucked them but that's as far as things went." He took one more toke from his blunt then put it out in the ashtray. He gripped me by the arm and pulled me over into his lap where I straddled him. "I promise that I love you and only you. I told you I wanted to give this relationship shit a try and I meant that. But you have to be willing to put in the work as well. If we do this, ain't no more breaking up no matter how hard shit get between us."

I gazed into his dark eyes and my heart thumped in my chest for him. Both of my hands went up to his face, palming it. "Of course, I want to give it a try. No more breaking up and no more women, Berlin. This my dick." I half-smirked, reaching down, gripping it through his shorts. It was already stiff probably from me sitting on his lap.

"Show me that's your shit then." He relaxed back on the couch with his hands resting behind his head and that sexy smirk adorned his face. He didn't have to tell me twice. I hadn't had any dick since the last time he was between my legs. The shit was long overdue.

I lifted up pulling his dick out and pushed my panties to the side. Easing down onto his dick, I slowly bounced up and down on it. My mouth formed a huge "O" feeling him fill up my insides.

Berlin roughly gripped me by my hair, jerking my head back. "If you ever fucking leave me again, I'll kill you." He sunk his teeth into my neck and I instantly felt my climax coming on.

"I promise you I won't leave you again." I kept bouncing on his dick and my fluids leaked all over the place. My pussy was so fucking wet that it was talking back to him every time I felt the tip of his dick press into my guts.

"Better not, now go on and take this dick."

"Oh, fuck I'm taking it!" I whimpered. He kept pounding into my guts repeatedly. "Oh, fuck I'm about to cum!"

Smack!

He slapped me hard on the ass then rubbed the place he hit me at to soothe the pain.

"Go on, cum on this dick." His hand squeezed tighter around my throat and for a second, I thought he was about to kill me until I felt the intensity of my climax.

"Unnngggghhhh!"

My fluids rushed all over his dick and my eyes crossed, that's how good the shit was. Soon as I finished climaxing, I felt another orgasm coming on. That's never happened to me before.

I released for the second time and watched as Berlin bit his lower lip and his head tilted back on the couch. He was cumming right along with me and the feeling was amazing.

"Got damn, girl."

Smack!

He slapped me on the ass again. I rested my head on his chest and listened to his heartbeat pace through his chest. He wrapped his big arms around me and I felt secure. Felt like he actually did love me even though I had my doubts over the last few weeks. I was where I belonged and I wasn't going to mess that up again for nothing in the world.

My phone chimed and I picked it up off the couch alongside us.

Sanaa: *I thought about it and I've decided that an abortion is best for me. I'm on my way to the clinic now to get it done if you want to meet me there.*

I wasn't sure what I was going to do. I tried to give her another option in hopes she would go with that one and somewhere along the line would want to keep the baby. Whether Sanaa wanted to admit it or not, she was making a fucking mistake by aborting that child.

"What's wrong with you?" Berlin questioned me. Guess the disappointment was written all over my face.

BERLIN

"It's Sanaa," she softly answered.

"What about her?" I stared into her eyes and waited for her to tell me what was going on.

Her eyes softened and she climbed over out of my lap. I knew something was wrong by the way she was acting.

"Promise me, you won't say anything to Soul if I tell you."

"I can't promise you that, now what is it?"

"Well, the other day she told me she found out she was pregnant. At first, she told me she wasn't sure what she wanted to do about it."

"The hell she mean?" I cut her off. Her brows wrinkled and I knew she was almost as frustrated as I was.

"She said that she thinks she wants to get an abortion. I told her to think about it but then she texted me a minute ago saying it's what she wants to do. She's on her way to the clinic to get it done now." I jolted from the couch, pulling my shorts all the way up.

"Wait, where you going?" She got up and came behind me as I made my way toward my bedroom.

"I'm about to go tell Soul."

"But, you can't tell him, Berlin! She'll get mad at me for telling you!"

"I can't just not tell him." I went into the bathroom and turned on the water at the sink. I grabbed a washcloth and wiped my dick down.

"Berlin, please," she begged, but all that shit went out the window. I was not about to withhold some shit like that from my brother. She should have never told me, if she didn't want him to know.

I brushed right past her and went into my walk-in closet, grabbing a pair of jeans. I slipped them on and a t-shirt over my head and slid my feet into my black Versace slides.

"You can either come with me or stay your ass here until I get back."

"I want no parts of this shit," she replied, folding her arms underneath her breasts and rolling her eyes.

"I'll see you when I get back then." I pecked her on the lips and was out the door.

I couldn't hold any shit like that from Soul. If he had some valuable information like that then I'd expect for him to tell me. I already knew he was about to raise hell once I told him what was going on. Soul has never said anything about having kids before, but I was sure if he knew he had one on the way then he'd be more than happy to take care of it. Finding out Sanaa wanted to strip him of that opportunity without even talking to him first, pissed me the fuck off like I was the damn daddy.

I already knew where Soul was because I talked to him earlier. He was at the warehouse on 19th Street in the middle of a meeting about buying some more property. That's the reason why I didn't try to call and tell him over the phone. He wasn't going to pick up. Hopefully, I'm able to make it to him in time and let him know what's going on.

I pulled into the first parking spot I saw outside of the warehouse and rushed inside heading straight for the conference room on the second floor of the warehouse. I burst into the room and all eyes fell on me. Soul stood from the head of the table with a mug on his face. He wasn't pleased with my grand entrance but once he found out the reason why I was there in the first place then I was sure he'd be.

"Berlin, don't you see I'm in the middle of a meeting right now?"

"I need to talk to you about something."

"Can it wait?"

"It's a matter of life and death," I replied. In reality, it really was. If he didn't listen to what I needed to say to him, then the seed he didn't even know existed would die.

"Excuse me, gentlemen." He buttoned up the buttons on his black Armani suit and strolled toward me with a scowl on his face. Little did he know, this little meeting of his was about to come to an end. "It better be something important, Berlin." He shoved me out the conference room and shut the door behind us.

"Look, you need to end this little meeting of yours and get your ass down to Planned Parenthood if you want to save your baby because Sanaa about to get that muhfucka sucked out like she sucked the nut out your dick head."

"What are you talking about? What baby?" His brow wrinkled.

"Naomi just came over to my house and after we made love all over the couch and shit, she told me that Sanaa is pregnant with YOUR baby and was on her way to the clinic to have an abortion because she doesn't feel like she wants the baby."

"Oh hell nah." He pushed the double doors back open on the conference room and everyone gazed over at him. "This meeting is over. We'll get together in a

couple of days. I'll get Emily to schedule another date that's suitable for everyone."
He turned around and strolled off so I went behind him.

"So, what are you going to do?"

"I'm about to go up there and see what the hell is going on. If she's pregnant by me then she's not about to have an abortion I don't give a damn what she says. She can push that baby out and never be a part of its life far as I give a damn but she's not about to kill my seed."

I followed him out the door and he hit the key fob to his Wraith. I know he was probably in his feelings about wrecking that Lambo but the nigga had the money to buy another one. I'm surprised he hasn't done it yet.

"Let me know how that shit goes then."

"Appreciate you looking out for me," he said over his shoulder and climbed into his car then pulled out the parking lot.

I hopped back into my Ferrari and pulled my phone out calling Naomi's number. The phone rang a couple times and she picked up.

"Yeah, Berlin?" She sighed into the phone. She could be mad at me all she wanted to for telling Soul.

"I'm on my way back to the house and a nigga hungry so you need to go in the kitchen and cook something by the time I make it back there."

"I don't know who you think you're talking to."

Click!

I pulled my phone away from my ear and stared at the screen in awe. She had hung up in my fucking face and I couldn't do anything but chuckle at her ass.

SOUL

When Berlin first burst into my meeting, I was angry as hell but quickly found out the reason for him being there. I couldn't believe Sanaa found out she was pregnant and didn't even say anything to me about it. Then, had the nerves to try and kill my fucking seed. I was not about to let that shit go down like that.

I sped all the way over to Planned Parenthood running every red light and stop sign I encountered. I had to get there before she killed my seed. If she did, then I don't think I'd ever be able to forgive her. Maybe that's how she felt about what happened with Yonnie. I can seriously say I actually see where she was coming from. Honestly, if she did, she might end up on the other end of my barrel. I was just that serious.

I know things between us were bad but I didn't think they were that bad to the point where she couldn't come to me and talk about it. The entire time I was driving, the only thing I could think about was me not making it there in time. I've lost one baby before that no one knew about and I wasn't prepared for that shit to happen again.

That was the reason why I didn't go up in anyone raw anymore. The girl I used to mess around with before Sofia, fucked everything up for everyone. Lola was batshit crazy. She got mad at me and did stupid things out of spite. Like drunk posion while pregnant with our daughter and killed her because we got into an argument about a chick she thought I was sleeping with. That shit fucked my mind up but I put it on the back burner and moved on with my life.

Pulling up into the parking lot, I got out the car. I went inside and my eyes roamed around the waiting area to see if I saw her but I didn't spot her anywhere. I knew she was still there because I saw her Maserati parked out front. Which only meant she had to be already in the back.

I headed to the back and one of the nurses tried to stop me but I kept walking. I pushed every door open back there until I found her in the last room sitting on the exam table talking to a doctor who was sitting between her legs.

Heat took over my body and I went inside and jerked her up off the table.

179

"What the hell are you doing, Soul?" she questioned me as I pulled her toward the door.

"I'm taking your ass home. You lost your fucking mind, thinking you're about to kill my got damn seed."

"Can I at least put my pants back on?" I stopped and looked down at her standing there in her white cotton panties. I was so angry at her actions that I almost dragged her out into the waiting area with no pants on.

"Go on put your pants on then we're leaving." I shoved her back toward the table.

"Does this mean that you're not getting the abortion today?" the doctor asked Sanaa.

"She's never getting an abortion, period. Not today, not tomorrow, not ever. If you even try to give her a fucking abortion then I'm going to abort your ass and every fucking one in this muhfucka. Are we clear?" She nodded and Sanaa eyed me suspiciously.

Sanaa pulled her pants back up and grabbed her things then stormed past me out the door. I fell in stride behind her. I knew she was angry from how she tried to slam the door on me when we were walking out but I didn't give a damn. I accomplished what I was aiming for.

"I can't believe you came in here and embarrassed me like that!" She stormed toward her car and I gripped her by the wrist stopping her.

"I can't *believe* you were trying to kill my fucking seed before talking to me first about it."

"What I want to do with my body is my choice, not yours."

"It is when you're carrying around my seed. I'm not about to let you kill my child like that. This isn't the first time something like this has happened to me and I'm just trying to stop it from happening again."

"What you mean this isn't the first time?" She brushed her hair back behind her ear and gazed up into my face.

"It's a long story but I got this girl pregnant one time before and she killed the baby when she was five months pregnant over something stupid. I'm not going through this again, Sanaa." I went over to her car opening the passenger's side door for her. "Get in the car and give me your keys," I ordered.

"For what? I can drive myself home."

"I just want to make sure you go there and don't make any detours at any other clinics along the way."

"What about your car?"

"I can come back and get it or send someone to pick it up for me. Get in the car Sanaa."

She sucked her teeth and slammed the keys down into my palm. I stood there, waiting until she was securely in the car before shutting the door and going around to the driver's side. I got in and backed out of the parking spot, heading for her condo.

God had to be on my side for me to get there just in time to stop her from killing my seed. If I had been a moment later, I'd probably be too late. On the ride to her condo, I kept glancing over at her as she stared out the window. The car ride was silent but that's probably for the best.

I pulled up in front of her building and exhaled. She glanced over at me, then rolled her eyes.

"I know you call yourself pissed the fuck off with me right now. You'll see that I was only stopping you from making a fucking mistake. You don't want to kill that baby for real, Sanaa. You're only doing the shit out of spite."

"You don't know what I want to do." She pushed the door open and climbed out the car so I followed suit. She went into her building and got on the elevator. "You don't have to follow me up to my condo. There are no clinics in this building." She pressed the number five and the doors shut.

"How long are you going to keep this shit up, Sanaa?"

"I don't know what you're talking about." She stepped off the elevator and tread to her door. "Can I have my keys?"

I handed them over to her and she unlocked the door. She tried to shut it on me when she stepped over the threshold but I pushed it back. I wasn't leaving there until we had a conversation together like a couple of adults. These childish ass games had to come to an end.

SANAA

Soul pissed me the fuck off. He just had to come along and ruin my plans. Everything was going just fine until he showed up. After days of contemplating, I finally talked myself into wanting to have the abortion. He didn't even know the real reason behind me wanting it but was determined to come in and regulate some shit.

When I see Naomi, my foot was going so far up her ass that it was going to come out of her mouth. I know she's the only one who spilled the beans because she was the only person who knew about my pregnancy. Sometimes, she just talked entirely too fucking much especially when a nigga was waving a dick in her face.

Soul followed me into my condo like a lost puppy. I thought once I made it home and he saw I wasn't going to go back to the doctor, he would have gone about his business. I was wrong yet again. I heard the door close behind me. I went into the kitchen and grabbed me a bottle of water out the fridge.

"Sanaa, we really need to talk," he said. I turned around and he was undoing his suit jacket and sat down on the couch like I invited him to stay there or something.

"Yeah, we do." I gulped down the water, trying to prepare myself for what I was about to tell him. I wasn't certain how he was going to act about the matter, but it was best I went on and got it off my chest. "Look, Soul," I nibbled on the corner of my lower lip and sat the bottle down on the countertop. "The real reason why I wanted to get the abortion was that I'm not sure if this baby is yours to begin with. I slept with Quentin as well, remember?"

From the twisted expression on his face, I could tell it was something he tried his hardest to forget. He brushed his hand across his waves while staring down at the coffee table. I stood there fidgeting with my fingers not sure what he was going to say next.

Sleeping with Quentin was becoming a bigger mistake with every day that went by. Now, I was standing here not even sure who was the father of my baby. I thought to abort it was the best and easiest option. I didn't want to know how long I had been carrying around the baby or get an ultrasound of it. All I wanted to do was get rid of it and be done with it.

"I have a strong feeling the baby is mine. You're not killing my seed, Sanaa, so you might as well get the shit out of your head."

I sighed a deep breath. Trying to talk to him was like talking to a brick wall.

"Well, since you want to be so stubborn, I'll schedule a DNA test to see whose baby it is."

"It's mine, Sanaa. You don't even have to take a DNA test. I'm taking care of this child no matter what." I was glad he was so confident about the matter but there's no nigga on this earth in his right mind who would take care of a baby that's not his. I couldn't believe a word that seeped from his mouth.

"Now, that I don't believe," I sarcastically stated.

He got up from the couch and came over to me palming my face. It took everything inside me not to slap his hand down.

"I promise you I'll help you take care of this baby, Sanaa. Plus, if it's Quentin's it will need a father figure in its life because I'm putting a bullet in that nigga the first chance I get," he warned and chill bumps took over my body. His eyes bored into mine and they told me he was serious as hell. I saw no hesitation in them. Quentin was, in fact, a dead man walking.

"If that's what you really want to do Soul then I guess I can't stop you."

He stroked my cheek and it felt so good. I almost shut my eyes and fell into him but I had to remember I was still supposed to be angry with him.

"I really want things to work between us, Sanaa."

I whacked his hand away. I almost fell into his trap and if I stood there in his alluring presence for a moment longer, I might have.

"I'm sorry Soul but I just can't do this." I went over to the front door and pulled it open. "You need to leave."

He nodded and buttoned his suit jacket back up then approached me, stopping directly in front of me. I directed my eyes to my feet not wanting to look him in the eyes. My chest ached from telling him he had to go but it was the best thing I could do at the moment. I wasn't sure what I wanted as far as this baby and relationship with him but I needed some time to think things over.

"Goodbye, Sanaa."

After he stepped over the threshold, I pushed the door shut and locked it. I slid down the door to the floor and rested my chin on my knee. The tears flooded my cheeks. I was tired of having this same reaction whenever I left Soul's presence. Why did he have to come along and mess up a good thing? Everything was finally falling together for us and boom! Life just had to throw a wrench in my plans and fuck everything up.

Taniece

I just wished I could go back in time and talk them out of killing my mother. That way, I could have her and the man I was falling for all in one breath. Life just didn't work out like that and now I had to play the hand I'd been dealt and try to figure out this messy shit that I call my life all on my own.

NAOMI

The Bluetooth speaker in my truck began ringing. I pressed the button and answered it.

"I swear to God I'm going to fucking kill you!"

I didn't even have to look at the screen to know it was Sanaa on the other end of the line. I get she was pissed at me for telling, that's the reason why I been trying my best to avoid her at all costs this morning. Berlin tricked me into telling him about her pregnancy and he went and gossiped to his brother like a little ho. I knew the moment he told because I began receiving death threat messages from Sanaa.

"I'm sorry, I slipped and told Berlin then he went and told Soul. Please don't be mad at me, Sanaa."

"I'm going to fucking kill you!" she repeated. I hated whenever she did that when she was angry. You know how some women get mad and they just say the same thing over and over in the argument... that was Sanaa.

"I have a bad connection." I rattled the chip bag that was on my passenger's seat.

"Naomi!"

"I'm sorry but I can't hear you. I'll have to call you back. Love you girl!"

Click!

If I didn't get her off the phone then she was going to scream my ear off and I just didn't feel up for that at the moment. I exhaled a deep breath and pulled away from the stop light.

After Sanaa told me about her pregnancy, I figured I should think about kids of my own. So I set up a doctor's appointment to get my IUD taken out. I wasn't sure how Berlin was going to react to it once he found out what I did but I was hoping I'd be pregnant by then and wouldn't have to worry about it.

I pulled up at the doctor's office and parked directly in front of the door. I sat in my truck for a moment, trying to see if this was what I really wanted to do. If I was to get pregnant then there wasn't any coming back from it. Berlin was going to be stuck with me forever.

Finally collecting my thoughts, I climbed out of the car and headed inside. I had an appointment scheduled so I signed in on the sign in sheet then took a seat and waited for my name to be called. I glanced around the waiting room at all the other patients who were in there. I saw this woman with her little girl and she was so gorgeous. It only made me know for certain this was what I actually wanted to do.

It was going to be hard being pregnant and trying to finish school but I was sure I'd be able to do it. That's the reason why Sanaa got all in her feelings that day she thought I was pregnant. She doesn't want anything to get in my way of completing college. She wanted what was best for me just as I wanted what was best for her.

In a way, I think she should give Soul another chance. I saw the impact he was making on her and I felt like she was going to miss out on a good thing. I wouldn't dare tell her that to her face though because she might think I didn't care about Yonnie when I really did but they killed her before he met Sanaa. That shouldn't have an effect on the love they have for each other.

"Naomi Copeland!" the nurse called out from the door and I hopped up from my seat and rushed over to her with a smile on my face. She probably thought I was a little too fucking excited to want to get off birth control.

"That's me."

"Follow me," she ordered and held the door open for me. She took me into room six and I sat down on the chair. "I see you're here to get your IUD removed. You sure that you want to do that?"

"I'm positive." I grinned up at her as she looked over my chart.

It didn't take them long to remove the birth control and I already felt like a completely different woman. I couldn't wait to get to Berlin and pop this birth control free pussy on his dick. I rushed out of the doctor's office and hopped back into my truck. As I was backing out of my parking space, I called Berlin's phone.

"Hey, bae, where are you?" I quizzed him when he picked up the phone. Music could be heard in his background so he was either in the car or out at a club or something. It was too early for the club part so maybe he was heading somewhere.

"On my way to my parents' house. I've been trying to call my Pops all day and he hasn't been answering the phone. Why what's up?"

"Oh, I was hoping you would have been at home or something where I could have come by." I grinned from ear to ear and my cheeks were on fire.

"From the sound of that, I already know what you want." He chuckled into the phone. "You want this dick, don't you?"

"Hell yeah, I'm fiending for it bad right now before I have to go to class. But, if you're busy with your parents then I guess I'll just have to wait until later." I sighed a deep breath. I wasn't expecting him to be busy at the moment. Well, at least if he was at the office or something, I could have gone there and jumped on the dick.

186

"You can just meet me at my parents' house, and I can give you a quickie before you head to class," he suggested and I was not about to turn down that proposal.

"I'm on my way to yoooouuuuuuu, daddy," I sang into the phone and giggled. He burst out laughing at me. I know my singing was horrible.

"Aight, but if you sing like that again, then I won't have much of a choice but to cut you off from the dick. I'll text you the address." He ended the call and my phone chimed with the address. I couldn't wait to get over there to him. We were about to make a baby and he didn't even know it.

BERLIN

Naomi was on her way to meet me at my parents' house. I been calling their phones all morning long and no one was answering. I knew something had to be wrong because my mother never missed a phone call from me. I just wanted to make sure they were all right over there.

I pulled up to the gate and put the code in then stopped in front of the house. I got out the car and went inside. The house reeked of death. Pulling my strap from my waistline, I rushed upstairs toward their bedroom.

"Ma... Pops!" I called out for them but wasn't getting any answers. I stepped into the bedroom and saw my mother lying on top of blood-stained sheets. Tears glistened in my eyes and I lowered the gun and hurried over to her. My knees grew weak and I dropped to the floor. "Ma!" I cried out, grabbing her lifeless body. Someone had come into my parents' house and killed my mother.

I felt like my soul been snatched from my body. My heart crushed in my chest and I felt like I no longer had breath in my lungs. "Ma just wake up," I pleaded, rocking with her head, resting against my chest. I knew she wasn't going to wake up because she was already long gone. Her body was lifeless—eyes wide open.

I realized my father was not in the bed alongside her, so I gently placed her down then searched the rest of the house, finding him in the study with a bullet in his head. The housekeeper, Sarah was shot to death beside his desk. Something was up since his pants were unbuttoned.

My pulse raced; I was furious as hell. I know damn well he wasn't in there getting sloppy toppy and shit cheating on my mother. I never expected him of cheating on her. They both seemed like they were so happy, but I guess everyone has their problems when it came to relationships. Nothing was really as it seemed.

I reached into my pocket and pulled my ringing phone out. Naomi was calling me so she was probably at the gate. I went around my father's desk so I could hit the button and let her in.

"I'm outside the gate," she softly spoke into the phone.

"Ahem," I quickly cleared my throat. "Aight, I'm letting you in now."

"Is everything alright with you?" she asked with much concern in her voice.

"I'll tell you when I come outside." I ended the call and pressed the button then stepped over Sarah's body leaving out the office. I went straight to the front door and soon as I pulled it open Naomi was pulling up behind my car.

She rushed up the front steps to me and gazed intently into my eyes. "What's the matter? It looks like you've been crying," she said, gently palming my face.

"I just found my parents in there with bullets in them."

Tears rushed to her eyes as well. It was like she felt my pain.

"Baby, I'm so sorry." She pulled me into her frame and I broke down crying, lying on her breasts while she stroked my hair. I didn't know what the hell I was going to do but I did know, once I found out whoever the hell did this shit, they were going to die a slow painful death.

"I have to call and tell my brother and sister about this shit. I don't want to be the one to have to tell them that our parents are dead." I pulled back from her and my glossy eyes poured into her watery ones.

"If you want me to, then I'll call them for you," she offered with a slight smile.

"No, I have to do this myself." I gripped her by the hand and pulled her into the house then called Soul's phone. I was sure he was going to go ballistic once he found out about our parents.

"Yeah, Berlin?"

"I just came by Ma and them house and found them dead." I almost choked when the words seeped from my lips.

Nothing came through the phone after I said that. We sat in a moment of silence, but I knew he was still on the line because it hadn't gone dead yet.

"Go into Pops's office and check the security cameras."

"Security cameras? Since when they had cameras?"

"Yeah, Pops has them outside the house all around. You know he was paranoid as hell."

Rushing to the office, I sat down behind the desk. I put his passcode into the computer and pulled up the security cameras while Soul was still on the phone. I was sure he'd want to know who had done it as well.

Naomi stood in the doorway with her back resting against the frame carefully observing me as I played the tapes back on the computer. I wasn't the best at technology like that but I did well enough to figure out this figure who was on the screen. I zoomed in and paused on their face. Lucky for me, the light on the gate shined at the perfect angle and lit his face straight up.

A flush of adrenaline tingled through my body as I stared at Quentin on the screen. My trigger finger itched and I knew exactly what I needed to do.

"Did you find something?" Naomi asked me and approached the desk. She rested both of her hands on my shoulders and leaned her face down at the screen. "Oh my God, that's Quentin! You really think he's the one who did it?"

"Did she just say, Quentin?" Soul's voice asked through the phone. I almost forgot he was on the line.

"Yeah, I'm pretty sure he was the one who did it."

"That nigga is going to fucking pay for what he's done," Soul said and disconnected the call.

I relaxed back in the chair just gazing at the screen. Quentin may have done some fucked up things but this was an all-time low, even for him. Little did he know, he put his life on the line and we were willing to do anything to find him. He was going to fucking pay for coming after my parents the way he had if it's the last thing I do.

SOUL

It's been a month since we laid our parents to rest and the shit still haunted me. I didn't know how I was supposed to handle this. My mind was all over the place and I been shut off from the outside world. I'm sure we were losing out on money from me not working. Berlin been trying his best to keep things afloat while I was on my hiatus, but I knew he wasn't going to be able to hold the fort down for much longer on his own.

With the way he ran things, I was sure they were running smoothly so there wasn't anything I had to worry about. At least not at the moment. So far, I hadn't heard anything about him killing anyone which was a good thing. I just needed some time to myself to process things. I figured I been away long enough and needed to fall back into stride with my personal life and business.

Guess I can say, I truly understood where Sanaa was coming from when we took Yonnie away from her. I didn't understand the way she felt then, but I completely understood now. It was rough not having your parents in your life. Especially when your mother meant so much to you. I owed Sanaa an eternity of apologies even though I knew she wasn't going to accept them.

Sanaa's been on my mind almost every single day since I found out about my parents. I'm sure she was angry as hell with me carrying around that baby and I hadn't been there to help her out like I told her I would.

I stared up at the ceiling in my pitch-black bedroom. I tossed and turned all night long trying to force myself to sleep but it didn't seem to be working out for me. I could have easily drunk some liquor to help me sleep but I hadn't touched a bottle since I had my accident. I was too close to killing myself and didn't want to ever go through that again.

I reached over picking my phone up off the nightstand. I saw it was going on three in the morning. Exhaling a deep breath, I climbed out of bed and went over to the dresser, grabbing me a pair of black sweatpants and slipped them on, then tugged a white t-shirt down over my head. I stuck my feet down into my white and black Jordan sneakers and grabbed my keys off the dresser along with my wallet.

I knew what I was about to do wasn't going to be a good idea but I was doing it anyway. Leaving out my front door, I hopped into my gray Tesla and pulled out the driveway.

I made it back to the city and stopped by IHOP to grab something to eat. Going by a pregnant girl's house this time of morning without any food was out of the question. We already weren't on the best of terms. I didn't want her to bite my fucking head off. I wanted to butter her up so I could be near her even if it was just for a little while.

After I grabbed the food, I made it to her condo. *Please, don't let her turn me around.* Sanaa was the only person I wanted to be up under right now. I fought the urge for as long as I could but I couldn't do it anymore. That's the reason why I was knocking on her door at the moment.

Knock! Knock!

I stood back with the food in my hands, patiently waiting for her to come to the door. I expected a scowl to be plastered on her face when she eventually did since I was waking her up from her sleep but instead of the scowl, her brows wrinkled and she looked like she was shocked to see me. Her belly had a small pudge in it. I couldn't believe she was actually pregnant right now.

"What are you doing here, Soul?"

"I couldn't sleep. I brought food in case you're hungry." I showed her the food in my hands.

She sighed heavily, then pulled the door all the way open. I took that as my invitation inside. Placing the food down on the coffee table, I made myself comfortable on the couch.

"Is everything alright?" she questioned me then flopped down on the couch beside me with one of her legs underneath her.

"My mind has been all over the place ever since I found out about my parents. I tossed and turned all night long like I've done most nights and you were the first thing that popped up into my mind." I turned to her and stared her directly in her hazel eyes. "I wanted to be near you even if it was just for a little while. And I also wanted to let you know how sorry I was for taking Yonnie away from you. I honestly know how you feel now and the shit is unbearable. I'm truly sorry, Sanaa and if I could take it back then I would. All I want... no need is for you to forgive me."

"It's alright, Soul. I forgive you."

"You're not saying that just to be saying it are you?"

She got up from the couch and straddled me catching me by surprise. Both of her hands palmed my face and she gazed deep into my eyes. "I forgive you." Her lips fell atop mine and she slightly parted her lips giving me entry to her minty tasting tongue. She must have brushed her teeth not too long ago.

Her kisses grew deeper and I took that as the okay to take things to the next level. Lifting up from the sofa with her in my arms, I carried her to the bedroom. I gently laid her down on the bed and cupped her face.

Her hands tugged on the waistline of my sweats. I eased them down some and she spread her legs for me. I slid her panties to the side and eased my way inside her.

"Ungh," she moaned and bit down on my lower lip soon I gained entry. I slowly stroked her g-spot and her sharp nails dug into my back deeper with every pump I gave her.

She stared me in the eyes not batting an eye. No matter how much she said she didn't want anything else to do with me, I knew she was lying. The connection between us was strong as fuck and I knew she felt it just as I did.

"I love you." I couldn't even catch the words before they escaped my lips. She didn't utter a word back and I didn't expect her to.

I held onto her hip as I pounded my dick in and out of her. It gushed, talking back to me with every stroke and I could feel myself close to my peek.

"Fuck," I groaned.

"I'm about to cum!" she screamed and her back arched deeply. I saw the vein popping in her neck and how far her nails went into my back I wouldn't be surprised I was bleeding afterward.

"Go on and cum."

"Fuck, I'm cuuummmmiiinnngg!" she shouted and I felt her pussy muscles squeeze my dick. I released my seeds right along with her then pulled out and fell over alongside her. She just laid there, staring up at the ceiling like she regretted letting me make love to her.

"I do love you, Sanaa."

"Get you some rest," was all she said before she snuggled underneath me. I felt her heartbeat pounding against her chest through her back. Just being able to smell her scent and feel her soft skin against mine, my eyes shut and it wasn't long before sleep took over my body.

SANAA

I laid there staring at the wall listening to Soul snore behind me. He shocked me showing up on my doorstep, but I couldn't turn him away with all the things he's been through lately. He didn't only lose one, but both of his parents and I'm sure that was far worse than what I've gone through.

Having sex with him wasn't part of the plan. It just happened. I been fighting to stay away from him, and he was just in my face. I couldn't help the shit. Blame it on my pregnancy hormones or some shit but don't charge it to my heart.

I looked back over my shoulder to make sure he was still sleeping. I eased out the bed and hit my toe on the nightstand.

"Unnngghhh," I lowly mumbled grabbing my foot. My eyes darted over to see if he was still sleeping. He turned over onto his back, so I went on into the bathroom.

Since he'd been gone for the last month doing only God knows what, I been trying to figure out who my baby's father was. It was driving me insane not knowing. I needed to know who this baby belonged to whether he wanted to know or not.

I grabbed a Q-tip and went back into the bedroom. I stood over Soul debating if I really wanted to go behind his back and do this. I'm sure he'd be angry once he found out what I did but he'll be all right.

His mouth hung slightly open, so I stuck the Q-tip inside and swabbed it then dropped it down into the Ziploc bag. I hid the bag inside my panties' drawer and first thing in the morning I was going to make a trip to the doctor and get this DNA test done. I wasn't sure if they would be willing to do it without his consent but I sure as hell was going to try. Slowly, I climbed back into the bed and pulled his arm around my body.

Thoughts of Soul telling me he loved me seeped back into my mind. He really caught me off guard with that one. Part of me wanted to say it back but the other part wanted to hold a grudge. I wasn't certain if I was ready to say those three words just yet. When or *if* I am, then I'll say it. Sleep soon washed over my body and I fell into a peaceful slumber.

* * *

The following morning, I woke up and Soul was still lying in bed beside me. I don't know why I thought he would have gotten up and left by the time I woke up. I remembered how he said he hadn't been getting much sleep so this must be the best night's rest he's gotten in a while. I didn't want to disturb him so I tried to get up slowly from the bed but he caught me by my waist, pulling me closer to him.

"Where you going?" He mumbled with his eyes still sealed shut.

"I was about to go brush my teeth and wash my face before you stopped me."

"Just lay down with me for a second," he said with his eyes still closed. I didn't know what he was getting at. Just because I was nice to him the night before didn't mean I was going to be this morning.

"For what? You act like I don't have a job to go to this morning or something."

I was the boss so, therefore, I didn't really have to go into work which I wasn't. He wasn't about to get in the way of my plans for the day, so he needed to get up off his ass and get ghost.

"You're the boss, Sanaa. You only have to go to work because you choose to." I rolled my eyes at him. He didn't see me since my back was to him. "I was thinking maybe we could do something today. We have a month's worth of lost time to make up for."

"Soul," I sighed heavily, "you're acting like we're together or something."

His eyes finally opened and he shot straight up in bed. "So, what was that last night? You used me for a booty call?"

"Pretty much." I pulled his arms from around my waist and climbed out of bed heading into the bathroom. He was probably feeling some type of way after I said that. Maybe one day, I'd be able to move on from this.

"But you told me you forgave me last night."

I placed my toothbrush in my mouth and turned to him. "I do, but that doesn't mean I'm going to forget." I mumbled, scrubbing my teeth. His eyes softened and his head hung low. "Look, Soul, maybe one day we'll be able to move on from this but right now, I'm not too sure. Can we just focus on the baby for right now then deal with whatever this may be later?"

"So that's a no for today?"

I spit the toothpaste out in the sink and turned to him with my brow raised. "What do you think?"

"I'll just leave." He left out the doorway and I sighed.

Soul was really trying to fix things between us but that didn't mean I was going to forget he was the one who put that bullet in my mother's skull. He was the one who had taken my entire world away from me. How was I supposed to look past all that? I wanted to love and be loved by him but things were just... complicated.

A few moments later I heard the front door open and close. I finished handling my hygiene then went into the bedroom to try and find me something to throw on. It didn't have to be anything fancy seeing how the only thing I was doing today was going to the doctor then coming back home.

I slipped on a white striped sundress then slid my feet into my Jimmy Choo sandals. I blow dried my hair dry by the time I was done, Naomi was calling my phone. I sent her to the voicemail. I'd just talk to her once I got back from the doctor. I'm sure she was going to have a fucking field day once she found out what I did. I shot her a text to let her know I wasn't ignoring her or anything.

Me: *Can't talk right now but I'll be by there after I'm done doing what I'm doing.*

I couldn't tell her what my plans were because no matter how much she said she supported everything I do, I knew she was going to have a few choice words to try and talk me out of it. I grabbed my keys and purse off the dresser and was out the front door.

QUENTIN

Boom! Boom! Boom!

Someone banged at my front door so hard I thought they were going to knock it off the hinges. I been cautious about answering the door lately ever since I killed Vanessa and Gabriel. I knew sooner or later Berlin or Soul would show up on my doorstep ready to put a bullet in my ass assuming I was the one who did it. *Hope that's not them on the other side of that door.*

Something told me not to come by the house in the first place. The only reason I had was so I could grab a few things. I hadn't been staying there so they wouldn't be able to find me. Guess I picked the wrong day to want to come home and grab fucking clothes and cash.

I slowly approached the door with caution. My first mind told me not to go to it at all but I went ahead anyway. My curiosity was getting the best of me. When I peeked out the blinds, I saw A'Karri standing on the other side. She kept peeking over her shoulder like she was scared someone had followed her here. It was a surprise because I thought she made it perfectly clear she didn't want to see me again and wanted nothing to do with me.

My curiosity reared its ugly head again and I pulled the front door open leaving only a crack in it. "What are you doing here, Karri?"

She pushed the door open on me almost hitting me in the face. "Did you do it?" Tears were in her eyes and her little fists were balled up like she was about to take a swing on me.

"Did I do what?" I opted on playing stupid with her to see what she was getting at. I was sure she was talking about killing her parents but I wasn't about to say it before her then she'd know I was guilty as fuck.

"Kill my parents! Don't play fucking stupid with me!" She shoved me in the chest and I stumbled back a little bit. "Did. You. Fucking. Do. It!"

"No, I didn't kill your parents. Why would I do that? I love you too much to do something like that." I took a couple steps toward her not breaking our gaze. I wanted her to believe the lie I was attempting to feed her. If she actually knew I was the one who stood behind the trigger then she'd without a doubt put a hot one in my ass.

She brushed her straight hair back out her face with her hands. "Berlin and Soul say otherwise."

I kept on easing toward her. I was now so close to her that I could smell the sweet scent of her perfume. A'Karri never really wore heavy perfume. Just sprayed once on her neck then her wrists.

"Well, they a muhfuckin' lie. I'd never do anything like that to hurt you, Karri. You should know that by now." I gripped her by the waist and pulled her body into my frame. I was surprised she hadn't shoved me away again. "I'm sorry about your parents but I wasn't the one who did the shit."

She gazed up at me with tear-filled eyes. "My brothers feel strongly about you being the one who did it. I'm sure you know they'll be coming for you soon. They have been looking all over St. Louis for you. I'm surprised they haven't gotten their hands on you yet."

"I've been hiding. Speaking of which, I need to get the hell out of here before they show up." I let go of her waist and went back into my bedroom to finish packing up the few things I needed.

"Maybe I can help you with that."

I glanced over my shoulder and A'Karri was standing in the doorway with her arms folded underneath her breasts.

"Why would you want to do that? Thought you didn't want anything else to do with me?" Her saying she would help me caught me totally off guard. I thought I completely lost her but maybe I haven't. This wasn't part of the plan but I was loving the direction it was heading in.

She approached me. This time she no longer had tears in her eyes. "Even though you've hurt me to my core, I still love you Quentin and don't want to see anything happen to you." She palmed my face and I knew I had her exactly where I wanted her.

"What you think is going to happen if they ever find out you helped me? Your brothers aren't going to stop looking for me."

"They aren't going to do anything to me. Sure, they'll be angry but that's about it. I don't think they'll ever find out unless you were to tell them."

"You sure that you want to help me?"

"I'm more than sure. Get your stuff together so we can go." I kissed her softly on the lips then finished packing my things.

I grabbed a Louis Vuitton bag down out the top of the closet and put the code in my safe that sat in the corner of the closet. I stuffed the bag full with cash so I wouldn't have to come back there for anything.

"I'm ready," I told her zipping the bag up.

"You sure you have everything?"

"Yeah." Grabbing the duffel bag off the bed, I tossed it over my shoulder. I followed her to the front door and made sure to lock it on my way out.

"I think you should just leave your car here and ride to my house with me. That way if they were ever to come by, they wouldn't see your car there," she told me, hitting the key fob unlocking the doors. She seemed like she had everything figured out with the way she was talking.

I tossed my bags onto the back seat and climbed into the passenger's seat alongside her. I didn't know how this was going to work out between us when I had the motive to kill her brothers. Hopefully, I'd be able to knock their asses out the way and she wouldn't even notice the shit or think someone else did it.

I glanced over at her as she was weaving in and out of traffic. "Do you think we will be able to fix things between us?"

She briefly glared over at me then took her eyes back to the road. "I don't know about all that, Quentin. I said I was going to help you; I didn't say we were getting back together."

"But, you do want to work on things, right?"

"I don't know," was all she said then turned the radio up on me.

She may not know now, but after I get rid of her brothers, I'd be the only thing she has left and wouldn't have much of a choice but to come running back to me. I'd be right there to comfort her with open arms too. I just have to take me killing her entire family to the grave.

NAOMI

I laid there in bed on my back with my legs propped up against the headboard toking on a blunt. I read somewhere online that it was the best way to get the semen to flow after sex. I know it was crazy but I was willing to do whatever to get pregnant by Berlin. Okay, I was sounding like a crazy side chick right about now. Some might look at it as I was trying to trap him or something but that was far from the case. I loved Berlin and just wanted to give him any and everything possible.

He didn't know what the hell I was doing. Probably just assumed I was comfortable like this and didn't really too much pay it any attention. He was sitting beside me scrolling on his phone with a blunt dangling between his lips. The entire room was smoked out from the two Kush blunts we had in rotation but that wasn't anything new dealing with Berlin.

I just laid there, staring at the side of his tensed face. He been like that a lot lately after finding his parents dead. Then, Soul just left my baby out there with the wolves trying to hold everything together on his own. I must admit, he was handling everything mighty well. I hated the fact he was out all times of night but I should have expected that sooner or later with the type of lifestyle he lived.

I can't lie and say the thoughts of him cheating hadn't crossed my mind a couple times because it has. I mean, I was in love with Berlin Maserati. Him being with all sorts of women was part of his lifestyle. I knew that shit when we got together but I took his word that he'd let all those bitches go to be with me.

"What you over there doing anyway?" I questioned him, taking another pull from the blunt.

"Texting this guy, Anthony about a meeting we were supposed to have today. He trying to cancel the shit on me last minute and shit."

"Is that why you have that mug on your face?" I smiled, leaned over and dumped the ashes in the ashtray then straddled him. His face scrunched up even more as he moved his fingers across the keyboard. "Stop looking so ugly." I leaned over causing his phone to press against his chest and pecked him on the lips.

"Why you want to come playing and shit while I'm trying to do something?" He pushed me over off him and I felt some sort of way with how he was acting.

"All I was trying to do was make you feel better. Damn." Now, my face was screwed up.

He took his face away from the phone long enough to glance over at me. "I'm sorry, bae. This shit just stressful as hell. I'm not used to having all this responsibility."

"Why don't you take your ass over there and grab Soul by his dick and tell him to fucking man up. I've been watching you handle everything on your own while he's out doing only God knows what."

"First of all, I'm not grabbing no other nigga's dick." I burst out laughing at him. I tried to hold it in but the face he was making made it worse.

"I'm sorry," I told him when he side-eyed me.

"Soul grieves a different type of way than others. It's just something I can't really explain but I'll be able to handle it until he's ready to come back. I'm sure it won't be long."

"You sure? Because I don't want you to end up chewing my head off only because I'm trying to make you feel better."

"You don't have to worry about that."

Smack!

He slapped me on the ass and I smiled at him. Yeah, he was saying that now but if he found out I tried to trap him into having a child, he was going to be saying otherwise.

Buzzzzzzz

I saw his jaw tighten as he stared at his ringing phone that was the only reason why I lifted up and peered over at it.

"What the hell she doing calling you? Better yet, why the fuck her number still saved in your phone, Berlin!" I yelled slapping him on his arm.

"Chill the fuck out and keep your hands to yourself. I never deleted her number. The shit never crossed my mind."

"I deleted every nigga number out my phone when we got together the first time. What she calling your phone for, Berlin?" My eyes grew wider, waiting for him to respond. It was already bad enough I been thinking he was cheating and now that didn't make the situation any better. If anything, it only made me suspect him. He did tell me he fucked her while we were on break. He could easily be slipping up in that shit when he's supposed to be working. I wanted to trust him but he was kind of making it hard for me at the moment.

"I don't know what she's calling me for."

Smack!

I fired his face up. "You're a fucking lie!"

"What the hell I told you about putting your hands on me!" he barked, tossing the phone to the side and grabbed me by the forearms pinning me down on the bed. I had tears in my eyes as I gazed up into his low dark ones.

"You still fucking that bitch, Berlin?"

"Nah, I ain't got no reason to lie to you."

"Well, I don't believe you! That bitch calling your phone for a reason!" Tears seeped from the corners of my eyes and dripped into my ears.

"That's your fault you don't believe me because I'm telling the truth."

"You still want to fuck her?" I couldn't help but want to ask. I wanted to see if there was any hesitation when it came to being with me.

"What the hell I'm going to want to still fuck her for? I got you to handle that shit unless you don't want to anymore..."

I wanted to slap the shit out of his ass again for that slick ass remark. He was lucky he still had me pinned down to this bed. I squirmed underneath him trying to get loose but it was like he had a death grip on my ass.

"Get off me, Berlin!" I shouted into his face but he wasn't budging.

"For what? So, you can hit me again?" He knew me all too well. "I ain't letting you go until I know you've calmed down."

His phone kept buzzing and I just wanted to knock him out with the muhfucka. If there wasn't anything going on between the two, she sure as hell was trying to get a hold of him badly.

"Why she still calling your fucking phone?"

"That ain't her. That's Mason."

"Why are you lying?"

He sighed deeply then let me go and grabbed his phone shoving it into my face. "What the hell that says?"

True enough, it said Mason clear as day but I won't tell him what it said. I so badly wanted to be right about that bitch calling his phone again. I sat there pouting on the bed with my arms folded underneath my breasts.

"I'm about to go because I'm not about to deal with this shit." He got up from the bed, grabbing his pants and shirt then went into the bedroom.

"Nah, what you're about to do is go running to that ho!" I yelled, getting up going behind him but he shut the bathroom door in my face then I heard the lock click. "Open this fucking door, Berlin!"

Boom!

The water began running but he didn't open the door. "Berlin!"

Boom! Boom!

"Berlin!"

My heart thumped rapidly in my chest and all I wanted to do was fuck his ass up in here. If that nigga went running to that ho, he and her was going to regret the shit.

The door snatched open and he was fully dressed. He brushed straight past me to the bed and stuck his feet into his Jimmy Choo sneakers.

"So, you're just going to act like you don't see me right here?"

He didn't utter a word just grabbed his keys off the nightstand and blunt, tucking it behind his ear then pulled the bedroom door open, shutting it behind him. I gripped the lamp off the dresser and lunged it at the door.

Crash!

"You better delete that bitch number out your phone!" I screamed. I rushed over to the door pulling it open and he was going out the front door. "I love you!"

Slam!

He slammed the front door shut frustrating me even more. It's all right though because pretty soon, I was going to have a little baby baking in my oven and that nigga would be stuck with me forever.

BERLIN

I can't believe Naomi thought I was cheating on her. I told her I loved her so why would I try to fuck things up between us by cheating? Yeah, I've done it in the past with other females but she was different. So far, I'd been doing good. With all the work I been doing, the thought of stepping out on her has never crossed my mind.

I had to get out of that condo before I ended up doing something I'd regret. She was really pissing me the fuck off with her accusations and putting her hands on me and shit when I asked her not to. I've never once laid a finger on Naomi and she got mad and wanted to hit me wherever her tiny hands could land. To keep from knocking her the fuck out, I left.

I jumped into my car and rode around to clear my mind. I don't know why Ivy called me. I'm not going to lie and say I didn't get the urge to call her back and see what she wanted but I didn't want to have to deal with the consequences later. Naomi got angry from her just calling, imagine how she'd feel if she was to find out I actually talked to her. These were the type of situations I was trying to avoid not being in a relationship. The things I'd deal with all for love.

My phone began ringing again. I almost didn't pull it out my pocket thinking it was Naomi's crazy ass calling to curse me out some more. Instead, it was Mason who I completely forgot had called me earlier. If he was calling again, then he had to needed something.

"Yeah, Mason?"

"I got that little information you had been waiting for." A smile replaced the frown I had been wearing since I left Naomi's place.

"I'm listening."

"She's at work right now. She works over there at the Shell gas station on South Grand Boulevard. She'll be there until seven tonight."

"Thanks for the info, Mas. I'll have something for you later."

"You know you don't have to give me shit for looking out for you niggas. Y'all like brothers to me." He chuckled and ended the call. I sped all the way to the gas station with one thing on my mind—murder. I hated she was about to be a casualty of war but that was just the price sometimes. Innocent people had to die to get a point across.

I pulled into the parking lot just scoping out the scene for a moment trying to figure out the best way to handle the shit. Too many people were going in and out and I knew I wouldn't be able to do anything until there were fewer witnesses out. I didn't want to leave bodies all over the place just so I could get that one.

I sat out there in the parking lot for what seemed like forever. The sun was slowly setting and fewer people began coming to the store. Reaching over, I grabbed my gun and silencer out the glove compartment. I watched my surroundings as I screwed the silencer on. The last woman came out of the store and I waited for her to pump her gas before slipping my piece down into the front of my pants and covered it with my shirt.

When she pulled out the parking lot, I climbed out my car and headed into the store. Quenby was behind the counter talking on the phone laughing and popping her chewing gum so she didn't notice me come in. I locked the door behind me so we wouldn't have any interruptions.

Easing my gun from my waistline, I strolled up to the counter. I reached across it taking the phone from her clutches and placed it on the receiver. She turned to me with her mouth fixed to say something but her words got caught in her throat when she realized it was me. Her eyes expanded and she stumbled back a little bit.

"Wh-what are you doing here?" she stammered over her words.

"I came to see you, baby girl."

"About what? Quentin's not here. I haven't seen him since—" I quickly cut her off.

"I want you to stop right there in that bullshit ass lie you were about to tell me. I know you saw Quentin. In fact, you've seen him recently so save yourself the breath and don't fucking lie to me."

"The last time I saw him was a couple days ago. He came by and stayed the night and by the time I got up the next morning he was gone. That's the God to honest truth." Her body trembled a little bit as she spoke to me. I could tell she was terrified, and she had the right to be.

After I found out Quentin killed our parents, I went looking for him but couldn't seem to find the nigga anywhere. He had Quenby hid off some fucking where and it took forever for us to get eyes on her ass. Now that I was staring at her, I wasn't about to let the opportunity slip through my fingertips.

"Slowly grab your phone, and don't try any funny shit." She eased her hand down on the countertop picking the phone up. "Now, call that son of a bitch brother of yours." I lifted my hand so she could see the gun in my hand. "If you try anything funny, I promise you I'll put a bullet in your ass."

Boom! Boom!

Someone banged on the store door. I glanced back and some guy was trying to peek through. "Store's closed. Come back later!"

"But the sign says open," he said, pointing up at the sign.

"I said the fucking store is closed. Fuck out of here!" I barked and directed my attention back to Quenby. "The hell you waiting for? Call that nigga." I pointed at the phone with the gun.

Her hand shook as she dialed Quentin's number.

"What do you want from me?" she questioned me.

"You'll see." I stood there listening to the phone ring then he finally picked up.

"Yeah, Quen?"

"Quentin, where are you?" she asked him, keeping her eyes trained on me.

"What you want to know where I'm at for? You don't ever call and ask me where I'm at."

"Quentin," she swallowed hard to fight back the tears that formed in her eyes. "Can you just tell me where you are?"

"They got to you, didn't they?" I heard shuffling in his background. "Where that nigga at? Is it Soul or Berlin?" Her eyes shifted to me searching for answers. I nodded my head letting her know it was all right to tell him.

"Berlin."

"Give that nigga the phone," he said, sounding confident as a muhfucka. Just the sound of his voice made me cringe.

"You're on speakerphone. She doesn't have to hand me the phone. I suggest you tell your sister where you are unless you want me to put a bullet in her ass."

He smacked his lips. "Nigga, you're bluffing."

"Quentin, you've been around how long? You should know I don't fucking bluff. You got to the count of two."

"I'm not telling you shit. It's alright, Quen, he's not going to do anything to you."

"You sure about that?" My hand rose again and I pulled the safety back off the gun.

Pew!

The bullet went right between her eyes sending blood and brain matter all over the cigarettes and Black & Mild's behind the counter. Her body slumped to the floor and the phone dropped along with her.

"Two." I half-smirk. "I'm coming for you nigga."

"Berlin! Berlin!" he called out for me as I tucked my gun back into my waistline and made my way to the exit. I glared out into the dark to make sure I didn't see anyone coming before I stepped out the door and jogged to my car.

If nothing else could bring that bitch ass nigga out then I knew it would be his sister's death. Quentin thought I was playing games with him but he was going to slowly but surely pay for our parents' death. I slung the car in reverse and peeled out the parking lot heading straight for Soul's place. He was going to kill my ass.

SOUL

Boom! Boom! Boom!

"Soul!" Berlin roared from the other side of my front door. I rushed to it knowing something was wrong by the tone of his voice. I snatched the front door open and he shoved straight past me.

"What's going on?" I asked him, shutting the door and following him into the living room. He began pacing and doing little hand movements like he was trying to figure something out in his head. It was only frustrating the hell out of me. Whatever he needed to say, he needed to go on and spit the shit out.

From the crazy expression on his face, I already knew he'd fucked up somewhere and that's what I get for letting him run things this long. How badly? I didn't know.

I went over to the bar in the corner of my living room and poured us both a shot of Louis Xiii. I was certain we both were going to need the shit for whatever he was about to tell me. Handing him his shot, he quickly tossed it back. I followed suit.

"Gone spit the shit out, Berlin. Whatever it is, I'm sure we'll be able to fix it." Actually, I wasn't positive about that, but I was going to try my hardest to.

"I fucked around and killed Quenby."

"That's what you're tripping about? I don't give a damn about you killing her."

"No, it's not that. It's where I killed her at."

"Where?" I quizzed him with a raised brow.

"At a gas station and I kind of left her lying there."

Wham!

I punched him dead in his shit and he stumbled back.

"Are you fucking stupid! You're trying to get yourself locked up!" The least he could have done was stayed at the store and called me over there. We could have handled the shit. How long it took him to drive up here, I was sure someone already found her ass and now he was risking himself going to jail.

He wiped the tiny trickle of blood from the corner of his mouth and met my gaze. "Bruh, I wasn't thinking straight. I was trying to find out where Quentin's ass was. He was pushing my fucking buttons."

"I'm going to push your fucking buttons alright." I scrubbed my hand down my face and sighed deeply. I had to try and figure out a way to get him out this mess. I headed for the garage and he was right on my heels. Grabbing the Escalade keys off the hook, I opened up the driver's side door.

"Where are you going?"

"We have to go and see if someone found her yet. Get your stupid ass in the truck." I slammed the door and started the truck and followed his directions to the store. Before we even got all the way there, the flashing lights could be seen lighting up the street. I just wanted to reach over there and punch him in his shit all over again.

Pulling over to the side of the road, I watched as they brought her body out the store in a body bag then placed her in the back of the van. "You see what the hell you did, idiot? Now the police going to be sniffing around because they got the security tapes I'm sure." I slapped him on the back of the head and pulled away from the curbside.

"I'm sorry, but I wasn't thinking straight. I should have just gotten the clean-up crew in there first then called you." He pulled a bag of weed out his pocket along with a swisher then rolled himself a blunt.

"You better smoke that blunt because it's going to be the last one in a very long time after you do about fifteen years for killing that damn girl." I sped through traffic going about twenty over the limit trying to get to my location quickly.

I stopped by the warehouse on 19th street and rushed inside while Berlin sat in the truck. That nigga was in time out for the bullshit he pulled. I headed straight to the vault room and placed my hand on the wall and waited for it to scan my handprint. The door opened up and I stepped inside. I grabbed two duffels and stuffed cash into both of them then zipped them up. I had to fix this shit and there was only one way I knew how.

Shutting the vault behind me, I listened to it lock before I walked off. I dropped both of the bags on the back seat then climbed back into the driver's seat.

"What you about to do with that?"

"You lost the right to question me when you put our entire family in jeopardy." I peeled out the parking lot. *Please, let me be able to fix this shit.* I was my brother and sister's keeper and I'll be damned if I let anything happen to either one of them even if they pissed me the fuck off and got on my nerves.

I pulled up in front of the police station and Berlin's eyes damn near popped from his head. "Don't tell me you're about to turn me in."

"I'm about to fix your shit." I grabbed the duffels and headed inside.

I felt eyes on me as I made my way through the building but I was used to it. They were probably wondering what the hell I was doing there. Most of them heard of me before and then there were others who hadn't. I know I could go to jail for the bullshit I was about to pull but I was doing it anyway.

I stopped right in front of the door and pushed it open without even knocking. The chubby white guy sitting behind the desk eyes peered over at me. He wrapped up his phone call.

"I have to call you right back." He placed the phone down on the receiver and I shut the door behind me. "What can I do for you, Soul?"

"I need you to take care of something for me. My brother did something stupid as hell and I'm sure you will find out soon rather than later. I need you to make the shit disappear and quick."

Boom!

The bags made a loud thud sound when they impacted the desk. He unzipped one of them and a half-smirk appeared on his face. He didn't even have to say anything for me to know he was going to do it.

"Pleasure doing business with you, Chief Jacobs." I shook his hand and left out of there. I didn't have any doubts he wouldn't help me because my father used to have him and several other officers in his back pocket when he was alive. I've never really had to come to him for help before but there was always a first time for everything.

SANAA

After a lot of begging, pleading, and cash being thrown around the nurse finally agreed to do the DNA test without Soul being present. I been going insane waiting on the results to come back. I received a call this morning saying they were finally back and asking me to come in to see them.

I rushed up to the clinic to view my results. I was nervous and my leg bounced as I sat in the waiting room anticipating my results. My heart thumped in my chest so hard I thought it was going to pop out soon or later.

I kept trying to change my train of thought so I wouldn't stress too much about it. But no matter what I did, my mind kept going back to the results. I know I wanted to know what they were but I hadn't decided what I was going to do with the information once I received it.

Rubbing my belly, my eyes danced around the waiting area at everyone who was in there waiting to be seen. This older woman sat a couple seats down from me and had one of the worst coughs I've ever heard. I wanted to run out of there to get away from her. I wasn't certain if she was sick or if she just had a bad cough. Either way, I wasn't feeling it.

"Sanaa Love," the nurse called out and I jolted from the seat not even looking back. With every step I took, my heart pounded even more. If it was to keep on, I was sure I'd have a heart attack before I even got my results. "Right this way, Ms. Love."

She gestured into a room and I went inside sitting down in the black chair. I chewed on my fingernails while she stood looking over my paperwork. I knew I was probably fucking up the acrylic but I'd just fix it later.

"Can you just tell me my results because I'm really nervous."

She opened the folder and stared down at it for a brief moment. "I did the best I could with the Q-tip you gave me, it came back stating that the baby is 99.9%, not his." I felt my heart collapse in my chest. The muhfucka fell into the pit of my stomach and I didn't know if it'll come back.

If Soul wasn't the father then it only meant Quentin was. That was even worse than Soul. How could I be so fucking careless? Now, I wished I never done the stupid DNA test in the first place like Soul told me. How was I going to explain that to him?

I sat there caught in my daze for a while, trying to figure out what I was going to do. "Ms. Love?" the nurse called out to me bringing me back from my thoughts.

"Yes? I'm sorry."

"Is there anything else you needed me to help you with?"

"No." I shook my head and got up from the chair. As I made my way out to my car, it was like time was at a standstill. "Quentin's my baby's father..." I couldn't even believe the shit that was seeping from my mouth. "Quentin's my baby's father," I repeated and it wasn't any better that time around.

I climbed into my car and headed to Soul's house so I could tell him what I just found out. All I could hope for was he didn't react badly to the news I was about to give him. I know he claimed he'd still be in the baby's life whether if he was the father or not, but would he actually once he was certain the baby didn't belong to him?

I pulled into Soul's driveway and sat in the car for a moment trying to collect my thoughts. Soul's front door pulled open and he jogged down the front steps. He looked back to his normal self in his charcoal gray suit and white button-up. He had a fresh lineup and of course, his waves were on swim as always. I just wanted to jump into his arms but I fought the urge. I exhaled deeply and climbed out of the car.

"Soul," I called out for him. I didn't have to say anything, he already saw me.

"What are you doing here, Sanaa?"

I tugged on my lower lip and directed my eyes to the ground. "I came because I needed to talk to you."

He hooked me by the chin and tilted my face back to him. "You can't talk to me staring at the ground. What's wrong?"

I rubbed my hands up and down the sides of my pants, trying to find the balls to tell him what I wanted to say. I knew once the words escaped my lips, they were probably going to crush him. He already been through enough and I was about to make things worse for him.

"The baby isn't yours, it's Quentin's," I finally blurted.

"And, how do you even know that?"

There goes my heart again thumping in my chest. "Because I swabbed your mouth and did a DNA test," I quickly rambled off hoping he didn't hear exactly what I said.

"You did what?" His hand dropped from my face and he stumbled back away from me. He was angry from the scowl which adorned his handsome face.

"I'm sorry, Soul but I just had to know. It wasn't fair to you to have you taking care of someone else's child not knowing if it was yours or not. I did it for the both of us."

"I specially told you that you didn't have to do a DNA test and you still do one behind my back." He tread off and snatched the door open on his Tesla.

I rushed over to him. "Don't act like you didn't want to know just as bad as I did. You can't stand there and tell me there wasn't a small part of you that wondered if the baby was yours. I was thinking about you when I did it. YOU, Soul." I went to touch him but he whacked my hand away.

Tears seeped from my eyes and I didn't fully understand what I was crying for. Even though I was still supposed to be angry with him, he was still tugging on my heartstrings.

"Soul," I cried out but he went on and climbed into the car shutting the door in my face. The car started up and I saw it jerk into drive so I stepped back where he wouldn't run over my toes. His car spent off as he pulled out the driveway.

"I did it for us," I whispered.

NAOMI

I was sitting in the middle of class when I got this weird feeling in the pit of my stomach. I felt vomit coming up my throat, so I jumped up from my seat and rushed up the stairs toward the exit with my hand covering my mouth. The bathroom wasn't that far away so I rushed for it, bumping into a few people along the way. I'm sure they were angry but I couldn't stop and say anything to them. I was too afraid that if I opened my mouth, puke would go everywhere.

I got into the bathroom and went into the first stall I saw. Soon as I dropped down to my knees, I vomited up my entire insides. It had been a week since I first tried to get pregnant by Berlin. Guess my tries had finally worked if I was in this nasty ass bathroom puking in the toilet like I had a stomach virus.

I finally pulled myself up off the floor and wiped my mouth with the back of my hand. I went over to the sink and washed my hands then splashed some water onto my face. After staring at my reflection for a moment, I left out the bathroom and went out to my car. There was a Walgreens by my house so I was going to stop there on my way home and grab a pregnancy test.

It wasn't solid that I was pregnant. I could easily be sick or something but it didn't hurt to try and find out. I went into the store and quickly grabbed a test. As I stood in line, people were eyeing me like I was doing something wrong. This woman behind me kept sticking her nose up in the air at me. I wanted to get smart with her but my mother always taught me to respect my elders so I held my tongue.

I paid for my test and got out of there. When I got home, I went straight into the bathroom and sat down on the toilet. I sat there for a moment with the test in my hand. My pulse raced just from the thought I could possibly be pregnant.

Taking a deep breath, I opened the test and peed on the stick then set it down on the countertop beside me. I scrolled down my Instagram, waiting for the time to go up. I didn't want to drive myself insane by keep checking it so I had to do something to take my mind off it for a second.

When my alarm on my phone beeped, I picked the test up and stared at the positive sign. A grin crept up on my face and I did a little happy dance on the toilet before getting up and slipping the test into my pocket. I was so excited that I couldn't wait to call Berlin and let him know the good news.

I dialed his number as I was leaving out the bathroom. His phone rung so many times that I thought he wasn't even going to pick up.

"Yeah?" was all he said into the phone. *Since when he started answering me like that?*

"Berlin, oh my God guess what?"

"I don't have time for your games right now. I was kind of busy so I'll just have to call you back when I'm done doing what I'm doing."

Click!

I know damn well he didn't just hang the phone up in my face like that. I pulled it away from my ear and was staring at my home screen.

"Muhfucka."

I dialed him right back and this time he sent me to voicemail. I was excited to tell him the good news but he pissed me off just that fast. No matter how hard he was out working, he's always had time to talk to me. But now, I felt like something wasn't right.

My gut was telling me he was out doing something he wasn't supposed to be doing. I pulled up my phone and used the find my phone application and searched for his iPhone. The dot pinged on Mississippi Avenue.

"I got you little muhfucka." I rushed out of the bathroom heading straight for the front door. Whatever he was out there doing he was about to be in for a huge surprise. Whatever party he was having, I was about to crash it.

I pulled up in front of the address that was on my phone and it was a restaurant called Eleven Eleven Mississippi. Brushing my hair back behind my ear, I got out the car. I had to mentally prepare myself for what I was about to walk into. He could be in there with Ivy or having lunch with another chick.

I stepped inside the restaurant and my eyes danced around until they landed on Berlin who was sitting at the table with a chick. All I could see was the back of her head but that was good enough for me.

I stormed toward the table with every right mind to whoop his and that bitch's ass. By the time I was done with him, they were going to ban me from the restaurant.

"What the fuck is this shit, Berlin! Is this why you rushed me off the phone so you could have lunch with a bitch!" I picked the cup up off the table in front of him and splashed it into his face.

"The hell, Naomi!" he barked and looked down at his drenched Versace shirt.

Snickering caught my attention so I looked at the girl who was in front of him. It was his sister A'Karri. Maybe I should have done better research than trying to jump to conclusions and shit. I could tell he was angry as hell from the mug that was plastered on his face. His jaws tightened as he gazed back at me.

"I need to talk to you right fucking now!" he roared, getting up from his seat and gripping me by the forearm. He pulled me out of the restaurant and took me outside so we could talk.

"You don't have to be so rough with me, Berlin," I whined, pulling my arm away from him. I rubbed my arm where he grabbed me to soothe the pain.

"You've been tripping ever since that day Ivy called my phone. That's why I been trying to stay away from you. I don't know if this shit between us is going to work."

My eyes watered. "What are you saying, Berlin? Are you breaking up with me?"

"I'm saying, you need to go home, Naomi."

"I only wanted to tell you that I was pregnant. But fuck you, Berlin!" I yelled and walked off hugging myself. Maybe getting pregnant by him wasn't such a good idea after all.

BERLIN

Naomi telling me she was pregnant caught me totally off guard. I wasn't expecting her to say anything like that to me. Really, I wasn't expecting her to do a lot of things she had been doing over the last couple of weeks. She had been tripping on me hard, that's the reason why I tried to drown myself in finding Quentin or work so I wouldn't have to deal with any of that nonsense.

I watched her as she peeled out of the parking lot then went back into the restaurant with A'Karri. There was a feeling in the pit of my stomach that she knew where Quentin was or had heard from him one. She hadn't been coming around either Soul or I lately and that just wasn't like her. She was withholding something from us and I was going to find out what it was.

When I got back into the restaurant, A'Karri was sitting at the table, sipping from her wine glass as if nothing had happened. Her eyes landed on me and she giggled.

"I don't see shit funny." I sighed heavily and plopped back down into my chair in front of her.

"Actually, it is funny because you're the one who chooses to deal with that crazy ass girl. Can you just tell me what you called me out to lunch for so I can get back to my day? I have a hair appointment in two hours."

"Damn, you around here MIA and shit and when I get you to sit down for a couple minutes, you trying to rush off somewhere."

"Come on, Berlin. I know you want something. You didn't just call me here for lunch." Sadly, she was right.

"I wanted to talk to you about Quentin."

"Oh my God, I'm not about to do this." She pushed her seat back from the table and stood up but I grabbed her by the wrist before she could walk away.

"Sit down, Karri. This shit isn't a joke."

She sucked her teeth and plopped back down in the chair.

"What about Quentin?" she questioned me, picking her wine glass back up sticking it to her lips.

"I'm sure you know where Quentin is but you just don't want to tell me."

"And, what makes you think that?" She stared me directly into the eyes and I peeped the hesitation in hers. A'Karri couldn't hide anything from me.

"Because I know you, Karri. Despite all the things that nigga has done to you, you still love him. You'd do anything to try and protect him." Her eyes glossed over and she turned away. That only confirmed my accusations. She knew where he was and I wouldn't be surprised if she was hiding him.

"Tell me where he is, Karri."

"I can't do that." The tears now streamed down her face at full force.

"I just want to talk to him about our parents' death, that's all Karri. I saw him on the tapes at the house and I just want to know if he had something to do with it. Don't you want justice for their death?"

She fidgeted with her fingers for a moment then her gaze met mine. "Of course, I want justice but I don't want anything to happen to him, Berlin. Promise me you won't do anything to hurt him."

"I just want to talk to him, that's all. Now, if he did kill our parents, that's a different story."

She swallowed so hard I could see it. "He's at my condo." Just as I thought, she had been hiding his ass. I don't know why I didn't think to look there in the first place. Out of all the stupid things she's done for him, this one should be at the top of the list. I jolted from the seat so fast that the chair I was sitting in fell to the floor. "Berlin! You promised me that you wouldn't hurt him."

"Go on to your hair appointment and I'll call you later. Whatever you do, don't call and tip that nigga off about me coming because he might run." I gripped her by her forearms and stared her into the eyes so she would know I wasn't playing with her. "Don't. Call. Quentin." She nodded her head with tears in her eyes. If only she knew that this was for the best.

I let her go and rushed out of the restaurant while dialing Soul's number.

"Yeah, Berlin?"

I hit the key fob unlocking my doors. "I know where to find Quentin."

"Where?"

"He's at A'Karri's. I'll meet you there."

218

QUENTIN

I been shacking up with A'Karri for the last week and things seemed to be going great so far. She was still being kind of closed off to me but I accepted that for the time being. I knew soon or later I was slowly going to break that wall back down she was trying to use to guard herself.

All I had to do was show her I wasn't going to fuck up again when it came to her heart. When I got her back, I had no plans of losing her again. I fucked up a lot in the past but I finally came to my senses. After all this shit was over with, I was going to propose to A'Karri like I should have a long time ago. Let her know this shit is real.

I already bought her ring and all. Just had to wait until the perfect time to ask her to marry me. I'd have to give her time to heal after losing both her parents and brothers but after that, it was on.

I glanced down at the ring one more time before getting up from the couch and taking it into the guest bedroom where I had been sleeping. I placed it into the drawer and went back into the living room. I grabbed the Kush bag and cigar off the coffee table and rolled me a blunt in my lap.

A'Karri had left earlier saying something about going to get her hair done or something. I wasn't sure because I wasn't too much listening. She woke me up out my sleep and knew how I could be in that state. I thought she would have been back by now. I placed the blunt between my lips and grabbed my phone to call her. The phone rung all the way out to voicemail.

Lighting the tip of my blunt, my fingers flowed across my keyboard to give her a very detailed message. It wasn't going to be anything bad just telling her I was missing her and she needed to hurry up and get home. Before I could press send, the front door pushed open.

"Damn, I was just texting you," I said, pressing home and tossing the phone to the side.

"Oh, you were, were you? Let me check my phone and see if I got it." I looked up and Soul was shutting the door behind himself and turned the lock.

A'Karri left out that tiny detail about them having keys to her apartment. They could have come at any time and found me in there like he just did.

"What you doing here?"

"I came looking for you." He half-smirked and I leaned over to put the blunt out in the ashtray. "If I were you, I'd go ahead and finish smoking that since it's going to be your last." I shifted my eyes over to my strap that was lying on the end table next to the couch. *Wonder if I can get there in time?*

"You know, I've been wanting to put a bullet in you for some time now but I've decided putting a hot one in your ass was too easy. Then, I thought about chopping your head off and serving it to your family on a silver platter surrounded by your organs, then I realized Berlin killed the last of your family so I can't do that either." He chuckled to himself.

"If you're here to kill me, why won't you go on and do it and get the shit over with?"

"Thought I should just wait until Berlin gets here so he can get in on all the fun."

If Berlin steps foot in that door, I was without a doubt dead. I was supposed to be the one standing on the other end of the gun.

"Too bad things aren't going to play out like that."

I jumped up from the couch and hurried over to the gun. I spun around backward aiming it toward him.

Pow!

Pow!

Both of the guns went off at the exact same time. I fell back on the floor and felt a burning sensation in my stomach. Before I fell, I saw Soul jerk back and fall into the front door, so I knew I had gotten him. I dropped the gun to the floor alongside me and touched my stomach then brought my hand up to my face. My entire hand was covered in blood.

The nigga almost got me but I'd be able to make it to the hospital or something if I was to get up and go now. I tried to pull myself up from the floor but was kicked right in the face.

Wham!

My head flew back and hit the floor.

"It'll take more than that got damn bullet to the shoulder to take me out, nigga. Next time aim for the fucking face." I was staring straight down the barrel of Soul's gold Glock. I never thought I'd be at this end of his gun but should have seen it coming sooner or later. "Muhfucka, I'm going to raise your got damn child like it's mine and have it calling me daddy."

"What child?" I gripped my stomach trying to slow the bleeding down, but I could feel it puddling underneath me. My vision grew blurry.

"You knocked my girl up and I think you did the shit on purpose to get back at me."

"Wait, Sanaa's pregnant?"

"Does it matter?"

"Wait!" I stuck my other hand up in the air to stop him.

Pow!

The bullet traveled through my hand and went straight into my skull. As I took my last breath, I saw Sanaa's smiling face in my head. If I knew I had a child on the way, then I would have played my cards differently. Soon, everything went pitch black.

A'KARRI

I felt like shit the entire time I was getting my hair done. My mind kept going back to Quentin especially after he called me and I just let the phone ring so he'd think I was busy. I wanted to warn him about Berlin coming so badly but he told me not to and I didn't want him to get angry with me about it. I took his word for it that he wouldn't kill him and left it at that.

I tried to stay away from the house long enough so they could have their talk. I had finished getting my hair done hours ago but stopped by Ices Plain & Fancy to grab me some ice cream to buy time. The urge to call Quentin and make sure he was all right was so strong, I actually thought I would cave before it was over with.

I sat there in the shop daydreaming while my ice cream melted. At a time like this, I couldn't really eat. I left my ex-boyfriend at home with my crazy ass brother who was capable of anything. Just the thought had my heart thumping in my chest and ringing in my ears.

"Quentin's okay. Quentin's okay," I told myself over and over but wasn't sure I believed it. I was sure people were looking at me crazy right about now but I didn't care. I didn't have anyone to assure me he was fine so I had to reassure myself. I didn't want or need to think the worst at this moment.

"Fuck," I groaned, digging into my purse and pulling out my phone. I couldn't torture myself any longer. I had to make sure he was all right.

I tapped my nails on the table while listening to the phone ring in my ear. It went straight to voicemail so I called him back and got the same thing.

"Something's not right." I jumped up from the table leaving the ice cream sitting on it and rushed out the door. I had to get home and lay eyes on Quentin because my heart told me something was wrong.

Jumping into my truck, I sped all the way to my condo. I stepped on the elevator and repeatedly pressed the number eight until the doors closed. I shook my hands waiting for it to come to a halt. Tugging on my lower lip, I looked up at the numbers.

When the doors opened, I stood there staring down the hallway at my door. My heart felt like it was about to burst out of my chest. I finally stepped off and the walk up to my door felt like the longest walk of my life.

"You're just tripping, Karri," I told myself and put the key in the door. I slowly turned the knob and stepped inside. When I saw Quentin lying on the floor on top of plastic my heart dropped to my stomach. Tears formed in my eyes and words got caught in my throat.

"What are you doing here, Karri?" Berlin asked, trying to approach me but I stumbled back away from him.

"You promised me, Berlin!" I rushed straight past him over to Quentin's body and dropped to my knees. "Quentin," I cried out for him and gripped the sides of his face. They fucking shot him. Put a bullet in his head. How could they!

"Karri, you shouldn't be here right now," Soul tried to tell me but I wasn't hearing anything he had to say.

"What did they do to you?" Tears poured down my cheeks and I rested my forehead on his.

"Get her out of her," Soul instructed Berlin.

Berlin grabbed my forearm but I snatched away from him. "Don't fucking touch me!" I yelled, giving him an icy glare. I wanted nothing to do with either one of them at the moment. Berlin promised he wouldn't kill Quentin and now the love of my life was lifeless on my living room floor. Then, they were in there trying to clean up their mess before I got here. If I hadn't come when I did, I wouldn't have known about him being dead. One of them would have come up with a lie to tell me just to keep me happy.

"Come on, Karri." Berlin went to grab me again. I kissed Quentin on his lips then he pulled me up off the floor. I stood there sobbing. It felt like they had snatched a piece of me away. My heart felt like it had a black hole in it.

"Sis, I promise you, you're better off without that nigga. I did all of us a favor," Soul said only frustrating me even more than I already was.

I sniffled and rubbed my nose with my hand. The tears were still falling and I honestly don't think that they'd stop any time soon. My eyes directed toward the gun that was sticking out of Berlin's waistline. I quickly gripped it and turned it on them.

"Woah, hold up," Berlin said, taking a few steps back away from me with his hands up in the air.

"What the hell are you doing, A'Karri?" Soul asked me and I saw his jaws tightening. He was getting angry which was good, that made two of us.

"I love Quentin and you two took him away from me."

"He killed Ma and Pops, A'Karri. I did what was necessary. Thought you would understand."

"We were going to get married and have kids together. You two ripped me of all that. Do you get a kick out of destroying other people's lives? If anything, I did Sanaa a favor by pushing her away from you. You were only going to fuck her over even worse. You ruin everyone's lives you touch. You even ran Sofia off!" Soul's fist balled up and he eased a little closer to me. "Take another step and I promise I'll shoot you."

"This girl has really lost her mind. I can't deal with this shit. When you calm your sister down, then hit my line." Berlin tried to leave but he wasn't going anywhere.

"BRING YOUR ASS BACK HERE BERLIN!" I yelled and he stopped in his tracks.

"I'm not doing shit. I know you're not crazy enough to shoot either one of us. If Soul wants to stand there and entertain your crazy ass then that's his business."

"I wish the both of you nothing but misery. Now you have to dig two graves."

"What the hell are you talking about?"

My tears blurred my vision and I placed the gun underneath my chin. "I love the both of you."

"A'Karri, no!" they both yelled in unison.

Pow!

NAOMI

A month had gone by since I got into it with Berlin and A'Karri killed herself in front of them. I know that was awful to see. I couldn't imagine what he was going through, but it wasn't enough for me to be willing to put up with his bullshit.

"Congrats, bih!" Sanaa sang, rubbing her belly when I appeared outside. She was holding five balloons and a dozen red roses for me.

I had just walked across the stage and I was happy as hell. I finally finished up with school and didn't have to worry about coming back there. At least not until next year. I was going to go back to school for another degree, but I hadn't figured out exactly what I wanted to major in yet.

Despite me being pregnant in my last month of school, I was still able to graduate at the top of my class. I didn't let my pregnancy get in the way of things for me. If anything, it motivated me to work harder.

"Thank you!" I pulled her in for an embrace.

"Sweetie, we'll see you later. Your father has to get to work but we're so proud of you," my mother, Angela beamed and pulled me in for a hug as well.

"Thanks, Ma." She kissed me on the cheek when she pulled back. My father, Rodrick kissed me in the center of my forehead and they both left heading for the parking lot.

"So, what are you going to do to celebrate? You can't go to the club in case you forgot." She laughed, rubbing my stomach. It was nowhere near as big as hers but I'm sure I'd catch up to her in due time.

"Uh, I'm not sure. Maybe we can go out to eat or something."

"That's fine by me. You know I'm always down to eat something." We both burst out into laughter and made our way across the parking lot. I pulled my gown off displaying the black two-piece skirt set I was wearing underneath. I could still get away with wearing things like this but I'm certain by this time next month, my stomach would be bigger than this.

"Where you want to meet up at or I could just follow you?" We had driven in separate cars and I just wanted to see what was best for her.

"What about Charlie Gitto's On The Hill?" I never heard of her wanting to eat there before but if she wanted to try it then I didn't mind. I'd try everything once. But if the food was nasty, then the shit was going to be on her.

"It doesn't matter to me because dinner is on you." I giggled and she side-eyed me. "What? It's only right?"

"You lucky I love your ugly ass." She rolled her eyes at me.

"I know, you love me oh so much." I cheesed then pulled my car door open. "I'll see you there."

* * *

I pulled up to Charlie Gitto's On The Hill and climbed out of my car. Sanaa was already there waving her hands in the air for me out on the patio.

"Naomi!" she yelled like I could miss her bright ass face or something.

I grinned at her shaking my head then pushed the patio door open and stepped inside shutting it behind me. When I got back there I was in awe. My parents told me they were going home but there they were sitting at the same table with Sanaa.

"Thought you two were going home?" I asked them then kissed both of their cheeks before pulling out the empty chair at the table.

"Sanaa had reservations here and we wanted to make it in time so they wouldn't give the table away," my mother answered.

"So, this was your little evil plan?"

"Guess you got me." She gave me a half-smirk.

As I sat down at the table and laughed at their silly little jokes. I could only feel nothing but love surrounding me. Even if I was to go through this pregnancy alone, my baby would still be loved. Sanaa had this huge smile on her face as she talked to my parents. This was honestly the happiest I've seen her in a while.

For the first time in a long time, I felt like things were going to be just fine. I finally got my degree and pretty soon I'd be opening my own practice while taking up classes online somewhere. I and my baby were going to be straight regardless.

I heard the patio door shut and it brought me back to reality. My eyes darted over to the door and they landed on Berlin. He was standing there with a dozen pink roses in his hand as well as balloons in the other. I wanted to kick Sanaa's ass because I finally put two and two together. This entire restaurant had to be his idea.

I couldn't lie, seeing him was like falling in love with him all over again. He stood there with that stupid ass smirk on his face that I loved so much. As always, his swag was on point. His black Balmain jeans had rips in them that went well with the tight black t-shirt he had on showing off his tattooed sleeve.

"Congratulations, Naomi," he said attempting to hand me the balloons and roses but I slapped them both from his hands and stood to my feet and walked away. I was not about to stay in his presence when I didn't really have to.

BERLIN

I knew Naomi was going to be angry at me for pushing her away but I had to do what I had to do for myself. The time I spent away from her I realized that being with her was the only thing I wanted. No, more like needed.

I stopped by the shop earlier and asked Sanaa to help me get her back. She was against it at first but then she eventually agreed to it. I made reservations at the restaurant and asked Sanaa to have her here. I knew I had to do something nice since it was also her graduation day.

Walking in seeing her sitting there laughing with her family did something to me. I was struck with Naomi's beauty all over again. It was like the first time seeing her and it stopped me in my tracks. She was gorgeous as hell with her long curly hair down her back.

Her slapping the gifts I got her out my hands wasn't expected but I should have known it wasn't going to be that easy to make things right between us. She was angry and when Naomi got angry, it was never a good thing. Anything could happen.

I stood there watching the *"Congrats"* balloons float up into the sky. She brushed straight past me and left off the patio so I went behind her.

"I wanted to see you, that's what I'm doing here, Naomi." I grabbed her wrist, stopping her and she looked like she wanted to slap the shit out of me but didn't which was shocking. I had gotten use to her licks.

The entire time I was away from her, all I could think about was if I was going to be a good father. I wasn't used to things like that but I guess with Naomi on my side, I'd make it through it. She turned me on to relationships and had me craving deeper things from her.

"Out of all this time, now you want to see me? Where were you when I was puking in trash cans because I couldn't make it to the toilet? Where were you when I tossed and turned at night because I couldn't sleep? Where were you when I went to my first doctor's appointment? Where were you when I—"

"I'm sorry, aight? But to be fair I was going through some things at the time."

"I understand that but I tried to give you your time to grieve your sister's death. I stayed away but then when I texted and tried to check on you, you didn't answer. I invited you to the doctor's appointment, you didn't show. This isn't how this is supposed to work, Berlin."

"I know and I'm sorry. I promise you I'm going to do better if you give me the chance to." I cupped her face and she shut her eyes at the feel of my touch.

"Why do I have to love you so much?" When she opened her eyes, they were misty.

"I love you just the same if not even more." I dropped down to one knee and heard Sanaa screaming in the background.

"Berlin, what are you doing? Get up off that ground!" Naomi glanced around at all the people who were looking on. Sanaa was standing directly beside us with Naomi's camera per my request. I knew how much she loved recording things.

"No, because I have something to say and you're going to listen." I reached into my pocket pulling out the velvet ring box and popped it open.

"I know that's not what I think it is, Berlin! Quit playing with me!" She stumbled back away from me and placed both her hands up to her mouth. "Berlin!"

"Naomi Copeland. You're loud, wild, you snore and slob in your sleep. You need anger management classes. You whoop my ass when no one else can or ever will. You accept me for the man that I am and love me for me. I've learned that you're the calm to my havoc storm. And another important lesson I've learned was that I can't live without you, Naomi." My eyes grew wet with tears and I quickly tried to blink them away before someone saw them. "I guess what I'm really trying to say is, Naomi," I popped the box open on her customized thirty-four karat diamond ring. The shit cost me a grip but it was worth it.

"Oh my God!" she shrieked with her hands still up to her mouth. I could see the tears flowing from her eyes.

"Will you marry me?"

She slowly nodded and said, "Yes."

I grabbed her hand and slipped the ring onto her finger. Everyone surrounding us began clapping as I got up from my knee and pulled her body into my frame. I kissed her gently on the lips and it was then I vowed I'd never let her slip away from me again.

SOUL

After losing A'Karri, I been fucked up in the head. I've lost too much to the streets and was second guessing if it's really what I wanted to do. I had more than enough money where I could live comfortably. Why should I keep risking my life and the ones I loved for that shit?

I sat there contemplating on the idea of giving up the game for the longest. I finally came to the conclusion I needed to have a talk with Berlin. I'm certain he wasn't going to be happy about it but it was my decision, not his.

Once I have this talk with Berlin, I was going to have a much-needed one with Sanaa. The shit between us had to come to an end. I was tired of playing these silly ass games with her. Even though the baby wasn't mine, I had yet to miss a doctor's appointment and was always there when she called. It really angered me when she went behind my back and did that DNA test. I had a feeling the baby wasn't mine that's why I didn't want to confirm it.

I got up off the couch and headed straight to the front door. Climbing into my truck, I texted Berlin and told him I was on my way over. I hoped this conversation between us played out far better than it did in my head.

Leaving everything to Berlin was kind of risky but I hoped that it worked out for the best. I remembered the last time I left everything for him to run and he almost ended up in prison. All I could do was pray he does a better job this go around.

I pulled up in front of his building and went inside. I knocked on his front door and waited for him to come to it.

Knock! Knock!

He pulled the door open and I stepped inside. "What you doing here?" he asked me with a bewildered expression on his face.

"I texted and told you I was coming by. Did you not get my text?"

"Nah, I heard it chime but didn't check my phone."

"What if it was something important, Berlin?" I questioned him, then scrubbed my hand down my face.

"You would have called." He brushed his hand across his hair. *Was this really who I was about to leave our family's legacy to?* Now, I saw why Pops was always on his ass the way he was.

"Look, I came over here to let you know that I'm out."

"What you mean you're out?"

I sighed deeply and plopped down on the couch. "I'm done with the street shit, bruh. It's cost me too much and I'm just over it."

"Damn, you for real?" he asked, sitting down beside me and grabbing his blunt from the ashtray. He placed it between his lips and fired it up.

"Yeah, I'm retiring from this mess while I still can. I'm handing everything over to you. If you need me I'd still be around to help out but as far as running it, I'm done."

"So, what are you going to do now?" He took a couple tokes from his blunt, then blew the smoke out.

"I'm about to settle down with Sanaa and raise my seed."

"You do know that baby doesn't belong to you, right?" He side-eyed me, then puffed on his L some more.

"You think I don't know that? It's still my seed though regardless. I love Sanaa, man and I'm just trying to make things right between us. Think I want to propose to her."

"Why don't you do it then? What do you have to lose?" I wanted to say my pride if she was to turn me down but I just kept that shit to myself.

"Everything if I'm being honest." Sanaa hadn't said anything else about it but I'm sure she's still carrying around that weight of her mother's death on her shoulders. I wish I could take it from her and bear it myself.

"Give it your best shot and if that still doesn't work then maybe she's not the girl for you." He tried to pass me the blunt but I declined.

"You know I don't smoke." I leaned back pulling my phone out of my front pants pocket and went to the text messages.

Me: *Can you meet me at the house in a couple of hours. I need to talk to you about something.*

I didn't even wait for her to text back just slipped the phone back into my pocket.

"I'm about to get going. I asked Sanaa to meet me at the house. Hopefully, she shows up."

"Good luck on your new endeavors." He laughed as I pulled the front door open.

"Try not to get yourself killed out there in them streets."

SANAA

When Soul texted and asked me to come to his house, I was visiting my mother's grave. It was her birthday and I had been sad the entire day. I didn't need him making the day worse for me.

Wiping the tears from my eyes, I rubbed my index finger across my nose. I laid the lilies down on her grave and walked away. Times like these were always hard for me. My mother and I were so close. She was like a sister to me as well. The only blood I had roaming this earth. That's why it was so hard for me to mourn her death.

I climbed back into my car and sat there for a moment debating if I wanted to go to his house or not. I could have easily pretended like I never got his message and just gone home but my heart was telling me I needed to go. I was angry and needed to get some things off my chest with him. My mind told me to take my ass home, it was a bad idea, but I didn't listen to it and was already in route to Soul's place.

It didn't take me long to get there. I got out the car and went up to the front door. I softly knocked on it, not even caring if he heard me or not. If he took too long to come to the door, then I was just going to turn around and head home.

The door pulled open and there he stood in a crisp white button-up and black slacks. *Why did he have to be so got damn sexy?* I cursed myself for craving this man. But that wasn't the reason I was there.

"I'm here, now what do you want? I'm tired and I'm hungry. All I want to do is go home and get some sleep." I was cranky as hell and he was about to catch all this backlash.

"It's a good thing you brought your appetite because I cooked for you." He smiled at me and it kind of threw me off. He gestured for me to enter the house. I stepped over the threshold and he shut the door. "I actually thought you weren't going to come."

I followed him toward the dining room. I stared at the long rectangular table that was set for two with two long stem candles sitting in the middle of it. Red rose petals were scattered on the floor around the table and candles were lit all around the room.

"What's all this?" I questioned him.

"I wanted to do something special for you, Sanaa. Do you like it?" He pulled one of the chairs at the end of the table out for me. I slowly tiptoed over to it and sat down.

"But why though?"

To show you how much I care for you." He sat down at the other end of the table. A guy came out of the kitchen with two plates in his hands and sat one down in front of each of us.

"You really didn't have to do all this," I said, looking down at the steak, potatoes, and brussel sprouts on my plate. I don't even know why I was sitting in front of him right now; I didn't want him to get the wrong impression.

"Actually, I really did. The last couple of months has been hard between us. Ever since you found out about Yonnie, you've been distancing yourself from me." He got up from the table and eased himself over to where I was sitting. I gazed up into his face and followed it as he kneeled down beside me. "All I want to do is love you, Sanaa." He pulled a box from his pocket and I squeezed my eyes shut.

Please don't be what I think it is. Please don't be what I think it is. I peeled my eyes open and a massive rock stared back at me. *Fuck, it's exactly what I thought it was!*

"I want to marry you, Sanaa. I want to be that perfect man in your life that makes you better. I want to take care of you when you're sick. Raise your child as if it's my very own. Love you for the rest of your life. Will you do me the honor of being my wife?"

I shook my head. "I can't do that Soul. I can't marry you knowing you were the one who killed my mother. As much as I try, I can't let go of that pain. It kills me every time I stare at your face. I get an aching feeling in my chest." I slid the chair back and stood to my feet. "When they were dropping my mother into the ground, I promised her that I was going to find her killer." I slipped my hand into my purse and pulled out the small Nine that was tucked away in there.

That's the reason why I had been crying all day. That's the reason why I didn't want to go to his house in the first place. I had to make good on my promise. I wasn't going to do it when I thought he was the father of my child, but now that I know he's not and I've thought long and hard about it. I knew it was what had to be done. No matter how much it hurt me.

"What are you doing, Sanaa?"

"A life for a life." I lifted my hand and pulled the safety off, shut my eyes, then squeezed the trigger.

Pow!

I pulled them open and Soul was dropping to his knees holding his chest. Tears welled up in my eyes and seeped from the corners. I didn't want to kill Soul, I had in fact fallen for him but I promised my mother...

"I-I wa-was going to t-tell you the truth."

Blood seeped from the corners of his plump lips. "What are you talking about?"

"It w-was Berlin."

My brows wrinkled. "What was Berlin?" I stood there trying to make out what he was trying to say. Oh my God! "Berlin killed my mother!"

I dropped the gun and rushed over to him, lifting his head up off the floor. "I-I was tr—" He coughed up a mouth full of blood. "Trying to protect him. I should have told you the truth sooner."

"I'm sorry, Soul," I wept still holding his head. "I'll call 911." I rambled through my purse looking for my phone. I pulled it out and Soul grabbed my hand with his bloody one.

"I love you."

"I love you too, Soul. It's going to be okay, babe. I promise you it's going to be okay." With shaky hands I fumbled through my purse and retrieved my phone. "I'm about to call for help. I'm going to get you some help." My tears blinded me, but I wasn't going to let that stop me from getting him help. The only thing I was able to dial was nine and looked down he was gone. He died in my arms by my hands only because I was being so stupid. Stupid to not let that man love me how I deserved. Revenge isn't always sweet especially if it takes the life of someone you love. I killed the man I loved all for vengeance. I leaned down and kissed him softly on the lips. "I love you, Soul."

Boom! Boom! Boom!

I gently rested Soul's head down on the floor and rushed to the front door to see who it was. When I pulled it open, all I saw was flashing lights behind two uniform cops and two EMTs.

Shit!

"We got a call about a disturbance. Someone heard a gunshot," the shorter chubby cop said with his gun already drawn. My heart thumped in my chest and was a few seconds away from bursting out. I could feel my body overflowing with sweat from me being so nervous. Going against my better judgement, I stepped to the side allowing them to come inside. "We got a body!" he yelled over his shoulder once his eyes landed on Soul lying on the floor in a puddle of his own blood.

I already knew I was fucked. He was lying there dead and the gun was only inches away from him with my fingerprints all over it. Without a doubt, I was going to jail for murder tonight and there wasn't anything I could do or say to get myself out of this shit.

At this point, I didn't really care what they did with me. They couldn't do me any more harm than I've already done to myself. I sat there and snatched the love of my life away from me and I don't think things could get any worse than they already had. If only he wasn't trying to protect Berlin, then he would have been the one on the other side of my gun instead of Soul.

Why Soul?

My heartbeat could be heard ringing in my ears, that's how strong it was at the moment. I stood off to the side with sweat beads dripping from my forehead as I watched the EMTs touch Soul's body looking for a pulse that I already knew wasn't there. He was lying there with his eyes closed. Of course, he was already gone, so what was the point in checking?

I could just run out the door while they aren't looking. But then, I'm sure my face and everything would be all over the news before I made it anywhere. And I wouldn't get far because my keys and purse were just a foot away from them.

"We got a pulse!" one of the EMTs shouted and I almost thought I was hearing things.

"Wh-what?" I asked slowly nearing them. All I wanted to do was make sure Soul was all right. He was the only thing on my mind, and I guess my body was craving to know since my feet began moving before my brain even told them to. "He's okay?" I asked with tears dripping from the corners of my eyes.

I went to go for him but the tall lean Caucasian cop stopped me, extending his arm out in front of me. "Please, just let me see him," I cried, tears blurring my vision. The other EMT came back into the house with the gurney and I watched as they lifted, putting him on it.

"Do you mind telling us what happened?" the chubby cop asked me but I wasn't worried about anything he was talking about.

I wanted my Soul. No, I needed my Soul...

"Please, just let me see him," I repeated, trying to get past him but he was steady holding me back.

"I think it's pretty obvious what happened." The chubby cop bent down and picked the pistol up with his index finger. "I think you're going to have to take a ride with us down to the station. You've got some explaining to do."

The lean cop pulled my arms behind my back, placing the cuffs on my wrists. They rolled Soul past me and I couldn't take my eyes off him.

"Soul!" I cried out in hopes he would somehow hear me.

They pulled me out of the house behind him and placed me in the back of the squad car. I'm not sure how I was going to get out of this one. I really fucked up and even if he was to survive that gunshot, I'm sure he'd never forgive me for shooting him in the first place.

BERLIN

When Soul told me, he was quitting the family business, I couldn't believe the shit but at the same time, I understood. We lost so much to these streets that he wasn't prepared to lose anything else. If he wanted to settle down and turn legit or live off the cash he saved up then I was with it. I was more than capable to run this shit on my own.

I grabbed my car keys off the dresser and headed for the front door. I had a shipment coming in soon and wanted to be there when it arrived to make sure everything was there. Niggas try to get you sometimes even when they know I'll knock they ass off the map for even attempting to play with my money. That still didn't stop a few from trying though.

As I locked the door, my phone began ringing so I dug into my pocket and pulled it out. An unknown number flashed across the screen and normally, I didn't really answer those phone calls but everything in my bones told me I needed to answer this one. I swiped the screen planting the phone to my ear.

"Who the hell is this?"

"Berlin, it's Chief Jacobs, I was calling you because I just found out that Soul got shot."

I stopped dead in my tracks and my heart dropped to the pit of my stomach. *Shot?*

Last I checked, he was going to cook dinner for Sanaa and propose to her. What the hell happened along the way to result in him getting shot?

I had to control my emotions because I was ready to go on a rampage. Heat coursed through my veins and all I could see was red. Whoever shot him was about to pay for this shit with their life. And they better hope they didn't kill him or else they were going to result to having a slow painful death.

"Do you know who shot him?"

"We actually have her in custody now."

"Her?" My brows furrowed when I asked that. I know damn well—

"Yeah, Sanaa Love."

"Make the shit go away. I'll send someone to get her," I told him and disconnected the call. I couldn't believe Sanaa actually had the fucking nerves to shoot my got damn brother. She was still walking around with that bullshit on her shoulders about me killing her mother. That's why Soul should have told her dumbass I was the one who did the shit. I would have sent her ass back flying not giving a fuck about ending her ass.

I dialed Naomi's number as I climbed into my car. She answered on the second ring so she must have been sitting by the phone.

"Heeeeeyyyyyyy babe," she sang into the phone.

"Naomi, I need you to go down and pick Sanaa up from jail."

"JAIL!" she frantically yelled.

"Yeah, jail. Her dumbass done shot Soul. I'm on my way to the hospital to make sure he's alright. And if he ain't—"

"Babe don't talk like that. He's going to be just fine, promise. But I'm about to go get her."

"Aight, thanks." I disconnected the call and dropped the phone into my lap. I punched the steering wheel hard, feeling tears drip from my eyes.

Here I was right back in the same predicament I was when he was in that car accident but this time, I'm not sure if I'll walk away from that hospital with my brother. Everything in me was telling me I might lose my fucking brother tonight and if I did, I was going to hunt Sanaa's ass down and make her pay for what the fuck she did. Show her ass no mercy.

I finally made it to Kindred Hospital. I hurriedly parked my car and rushed inside. I stopped at the nurses' station grabbing the first nurse I saw. "I need some info on my brother Gabriel Maserati. He was brought here not too long ago with a gunshot wound."

"Sir, if they just brought him in, then we won't have any information on him at this time. You'll have to take a seat in the waiting area and I'll let them know that you're here so when they do have something, they'll come out there and let you know."

"So, you mean to fucking tell me that you want me to sit my ass down and act like everything's all cool while my brother is back there damn near dying? You got me fucked up!"

She eased her forearm away from me. "Sir, I promise you that as soon as I find something out about your brother, I will personally come and tell you. Now, if you will excuse me, I have to get back to work."

I scrubbed my hand down my face as I watched her walk away from me. I wouldn't be able to just sit down not knowing what's happening to Soul. The shit was going to drive me fucking insane. Naomi needed to hurry up and do what she was supposed to so she could come up here with me before I went fully crazy.

I plopped down in the first chair I saw propping my elbows on my thighs and resting my face in my palms. I didn't know how to deal with the situation. I wanted to go after Sanaa for hurting Soul but then if he was to survive, I'm sure he'd be fucking pissed at me for the shit I've done. And if I didn't and word got out about what she did, everyone would think that it's all right to come for our heads. I couldn't have that shit. It was like I was in a lose, lose situation.

I jolted from the chair that I only been sitting in a good five minutes and went right back up to the nurses' station. Someone was going to tell me what the hell I wanted to know or else.

I snatched my gun from my waistline and slammed it down on the desk. All their eyes expanded and fell upon me. "Now, that I have your fucking attention. Someone better take their ass to the back and find out what the fuck is going on with Gabriel Maserati before I start knocking people off one by one in this muhfucka!"

SANAA

I walked out the door and Naomi was standing beside her truck with her arms folded across her chest and a scowl on her face. I knew she was pissed at me for what I did. What I really wanted to know was how she even knew I was locked up in the first place. They wouldn't let me have my phone call for whatever reason, so I wasn't able to call her. Everything seemed fishy to me.

Ever since they brought me in there, they tried asking me questions about what happened but I wouldn't talk to them unless I had a lawyer present. They wouldn't let me call one of them either. Something about my entire visit there was... weird. I mean, I knew my rights. They had no other choice than to let me have a lawyer present, yet they were still trying to deny me that right. Then on top of that, they just let me go without even signing one piece of paper or paying a bail.

"Please don't look at me like that Naomi."

"REALLY, SANAA! You fucking tried to kill Soul! You should have just left the shit alone but nooooo, you couldn't do that, could you? Do you not know what disaster this shit is going to cause not only to my relationship but to your wellbeing once I have to beg and plead with Berlin not to cause any harm to you?"

I knew she was angry with me from the way her nose flared and how she snatched the door open on her truck. I should have just gone with my first mind and not took my ass to Soul's house after I left the cemetery, then I wouldn't be in this shit. That little voice in the back of my mind was telling me not to go, but I just had to. My heart yearned for Soul but the anger I had for my mother's death weighed heavier on it.

Tears dripped from my eyes as I pulled the passenger's side door open and got in alongside her. For a moment, we just sat in silence. Me staring at the side of her angered face. Her jaw twitched as she stared straight ahead out the window.

"Out of all the things you've ever done, Sanaa, this is by far the worse." She finally turned to face me, and she had tears in her eyes as well.

"I'm sorry, Naomi. I wasn't thinking when I did it. I was just so angry. I'm hurting and I don't know what to do with this pain." I broke down right there in the front seat of her truck. I expected her to just pull away from the curb but instead, she reached over, wrapping her arms around me.

"We will get through this together. Just promise me that you won't do anything else stupid. I already have to sell my soul to get you out this shit. I won't have anything else to give." She kissed me on the cheek as she pulled back from my embrace and put the truck in drive.

I nibbled on the corner of my lower lip preparing myself for the other lashing she was about to give me once the next sentence seeped from my lips. "Naomi, can you take me to the hospital? I just want to make sure Soul is okay." I poked out my lower lip, hoping that would help me plead my case.

She gave me the side-eye. "I really don't think this is a good idea." She sighed heavily.

"Please."

"Fine."

When Naomi pulled up in front of the hospital, I fumbled with the door trying to open it before she even came to a complete stop. I rushed inside the hospital and the first face I saw was Berlin's plastered with a scowl. I knew he was going to be furious with me but at this moment, we needed to put our differences to the side. The both of us were there for the same exact reason. Soul. Just as he, I wanted to make sure he was okay. I know I probably didn't have the right to be there considering I was the one who put him there to begin with. We had to look past all that for now.

"The hell you're doing here!" he roared as he peeled his bottom from the chair he'd been occupying.

"Berlin, babe, please calm down," Naomi intervened. I didn't really need her to come between us. I was pretty certain I could stand my own ground with Berlin.

"Nah, she needs to fucking hear this shit." He lightly shoved Naomi out of the way and closed the gap between us. "You're angry with us because *I* killed your mother. Not Soul, but ME. We didn't know you at the time and it's in the past. You need to get over that bullshit before you end up getting yourself hurt. Your mother knew the risks of working for us and she also knew what the hell would happen if she ever crossed us. That shit was all on her. So, it's about time you let the shit go!"

His chest heaved as he glared down into my face with his dark eyes. I couldn't stop the tears that were slowly seeping from the brim of my eyes.

"Don't fucking cry now, you weren't crying when you pulled that got damn trigger and almost killed my brother!" He's right, I wasn't crying then, but I damn sure was after I pulled the trigger. That shit hurt me just as bad as it hurt him. If not even more.

"This is the guy I was talking about; he's Gabriel's brother." A nurse caught all of our attention and we turned to her. "Berlin, this is Doctor Trisha. She's going to explain to you about your brother." She dismissed herself.

"Okay, your brother is finally stable. We lost him a couple times when they first brought him in but he's finally out of surgery now and you can go back and see him if you'd like but I'm going to let you know now, he's pretty out of it."

I jumped and screamed in my head at the wonderful news she just shared with us. That's all I wanted to know. To make sure he'd make it. I don't think I'd ever be able to live with myself if he was to die.

"Thank you so much, Doctor. What room is he in?" Berlin quickly asked her.

"Room 314." She shook Berlin's hand then walked away.

I went to head to the elevator but Berlin stuck his arm out stopping me in my tracks. "The hell you think you're going?"

"I'm about to go up there and see Soul."

"Like hell you are. Don't you think you've done enough damage for a lifetime, Sanaa? Just go home and try to stay the fuck away from my brother." When he said that, I felt my very existence shattering. My heart dropped to the pit of my stomach and my entire body felt heavy. The tears were now coming down full force blinding me.

I slowly walked toward the exit. "That was kind of harsh don't you think?" Naomi asked Berlin and attempted to stop me. "Sanaa wait up." My feet pounded against the pavement as I took off running across the parking lot. I deserved everything Berlin said to me and more. If he wanted me to stay away from his brother, then that's exactly what I was going to do.

SOUL
Five months later...

I t's crazy how it's been five months since Sanaa shot me. Five whole months since I last saw her face. I thought that maybe she would have tried to reach out to me by now since she knew I was doing fine but guess not. Maybe she wanted me to die that night. Take my last breath to pay for her mother's death. Or it could be that she felt guilty as hell for shooting me and can't really show her face. Either way, I just wanted to see her. Even if it was for a moment.

I thought about going by the shop several times, but I wasn't certain how she was going to react when I got there. I didn't want to run her away or put too much pressure on her by just being in her presence. I had been trying to give her enough time to come to her senses, but I think five months was far too long. Everything I had been telling myself for the last five months had gone completely out the window.

I couldn't keep myself away from her any longer. I was yearning to be near her. Smell her fragrance. Touch her baby soft skin. Kiss her full lips. Brush my fingers across her freckled face. See her brush her hair back behind her ear whenever I stare at her beautiful eyes for too long or she got nervous.

Those eyes...

I miss those eyes so damn much. The way they poured into my soul whenever she gazed into mine. The sparkle that was always evident in them.

I found myself in my car and pulling up in front of the shop. I couldn't fight the urge to be near her any longer. My heart pounded in my chest as I sat outside in my car. I don't think I've ever been nervous before but the thought of walking into there and seeing Sanaa made a nigga get cold feet.

What if she didn't want to see me?

That was the same question I been asking myself for the longest. The thought of her turning me around was heartbreaking.

I climbed out of my car and stepped up onto the curb. When my eyes landed on Sanaa through the glass, I was stuck in awe. She'd gotten so big since the last time I've seen her. She was carrying her baby weight extremely well. Its been so long since I've last seen her that I almost forgot she was pregnant.

She stood there rubbing on her protruding belly through her knee-length white floral dress. Her hair even began growing. It now stopped at the nape of her neck with chestnut brown roots. Her face was a little fuller in depth but she was still beautiful. Wide nose and all.

Staring at her had my heart racing. Goosebumps took over my entire body. I swear I felt like I was falling in love with her all over again. I just stood there for a moment just admiring her beauty.

Pulling the door open, it chimed. All eyes fell upon me but the only ones I was worried about was Sanaa's. I saw the anxiousness in her eyes and it only made me wonder how come she'd stayed away from me for so long. When she thought I was dying, she told me she loved me and I thought it would have been enough for her to come looking for me once she knew I was fine. I was willing to look past her shooting me, so why she couldn't do the same?

What was holding her back?

I had so many questions for her and prayed that she was willing to answer them.

"What are you doing here Soul?" Her lips finally parted and I almost forgot what her voice sounded like. It was like a mixture of music and heaven all in one.

I grabbed her by the hand and led her to her office. When she stepped inside, I shut the door behind her. "I'm sorry to just drop by on you on such short notice but I needed to see you. You know, seeing how you hadn't even tried to after you damn near tried to kill my ass."

Her eyes lowered and she diverted them elsewhere. I could tell that she felt guilty for shooting me but I wasn't about to hold the shit over her head. I think she did what most normal people would do in her situation. Okay, not really but still...

"I'm so sorry for shooting you, Soul. I really am." Her eyes glistened when they gazed upon me once more.

I didn't come all the way there just so she would apologize to me. That's not what I was looking for. Yeah, I wanted an explanation for why she stayed away from me but that apology, she could have kept.

"You told me you loved me, so I'm trying to understand how come I haven't seen you. What's really going on Sanaa?"

"It's not that simple Soul."

"Why the hell not?"

I closed the gap between us and cupped her face. It felt weird feeling her belly pressing against my midsection. I know she was probably angered by the fact I hadn't been here to help her like I told her I was. I missed all the doctor's appointments and don't even know what she was having.

"I came to the hospital to see you after I shot you."

"How come I didn't see you, then?"

Berlin nor Naomi mentioned the fact that she was there. What was the whole point in her coming when she didn't even make it to the room?

"I tried to see you..." She gently grabbed me by the wrists and pulled my hands down from her face then took a couple steps back away from me, hugging herself. Her eyes were gazing at the floor like she didn't want to look me in my face any longer.

"But what?" I hooked her chin forcing her to stare at me.

"But, Berlin wouldn't let me go see you. He told me to go home and leave you alone. So, that's what I did."

I let go of her face and stormed out of there. My jaws tightened with every step I took to get back to my car. How the hell Berlin tell her to stay away from me? He had no right making a life-altering decision for me. Now, I see how A'Karri felt when we made decisions for her. I'm a grown ass man if I choose to be with Sanaa, then that's my fucking business. He had no business running her away from me like that and now he had to fucking answer to me.

BERLIN

I stabbed the knife into the key then dabbed my finger in it and brushed it against my gums. My gums immediately went numb letting me know it was some pure, good shit. I nodded my head and placed the key back into the cereal box and stepped back, waiting for my men to unload the truck.

It didn't matter that I always got my product from the same guy and he's never given me a reason to think he'd fuck me over. I always tried my shit out to make sure it was good before I even thought about distributing the shit.

I stood there watching them as they unloaded every single cardboard box that had different brands of cereal boxes inside them. This was one of the biggest shipments I've received in a while. After Soul had gotten shot, I kind of stepped away from the dope game for a while and focused more on our legit side of the family hustle just so I wouldn't be working as much and could be by his side most of the time. Eventually, he got sick and tired of me and sent me on my way.

A month ago, when I came back to the home front to make sure everything was running smoothly, we were low as fuck on product. I had to put in a special order just to get us back to where we were. If the FEDs were to get a whiff of that truck, with how much product was in there and how much it was worth, I'm sure we would have ended up doing at least four life sentences. If Soul was here to see the shit I was doing, he'd say I was fucking crazy and wouldn't be able to pull this shit—

"Berlin!" his voice barked and before I could even turn around, he grabbed my body and shoved me up against the wall. I felt the cold steel of his gun pressing underneath my chin. This nigga really lost his got damn mind coming in here manhandling me like that and shit.

My eyes roamed around at my men and all of them were still tending to their businesses like nothing was going on. They all knew better than to get in our business so it was best they just ignored us.

"The hell is your problem?"

"Why the fuck did you tell Sanaa to stay away from me?" His nostrils flared. I should have known he was going to find out sooner or later. She hadn't been around in months and quite frankly, I thought he had forgotten all about her ass. Guess he went checking for her if he was ready to send a bullet through my chin.

"I did it to fucking protect you. She was going to be nothing but the downfall of you. She tried to kill your ass, I'm sure you would have done the same. Now, can you get that got damn gun out of my face?"

At least I thought he would have done the same thing when it came to me. I would have understood why he told her to stay the hell away but I guess he was so fucking in love with her ass that he was blinded.

"That wasn't your fucking place. If I didn't want to see Sanaa, then I could have told her that on my own. I don't need you doing shit for me." He shoved me harder into the hall before letting me go.

"You're always looking out for everyone else, thought it was time someone looked out for you for a change."

"I thought she was fucking mad at me. But you pushed her away from me."

Soul was really acting like a bitch over Sanaa when he should have been the one angry with her. How could he still want to be with someone who tried to kill him over something he didn't do in the first place and that happened months before he even knew she existed? If Naomi would have pulled some shit like that on me, the both of us would have been lying there bleeding to death until someone found us. She knew not to play with me.

"Damn, I'm sorry just thought I was helping. You don't have to come all up in here, waving your gun in my fucking face like you going to fucking shoot me or some shit."

"What you need to do is stay the hell out my business or the next time I will *shoot* you." I didn't think he would get that serious about her to stand there in my face and threaten me over her. Soul was turning into a completely different person before my eyes and I wasn't sure how to feel about the shit.

"You're the only person I have left in this world, Soul. I can't let anything happen to you, so if that meant I had to run Sanaa off to protect you, then I did it. And you know what, I'm not even fucking sorry about the shit. You can be mad all you fucking want to but I did what I had to do." I was not about to apologize to this nigga for trying to watch out for him. It's what family does and who was to say that Sanaa wasn't going to go up to the hospital room and finish the fucking job? If it wasn't for me, then he probably wouldn't be alive today. If anything, he should have been thanking me but he'd never do that.

"Stay out my fucking business, Berlin," he warned then headed for the door.

Boom!

It slammed behind him when he shut it. I know that he might be angry now, but he'd get over the shit in due time. Right now, I had bigger things to worry about other than Soul's fucking attitude. I had almost an entire room of product that I had to get out there on the streets and quick to make up for lost time.

"What the fuck y'all standing around for? Get a move on your asses!" I barked, scrubbed my hand down my face, then headed for my office.

SOFIA ROMANO

When I found out about Soul getting shot, I wasted no time to get back to St. Louis to check on him. I had left after A'Karri's funeral knowing that he was probably still angry at me for getting into it with Sanaa. Just thinking of that bitch's name angered me to the core. She must didn't give a damn about shooting his ass since she's been completely out the picture for the last few months. I can't say that I wasn't loving it, because I definitely was. Doesn't really matter how she got out of our lives but it was good she did.

I nurtured Soul back to health and it was amazing being able to be around him basically 24/7. It had me feeling some type of way, knowing that Sanaa was the reason why he even allowed me to in the first place. I had been working so hard to get Soul to the place I wanted him at yet she came in and he just up and changed all for her. It was nice not having to argue with him about spending the night over his place. It took some getting used to though, but he finally came around.

Now that he's feeling better, I thought it was a good time to talk to him about *us*. I had been wanting to do that forever but couldn't really find the right time. The entire time he was gone, I found myself walking around the house talking to myself, trying to get my words together about what I wanted to say to him. Unbeknownst to him, I was already telling everyone we were back together. I just needed for him to get on the same page. I hope he didn't think I was taking care of him for nothing. I was trying to work my way back into his heart where I belonged.

Hearing the garage door let up, I instantly got nervous. My palms began sweating so I wiped them on my jeans but that didn't really seem to help my case. It was like they had been drenched in water or something. That's how bad I was sweating.

I nibbled on my thumbnail anxiously waiting for him to grace me with his presence. When the door pulled open, I damn near dashed over to it. "Hey Soul!" I grinned, not even being able to hide the excitement that was written all over my face. I was ready to have this talk with him. Quite frankly, it was long overdue.

"Hey Sofia." He sighed deeply and rubbed his hand down his face. I knew something had to be bothering him. I followed him into the kitchen like a lost puppy and watched as he grabbed a bottle of water out the fridge and turned it up.

"What's wrong with you?"

"Nothing, I'm good."

"You sure?" He may have been saying he was good but his twisted facial expression was saying otherwise.

"Yeah." He went to brush past me but I grabbed him by the wrist stopping him.

"I wanted to talk to you about something if you don't mind." My face held a half-smirk just to see what he was going to say.

"What is it Sofia?"

"Weelllllll," I pulled him back to the living room and sat him down on the sectional. "I thought this would have been a good time to talk to you about us."

"What you mean about us?" His forehead wrinkled as he gazed at me.

"Well, you know... us."

"There's really no us, Sofia."

"Yes, it is. About us getting back together." His lips parted but I pressed my index finger against them to stop him from speaking. "Before you say anything, I just wanted to say that I know things have been hard lately that's why I've been trying to give you your time and space to sort through them. I figured that you wouldn't mind getting back with me since we've been together a lot lately over these last five months. I've been taking care of you in more ways than you can count."

"Wait, wait." He rose from the couch and took a couple of steps away from me. "I'm sorry you got that impression Sofia, but I've never said anything about us getting back together. Sure, I liked having you around and I'm truly grateful that you were there for me when I needed you but you need to pump your brakes for a minute."

My mouth fell agape. I really wasn't expecting him to say anything like that. Actually, I thought the both of us were on the same page for a change.

"Close your mouth, Sofia." He shook his head and headed for the stairs, so I jumped up and went behind him.

"So, what you trying to say? All this I've been doing was for nothing?"

"No, that's not what I'm saying at all."

"Well, what are you saying?" I asked him, grabbing him by the forearm, stopping him since he was walking so fast, I could barely keep up. He gazed back at me with those low dark eyes of his. The ones that always caused me to melt whenever I was near him. Yeah, those.

"I'm not trying to get back with you right now. I have other things to figure out at the moment." His response triggered something in me. Something I should have known was going to come soon or later.

That bitch!

He went and saw that ho. I know he did.

So, I asked, "Soul, where did you go today?" My brow rose damn near touching my hairline. Before he left, he told me that he was going to check on Berlin to see how everything had been going. It was something he'd been doing at least once a week. I was sure Berlin was tired of his older brother hovering over him like he was a child. But now I think about it, he probably wasn't even going there at all. It made me actually question his whereabouts.

"I went to see Sanaa."

"You did what!" I shouted loud enough that his neighbors could hear me and they were miles away.

"You heard me. Did I stutter?"

He snatched his forearm away from me and went into the bedroom. I stood in the hallway for a moment trying to process the shit he'd just told me.

"Is that where you've been going every time you've told me you were going to check on Berlin?" I stormed into the bedroom behind him.

"Sofia don't start that shit."

"Answer my fucking question!"

"You're going to tone your voice down in my presence—"

"Or else what?" I was fucking livid and he was going to know exactly how I felt. I had been busting my ass taking care of this nigga and now it was like history was repeating itself. She was going to come right back in and swoop him up the same as before. Well, this time, I wasn't having that shit. I wasn't going anywhere without a fucking fight and if I had to go out kicking and screaming then so fucking be it.

"Know what? I'm not about to do this with you right now. I'm tired and I just want to take a nap. My day has been exhausting." He roughly gripped me by the forearm and pulled me out the bedroom and down the stairs to the front door. He snatched the door open and tossed me on the other side of it. "Come back when you calmed your fucking nerves."

Boom!

The slam of the door caused me to jerk. I was so terrified to even knock on the muhfucka to let him know I didn't have my keys nor my purse so I just sat down on the steps and tried to give him enough time to calm down.

NAOMI

My wedding day was slowly approaching so I had begun making arrangements for it. I wasn't sure how Sanaa would have felt so I left her out the loop about a lot of things lately. I know Soul proposed to her the night she shot him and I didn't want her to feel a certain type of way bringing my excitement to her door, so most of my planning I've been doing alone. It wasn't something I've wanted to do, but it was what I needed to.

I've always seen my wedding planning going as doing it with my mother and best friend. My mother has been helping me here and there for the most part but the person I craved to be near me, I had to keep at a distance for the time being to spare her feelings. I know it's crazy how it's my day but I'm thinking of everyone else and their feelings. Sanaa would have told me that I deserve to be a little selfish for once and honestly, I really do but that's just not the way my heart was set up.

I was getting ready to head out the door to take a look at a couple of venues. I had appointments set up and couldn't be late or else someone else might swoop in and steal the locations from underneath me. For the life of me, I couldn't find my keys anywhere and it was becoming frustrating as fuck. I grabbed my phone and checked the time. If I didn't get out of there and soon, then I'd miss my first appointment.

I dialed Berlin's number to see if he had seen my keys. "What's up, bae?"

"Babe, have you seen my keys? I can't seem to find them anywhere." I sighed into the phone, brushing my curly hair back out my face, then sat down on the coffee table I'd just bent down looking underneath. I felt exhausted and I had only been looking for the keys for a good five minutes. Why this got damn baby had me feeling like I just run a 20k marathon?

"Why are you breathing so damn hard? Sound like you been fucking."

"Because I'm fucking tired! Now, have you seen my keys or not?"

"You and them hormones, I swear. No, bae, I haven't seen your keys. Slow down for a sec and take your time looking for them. You're probably overlooking them knowing you."

Knock! Knock!

The knock at the front door startled me a little bit. I wasn't expecting anyone. "Yeah, okay, I have to go." I ended the call and tossed the phone onto the couch then got up. My hand immediately went to my lower back. It was killing me and Berlin needed to get home so he could rub it for me.

When I pulled the door open, I was greeted by Sanaa's wide, bright smile and even bigger belly. "Look like that baby is weighing you down," she joked then brushed past me into the house.

"Swear you don't even know the half. I'm actually glad that you're here."

"Why what's wrong?" Both of her brows rose as she stared at me.

"I actually need a ride somewhere right quick. I can't find my keys and I don't want to be late."

"You know I got you, girl. But, if you can't find your keys, how are you going to get back in?"

"Berlin has a key. I'll get back in." I grabbed my phone off the couch and purse off the countertop. "Come on, let's go." I made sure to lock the bottom lock before pulling the door closed.

"Where you heading to anyway?" Sanaa asked me when I climbed into the car alongside her.

"Don't get mad at me but I was actually going to look at some venues for the wedding."

"Why would I get mad?" Her brows furrowed and she started the car.

I fidgeted with my fingers before saying, "Because I've been planning without you."

"Naomi!" she shrieked.

"I know, I'm sorry but I didn't think you would be up to it with what you've been going through lately."

"Don't ever think that. I'll always be here for you and excited no matter what I'm going through. You're my best friend. So, where we going?"

"My first stop is Lumen Private Event Space on Locust Street," I answered getting comfortable in the seat.

Honestly, I was anxious and nervous at the same time to get married to Berlin. I couldn't help but keep thinking about my wedding day and praying that everything goes according to plan. So far, being with him, I've been in for a wild ride and I'm sure that wouldn't stop once we said I do.

It didn't take us long to make it to the venue. Samantha was waiting inside for me. She showed me around the place and I could already envision how I wanted everything set up. I was sold and hadn't even looked at any more venues. This was it for me. I didn't need to hear the speech she was trying to pitch to get me to settle on the place. In my mind, I already had made my decision. I'm not sure how Berlin would feel about the space. He gave me free reign to do whatever I wanted at his expense. Said long as I was happy it didn't matter if we got married on the corner in front of a convenient store. He was good. That's what I loved about him.

"I'll take it!"

"But you haven't seen everything yet."

"Doesn't matter. My heart is set on this place so it's what I want. What do I need to sign?" My eyes lit up as I stared at her.

As I waited on Samantha to get the paperwork in order and make sure that my date was available, I went back to the front of the building and found Sanaa sitting down staring into space. I could tell something was wrong with her and kind of had a feeling that I already knew what it was.

"You want to talk about it?" I asked her, taking a seat in the chair beside her.

"It's just I see how happy you are planning your wedding and it makes me sad knowing that I'm supposed to be getting married to Soul but I just had to hold on to that damn anger and shoot him. I don't know if I'll ever have that now." She sighed deeply then her gaze met mine. I could feel my friend's pain. "I miss him so much and don't know what to do."

Tears slipped from the corners of her eyes. I reached out and wiped them away. "Babes, if you miss him then go get your man back. That's the best advice I can give you. If he loves you, then I'm sure that he can look past all the bullshit and make things work. Stop beating yourself up about the past and try to focus on your future. The longer you dwell on the past, the more miserable you'll be."

"Okay, Ms. Copeland, I just need for you to sign right here." Samantha reappeared with a clipboard in her hand.

"Just think about it," I told Sanaa as I rose from the chair beside her. I just hope for her sake and his too, that they fix things. All I ever wanted was for her to be happy. She deserved the shit and should make the best out of her second chance with him on this earth. God spared his life for a reason, they both just had to figure that out.

SANAA

I was trying to take heed of the advice Naomi had given me the other day but I didn't know if the both of us were capable of moving on from our past. There was just so much that had transpired there that was making things so difficult for me. I wanted to be with Soul. Everything in me desired to be with that man but I wasn't certain if things were really going to work out between us.

I hadn't seen him since that day he showed up at the salon a couple days ago and I told him what Berlin said. He left so quickly before anything else could be said. I knew he was angry from his facial expression but I at least thought he would have come back or something. Maybe Berlin had talked some sense into him about not being with me. Who knows? I couldn't really too much worry about all that at the moment. The only thing I had the time to stress over was this baby growing inside me.

With every day that passed, I'm closer to pushing this baby out and becoming a mother. I'm not sure how things were going to work once the baby got here. I knew nothing about being a mother and I had to be a single one at that but I damn sure was going to give that baby my best. It wasn't going to have to worry about anything once it came into this world. Not even the fact it was fatherless. I was going to be mother and father to my child. Women do it all the time so I'm sure I'd be able to.

This morning I had a doctor's appointment and didn't really feel like going alone so I went over to Naomi's apartment to see if she wanted to tag along with me. I stood out in the hallway rubbing on my belly waiting for her to come to the door.

When Naomi pulled the door open, she looked completely like shit. I was starting to believe that she was having a worse pregnancy than I was. Her hair was all over her head. Her eyes were low and I could have sworn I was staring at puke on the corner of her mouth. The clothes she wore were baggy as fuck so they had to have been Berlin's. She definitely wasn't wearing pregnancy well at all.

"You feeling alright?" I questioned her. Soon as her mouth parted, her hand went up to it and she waddled toward the bathroom. I shut the door behind me and followed closely behind her. "Take that as a no."

She got down on her knees in front of the toilet and began vomiting. I grabbed her curly hair, pulling it back out her face so she wouldn't get puke in it. I rubbed her lower back in a circular motion as she threw up what seemed like her insides. When she pulled back from the toilet and I saw all the throw up in there, I couldn't help but vomit myself.

I pulled myself up off the floor and rinsed my mouth out then handed her a wet rag so she could clean her face. "I need to get the hell out of here before you have me sick as fuck like you." I couldn't be around people when they were puking, it only made me join in with them.

"I'm sorry," she said, sitting with her back resting against the bathtub.

"I was going to ask you if you wanted to go to the doctor with me but I think I'll pass on that one."

"You sure? Because I'll go if you really want me to." Naomi hasn't missed a doctor's appointment with me since she found out I was pregnant and I knew she was going to feel bad, knowing she wasn't going to be able to make it to this one. No way I was taking her out the house behind me vomiting like that. I'll pass on that one. I wasn't about to be cleaning no throw up out my car and puking all over myself in the process.

"Nope, I think you're good exactly where you're at." I eased toward the door with my hand up in the air, palm facing her. "Just stay where you're at. You know, just in case you have to throw up again. Call me if you need me." I rushed toward the front door and before I could even get my hand on the doorknob, I heard her insides coming up through her mouth. "Love you girl!"

* * *

I ended up going to the doctor alone. It felt weird every time I came to the place looking around the waiting area. I would see all the women there with their men and baby daddies but not once was mine even able to step foot through the door thanks to Soul. That was someone else who had been taken away from me by the hands of that man. And the crazy thing about it, I still loved him more than anything in this world.

I exhaled, gazing around the room. I constantly had to tell myself that everything was going to be all right and I'd be able to handle this all on my own. Daily, it became even harder to convince myself of that lie. I wanted someone to help me. I wanted my baby's father to be present. I wanted the small little family and to get married like Naomi and live happily ever after. Unbeknownst to her, I envied her life at the moment. She had every damn thing I craved. But I'd always be happy for my girl no matter what. No matter how miserable I was inside.

"Sanaa Love!" the nurse called out and I rose to my feet. I followed her to the back and she put me up into a room. "How are you feeling today, Sanaa?" she queried with a wide smile on her face.

"I've been better."

"Don't tell me that little angel has been giving you trouble."

"No, she's been perfect." I couldn't help but smile. I still remembered the day I found out I was having a girl. My glow was radiant and all I could feel was excitement. I was six months pregnant and had yet to figure out what I wanted to name her.

"Climb up on the table and pull your shirt up so we can check on baby girl." I did as I was told.

Knock! Knock!

The door slowly pushed open and Soul's head popped in. "I was just making sure I had the right room." I couldn't believe he was standing before me. I wanted to ask him what he was doing here but then Naomi popped into my mind. She had to have called him feeling bad about me coming to the doctor alone. I was glad he was here though.

"You must be daddy?" Amanda asked with a smile.

I was about to tell her no but he beat me to the punch. "Yeah, sorry I haven't been here but I'm here now." My eyes glistened as I stared at him. How could I keep being angry at this man?

SOUL

When Naomi called and told me about Sanaa's doctor's appointment today, I wasted no time getting there to be with her. I don't know why she didn't call me herself and let me know. Guess maybe because I hadn't really been there like I was supposed to be in the first place. Like I told her, I'm here now and she doesn't have to worry about going through this alone anymore.

When I stepped through the door and saw her lying on that table with her belly out it's like I got butterflies in my stomach. Time stopped and she and her belly was the only thing I saw, along with the tears, she was trying her best to blink back. I thought she wasn't going to want me there until her eyes landed on me and they told me she was just as happy as I was about me being there.

"Just in time, daddy. We were just about to listen to your baby girl's heartbeat," the nurse spoke, bringing me back from my thoughts.

"Baby girl?"

"Yeah, it's a girl," Sanaa answered and turned her face to the screen. I watched as the nurse squeezed some gel onto her stomach. My eyes darted over to the screen as well and suddenly my heart began pounding in my chest hearing the baby's heartbeat. It was strong and loud.

Moisture filled my eyes as I watched the baby balled up on the screen. I moved closer to Sanaa and before I knew it, I felt her hand grip mine. It was unexpected but I liked it so I squeezed it just to give her clarification that I meant she wasn't going to do this alone. I didn't give a damn if the baby was Quentin's. I was going to love her like she came from my nut sack and not his.

"I'll print out the copies of the ultrasound for you two," the nurse said and got up from her seat, leaving out of the room. Sanaa wiped the gel from her stomach and I helped her sit up so she could pull her shirt back down.

"Can't believe you showed up. Naomi must have called you?"

"Yeah, did you really think I was going to let you come here by yourself? If you would have called and let me know about your appointment, I would have come by and picked you up."

"I just didn't want to be a burden." Her eyes shifted away from me and stared down at her dark pink toes in her gold sandals.

Hooking her chin, I tilted her face back to me. "You could never be a burden to me. Remember that."

When the nurse came back with the pictures, I walked Sanaa out to her car. I didn't want to leave her side so quickly so I asked, "Can I take you out to lunch? Before you say anything, it's just lunch and that's it." I leaned down gazing into her eyes as she sat in her driver's seat. Silence lingered over us for a moment and I actually thought she was going to turn me down if she had to think about it that long.

"I guess it couldn't hurt."

"What do you have a taste for?"

"I don't really have a taste for anything so I guess it doesn't matter."

"Alright, follow me then."

I hopped into my car and took her to the soul food place I had taken her on one of our dates before—Gourmet Soul Restaurant and Catering. I knew it was one of her favorite spots, that's why I took her there.

I wasn't really hungry but I sat across from her at the table and just watched as she ate her food. The only reason why I offered to take her to lunch was only so I could spend more time around her. I missed being in her presence. I missed the way she brushed her hair back behind her ear. The simple wrinkle of her nose. Her soft lips pressing against mine. I had it made up in my mind that I wanted to get her back. I wasn't sure how but I was going to do it.

"Why you keep staring at me like that?"

"Because you're beautiful. Is that a problem?" I noticed her face turn beet red. She didn't have to be ashamed of being gorgeous because she was. The most beautiful woman I've ever laid eyes on before.

"I don't know why you're lying to me. I'm fat as fuck. My nose damn near taking up my whole face. I look like Mrs. Piggy and you're trying to tell me I'm gorgeous. Stop fucking lying to me, Soul." I chuckled at her screwed-up face. She was serious as hell too.

"Sanaa cut that shit out. You are beautiful to me. You always have been and always will be. I don't give a damn if you were wider than this got damn restaurant."

"Yeah, you're saying that now but just wait until I am and can swallow you whole, then you won't be."

"You'll still be gorgeous."

"Yeah, whatever."

She finished up her food and I walked her outside to her car. Just like earlier, I wasn't ready for her to leave but I knew I had to let her go. I didn't want her to think I was getting all clingy and shit. My day was made just by seeing her.

"Guess I'll get going," she said, pulling her car door open but she was kind of hesitant. I could sense she didn't really want to leave but didn't want to stay either. She was confused and had the right to be. "Thanks for the lunch and most of all thanks for being there for me today. I really appreciate it."

"You know it wasn't a problem but you can thank me properly." I grabbed her by the wrist and pulled her body into my frame. It felt like forever since she's been this close to me and I damn sure didn't want to let her go now. She wrapped her arms around my midsection and hugged me as tightly as she could.

"I'll see you around," she said when she pulled back from my embrace.

"See you." I stood there and watched as she climbed into her car and pulled out of the parking lot. "See you very soon."

BERLIN

y mind had completely been all over the place lately. It did something to me losing my parents and sister then almost Soul. I was tired of trying to be strong for everyone all the time. I didn't want to bug Naomi with my problems because she already had a lot of stress on her trying to plan our wedding all the while being six months pregnant.

I knew I wasn't going to be good with that sort of thing that's why I let her just do whatever she wanted and told her to let me know how much I had to spend and what day I needed to be at the altar.

Naomi was in the house not feeling too well. She's been like that for the last couple of days. I tried doing whatever I could for her to make sure she was comfortable but her and those got damn hormones were pissing me the fuck off per usual, so I had to get the hell out of there. I found myself sitting outside of *Phoenix*, this strip club that was downtown. I was debating if I wanted to go inside or not. I knew that if I did, I was probably going to end up sloppy drunk which wasn't going to turn out to be a good thing.

After debating with myself for a while, I finally climbed out of the car and went inside. There weren't that many people in the club like I thought it would have been since it was late as fuck and a Friday at that. I went up to the VIP section and took a seat. One of the bottle girls immediately came up to take my drink order. I couldn't ignore the fact that she was fine as fuck. The only thing I could pay attention to was all that ass in those white boy shorts she wore.

She was built kind of similar to Naomi but had a little more pudge in her stomach than her. She had a bright skin tone without a blemish in sight and her facial features were sort of doll-like. She looked plastic as fuck.

"What can I get for you today, handsome?" She nibbled on her lower lip as her eyes peered into mine. My first thought was, for me to tell her to go and find me the ugliest bottle girl in the club but I just went on and ordered my drink.

"Bring me up a bottle of Louis Xiii." I slumped back on the couch and pulled out a pre-rolled blunt from my front pants pocket and stuck it between my lips. I watched as her ass swayed side to side as she strutted away. Quickly, I shook my head to bring me out the daze I was in. I had a perfectly good woman at home who I loved and was carrying my seed. No need for me to slip back into my old ways now.

She brought the bottle back and I sat there for hours just drinking alone. Strippers came up to my section offering me dances but I wasn't really paying them any mind. I was feeling the effects of the Kush I had been smoking and liquor I been drinking. My mind kept roaming off to the bottle chick. I knew it wasn't supposed to but I couldn't help myself at the moment. She came back into my section to make sure I didn't need anything else.

"You good?" she asked me with a wide smile on her face, displaying her perfectly shaped pearly whites.

"I'd be better if you gave me a little of your time." I shot her a half-smirk.

"Nigga, you're just drunk that's all." She laughed trying to play it off like she didn't want to get with a nigga like me. I hadn't come across any chick that I wasn't able to pull if I put in the effort for it.

I gripped her by the wrist pulling her into my lap. "That may be true but still..." I brushed her wavy brunt orange hair back out her face and stared her into the eyes. "So, what are you going to do? You going to show me what that muhfuckin' mouth do or nah?"

She brushed the tip of her tongue across her upper lip and I knew I had her exactly where I wanted her. "I don't go on break for another hour or so."

"Who gives a fuck?" I lifted from my seat and she dropped straight to her feet. "If you not scared, I'm parked right out front in the Ferrari." I headed straight for the exit knowing that she was going to be right on my heels. I needed to get some steam off by busting a quick nut. Lately, Naomi had been acting stingy as fuck with the pussy and I was never the type to take the shit even if she was my girl.

Soon as I pulled the door open to climb into the car, I heard her voice behind me. "Hey, wait up!" I directed my attention in her direction and she was jogging across the parking lot. "I—" I quickly cut her off before she could even get a word off by grabbing her by the wrist and pushing her body up against the side of the car. My dick was on brick and I needed to empty that shit before it exploded in my boxers. I had to be faded if I was willing to do that shit right there in the parking lot of the strip club and there was no telling who could see me.

"Ungh!" she whimpered when I found her entrance and shoved my way inside her. Her shit was so tight that it was gripping the hell out of my dick.

I held on to her waist and roughly pumped in and out of her. The entire car rocked with every stroke I gave her. I gripped her by the hair and snatched her head back.

"You tell anyone about this and I'll kill you," I warned, meaning every word of it. I couldn't allow Naomi to find out I had cheated on her. It would crush her and

I couldn't hurt her. Not right now. Especially when we were so close to getting married and her having my baby boy. Nothing could get in the way of that shit.

"I won't tell," she moaned and shut her eyes. She was enjoying every moment of this dick and she better had because she'd never taste this shit again.

I felt myself nearing my peak and I was sure she was too since her pussy muscles were beginning to contract. I let her hair go and reached around roughly rubbing her clit to intensify her orgasm.

"Fucccckkkk!" she cried out. She bounced back harder on my dick. Her pussy was dripping wet so much so that I felt her juices wetting up my boxers. I pinned her up harder against the car and pounded the hell out of that pussy until I released my seeds.

I pulled my dick out and stuffed it back down into my pants. "I'm not playing with your ass. You better not tell a soul about what happened here." I shoved her away from my car and climbed into the driver seat and sped out of there.

NAOMI

I tossed and turned in the bed, trying my best to get comfortable so I could sleep. I knew that sleep was never going to find me especially since Berlin wasn't in bed alongside me. I reached over grabbing my phone off the nightstand. I saw it was going on 3:00 in the morning and he had yet to come in the door. I knew damn well he wasn't out working this late. Berlin knew that ever since I became pregnant, I wasn't able to sleep without him lying next to me. That's the reason why I had been staying over his place and abandoned my own.

I called his phone repeatedly to see if he would pick up so I could see where he was. The only thing I was getting was the voicemail which frightened me. *What if something had happened to him that I wasn't aware of?* Crazy thoughts began running through my mind. It honestly had me wondering if I was really ready for this lifestyle like I thought I was.

"Answer the fucking phone, Berlin," I mumbled, pressing dial on his number for what seemed like the millionth time. I'm not sure how I would feel if something was to happen to him. I needed him in my life. I can't raise a baby all on my own. Shit, I don't even think that Sanaa can as much as she tried to make it seem like she could. That's why I tried my hardest to push her and Soul back together. "Lord, please don't let anything be wrong with him," I prayed as I tossed the covers back and climbed out of bed.

I went into the bathroom to empty out my bladder. This darn child of mine was always sitting on my shit causing me to continually have to use the bathroom. I couldn't wait until I pushed his little ass out.

When I came out of the bathroom, it sounded like I heard the front door shut so I headed for the living room. Soon as I bent the corner, I saw Berlin stumbling and bumping into almost everything he encountered.

"Are you drunk?" I went over to him to sniff him but he held his hand out stopping me in my tracks. I didn't even have to go any further to smell the liquor radiating off his skin. He reeked and needed to do something about that shit ASAP before he had me bent over the toilet vomiting all over again. I finally had that shit under control and wasn't trying to go back down that road. Not tonight.

"I only had a few drinks that's all."

"Smells like more than a few to me." I mumbled, scrunching up my nose. "The way you're stumbling, I'm surprised you even made it home." I was about to help him to the bedroom then I realized what time it was and he was just now coming in. My ears became hot as my body's temperature rose. "You've been out drinking while I was sitting in here worried sick about you!" I shoved him in the chest and he stumbled back falling into the side of the sectional. "I've called you I don't know how many fucking times and you couldn't pick up the phone not once?" I mushed him in the center of his forehead and he whacked my hand away.

"Keep your fucking hands to yourself, Naomi."

"Know what? I'm not even about to deal with this shit with you. I'm going to my place." My feet tapped against the hardwood floors as I made my way down the hallway to his bedroom. I don't give a damn if he was drunk, he still should have picked up the fucking phone and let me know he was all right. I was sitting in here thinking that something terrible had happened to him. He was skyrocketing my pressure only because he wanted to go out and have a little drink... no, the entire fucking bar from the way he smelt.

"Naomi, you're not going anywhere, it's late."

"The hell I'm not." I yanked the dresser drawer open and snatched out a pair of tights and a t-shirt. I was not about to stay in here with his drunk ass tonight.

"I said you're not going anywhere." He roughly gripped me by the forearm and spun me around to face him. He glared at me with his dark eyes. I saw something in them that I've never seen before. They were emotionless. And I couldn't lie and say they weren't scaring me.

Tears filled my eyes as they gazed down at the tight grip he had on my arm. "Can you let my arm go? You're hurting me."

"Your ass ain't going nowhere." He snatched the clothes from me with his free hand and tossed them to the floor. "Get your ass in the bed. I'm about to take a shower." He slung me toward the bed and I barely made it. I sat there with my mouth wide open. I couldn't believe he was handling me like that. I've never seen him act this way before and it was only pissing me off more.

I jolted from the bed and slapped the shit out of him.

Smack!

"Don't ever fucking handle—" Before I could even finish my sentence, I was met with the back of Berlin's heavy hand.

Smack!

Tears poured down my cheeks. I could taste the blood forming in my mouth. This nigga really just hit me. His posture stiffened as he gazed back at me.

"Damn, I'm sorry Naomi." He slowly stepped toward me and I backed away from him with every step he took. I didn't want to be near him. Not if he was going to put his hands on me again. That alone told me I needed to get out of there before things got worse.

I stared back at the man that I didn't even recognize as my own anymore. "I'm sorry, babe. Don't look at me like that."

"I don't even know who you are anymore." I ran as fast as I possibly could with me being pregnant and all. I scooped my keys off the counter in the kitchen and kept trekking toward the front door.

"Naomi!" Berlin's voice roared in the distance but I wasn't about to stop running. I didn't even bother to use the elevator just pushed the exit door open that led to the stairs. I had to get out of there as quickly as possible. My lungs felt empty. My heart ached. I needed air or I felt like I was going to collapse.

I didn't even stop to breath until I made it outside and climbed into my car. Pains shot through my body but I just ignored them. I wanted to take a breather just to cry but I knew if I sat there too much longer, he would have caught up to me. I started the car and pulled out of the parking deck heading straight for Sanaa's house. I couldn't go to my own because that would have been the first place he'd go looking for me. At least I knew when I made it to Sanaa's and he was to show up, she wouldn't allow him past the front door. I'd be safe for a while, but the question was... how long?

I found myself standing on the outside of Sanaa's front door with nothing but tears in my eyes. They were coming down nonstop that I couldn't even make out the gold numbers on her door. The door pulled open and Sanaa stood there with a bewildered expression on her face. She didn't speak any words, just grabbed me by the wrist and pulled me into a hug.

"I don't know what happened, and you don't have to tell me if you don't want to. You're more than welcome to stay here for as long as you need."

"Thank you," was all I was able to get out because my heart ached too much.

SOFIA

Soul was acting all funny and shit toward me and it was only Sanaa's fault. She should have just stayed her ass where she was. My life was going just fine until she popped her ass out the blue on me all over again. I tried to give him some time to come back to his senses but I knew he wasn't going to be able to do that with her in the way.

I found myself sitting outside of the shop in my car debating on what I was going to do. I thought about not going in there at all until I saw her waddle across the salon. My cheeks immediately flared up. There was no way I could be able to leave there now without going inside. I just had to know if the baby she was carrying inside her belonged to Soul. My heart wouldn't allow me to walk away from the situation.

How come I had to love that man so fucking much?

Love drove you to do crazy things. The unthinkable. Unimaginable. If she was indeed carrying his baby then it was going to be harder than I thought to get her away from him. Once she walked the last customer out. I climbed out of my car with my blade in my hand and went over to hers. I kneeled down beside every single tire and jammed my knife into it.

"Hmph, that bitch ain't going nowhere tonight." I mumbled, snatching the knife out the last tire. "Not if I can help it."

I slid my blade into my purse then went inside the shop toward the back where her office was located. I remembered exactly where it was from when A'Karri and I took our anger out on the place. I could have just done the same thing again but I knew Soul would only play Captain Save A Ho again and get everything replaced.

I stopped in the doorway and just stared at her for a moment not even making a peep. Something on that phone must have really had her attention if she didn't hear me come in or notice me standing there. I could have easily done anything to her and she wouldn't even know who done it. Not even see it coming.

"Does it belong to Soul?" I asked her and she jumped grabbing her chest. Unlucky for me, she didn't actually have a heart attack.

"What are you doing here, Sofia?"

"I came to have a little talk with you." I eased on into the office and glanced around at the décor. It was cute and all but not my taste. From the expensive taste of it, I could tell Soul was the one who decorated in here. "You know, woman to woman." I planted both of my hands face down on the desk and gazed straight into her eyes. I wasn't worried about her doing anything crazy or trying to whoop my ass like she did at the club that night. She caught me off guard and I'm sure if I had known it was coming then I would have handled the situation a little better.

"We don't have anything to talk about, so you can just get your ass out of my shop!" She went to rise up from her seat, so I took my blade from my purse and twirled it on the desk.

"See, that's where you're wrong. We have plenty to talk about and you're going to listen." Her eyes darted straight to the blade and they grew wide as saucers.

"What the hell do you want, Sofia?"

"I told you, I just want to talk woman to woman."

"About what?" she asked, relaxing back in her chair and placing both of her hands onto her belly.

"That for starters." I pointed at her stomach so she would know what I was talking about. "Does it belong to Soul?"

"No, I don't know why you're sweating me and Soul in the first place. There's nothing going on between us."

"You're lying. He told me about his little visit with you the other day. I can tell he wants to be with you and I can't understand for the life of me why when you fucking shot him! You wanted to take his fucking life! I give him my all and he tosses to me to the side every fucking time." I picked up the knife and paced back and forth in front of her desk. I just couldn't wrap my mind around this shit. He'd rather be with someone who tried to kill him than someone who loved the shit out of him.

"Sofia, I just think that you're overreacting. Soul doesn't want me not after what I've done." Her eyes stayed trained on the knife like I was going to use it on her. I may have been a little crazy but I wasn't that crazy. I loved my freedom way too much for that.

"No, I'm not." Tears came to my eyes and flowed quickly. If I wanted to stop them, it was too late. She already spotted them on my face. Her eyes softened and it was almost like she felt sorry for me. Maybe it was just the hormones getting to her. I rushed over to the desk and locked eyes with her. "Your ass is going to stay away from Soul or else."

Sanaa slowly rose from her chair. I could tell she was no longer worried about the little blade that was resting in my hand. She took my little remark as a threat.

"First of all, don't bring your ass in my shit and tell me what the hell to do. I don't know who the hell you think you are walking up in here with a knife and shit thinking that you're going to scare me into my place. Sofia, I swear to God you're lucky as shit that I'm carrying my baby because if I wasn't you would have been got these hands like you did the last time. I'd drag your ass all up and down this fucking office. Don't play with me." Her chest heaved as she glared at me. She looked like she was almost out of breath.

"Bitch, do you really think I'm worried about all that shit? The only reason you whooped my ass that day was only because you caught me off guard. Don't take your little sneak jumping as a win because I could whoop your ass with my eyes closed and one hand tied behind my back. Want to find out? Keep fucking with Soul." I headed for her office door so I could leave. I've said what I needed to say and was leaving it at that.

"Ho just wait until I drop this fucking load! Swear to God I'm going to hunt your ass down and beat the shit out of you!" she shouted behind me but I kept on walking. She kept running her fat ass behind Soul and she was going to be the one with her ass beat. I don't give a damn about her being pregnant. Especially now that I know the baby didn't belong to Soul. She and that bastard were a nonfactor.

SANAA

I couldn't believe that bitch just brought her little ugly ass into my shop and tried to threaten me over Soul. He and I weren't even on greatest of terms at the moment and she was trying to come at my throat for the shit. Yeah, I've seen him a few times over the last few days but that was just about it.

I swear she doesn't know how lucky she is that I'm pregnant or I really would have whooped her ass for the little stunt she just tried to pull. I wasn't about to let her scare me away from Soul. If I wanted to be with him then I would be. But at the moment, I wasn't certain how we were going to turn out. We had a lot of things to work on before we even uttered the word relationship to one another.

I locked up the shop and hit the key fob on my car. When I stepped down off the curve, I noticed my front tire was flat. My first thought was I caught a flat until I looked and saw the back one along with the other two tires were slashed.

"Sofia!" I shouted and stomped my foot as I glanced around the parking lot to see if I could spot her car. Ain't nobody did this bullshit but her. Clearly, she was all in her feelings over a man that didn't even belong to her.

I pulled my phone out and dialed Naomi's number to see if she could come and pick me up. I was too tired to deal with this car tonight so I'd just get it towed to a shop or something in the morning. The only thing I wanted to do at the moment was grab me something to eat and go home to my comfy bed. Sofia just had to put a wrench in my plans.

Naomi didn't answer the phone and I thought about calling Berlin but I knew that those two weren't on the best of terms right now and didn't want him to end up finding out she was over my house. The last thing I wanted to do was go home to an argument between the two. Going against my better judgment, I dialed the ten numbers I thought I'd never had to dial. Soul. Lucky for me, he picked up on the second ring.

"What's up Sanaa?"

"I'm sorry to bother you but were you busy?"

"No, I was actually about to sit down and eat. Is there something wrong?"

I sighed deeply debating if I actually wanted to tell him the truth. I almost parted my lips to tell a lie then I knew it was only going to make him angry once he found out the truth anyway so I decided to save myself the trouble. Truth it is.

"Uh, I'm kind of stuck at the shop right now and need a way home."

"What do you mean you're stuck?" I heard shuffling noises in his background. Even though all the things we've been through, it felt good knowing I could still count on him.

"Well, Sofia came and paid me a visit. You know how she can get. She was angry thought I was pregnant by you and started threatening me and—"

"Wait, what you mean threatening you?" he quickly interrupted me. A few moments later, I heard a door shut and then the sound of his garage let up.

"I'm not too much worried about her. Sofia isn't anything but lightweight."

"What did she say Sanaa?" I could hear the anger rising in his voice.

"Well, she only told me to leave you alone or else. Normally, I wouldn't take her remark as a threat but with me being pregnant and all—"

"I know," he sighed heavily. "Did she say anything else?"

"Not more so what she said but it's what she did. She flattened all my tires," I huffed and squatted down on the curve with my feet stretched straight out. I don't know why I did that knowing my fat ass wasn't going to be able to get up afterward. Hopefully, I don't have to pee or anything because I'd definitely be stuck down there until he arrived.

"It's fine, I'll handle it." I wanted to tell him that he shouldn't and that I would but I knew it was probably only going to turn into an argument. That was something I was trying my best to avoid.

"You sure because I can really take care of it myself?"

"No, I got you. I'll be there in a few," he said then disconnected the call.

I sat there on the curve playing Words with Friends on my phone certainly getting my ass kicked but it was passing the time. I knew it was going to take him a while to get to me since he was leaving his house. I wasn't really in a rush to get home but my stomach definitely was grumbling. Something needed to be put on it and quick.

Headlights shone directly on me as a car pulled into the parking lot. I shielded my eyes with my hand so I could get a look at who the car belonged to. When I noticed it was Soul, I tried to get up off the ground but it seemed impossible.

"Let me give you a hand," he said, rushing over to my side and grabbing me underneath my arm lifting me up.

"Thanks."

I observed him as he walked around the car taking a look at the damage Sofia had done. I couldn't help but smile at his tensed-up face. He was definitely displeased with her actions.

Every time I saw Soul dressed down, he looked weird to me. This time was no different. From the gray sweats he wore and white plain t-shirt, I could tell he was at home for the night.

"I'm sorry I disturbed you. Maybe I should have called an Uber or something."

"You're good."

"You sure?" I just had to make sure I didn't disrupt any plans of his or anything.

"What I tell you about that, Sanaa?" I shrugged my shoulders at him. "I made arrangements for someone to pick the car up in the morning. You should have everything fixed by that afternoon. Did you lock up?"

"Yeah."

"Come on let me get you home." He opened the passenger's side door for me and stood there waiting for me to climb inside. The scent of his cologne immediately attacked my nostrils as soon as I planted my butt in the seat. It seemed like forever since I was this close to him. My heart thumped in my chest rapidly as I watched him get into the car from my peripheral. "I brought you something." He reached into the back seat and handed me a plastic container.

"What's this?"

"Your dinner." He slung the car in reverse and back up out the parking spot.

"How did you even know I was hungry?" I lifted the corner of the lid and my stomach growled even more at the smell of the food. I was so hungry that I couldn't even wait to get home to eat. I snatched the top all the way off and picked up the fork digging right into the cream mashed potatoes. "Mhm," I moaned, closing my eyes savoring the taste.

"Just a hunch."

SOUL

I kept glancing over at Sanaa every chance I got while she wasn't looking as I zoomed in and out of traffic. I jumped at the opportunity to come and pick her up. It frustrated me when I found out that Sofia had threatened her. The old Sofia I knew wouldn't harm a fly but I couldn't say the same about a woman scorned. They'd go to any lengths to inflict pain upon another person that wronged them. I should have never opened the door and invited her back into my life. No matter how much I may have needed her.

Pulling up in front of her building, I put the car in park. I wasn't sure if I was ready for her to get out and she must have felt the same way because she was kind of hesitant. She closed the empty container and her gaze met mine.

"Thanks again for coming to get me." She smiled displaying those deep dimples I loved. so much. In fact, I loved damn near everything about Sanaa. She made it impossible for me not to fall in love with her.

"Of course, I came to get you. As long as you call, I'll always come, Sanaa," I told her honestly. She went to get out the car but I grabbed her wrist stopping her. Her eyes met mine again and I spoke. "I'm sorry for not telling you the truth about Yonnie's death. I actually thought I was doing a good thing trying to protect my brother. Truth is, I wasn't there when he killed her. I was nowhere near St. Louis when the shit went down. I found out about it when I came back home from a business trip. I'm sorry—"

She placed her index finger up to my lips silencing me. "It's okay, Soul. I forgive you. I know that I've said this before, but I'm really sorry about shooting you. I wasn't thinking with a clear mind. Both of us have done some questionable things. Let's put it behind us and worry about this baby girl for the time being." She grinned and rubbed her belly.

I hesitantly reached out to touch her stomach. "It's okay," she said, grabbing my hand and placing it on her stomach. The baby immediately began kicking like crazy. "Ooh, she's never done that before."

"Does it hurt?"

"I'll be fine. I'm tired though so I'm going to head on inside and take a bath then climb into bed. See you later." I sat there watching her as she climbed out of the car and headed up to her building. From where I was sitting, I could see up to her condo so I sat there until the light came out to ensure she got in safely. When the light popped on, I pulled away from the curve heading to Sofia's house. I was not about to let the night go by without letting her know exactly how I felt about her showing up to Sanaa's and her little threat. I've told Sofia to leave Sanaa alone before and she thought I was playing games with her but this time I was going to have to show her.

Boom! Boom! Boom!

I stood on her front porch with both of my hands balled up into fists. I was ready to knock the living hell out of Sofia for trying me over and over again. If anything was to happen to Sanaa or that baby, I'm not sure what I'd do to her ass. So, her best bet is to stay as far away from them as possible before she ended up dead somewhere.

She swung the door open with a bright smile on her face that quickly disappeared when she noticed the mug on mine. I pushed straight past her into the house and she shut the door.

"What's wrong with you? Thought you would have been happy to see me." She slid her hands up to my chest and I snatched her by the wrists.

"You went up there to Sanaa's shop and flat her tires?"

"I don't know what you're talking about."

"Don't fucking lie to me, Sofia. I'm not in the fucking mood."

She snatched her wrists away from me and flopped down on the couch. "So, what if I did? They're just tires anyway."

"So, that also means you threatened her as well right?"

"You're making a big deal out of nothing. I was being friendly when I went by there but I wasn't playing with her when I told her to leave you alone."

Before I knew it, I had Sofia's neck clutched in my hand. "If you harm any hair on Sanaa's head and I mean one tiny strand, I will kill you." I let her neck go and stepped back away from the couch before I ended up killing her ass right then and there. I saw the tears forming in her eyes as they glistened, gazing up at me.

"All I want is to be with you, Soul."

"I shouldn't have ever started this shit back up with you. I should've just left you where you were."

She got up from the couch and rushed over to me. "No, don't say that." I observed as the tears flooded down her cheeks. "I love you Soul and I know you love me too."

"I love you, but I'm not in love with you. You're tripping because I don't want to be with you and I can't deal with this shit anymore."

"Soul... please." Snot dripped from her nose as she tugged on my arm. I snatched away from her.

"We're done for good this time Sof. I just can't..."

"You don't really mean that."

"Yes, I do. I love Sanaa. I'm in love with her and I'm pretty sure that's where I want to be."

"You're fucking stupid! You want to be with a bitch that fucking shot your dumb ass instead of with one who actually loves you and wouldn't do anything to harm you in any way." It's like her tears automatically shut off like a faucet when I said that. That alone let me know the bitch was fucking crazy.

"You tripping."

"No, you're the one that's tripping! GET THE FUCK OUT OF MY HOUSE!" she screamed pointing her index finger toward the front door.

"I don't give a damn about you being mad as long as you stay your crazy ass the hell away from Sanaa and my baby."

When I said the words, *my baby*, the tears began again. "GET OUT MY HOUSE, SOUL!" I took one last look at her then pulled the front door open and stepped out shutting it behind me. I wasn't playing with Sofia, if she did anything to either one of them, her family was going to be filing a missing report on her ass. She can play with me if she wanted to.

BERLIN

It's been a few days since I last saw Naomi. I knew she was still angry at me for putting my hands on her. Shit, I was angry with my damn self. I never should have allowed myself to get that drunk where things would escalate in that manner. But at the same time, she needed to fully understand that I was dealing with so much stress and loss. The shit was getting to me mentally and pretty soon, I was certain I was going to go crazy if I didn't deal with it.

I had been beating myself up on the inside for not only putting my hands on my babe, but also for cheating on her as well. If I could go back in time, I'd change my route to the strip club altogether. I had been debating if I wanted to tell her the truth or not before she found out from the streets which were only going to make matters worse for me. Since I couldn't fully come to a conclusion, I decided to go and pay Soul a visit. He was older and much wiser than me, so I was certain he probably knew what to do in my situation and give me the best advice.

"Is everything all good with you?" Soul asked me bringing me back from my thoughts. I had completely zoned out on his couch while he was talking to me trying to figure out what I was going to do about my spiraling life. When I looked up at him, he was standing over me with two glasses in his hand. He handed me one and sat down on the other end of the sectional.

"Nah, man I really fucked up big time." I sighed deeply still not knowing if this was going to be fixable. I did two of the worse things a man could ever do to a woman and now I wanted her to forgive me. It was going to be far from easy.

"What did you do? Don't tell me you already destroyed the family business. I knew it was—"

"Nah, it's not that," I quickly cut him off before he began telling me how disappointed he was in me and try to come take back over the business. That was the only thing in my life at this present time I had under control. "I fucked up with Naomi, bruh." I tossed the shot back and scrubbed my hand down my face. "I got drunk the other night and ended up putting my hands on her. Even though it was out of reflex because she hit me first, I still should have been able to control my anger."

"Yeah, you really did fuck up." He took a swig from his drink. "Did she break up with you afterward?"

"I wouldn't really say that she broke up with me but she did leave the condo and I haven't seen or heard from her since."

"You tried calling her?"

I rubbed my hand up and down the back of my neck. "I tried, but she had to have put me on the blocklist because my calls going straight to voicemail. I told her I was sorry before she left and it's like it fell on deaf ears. I went to her apartment but she wasn't there. I honestly don't know what to do right now." Obviously, I didn't if I was sitting on his couch prepared to break down like a little bitch. Who would have known relationships were going to be this complicated?

"Well, if she hadn't officially broken up with you yet, then you might have a chance to get her back. You just have to show her you're sorry not just say it. Actions speak volumes, little brother."

"It might not be as easy as you think it is. See, the same night before I came home, I also fucked a bottle girl in *Phoenix* parking lot."

"Yeah, you're most definitely fucked." I blew air from my lips because he was already telling me something I knew.

"Do you think I should tell her? I don't want her to end up finding out from the streets. That shit will crush my girl, bruh."

"Nigga, that's the type of shit you take to the grave. If you tell her, it's still going to crush her. Just make sure she never find the shit out." I brushed my hand across my waves and relaxed back on the sofa pondering on what I was going to do to show Naomi how sorry I was. There really wasn't much I could do. I didn't want to go out and buy her something then she thought I'm one of those guys who fuck up and thought buying her expensive gifts was going to fix everything. An idea struck me and I jolted from the couch.

"I'll hit your line later." I rushed out the door.

* * *

I popped up at Sanaa's condo with every single piece of food I could think of that Naomi loved. She was pregnant and angry with me so I just knew buying her all her favorite foods would do the trick for me. I stood out in the hallway waiting for someone to come to the door. When it pulled open, I was expecting to see Naomi but Sanaa glared back at me with a scowl on her face. From her facial expression and the knife that was in her hand, I was sure she wanted to kill me.

"I come in peace and baring food." I lifted my hands, showing her the dozen glazed doughnuts in one hand and the Carmine's Steak House bag and

Peacemaker Lobster & Crab bag in the other. Sitting on the floor at my feet was two Walmart bags filled with nothing but all the junk food and sodas she loved. "I just want to see Naomi. Can I... please?"

Sanaa sighed and her chest heaved. She stood there for a moment then shut the door in my face. I should have known that was going to be the reaction I got. As I went to knock on the door again, it pulled open.

"What are you doing here, Berlin?" I felt like shit staring at her gorgeous face and noticing the split on her lip.

"I missed you and look, I brought all your favorite foods."

"I don't want it," she said, folding her arms across her chest.

"Girl, you're crazy. I haven't eaten anything all day. Do you really think I'm about to let this good food go to waste?" Sanaa shoved past her and snatched the Peacemaker Lobster & Crab bag out of my hand and grabbed one of the Walmart bags. She nudged Naomi out the door and shut it behind her.

"I'm really sorry for putting my hands on you. I know I told you that the night I did it but I wanted to show you how sorry I am, bae. All I want is for you to come home and I promise I won't ever put my hands on you again. I miss you like crazy, girl."

I saw the tears forming in her eyes. She turned her head away from me and gazed down the empty hallway. I knew she had to be thinking about the things I said. I just hoped she'd be able to forgive me because if she couldn't then I knew I'd never be able to forgive myself for what I've done.

"Babe say something." I sat the bag and doughnut box down on the floor then closed the short gap between us with one step. I tilted her face back to me by her chin and saw all the tears that were cascading down her cheeks. *Fuck!*

NAOMI

As I gazed into Berlin's eyes, I could tell he was sorry for putting his hands on me. My heart wanted to forgive him but at the same time, my mind didn't want to. I wanted to believe that he'd never put his hands on me again then there was the little voice in the back of my mind that I couldn't shake. *"If he did it once, he'll do it again."* I was having an entire war inside me not knowing what I should do.

The love I had for Berlin was obvious. If I didn't love him then I wouldn't be with him at this moment. I wanted to marry this man. That's the reason I told him yes when he proposed. Had I known he acted out when he got sloppy drunk, then I probably would have run the other way but I was here now and needed to make the best out of our situation. We had a baby that was going to be here soon, so the both of us needed to get our act together.

Was I going to go flying back into his arms after the first apology or because he brought me food? No. He needed to know that it wasn't okay what he did and the shit couldn't happen again.

Our time apart, it got me to thinking about things. My mind was all over the place and I had questions I needed to get off my chest before I drove myself mad. Did I want to actually hear the answers to those questions? No, but I was going to ask them anyway. I'd rather know the truth than to be blindsided by a lie.

"Babe," he spoke and I pulled myself from my daze. "Are you going to come home?"

"Did you cheat on me, Berlin?"

"Huh?" he asked but I know damn well he heard me perfectly fine.

"You heard me. Did you cheat on me?"

"No, I didn't cheat on you. Where did you get that bullshit from?" His forehead wrinkled when he asked me that and he took a couple steps back away from me.

"I didn't get it from anywhere. It's just when you came in late and smelling like liquor, it was my first thought."

"Does that mean that you're going to come home now?"

"I can't Berlin, not right now. I need some time to think things over," I tried to explain but he wasn't really feeling that.

"What you mean think things over? Ain't nothing to think over. I love you and you love me. We're meant to be together."

"But not like this." I could feel my eyes watering and I knew I needed to get into the condo. If I didn't go right then, then I might give in and end up going back to his place with him. I couldn't have that right now.

"You breaking up with me?" I saw the tears forming in his eyes. He was hurting but I'm sure it wasn't as bad as me. I was breaking my own heart keeping myself away from him.

"I don't know. I gotta go." I hurriedly pulled the door open and rushed into the condo before I broke down right there in his face. I shut the door and leaned my frame against it.

"Aw, I take it that you didn't forgive him." Sanaa dropped her fork and got up from the table and came over to me. I gently shook my head and finally let the tears flow freely. "I'm sure that everything is going to be alright," she assured me but I wasn't that sure. I didn't know if I'd ever be able to forgive Berlin and it was killing me inside.

"I don't know if I can forgive him after that." This was the first time I've ever had to deal with a boyfriend putting his hands on me. He caught me off guard when he did it and I think that's what bothered me the most. I always knew that he was kind of a hothead, but I didn't expect him to actually hit me. Guess I should have seen it coming that night I tried to break up with him and he punched a hole through the wall. Something should have told me that then. But then, there was a part of me that felt like he would never do anything like that to me. I felt like maybe he would be able to control his anger but I was wrong.

"How could he do me like this?" I sobbed. She held me as best as she could despite both of our bellies trying to get in the way.

"Babe, honestly, I don't know why men do the things they do. I found it best to stop trying to figure them out. The best advice I can give you is that if you really want to be with him then you should try to work things out. It's hard finding a good man especially when you have a child. Berlin may have put his hands on you but at the same time, it was an honest mistake. He's apologized for it and maybe it won't happen again. Who knows? I just want you to be happy so can you do me a favor and just think about it?"

"I'll think about it but I still don't know if I can forgive him."

She stepped back away from me and lifted my head by my chin where I was staring her straight into the eyes. "You have to forgive him sooner or later. You might not forget but it's best you forgive. You have to do it for yourself, Naomi. Protect that peace, sis." She went back over to the kitchen table and closed the container she was just eating out of. "I'm going to head to the shop for a little while. Call me if you need anything and I'll come running." She placed the food into the fridge then kissed me on the cheek before she went out the front door.

I stood there with my feet still planted to the floor not knowing what I was going to do about my relationship. I was lost. Conflicted. Unsure if it was the best thing for me even though in my heart, I knew it was. Berlin loved me like no other has ever besides my parents and Sanaa. I'd be a fool to let all of that go but at the same time, I had to do what was best for me and my baby. And if that meant leaving Berlin alone for good, then I was going to do it with no hesitations.

I dried my tears and wiped the snot from my nose then finally unglued my feet from the floor. I went into Sanaa's bedroom and climbed over into her bed. I needed some time to myself to think about things. Berlin had to respect that and stop trying to force me to forgive him when I wasn't ready. When I wanted to talk to him about our situation, then I'd find him. But for now, he needed to let me be. I pulled the pillow over my head and dozed straight off to sleep.

SANAA
A month later...

Naomi and I's baby shower rolled around. Since we were so close in due dates, we decided to get together and have adjoined baby showers. I was the one who came up with the idea and thought it would have been cool. For the last month, we were planning everything, and it turned out to not only be a struggle but stressful as hell. To say the least, everything turned out perfectly fine when the day arrived.

It took us forever to agree on a color scheme. We had to choose neutral colors since I was having a girl and she was having a boy. Of course, we bumped heads a lot when it came to certain things but we finally agreed on everything.

I stood there staring at myself in my floor-length mirror admiring the teal floor-length gown I had on. When I spotted it in Saks Fifth, I knew I had to have it. My hair was freshly dyed and cut into a bob. I was loving my new hairstyle and baby girl was causing my hair to grow very quickly. I wasn't certain if I was going to keep it or cut it again once I popped her out. But for now, I was loving it.

Knock! Knock!

I grabbed my gold clutch and keys off the dresser and rushed to the front door. With it going on 4:00 p.m. I knew that the only person who could have been on the other side of that door was Naomi. She was meeting me at my house so we could ride to the baby shower together.

I pulled the front door open and a smile graced my face when I was met with Naomi's bright grin. My girl looked beautiful and definitely was glowing in the white flowing knee-length dress she wore.

"You look so pretty. Tear." I wiped the fake tear from my eye and pulled her in for a hug. I held my face out so I wouldn't get any makeup on her dress.

"You look good too, bih!" she beamed, then grabbed me by the hand and made me do a 360.

"I know right." I smiled, then shut the front door locking it.

I climbed into the passenger's seat of Naomi's Audi Q3. I was nervous and kind of excited to go to the baby shower at the same time. It also upset me because I knew that my mother wasn't here to be there. She wouldn't be there in the delivery room when I have my baby and it bothered me deeply. That was always something I wanted my mother for. I thought that she'd be there. Now I just had to deal with it.

I quickly pulled myself from the thought. I told myself I wasn't going to get upset today. This was a joyous occasion and I wasn't going to let anything get me down.

I looked out the window and saw we were pulling up to Randell Gallery where we were having the baby shower. Naomi pulled straight up to the door and valet pulled the doors open for us. She came around the truck and locked arms with me and we entered the building.

As we walked through the door, there were pictures covering the walls of Naomi and me during our pregnancy. The entire place was teal, gold, and white. Everything was just beautiful. The teal and white shower cake was almost as tall as me sitting on top of the white table in the back corner. It was the first thing I laid eyes on when I walked through the door. Naomi went a little overboard with the decorations. She didn't spare Berlin period when it came to his pockets. Don't get me wrong, I pitched in too of course, but he told me I didn't really have to, that everything was covered. He was still trying to get himself back into Naomi's good graces. So far, it wasn't working.

"Oh my God, you two look so beautiful!" Naomi's mother, Angela excitedly beamed as she approached us. She pulled Naomi in for a hug then grabbed me.

"Thank you," we both said in unison.

My eyes danced around the place to the two huge white and gold studded throne chairs that sat against the wall that was surrounded by two rather large tables which were filled with gifts. We were surrounded by nothing but people who cared about us. I could feel nothing but love radiating in the air.

My eyes stopped when they landed on a figure, I knew all too well. His back was facing me but I knew that stance and those deep jet-black waves from anywhere.

Soul...

My heart sped up in my chest as I gazed at him. Butterflies swarmed in my belly or it could have just been gas from the burrito I ate earlier. I'm sure he looked heavenly in his white button-down and black slacks. *Please turn around.* I wanted him to grace me with his handsome face even if it was just one time. I could hear Angela rambling off at the mouth but I had long tuned out whatever she was saying.

"Un-huh, I'll be right back."

I slowly eased across the floor. My feet were moving toward him without me even telling them to. Even my body craved to be close to this man. Guess you couldn't fight what the heart wanted.

"Soul?" I softly spoke behind him. He turned around with a champagne glass in his hand and a half-smirk plastered on his lovely face. I watched as his eyes roamed up and down my body as he licked his pink plump lips.

"You look beautiful."

"Thank you," I blushed and brushed my hair back behind my ear. "I wasn't expecting you to show."

"Why not? You sent me an invitation and you are carrying my baby." It crazy how he was still saying that even though he knew this baby belonged to Quentin. After he spoke, she immediately began kicking me like crazy.

"Oooh." I placed my hand on my stomach where she was just kicking.

"You okay?" He placed his glass down on the table and grabbed my arm leading me over to one of the throne chairs.

"I'm fine; it's nothing." I sat down for a moment just rubbing my hand in a circular motion over my stomach.

"I got something for you." He reached into his back pocket and pulled out a white square box with a teal ribbon on it.

"What is it? You know you didn't have to do this."

"I didn't have to but I did." He handed me the box and I pulled the ribbon off opening it. Inside was a gold keychain. One set of keys looked like they belonged to a house, the other was a Rolls Royce car key.

"Soul, you didn't." I rose from the chair as fast as I could. "I can't accept this." I shoved the box back into his chest and headed for the door.

"Sanaa wait up!" He caught up to me, gripping me by the forearm. "Why not?"

"Because..."

"I told you I was going to take care of you and help with the baby. Will you just let me? I bought you that because I know that you need a new place to stay. You can't raise a baby in a one-bedroom condo, Sanaa. Will you just say thank you and take the gift because I'm not taking it back from you?" He grabbed my hand and firmly placed the box into it.

"But Soul—" He silenced me with his lips. Something I wasn't expecting at all. I closed my eyes and melted into his lips.

His soft, plump lips...

They took me to another universe. Sparked the flame between my thighs. Pumped more blood through my heart.

I shoved him back away from me. "I have to go." I quickly rushed off not wanting to accept my feelings.

SOUL

Whent I kissed Sanaa, I didn't expect her to shove me away. I felt the connection between us and she was only trying to push me away from her. I don't understand why she wouldn't just allow things to happen between us and leave it alone. Everything with her had to be complicated as hell.

I was willing to look past everything in our past and be with her. I told her that I'd take care of her baby even though it wasn't mine. I don't understand what else she wanted from me. The closer I got, the further away I seemed.

She ran out of the building without once looking back. The baby shower had just begun and I felt bad that I ran her off the way I had. I wanted to go behind her but I knew she just probably needed her space. Instead of staying at the baby shower, I decided to just head on home. There was no point in me staying there.

I went and found Berlin and Naomi and said my goodbyes. I didn't want him to come searching for me when I left. As I climbed over into my car, my mind kept going back to Sanaa. I so badly wanted to fix things between us and take it back to where we were. We were happy before A'Karri ruined everything. I don't know how come I didn't see that coming. If only I could go back in time and fix shit.

Sometimes I wished that I had just told Sanaa the truth when it came out about her mother's death. I could have easily avoided all of this shit. I was too blinded by desiring to be with her to do so. Everything seemed like it was a complete mess now.

It took everything in me to stay on route to my house and not make a detour to hers. I didn't want to keep pushing her and she just shut me down altogether. If she didn't come around by the time the baby was born, then I'll just give up. Giving up wasn't in my blood but I knew when enough was enough. I'd just help her take care of the baby like I said I would and leave our situation at that.

When I pulled up to my house, I hit the button to open the garage. As I turned into the driveway, I saw Sofia's car parked and her sitting on the steps. I didn't know what she was doing there when I told her that we were done. I made it pretty clear I wanted nothing else to do with her before she tossed me out of her house. The hell was she doing here?

Not being in the mood to deal with her at the moment, I pulled up behind her car and sat there. If I smoked, this would be the perfect time to do so. I already knew she was about to be on some bullshit. Her eyes lifted from her phone and she gazed in my direction.

My eyes narrowed and my lips contorted into a frown. I pushed the car door open and climbed out after sitting there watching her dumbass stay glued to the step for a good five minutes. I figured that she wasn't going anywhere, and I might as well go on and face her. Even though I wanted to drive right back out my driveway. I wasn't about to let anyone run me away from my own fucking house.

"What are you doing here Sofia?" I quizzed with a deep sigh.

She slowly rose from the step and crossed her right arm over her chest rubbing up and down her arm. She was avoiding eye contact with me but at this moment, I didn't really care. I wanted her to go on and say what she wanted, so she can get the hell away from my house.

"I needed to talk to you."

"About what?" I leaned up against my car and waited for her to speak.

"Since I last saw you, I've done a lot of thinking." She paused and gawked at me.

"I'm listening."

"I don't think that you really want to be with Sanaa. You just keep trying to push me away because you're afraid of commitment. Look how long it took for me to be able to stay the night over your house after all those years of being together? I finally get it." A smile crept up onto her face and it was then, that I realized she was fucking crazier than I thought. And I don't mean the little crazy where dick could fix the shit for a while. I'm talking about the crazy where the bitch stalked the shit out of you and come up with an entire relationship in her head. That kind of crazy.

"Let me stop you right there. You're really fucking tripping. Obviously, you've been doing too much damn thinking if you came to that conclusion. I don't want to be with you, Sofia. I want Sanaa." I peeled my body from the car and took the few steps to get to her and grabbed her by the shoulders. I glared her straight into the eyes. "I. Don't. Want. You. Sofia," I said so she could understand me this time. I don't want her to get to *overthinking* things again.

"You don't really mean that."

"Yes, the hell I do. Now can you go on and get out of here?" I let her go and headed up the steps to the front door.

"SOUL!" she shouted, stopping me in my tracks. I turned back around to face her. Tears cascaded down her cheeks and quite frankly, I was getting beyond tired of seeing her that way. "You're going to be with me or no one at all!"

I wasn't certain what she meant by that. But I damn sure wasn't trying to find out either. I rushed down the steps to her and snatched my strap from my waistline and placed it underneath her chin. "The fuck you mean by that?" I saw her swallow hard but she didn't utter a word. "You keep thinking I'm playing with your ass all you want to. If you touch Sanaa or that baby, I'm going to fucking kill you. This my last time warning you. Now, get your ass the fuck away from my house and don't ever fucking come back."

I shoved her away from me and watched as she ran to her car and hopped inside. With the way she had been acting, I knew I was going to have to keep an eye on her ass. Promise I wouldn't hesitate to put a bullet in her if she stepped out of line.

BERLIN

Naomi and I still weren't on the best of terms. It seemed like I've tried everything to get back into her good graces. That baby shower I payed for damn near cost me a grip but I wasn't complaining. Even after that, she still didn't really too much say no more than two words to me. Honestly, I didn't know what I was going to do but I damn sure didn't plan on giving up on her. I loved her way too much for that.

I picked up my phone off the coffee table and relaxed back on the couch. "Were you busy?" I asked Naomi when she picked up the phone. I truly didn't expect her to answer.

"Not really was just laying here watching *Sex and the City*. What's up?"

"I was wondering if you felt like going to lunch with me?" A silence loomed over us for a moment. I know she was trying to debate if she really wanted to go or not. "You don't have to stay long. You don't even have to say anything to me if you don't want to. You can just eat while I watch, then leave. Just come out with me."

"Alright, I'll give you thirty minutes but that's it."

"Okay, good. Meet me at Pappy's Smokehouse."

"Fine." She disconnected the call and I hopped up from the couch, heading into my bedroom. I had been lying around the house for the most part of the day so I went into the bathroom and started the shower.

After I handled my hygiene, I threw on some black Levi jeans, a brown and gold Versace shirt and slipped my feet into my Jimmy Choo red bottom sneakers. I grabbed my keys and was out the door.

It didn't take me long to make it to Pappy's Smokehouse. When I got there, Naomi hadn't arrived yet. *Hope she didn't try to stand me up.* I got out of the car and went inside. The hostess set me down at a table.

"Can I start you off with something to drink?"

"Just a glass of water. I'm waiting for someone," I told her and she nodded her head then bounced off.

I leaned back in my seat and pulled my phone out. I went to call her again to see if she was coming then I felt a presence standing over me. When I looked up I came face to face with Naomi. Her beauty caught me by surprise like it always did whenever I was near her. She stood there with that beautiful glow on her bronze face. Her curly hair flowed freely down her back.

I immediately rose from my seat and pulled her chair out so she could sit down. "I thought you weren't going to show."

"I don't know why when I told you I was coming."

I waved the waitress over so she could take our order. I knew she didn't want to be here with me long so I didn't want to waste her time. I sat there as Naomi rambled off her order to the waitress.

"Do you want anything, Sir?" she questioned me. I simply shook my head. I wasn't really hungry. The only reason I came here in the first place was so that I could see Naomi. I wanted to try and fix things between us if it was even possible. She's had more than enough time to think things over. It was either she wanted to be in this relationship or she doesn't.

The waitress left the table and I used that as my opportunity to talk to Naomi. "You already know why I called you here." She just sat there with her hands resting on her belly and gazing at me. "I want to try and fix things, Naomi. I miss you. What do I have to do to show you how sorry I am?"

"I miss you too, Berlin. Like a lot. I've been doing a lot of thinking since we've been apart and I really do want to work on things. Before I agree to it, is there anything you need to tell me? This is your only chance." I swallowed hard. She kept bringing that up like she just knew I had fucked up somewhere along the line.

"No," I lied and prayed she didn't know anything.

"Good because I don't think I can take anymore heartache." The waitress came back to the table with her food and placed it down in front of her.

"Let me know if you need anything else," she said and walked off.

I got excited as shit that we were finally about to work on us after so long. I was just about to ask her to move in with me when a woman walked up to the table. She caught me totally by surprise because I thought I'd never see her again. I managed to stay away from the strip club for that purpose. My hand eased to my strap when I saw her lips part. I was prepared to take my ass to jail for killing her if that was going to protect the secret I was hiding from Naomi. But then, I knew I wouldn't be able to help her raise a child from jail. *Calm down, Berlin. Maybe she's just speaking or something.*

Sweat beads formed on my forehead as I watched her mouth. "Hey, I never thought I'd bump into you again." Naomi looked up from her plate and glanced from me to old girl.

"Who the hell is this, Berlin?" she questioned me with her brow raised. She dropped her fork on the plate and relaxed back in her chair. I was trying my hardest to come up with a lie in my head.

"I'm his baby mama," the girl spoke and I wanted to slap that nappy ass pink wig flying off her fucking head.

"Excuse me?" Naomi slid back some so that the girl could see her stomach. "Last time I checked, he only had one baby mama."

"Well, guess I'm joining the family because congrats daddy! You're about to be a father... again!" She dropped the positive pregnancy test on the table in the center right in front of Naomi's plate. Her eyes quickly zeroed in on it and she immediately rose from her chair grabbing her cup in the process. Before I even realized what was about to happen, the water went flying straight into my face.

"YOU SON OF A BITCH!" she shouted and stormed out of the restaurant.

"What's her problem?" the girl asked me. "I only wanted money for an abortion."

"You stupid little—" I jumped up from my seat, snatching my piece from my waistline. I roughly gripped her by the neck and slammed her body down on the table, placing the gun at the side of her head. When I heard people gasp and scream, it brought me back to reality. I had completely forgotten where I was and was about to blow her fucking brains out all over the got damn table. I let her go and reached into my pocket tossing a few bills down onto her then rushed out the door. I had to catch up to Naomi and see if I could get myself out this deeper hole, I had dug myself into.

I stepped out the door and she was long gone. She must have hauled ass out the parking lot so I wouldn't catch up to her. I pulled my phone from my pocket and tried calling her, but she sent me straight to voicemail. I had really fucked up this time. When she asked me that, I should have just told her the fucking truth. Instead, I tried to use a lie to cover up another lie, ultimately ending in failure. Our relationship was doomed, and it was nothing but my own fault.

NAOMI

It's been a couple of days since I'd last seen or heard from Berlin. Before that girl walked in, I was happy to be thinking about getting our relationship back on the right track. I asked him if there was something he needed to tell me and he lied right to my face. It was like something in my gut telling me that something wasn't right. But I just couldn't figure out exactly what it was. Now that I know, I wish I had never found out. It crushed my soul and heart all in one and I've been aching ever since.

I've been locked away in my apartment since I ran off from Berlin. I wasn't taking calls from anyone, not even Sanaa. I definitely had him on the block list. I didn't want him reaching me whatsoever. He popped up at the house a few times, even went as far as sitting outside the door for hours hoping I would let him in. I didn't want to see his face. I was too hurt and ashamed.

Because of his infidelities, I had gone by the clinic for a checkup to make sure that everything was good with me, my baby, and my pussy. If he had gotten her pregnant, then that only meant he went up in her without a condom. I'm not certain how many times they've had sex or when the affair really started. I don't even know if I wanted the answers to those questions.

What really killed me was the fact that I had actually thought I'd be able to change him—make him a better man. He'd want to be with me and only me. Like what was I really expecting when I already knew his reputation when I started screwing around with him? I put myself in this predicament and was ready to kick my own ass for setting myself up for heartbreak.

I sat there in the lobby bouncing the hell out of my leg. The nurse had called me back into the clinic to review my results for the testing I did. I really hoped Berlin wasn't so fucking careless that he'd given me something to harm our baby. If I had anything, then we really were going to have an issue. I can't say I wouldn't find my way over to his place and he ended up on the other side of his own gun. He'd be the second Maserati boy shot and I can't make any promises that I won't aim to kill either.

"Naomi Copeland!" the nurse called out and I got up from my seat. I went behind her into exam room seven. I was so nervous about my results that I couldn't even sit down if I wanted to. My body trembled as I watched her open the folder and read over my paperwork. I nibbled on every single fingernail I had to try and calm my nerves but it seemed impossible.

"Can you just go on and tell me my results? You're killing me here." I nervously chuckled.

"I'm sorry but everything looks fine. Everything came back negative."

I finally exhaled. If I held my breath any longer I was sure I'd go blue in the face. That was all I needed to know. I and my baby were fine so I could stop stressing myself about that part. Obviously, the stress was still going to be there seeing how I wasn't certain how my relationship was going to turn out at this point. I knew that there was only one person I could go to talk about this... my mother.

After I left the clinic, I went to my parents' house. It's been a while since I've seen them but I was sure they'd welcome me with open arms. Sanaa was usually the person I talked to about these things but at this point, I wasn't certain if she would even know what to do.

I pulled into the driveway behind my mother's black Tahoe truck and sat in the car for a moment just observing the two-story tan brick home I grew up in. I loved this house just as much as my mother did. To me, it was like a safe haven. Whenever things got to the point where I couldn't bear, I'd find my way home in my old bedroom. At this point, things were beyond the point of I what could bear.

Slowly, I climbed out of the car and entered the house using my key. I inhaled the lavender and vanilla scent. It always smelled like that; it was one of the best parts. I made my way upstairs to my bedroom which was the first door on the left. Pushing the door open, I tossed myself onto the purple and gold comforter on my queen-sized bed.

"Naomi is that you?" my mother's voice asked from the hallway. Pretty soon, her beautiful bronze face peeked into the bedroom. "You alright, sweetheart?" I sat up in the bed Indian style and the tears instantly began flowing.

"I don't know what to do, Ma," I admitted in between sobs.

"Oh, honey." She entered the room with her arms stretched out wide. She sat down on the bed beside me and pulled me into her embrace. I just sat there, freeing all the tears I had been holding in over the last couple of days.

After crying for what seemed like hours, I finally spoke. "Things between Berlin and I are getting rough. I'm not even sure if we are going to survive until the baby is born let alone afterward."

"Relationships are hard, sweetheart. If they were easy, then everyone would be in one. The longer you're with someone, the tougher things become between you two. There will be times you'll get hurt. There will be others when you're so angry that you want to kill each other. Then you have to think about the good times. How much you love each other. If you love each other enough and really want to be with each other, then you should try to stick it out—make things work. But don't do it for all the wrong reasons, Naomi."

"I love Berlin, Ma, I really do. But I just don't think we can work through this."

"Through what?" She held me and stroked my hair. I leaned back so I could stare her into the eyes.

"He cheated on me, Mama. Then the other girl says she's pregnant."

"It was only a slip-up. Berlin is human just like everyone else. Give him a second chance. Try to talk things out and get everything out on the table."

"How do you know he's worthy of a second chance though Mama?" I sat up straight on the bed and rubbed my belly. My heart wanted to give him a second chance but I just didn't want to end up in the same place all over again. For me and my baby's sake.

"Everyone deserves a second chance. I should know because your father gave me one." I gasped and my mouth fell all the way open. For as long as I could remember, my parents had the perfect marriage or so I thought. Now she was telling me everything I knew was a lie. "Don't look at me like that. I'm human as well, Naomi. We all make mistakes."

She got up from the bed and kissed me in the center of my forehead. "I made chicken quesadillas for lunch if you're hungry." She headed for the door then stopped in her tracks and turned back to me. "Just think about it Naomi. He just might be worthy of that second chance. You know I wouldn't steer you wrong." She winked and left out the bedroom. I balled up on my bed, holding one of my pillows. Berlin was the last thing on my mind before I drifted off to sleep.

SANAA

"You sure you got all that?" I asked Layla as I sat at my desk with her standing over me. Since it was getting closer to my due date, I was trying to groom her the best I could, so she could take over while I step away. I was hesitant about leaving the shop in someone else's hands but she was the best candidate I had. Hopefully, things run smoothly.

"Yes, I got it," she responded with a wide smile on her face. I could tell she was anxious to take over my job while I was gone. Hopefully, not too anxious where she tried to push me out my own spot while I'm away.

"If you run into any trouble, I'm just a phone call away," I assured her and stood from my desk. "I'll be in once a week until I go into labor to check on you." I gathered up all my things along with my Apple MacBook Air and headed for the door.

"I won't let you down," she said behind me.

"I know you won't. That's why I chose you in the first place." I winked at her and left out the door. I was going to miss being around this place like crazy, but I had to prepare myself and my home for my baby girl. I was a little over seven months and hadn't even picked up anything to put her nursery together. I was still calling her no-name because that's what she was. I had yet to give her a name. I was behind on everything, and that's the reason why I was stepping away from the shop early—to get myself in order.

I hit the key fob on the pearl white Rolls Royce truck Soul had bought me. I didn't really want to accept it, but he wouldn't take the keys back from me. I had been trying my best to avoid him ever since the little kiss we shared. It made me even more confused than I already was. As if the truck wasn't enough, I went to the house he bought me and it was huge as fuck. Almost as big as his and fully furnished except for the nursery. I guess he wanted me to do that one myself. I felt bad for accepting those gifts from him but I did need more space for the baby.

Just as I reached for the truck door, my phone began ringing in my purse. I fumbled with my things trying my best not to drop my laptop on the ground as I rummaged through my bag for my ringing phone.

"Hello?" I placed the phone between my face and my shoulder as I pulled the door open and climbed inside.

"Is this Sanaa Love?" the woman's voice asked.

"This is she." I placed my things on the passenger's seat then stuck the key in the ignition and started the truck. I hadn't been outside long and was already sweating bullets. I had to turn the AC up on full blast before I had a heat stroke.

"This is Bethany at *Mercy Clinic*. I'm not sure if you remember me, but I was the one who had done that DNA test for you."

"Oh, yeah, I remember." I wasn't sure what she was calling me for. I hadn't been there since I did the DNA test.

"Well, I was calling you because there seems to have been a mix-up. The results I gave you for the DNA test were false. Turns out, the Q-tip is the father." My heart damn near burst in my chest when she said that.

"You sure?" I wanted her to be extra positive because I didn't want to go running to Soul with false hope.

"Yes, I'm sure. Sorry about the mix-up and have a nice day."

I sat there in my parking spot in awe with the phone still glued to my ear. Guess that explained why she always got excited whenever he was around. She knew who her father was all along even when I didn't. Ain't that some shit?

I placed my phone in the cup holder and rubbed my hands on my belly. "Did you hear that little munchkin? Soul is your father." It sounded weird rolling off my tongue. "Soul's the father..." I could only imagine how he was going to react once he got the news.

Instead of heading home like I was intending on doing, I went in the opposite direction and hopped onto the interstate heading to Soul's house. I would have called to see if he was at home, but I wanted the entire thing to be a surprise.

As I was driving, I saw this billboard with a bakery on there that was coming up on the next exit and an idea struck me so I quickly hopped off. I pulled up to the bakery and got out the car heading inside.

"Welcome to *Divine's*," the African American woman said behind the counter. She had a huge grin on her face and I couldn't help but smile in return. "What can I do for you?" I glanced at the cupcakes, cookies, and cakes through the glass counter. When I made it to this cake with pink frosting and roses on it, I pointed at it.

"What flavor is that cake?"

"Strawberry."

"I want that one." I straighten my posture and looked her dead in the eyes. "Can you do something for me?"

"Un-huh, sure."

"Can you write on there *Congrats You Are the Father!*"

"Yes, ma'am and I'll package it up for you."

I stood back smiling from ear to ear anxiously waiting to see Soul. I paid for my cake and got back on the road. It didn't take me much longer to get to his house. When I got there, I hopped out of the truck so fast that I almost forgot to grab the cake.

"Shit." I leaned back into the truck and grabbed the cake box and walked up to the front door with a smile on my face. I didn't know if he was there or not because there weren't any cars in the driveway. But I still knocked on the door anyway.

Soul swung the door open in one of his black Armani suits with a fresh lineup and haircut. He looked so heavenly and it almost distracted me from the reason why I was there in the first place.

"Sanaa, what are you doing here?" I just smiled and brushed right past him into the house. It felt weird being in there since the last time I was there, I shot him almost killing him. I quickly shook the eerie feeling replacing it with the excitement I had. Nothing was about to put a damper on my mood. Nothing. "I'm not complaining because I love the hell out of your smile, but given the circumstances, I'm kind of worried right now. Can you just tell me what's—"

I immediately shut him up by opening the cake box.

SOUL

I just stood there, staring at the words on the cake. *You're the father.* At first, I thought I was reading it wrong but the more I read over it the more I realized what she was talking about. The baby she was carrying around in her womb actually belonged to me. It's funny because the entire time I was saying she was mine, to begin with. But to actually know that she was brought tears to my eyes. At this moment, I didn't care about Sanaa seeing me cry. I was really about to be a father.

"Are you for real?" I asked her finally lifting my eyes from the cake and meeting her gaze.

She nodded her head. "Un-huh. I found out not too long ago and I had to come and let you know. You were right all along. She belongs to you, Soul." The rather large smile was still evident on her face. She seemed just as excited about it as I was. Maybe there was hope for us after all.

I swiped my finger across the icing and stuck it up to her lips. Without even thinking twice, she pulled my finger into her mouth and sucked the icing off. "Mhm," she moaned as she was sucking it off. My dick immediately sprung to life. It had been so long since I've heard that sound that it was like music to my ears.

She dug her index finger down into the icing and place it up to my mouth. I took her hand and sucked the icing then kissed her from her hand down to her arm. She giggled so I decided to take it a bit further. I wasn't going to stop until she told me otherwise. I placed some icing directly down the center of her lips. Grabbing her by her lower back, I pulled her body into my frame and attacked her lips with mine. I kissed, licked, and sucked both her upper and lower lip. The cake fell from her grasp dropping to the floor. Light moans seeped from her lips as we kissed.

Scooping her up into my arms, I carried her upstairs to my bedroom. When we got in there, I gently laid her down on the bed. I planted one more sweet kiss on her lips before pulling her shirt up over her head. I pulled my suit jacket off, tossing it onto the bed alongside her and unbuttoned my shirt then dropped down to my knees, planting sweet sensual kisses all over her round belly. She giggled and rubbed her hand in a circular motion over my head.

"I love you; you know that?"

She nibbled on the corner of her lower lip for a second. "I love you too."

Without saying another word, I slipped my fingers inside the waistband of her tights and pulled them down. Instead of being bald, her pussy was neatly trimmed. *I can work with that.* I eased her closer to the edge and spread her legs as far as they would go then dove straight into that pussy.

I French kissed the muhfucka and planted soft kisses on her inner thighs. I gazed up at her and her head tilted back. She unsnapped her bra and her plump breasts were free. They were juicier than I remembered. Maybe from her being pregnant.

"Hold them legs wide for me."

With one hand, I groped her breast and the other, I spread her pussy lips with my thumb and index finger. I sucked on her clit then flicked it with the tip of my tongue.

"Mhm, Soul," she whimpered.

I dipped my long tongue inside her then swept it back across her clit. I kept licking and lapping up all her juices until I felt her body shivering like an earthquake. Pretty soon, she released all over my tongue.

"Fuuuccckk Soul!" she cried out.

I sprang straight to my feet while her body was still climaxing and shoved my slacks down along with my boxers. "Keep them legs right there," I instructed, positioning myself at her opening. I rubbed my dick up and down her slit. Her shit was so wet that I looked down and saw a string of her juices coming from her pussy to my dick. "Got damn girl." I was kind of afraid to go inside her; I might cum too quick.

"Please stop teasing me and just give me the dick."

"Oh, you want the dick, huh?"

I gently eased him inside her. "Ungh!" she whimpered when I entered.

I tenderly eased her back onto the bed, giving her slow deep strokes. I didn't want to get too rough with her and hurt her or the baby. I held her legs at my sides and stroked her deeper with every thrust I gave. I missed being inside the pussy. It was so wet that it felt like I was swimming in the muhfucka.

"Faster, Soul."

I glanced down and saw her biting on her lower lip with her eyes closed. Spreading her legs as far as they would go, I leaned into her on my tippy toes. My ass flexed with every stroke I gave her. Sweat beads formed on my forehead. Heat radiated off of both of our bodies.

"Yes, right there!" I could tell I was tapping her spot. Her hands tightly gripped the sheets. "Yes!" Her back arched deeply.

I hovered over her body with my hands planted on either side of her head and gawked down into her face. Her eyes shot open and she stared back at me with those beautiful hazel eyes of hers as her pussy muscles contracted. Her lips formed an "O". I felt my own climax building up knowing that she was getting pleasure with every thrust I gave her. I tried to hold out but I knew I wasn't going to be able to any longer.

"Cum with me," I told her.

"Okaaaaaaaaayy!" she screamed and I could feel her creaming all over my dick as I released my seeds deep inside her.

I leaned down kissing her softly on the lips then eased out of her and went into the bathroom to grab us a rag. I cleaned myself off first then went into the bedroom and wiped her up. She was laying there on the bed seemingly unconscious. All I could do was shake my head. The aftermath of my dick was already taking effect over her.

I climbed up on the bed and pulled her up beside me. Her back pressed against me as I wrapped my arm around her. This was where she belonged. Right here in my arms. She knew it, I knew it, everybody knew it.

"You know I'm not letting your ass go anymore, right?"

"Soul take a nap with me." she mumbled, then yawned.

"I'm being serious, Sanaa."

"I heard you, now go to sleep because I'm tired."

I brushed her hair out her face back behind her ear and kissed her on the cheek. Now that I had her back, I was going to do everything in my power to keep her. No more secrets. No more lies. Just the truth from now on and I was going to make everything right. In due time.

BERLIN

I was going crazy not being around my girl. She was really the only thing I could think about. After that little stunt with old girl at the restaurant, she'd cut all ties with me. I was completely on the block list and couldn't get through to her. I tried coming by her place but she wouldn't let me inside or talk to me. I was about to go so insane that I was thinking about writing her a letter or some shit, but I knew once she saw it was from me, it'd likely get ripped to pieces.

At this point, I didn't know what the hell to do. I had been sitting outside her apartment on the floor waiting for her to get home. I knew she wasn't there because I didn't see her car anywhere outside. If I had to wait the entire day for her to get there, then I would. I needed to talk to her something serious. I don't know if she was going to listen to me, but I was going to tell her how I felt regardless.

The elevator dinged and she stepped off with some bags in her hands. I noticed a guy walking behind her with some as well. I'd never seen him before. *I know damn well she hadn't moved on that fast.* I jolted from the floor. Heat coursed through my body and my fists balled up. She hadn't even noticed me standing there. It angered me even more just watching her laughing and talking with this nigga.

I snatched my strap from my waistline and charged toward them. Before they even knew what was happening, I had old dude pinned up against the wall with my gun shoved into his mouth. Every single bag he had, was lying on the floor at our feet. The groceries were spilled everywhere mainly the milk that had wasted onto the floor pooling at our feet.

"Berlin! What the hell are you doing?" Naomi yelled tugging on my arm but I just brushed her off.

"So, this why you weren't talking to me? You were getting cozy with the next nigga?" My eyes shifted from the nigga who was breathing heavily over to her who stood there with wide eyes.

"Berlin, it's not what it looks like. Put the gun down." That shit sounded like something I would have said when I got caught doing some bullshit. That's why I couldn't believe her.

"Nigga, you fucking my girl?" My nostrils flared as I gazed into her eyes. They were laced with fear. It's funny how she tried to upgrade from me but found herself downgrading. Everything about this nigga screamed bitch. Even the scent he wore smelled fruity as hell. Nothing about this nigga was masculine.

"Ain't nobody fucking me! Put the gun down Berlin!" She tugged at my arm again but my finger rubbed against the trigger. I was eager to pull the muhfucka. End this nigga's life. Show her I wasn't playing games when it came to her. I loved her and was willing to do anything, so she would know just how much. Even if it meant taking this nigga's life. "He's gay!"

When those words left her mouth, I eased the gun from his and took a step back. Now that I wasn't looking at him out of anger, I could tell he was gay. From his tight ass clothes to his arched eyebrows.

"My bad." I tucked my gun back into my waistline.

"Yeah, your bad," she mocked me. "I'm so sorry, Christopher."

"It's okay." He hurried off probably scared I was going to shoot him in the ass and not in a good way either.

"He saw me struggling with my groceries and offered to help me. If I had known your stalker ass was up here then I would have told him not to," she sighed and bent over trying to grab the stuff off the floor but her belly was in the way.

"I got it," I told her, grabbing her by the arm straightening her posture.

"That's one reason why we're not together now, Berlin. You have an anger problem that you need to work on."

I dropped the stuff back to the floor and stood straight up. "I'm willing to work on it, Naomi. I just want you back. I know I fucked up majorly, and I'm truly sorry for that but I'm willing to spend the rest of my life making it up to you if you let me." I glanced down and saw she was still wearing the ring I had given her. *That's a good sign, right?*

"I went and had a long talk with my mother a while ago."

"Great, now she knows I fucked up too." I scrubbed my hand down my face. Even if we were to fix things and stay together, the relationship with her mother was going to be off to a rocky start.

"No, listen..." she paused a moment and peeled her frame from the wall stepping closer to me. "It's nothing like that. She's not angry with you or anything. If anything, she shed some light on me and got the wheels to turning in my head. "I know that you love me, Berlin. If you didn't, you would have been given up a long time ago on trying to fix things between us and I thank you that you didn't. Times are going to get rough between us, we just have to learn how to communicate and work through the bad if we are going to stay good."

She palmed my face and a smile found hers. "I want to work on us, but you have to promise me that you're willing to put forth the effort as well. You have to work on yourself and your anger. That's the only way that we're going to work out."

I grabbed her hand softly kissing the palm of it. "I can do that. For you and the baby."

"You have to be willing to do it for yourself as well."

"I want to do it."

Smack!

Her free hand went across the side of my face. "What was that for?" my brows furrowed.

"It was long overdue. Now clean that shit up and you owe me some more fucking groceries." She stepped over the mess I made on the floor and unlocked her apartment door.

I thought she was going to shut and lock it behind her but she left it wide open. I cleaned up all the stuff off the floor and threw it away in her trashcan in the kitchen. Once I was done, I found her lying in the bed on her back scrolling through her phone. I stood there in the doorway with my back pressed up against the doorframe just gawking at her for a moment. I loved this girl more than I could even imagine. There was no way I was willing to lose her again.

"I love the shit out your ass," I told her then eased on into the room. I lifted her legs up off the bed and placed them into my lap when I sat down. I gently rubbed her feet and light moans escaped from her lips.

"Mhm, that feels so good."

"Does it really?" I pressed my fingers deeper into her foot and I saw her eyes shut and she pulled her lower lip in between her teeth. I lifted her foot up to my mouth kissing the bottom of it.

NAOMI

"Mhm," I moaned as Berlin licked and sucked on my toes. It already had me creaming in my panties. I was ready to feel his dick inside me. Using my bullet was getting tiring. I needed some real action and it seemed like forever since the last time I had some real dick.

His fingertips tickled my thighs as he brushed my dress up to my stomach. Gripping me by the legs, he pulled me down onto the bed where my head was lying on the pillow. His fingertips brushed against my hips as he tugged my panties down and tossed them to the floor.

"That shit already dripping wet." He slipped his index finger inside me roughly fingering me then pulled it out and sucked the juices off. "Damn, I missed that pussy," was the last thing he said before he dove into my shit headfirst.

I immediately creamed, feeling the light strokes of his tongue against my clit. His licks sped up and I ground my pussy on his tongue. I was too anxious to cum, feeling my orgasm raging inside me. He slipped two fingers inside my pussy and curved them. They instantly tapped my spot as he licked and that was the tip of the iceberg for me. My body shuddered and the faucet broke between my legs.

"Oh fuck!" I was cumming uncontrollably. My climax took over my entire body and I kept cumming. It was like I couldn't stop cumming if I wanted to.

Finally, he let go of my pussy and slapped it.

Smack!

He stood straight up and pulled his gun from his waistline, placing it down on the nightstand. I licked my lips knowing he was about to give me some of that dope dick. I was kicking my own ass for me staying away from him as long as I have.

He stripped out of his clothes and climbed into bed behind me. He lifted one of my legs and eased his dick inside. It was kind of a struggle at first because it was tight but once he got in there, all hell broke loose. His strokes were subtle and slow at first. I think he was trying to take his time with me since I was pregnant.

When he lifted that leg some more, those thrusts sped up. His dick ripped up my insides and felt like it was going to burst out of my chest.

"Fuck, right there," I whimpered.

My pussy gushed all over the place and talked back to him. I felt another climax forming and wasn't certain if I was prepared for this one. Especially if it was going to be anything like the first.

"That pussy squeezing that dick. You're about to cum?" He quickly snatched his dick out of me and slapped me on the ass.

Smack!

"Turn that ass over."

"Why you playing with me, Berlin?"

"Turn that ass over," he instructed again.

I got on all fours and arched my back as deep as it allowed me to.

Smack!

He kissed my ass in the exact spot he slapped me in, then I felt his dick head playing peekaboo at my opening. He rammed that big muhfucka up in me so fast, I had to grip the pillow to brace myself. After a good two strokes, I felt ready to climax again.

"Ungh, Berlin," I whimpered.

"Your ass better not cum until I tell you to."

I sunk my teeth into my lower lip, trying my best to hold off on that orgasm. It seemed impossible because it was ragging to get free.

"I can't... hold it."

"Yes, you can. Hold that shit."

He held onto my waist and pounded his dick in me from behind. I threw my ass back on his shit, trying to break it. His hand snaked around underneath me and he rubbed my clit.

"Pleeeeeaaaasse let me cum," I cried. My body shivered and he pulled out of me again.

"Hold it until I tell you to cum."

I looked back at him over my shoulder. "Why you torturing me? If you're rubbing on my shit, then I'm bound to cum."

Smack!

"Shut up."

He dove his dick right back into me. My pussy throbbed. My heart banged in my chest. My legs wobbled. Adrenaline skyrocketed.

"I can't hold it no more!"

His fingers dug into my hips and I heard him groan. He had to be close to getting his and must didn't want me to cum until he did but this shit had to be released or I was going to go insane.

"Cum."

As if on command, my shit flowed. My head flew back. My thrusts got harder. My fingers dug deeper into the pillow. I felt like my heart was bursting out of my chest.

"Oooooh fuck!" His fingers roughly rubbed on my clit and I just kept cumming.

When I was done, I fell down onto my side and tried to regulate my breathing. I wanted to get up and go get in the shower but didn't have the strength to do so. The bed dipped down as he climbed out and went into the bathroom. I heard the water running so I knew he had to be in there cleaning himself up. Moments later, he came back into the room with another rag.

"Turn over so I can wipe you," he instructed.

I used all the strength I had left in my body and turned over onto my back so he could clean me up. Once he was done, he took the rag back into the bathroom and put it in the dirty clothes' hamper. I laid there on my back, thinking about the sex we just had. I couldn't help but wonder about the girl who said she was pregnant by him.

"What's wrong with you?" he questioned when he climbed in bed alongside me, lying on his back.

"I was just thinking about you and that other girl. She's pregnant by you. What are you going to do about her?"

"She's not pregnant anymore. I highly doubt she was in the first place. She claimed that she only wanted money for an abortion so I gave it to her. I'm really sorry that I fucked up the way I did and I promise you that I'll do whatever to ensure that it doesn't ever happen again."

I laid there in silence. I know damn well it wasn't going to happen again. I forgave him that time, but if it was to reoccur, I won't forgive him the next. His light snores could be heard. Lifting up some, I gazed over and saw he had fallen asleep. My eyes wandered from him to his gun that was resting on the nightstand.

I climbed on top of him and his arm wrapped around my waist. Reaching over, I grabbed the gun and cocked it. When he heard the clicking sound, his eyes shot straight open.

"What are you doing, Naomi?"

"Making sure that it won't happen again." I placed the gun at the center of his forehead and peered right into his eyes. I've never used one before, but how hard could it be? All you have to do is pull the trigger and POW one bullet gone straight through his skull.

"Put the gun down, Naomi."

"I won't until I've gotten my point across. Berlin, I mean this in the nicest way possible. If you ever cheat on me again, I'll fucking kill you and raise this baby on my own. And trust me, when I shoot the muhfucka, it's not going to miss like

Sanaa did Soul." I pulled the gun down from his head and kissed him softly on the lips. Berlin could play with me if he wanted to, but I was serious as a fucking heart attack.

Taniece

SOFIA

It's been a month since I last laid eyes on Soul or Sanaa. I was angry as hell for how he had been treating me. In my opinion, it wasn't fair and he was plain down crazy for still wanting to be with her. If she tried to kill him once, then I'm pretty sure she might try to do it again.

Even though Soul threatened me, I didn't take that shit serious. I knew he wouldn't cause any harm to me. He knew me far longer than Sanaa and we definitely had way more history than those two.

For an entire month, I had been trying to figure out what I was going to do about the matter. Weigh my options on how I was going to get my man back. Figure out how I was going to make Sanaa pay for coming in between us. The only thing I could come up with was the bitch and the baby had to go. Soul was only drawn to her because she was carrying that damn baby. If she didn't have that thing growing inside her, I was pretty sure he would have left her alone by now. Getting rid of them wasn't going to be an easy task. And I knew I had to do it discreetly because then he'd definitely be pissed if he knew I had something to do with it.

Soul was so angry with me about the little threat I had given Sanaa that he switched his phone number up on me. I tried to give him some space to calm down, that's the reason why I hadn't gone by his place. But I was going crazy being without him.

I found myself driving by the shopping center that the shop was in. I wasn't going to stop but I saw Sanaa coming out and placing something into the trunk of a truck. An expensive one at that which only made my blood boil even more. I knew she couldn't afford that truck, so it only meant Soul had bought it for her.

I quickly whipped into the parking lot and jumped out my car just as she was shutting the trunk. I struck her in the back of her head with my fist. Her hand immediately went up to her head. Before she could turn around and see who had hit her, I kicked her in the back of her leg dropping her to the ground.

"I told your stupid ass to stay the hell away from my man! Now, he eyeing me funny and shit!"

Wham!

I kicked her in the face and blood and spit flew from her mouth. "You should have just stayed away like I fucking told you to!"

"Sofia... stop! Have you forgotten that I'm pregnant!"

"Fuck you and that baby!"

Wham!

I gave her one hard blow to the stomach and she balled up into the fetal position. "I'm sick of hearing about you and that stupid ass baby!"

Wham!

I kicked her in the back.

"Ahhh!" she hollered out in pain. "Please just stop, Sofia!"

"This shit ain't nothing but your own fault with your stupid ass."

Before I could get another lick in, people came running out of the shop. I coughed up a mouth full of saliva and spit on her. "Stay your ass the fuck away from Soul or else next time I won't be so nice."

I ran off and jumped into my car speeding out of there before anyone called the police on me. Lucky for me, none of those people recognized who I was to be able to snitch to Soul about what I've done. I was going to go home and pack a bag and head out of town for a while so he wouldn't expect it was me. And if he called and asked, I was only going to deny the shit and show him receipts of where I'd been. Hopefully, he doesn't take her word over mine or else I'd really be screwed.

My heart thumped in my chest as I pulled into my driveway and rushed into the house. I booked a flight on my phone that left in an hour. I wasn't actually going to get on the plane. I just needed for it to seem like I had gotten on it. I was just going to lay low in a hotel until things died down a little bit.

I prayed Sanaa lost her baby. If she was to lose it, then I knew she would be so angry with Soul that she wouldn't want anything else to do with him. She'd push him away and I'd be right there to pick him up again just like the last time when she shot him and left him for dead.

After I finished packing my overnight bag, I tossed it into the passenger's seat as I got back into the car. Ballwin was my destination. I was about to hop on the interstate and not look back until I reached it.

Just as I got on the interstate, my phone began ringing. I looked down at it and Soul's number flashed across the screen. I know like hell he hadn't found out about Sanaa that fast. I wasn't really prepared to deal with him at the moment so I didn't pick up or send him to voicemail. I needed some time so I could figure out my next move.

Buzz, Buzz

I grabbed my phone and stared down at the text message I had just received from Soul.

Soul: *Pick up the phone, Sof. We need to talk.*

My heart thumped so hard in my chest that I could hear it ringing in my ears. Terrified was an understatement. There was no need for me to be scared now. I had done the shit and had to be a big girl about it. But I damn sure wasn't about to be one at this moment. I powered my phone off so I couldn't receive any more calls or texts from him for the time being. Also turned it off so he wouldn't be able to track me.

I knew Soul all too well and if he wanted something bad enough, he was going to fucking get it. That text he had sent me was a little too calm for someone who had just found out I beat his girl's ass. Once I get my mind in order, then I'll call him back but it won't be a moment sooner.

As I sped down the interstate, I turned the radio up and let the music blast in my ears to take my mind away from what was going on around me. I brushed my clammy hands on my jeans and totally zoned out when Cardi B's *"I Like It"* came onto the radio.

"You're going to be fine, Sofia. It'll all blow over pretty soon and everything will be right back to normal," I told myself with a smile.

SANAA

I stayed balled up in the fetal position even long after Sofia had run off. I was terrified to move thinking that something was wrong with my baby. I was pretty sure that it was because I could feel the wetness between my thighs.

My heart banged in my chest. My ears rang uncontrollably. The aching feeling in my chest was growing stronger with every second that passed by, I laid there on the ground.

"We called 911 for you, Sanaa. Just hang in there," Layla said, reaching down to touch me. The only thing that was on my mind was if my baby was okay. Not Sofia. Not the fact I had just gotten my ass beaten for the first time in my life. Not Soul. All of that was irrelevant at the moment.

I could hear the sirens nearing me. But it seemed like they were trying to fade out in the distance. They weren't coming fast enough for me.

"Ahh!" I cried out, feeling a sharp pain shoot through my stomach. I wasn't sure what the hell it was until it hit for me a second time. "I'm having contract— ahhh!" I planted a hand on my stomach and tried to breathe. Tears seeped from the corners of my eyes. "No, baby girl it's not time for you yet. You have to stay in there a couple more weeks."

"Everything's going to be fine," Mia tried to assure me but I knew it was a lie. Nothing was fine in my book. That stupid bitch had jumped on me, catching me off guard and now because of her actions, I was going into labor early. How was any of that fine?

"Someone call Soul for me. My phone is in my purse," I pointed over to my purse that lay directly behind my truck. I had dropped it when I felt the first blow to my head she had given me. Layla rushed over and grabbed my purse then fumbled through it trying to find my phone. I watched her as she scrolled through it then placed it up to her ear.

The paramedics and the ambulance pulled into the parking lot. The bright lit up the dark sky. I heard the doors as they pushed them open and rushed over to my side.

"What happened?" the Caucasian woman asked me as she kneeled down beside me.

"Some crazy woman attacked me and now I think I'm going into labor." The other EMT rushed over to the opposite side of me with the gurney.

"Okay, we're going to lift you up and place you on the gurney." She grabbed my upper half while the guy grabbed my legs. "On a count of three. One, two..." Before she could even say *three*, they lifted me up just inches from the ground and placed me on the gurney.

"Did you talk to Soul?" I asked Layla when she appeared back at my side.

"He said that he'll meet you at the hospital. Excuse me, but her boyfriend wants to know what hospital you're about to take her to."

"Kindred," she answered as they rushed me over to the ambulance.

"I'm riding with her." Mia snatched my things away from Layla and went to climb up into the back of the ambulance with me.

"Are you family?"

I gripped the male EMT by the collar of his shirt, pulling his face down to me. "I got a baby that's trying to come out of me as we speak and you want to worry about if she's family or not? Just let her in the fucking truck so we can get to the hospital."

"Alright," he groaned and I let his shirt go.

They placed me in the back of the ambulance and Mia climbed in alongside me.

"I don't know if I'll be able to do this," I told her and she gripped me by the hand. I steady took deep breaths but it didn't seem to be helping with the pain. Those contractions were worse than cramps. And to think I told my doctor that I wanted to do it naturally.

"You got this, Sanaa and I promise that baby girl is going to come out healthy and strong just like her mother."

"Did anyone call and tell Naomi?"

"I'm texting her now."

I laid there gazing up at the ceiling silently praying for my baby's well-being. It's crazy because when I first got pregnant, I didn't even want to keep her. A lot had changed over the course of the last eight months and my bond to my baby grew stronger. I'm not certain how I would feel if I was to lose my baby. I couldn't.

The ambulance came to a halt and the back doors flew open. "You got this. I'm going to be with you until hubby shows up." Mia smiled brightly at me.

They rolled me into the hospital and I was met by my doctor, Dr. Stern. They took me to the back and put me in a room. At first, they were tripping about Mia coming along with me but I told them I wasn't doing it without her.

"Let's take a look at that baby," Dr. Stern said, rolling the ultrasound machine into the room. I laid there as she rolled the ball over my stomach. I gazed up into Mia's face with worried eyes. They were glossed over because I was scared as hell. "From what I'm seeing, the baby looks fine except for the fact that the umbilical cord is wrapped around her neck. We're going to have to prep you for a caesarean."

My eyes grew wide. I'd never had surgery before and here they were trying to cut me open to save my baby's life. Of course, I was going to go along with it. I just wished that Soul was there with me instead of Mia.

The nurses busied themselves around the room, preparing me for surgery. Mia tried calling Soul again but he wasn't picking up the phone. There was no way I was going into that room alone so I told Mia to get dressed to go in there with me. It wasn't the ideal person but at least she was there.

Knock! Knock!

The door pushed open and I nibbled on my lower lip. My heart pounded in my chest as I waited to lock eyes with whoever was on the other side. Naomi popped her head in. "I was just trying to make sure I had the right room." She pushed the door on open and shut it behind her. "What happened? You're not due for another couple of weeks."

"It was Sofia. That bitch caught me slipping and whooped my ass."

"Swear that bitch got an ass whooping coming her way when I drop this load!" Naomi scrunched her face up then sat her purse down on the chair.

"You don't even have to worry about all that because I'm going to beat her ass. She better pray to God that nothing comes out wrong with my baby!"

"Where's Soul?" she quizzed finally realizing that his presence wasn't in the room.

"I don't know. We tried calling him but he hadn't been answering the phone. Guess you're just going to have to go into the room with me."

"You might make me have a heart attack." She planted her hand over her heart.

"You might as well gone prepare yourself for what you're going to go through."

"Are you ready, Sanaa?" the nurse peeked her head into the room and asked.

"No, but I might as well be."

They pulled me out the room and I laid in the bed staring at the lights on the ceiling as I rolled down the hallway. "I'm here. I'm here." I heard Soul's voice before I saw his head lean over the bed.

I exhaled.

Knowing that he was going to be in the room with me was all I needed to feel relieved. Secure. Safe.

"Where have you been?"

"I had to come all the way from home."

"I thought you were going to miss out on your child being born."

"Never that."

We got into the room and Soul stood by my side the entire twenty minutes it took for them to get my baby safely out. When I heard her cries, I cried myself. It was then that I knew she was going to be all right. They wrapped her up in a blanket and brought her over to me.

Soul stared down into my face with tears in his eyes as well. He was excited. It was written all over his face.

"I love you," he spoke, leaning down kissing me softly in the center of my forehead.

"What did you name her?" the nurse asked.

I took one look at Soul and smiled. "Gabrielle Shantel Maserati." I didn't even have to think about the name. It just came to me naturally just like the love that I had for Soul.

"Marry me, Sanaa. We don't have to have no fancy wedding. Hell, I don't even have to put a ring on your finger if you don't want me to. Just marry me."

"Of course, I will." I cupped his face and he brought his lips down to mine, kissing me deeply.

SOUL

I got scared as fuck when I got that call about Sanaa. I actually thought the baby wasn't going to make it. I was doing the entire dash down the interstate trying to get to her. On my way there, I called and texted Sofia but she wouldn't answer. Every bone in my body was telling me she was the one who had done that shit. I asked old girl who called if she knew had done it and she said it was a girl she had never seen before but she kept saying my name. It couldn't be anyone else but her.

Sofia knew she fucked up that's the reason why she wasn't answering my fucking calls. I told her what was going to happen if she harmed even one hair on Sanaa's head. She could have easily killed my baby and I wasn't about to stand for that shit. I was going to get her one way or another.

Now that I knew the baby was all right, I had to go and take care of Sofia. She couldn't roam this earth another day after the stunt she pulled. They placed Sanaa into a room and she immediately fell asleep. Naomi was in there with her and the other chick had left to get back to work.

"Can you watch out for Sanaa for me? It's something I have to go and take care of right quick."

She got up from the couch and rushed over to me with wide eyes. "You're going after Sofia aren't you?"

"I'm not answering that question." I grabbed the doorknob and she clutched my wrist.

"Just make sure you make that ho pay. She could have killed my niece with her stupid ass." She let go of my wrist and without uttering a word, I pulled the door open and shut it behind me. She didn't have to remind me that she could have killed my baby. I somewhat felt like it was all my fault. I should have taken her ass out when I had the chance. I just didn't think that she would take things this far. Guess you never knew what a person really could do.

Climbing into my car, I headed to her house to see if she was there. When I got there, her car wasn't in the driveway, so I leaned back, pulling my phone out my front pants pocket. Reluctantly, I dialed her number again and hoped she answered.

At this point, I didn't know where the hell she was at or how long she was going to try to stay in hiding.

"Hello?" I exhaled when her voice came through the phone.

"Why you haven't been answering the phone? I've been calling and texting you."

"I'm sorry. I had left my phone in the room. I'm out of town right now."

"What are you doing out of town?" I questioned her, took one last look at her house and pulled away from the curb.

"I had to go take care of something for my father. I should be back the day after tomorrow."

"Where exactly are you? I've been doing some thinking and maybe you're right. Things between Sanaa and I would never work. I'd never be able to trust her again after she shot me."

"Are you serious?" I could hear the excitement in her voice and knew I had her dumbass exactly where I wanted her at.

"Yeah."

"Well, I'm in Ballwin staying at the Marriott on Maryville Centre Drive."

"Aight, give me a few and I'll be there." I quickly ended the call and dropped my phone into the cup holder. I wasted no time getting on the interstate heading toward Ballwin. It amazed me that she was dumb enough to fall for that bullshit but she had been acting crazy lately, so she might have believed me if I were to tell her the sky was red outside if she thought that was a way for her to get closer to me.

I did damn near the whole dash just so I could make it to Ballwin. I pulled up to the Marriott and parked in the back of the building. I went inside up to room 223 that she texted me and knocked on the door. I stood there stroking on my goatee, waiting for her to answer.

Sofia swung the door open with a wide smile on her face. It took everything in me not to pull my piece and shoot her right between the eyes at that very moment. My finger was itching like a muhfucka but I remained cool for the time being.

"I didn't actually think you would come." She stepped to the side, inviting me inside her suite.

"What? You thought I was just talking or something?" My eyes roamed around the room then landed back on her.

"No..." I sat down on the couch and she came, taking the seat beside me. "I'm so glad that you finally came to your senses. We made the perfect power couple. You just had to remember why you fell for me in the first place." Her hand landed on my thigh as she gazed into my eyes. I had to keep unclenching my fists to stop myself from knocking her the fuck out.

I didn't utter a word, just pulled my phone out and shot the clean-up crew a text. "You look tensed." She got down on her knees and tugged at my Versace belt. "Let me relax you." She was so in her zone that she didn't notice me reach behind my back and pull my strap out.

Before she could even pull my dick out the hole, I roughly gripped her by the hair and snatched her up to her feet as I rose from the couch. "I told you not to harm a hair on Sanaa's head but you just couldn't help yourself. Now could you?"

"Soul, what are you doing?" I could see the tears forming in her eyes.

"Did you really think I was playing with you when I told you, I'll kill your ass?"

"No, Soul, please don't!" she whimpered and tried to pry my fingers from her hair.

"Ain't no point in doing all that now." I pressed the silencer at the center of her forehead. "I never loved you."

Pew!

The bullet went straight through and I let her hair go. Her body slumped to the floor. I kneeled down, wiping the blood off my gun with her shirt then slipped it into my waistline. I took one last look at Sofia before heading to the door and grabbing the do not disturb sign and slipping it on the knob then headed downstairs and out the side door. I didn't have to stick around for the clean-up crew because I knew they were going to get here, do their job, and get out.

If I had to drop every muhfucka in St. Louis to make sure my girl was straight then I would. People better tread lightly when it came to her. She was officially about to be my wife, and I'd do any and everything necessary to protect my family. It was all I knew how to do.

BERLIN

When Soul called and told me about Sanaa going into labor, I wanted to put everything on hold and rush up there but he told me to go on and finish handling my business. I knew he was scared as hell from the tone of his voice but like always, he put on a front to remain strong. I wish he knew he didn't have to always be strong around me. I understood where he was coming from when he told me what happened. If I was him, I would have been dealt with Sofia's crazy ass. That bitch needed to be locked up somewhere and they throw away the key.

Knowing Soul, he was going to kill her ass before the night was even over with. My assumptions were proved correct when Steve received the clean-up text from him. All I could do was shake my head.

After I finished handling business, I headed up to the hospital where I knew Naomi was going to be. I had to come there anyway. No way I was going to miss seeing my niece. Shit sounded funny to me. Turned out, Soul actually was the father and I been calling him crazy all along for claiming a baby that didn't belong to him. Guess he knew something we all didn't.

Tap! Tap!

I lightly tapped on the room door with my knuckle. It was kind of late and I wasn't sure if they were sleeping or not. Then again, I didn't want to just enter without making my presence known first. I didn't want to walk in and see something I wasn't supposed to be seeing.

I pushed the door open and entered the room. Sanaa was sitting up in bed watching television and Naomi was lying on the couch fast asleep with cover on top of her.

"Congrats, Sis." I placed the bouquet of pink roses on the window sill then went over kissing Sanaa on the cheek. "She's gorgeous," I told her after I caught a glimpse of the baby that was sleeping in her arms. She was bright as hell just like Soul and me with a head full of jet-black curly hair. Messing around with her and Soul, that baby was going to be spoiled rotten. I couldn't really talk because my son was going to be spoiled as well.

"Thank you."

"Where's Soul?" I asked her.

"I'm not sure. He's been gone a while. I was sleep when he left."

I went over to the couch where Naomi was and brushed her curly hair back out her face. We had been through so much together lately. I was glad that we were finally back on the right track.

"She loves you a lot. You know that right?" Sanaa said, catching me off guard.

"Yeah, I know."

"She may act tough but she's still a woman, Berlin. She's given you a second chance, so you need to do right by her this time."

"I plan on it."

I lightly shook Naomi, trying to wake her from her sleep. She stirred softly and groaned before her eyes finally peeled open. "Hey, get up. I want to show you something."

"Isn't it late?" She wiped her eyes and sat up straight on the couch.

"It is, but I still want to show you something. Are you going to come with me?"

"This better not be no bullshit, Berlin." She mugged me then slowly rose to her feet. I could tell she was sleeping good as hell on that little ass couch from the drool that was on the corner of her mouth. I stroked my thumb across it, wiping it off for her.

"Just come on." I interlocked my fingers with hers and led her out of the room to the elevator.

"Where are you taking me?"

"It's a surprise."

"Well, that surprise better have food involved if you woke me from my sleep." She pouted as we stepped onto the elevator. I took her down to the first floor. She followed closely alongside me as I led her to a pair of double doors. "What are we going in there for?"

"You sure asking a lot of questions."

"Damn right because I be wanting to know stuff." I gave her a half-smirk and pushed the doors open. "What's all this?" she queried after her eyes roamed around the chapel. On my way there, I called Emily and got her to come to the hospital and make the chapel all romantic and shit for Naomi. I know I had cashed out on this big ass wedding but I couldn't let another day go by without her being my wife. I wanted to show her I was serious about she and I. I thought what better way to do so than giving her my last name?

"Did you really do all this for me?" She stared at me with tear-filled eyes.

"Of course, I did. I couldn't wait for you to be my wife."

She stepped further into the chapel. I glared at her watching her eyes glisten. The priest stood at the end of the aisle in his all-black. In the aisle next to each pew was white lit candles. Scattered on the floor were white roses.

Emily popped out with a bouquet of pink roses. Naomi stood there letting the tears cascade down her cheeks. I hooked her chin, tilting her face to me and wiped them away with my fingertips.

"I can't believe you did this."

"Believe it."

I walked down the aisle and stood beside the priest. A wide smile spread across Naomi's face as she gawked down at me. I know it probably wasn't the type of wedding she would have wanted but it was perfect for me. Me and her, that's all I really needed.

Naomi slowly walked down the aisle. Her eyes never left mine. I half-smirked knowing that I was just moments away from making her, my wife. She was about to make me the happiest man alive.

She made it to me and I grabbed her free hand. Tears were still evident in her eyes as her gaze met mine.

"Do you, Berlin take Naomi as your lawful wife, to have and to hold, from this day forward, for better or for worse, for richer or for poorer, in sickness and in health, to love and cherish until death do you part?"

"I do," I responded with a grin.

"And do you, Naomi take Berlin as your lawful husband, to have and to hold, from this day forward, for better or for worse, for richer or for poorer, in sickness and in health, to love and cherish until death do you part?"

"I do."

I took her ring from my pocket and slipped it onto her finger. After that ring touched her finger, everything else didn't really matter. I gripped her by the back of her head and pulled her lips to mine.

"How does it feels to be Mrs. Maserati?" I questioned her when we pulled back from our kiss.

"It feels—" Her eyes darted to the floor catching me totally off guard. They lifted up and met my gaze. "I think my water just broke."

NAOMI

I t's crazy how I ended up going into labor early. Then it was the exact night Sanaa had to have a c-section. I had too much pressure on me and I guess the baby wanted to come out early. It was a good thing that it waited until after Berlin and I had gotten married.

They rushed me upstairs because the baby felt like he was crowning while I was in the wheelchair. I know he wasn't that excited to come into this world. If only he knew what he was coming into.

After a few pushes, a million of curse words, slaps, and cries later... I finally gave birth to a healthy baby boy. He may have been premature but he seemed healthy nonetheless.

Berlin Maserati Jr.

I was finally able to hold my baby in my arms. See his sweet little face. He was bright as hell and everything about him looked like his father. Of course, he had a head full of hair. I was hoping that he would have come out with something like me but I guess I hated and talked about Berlin so much during my pregnancy he didn't have a choice but to look like his ugly ass.

They rolled me into the room right alongside Sanaa. It was a request I made and she agreed to it. We went through our entire pregnancy together and our babies were born hours apart. If only Junior had come a few hours earlier, he'd have the same birthday as his cousin. Maybe, he and Gabby would be best friends just like their parents. That was a thought.

"Hey, Naomi!" Sanaa shrieked when I got into the room. "Sorry, I tried to make it to your delivery but they wouldn't let me out the room."

"It's fine." I was beaming with a smile going from ear to ear. I may have been tired but at the same time, I was happy as hell. I had married the man I love and given birth to my first child who I instantly felt connected to. I wanted to protect him from everything. Everyone.

"Where is he?" she asked me.

"They took him to the nursery. Think they just wanted to make sure everything was good with him."

"Yeah..."

Berlin pulled a chair up beside my bed and plopped down in it. I knew he was tired himself because he had been going nonstop since he left the condo this morning. But I doubt very seriously that he was tired as me. I had just gotten done pushing out an entire human being. That shit was exhausting as fuck. All of us had a long ass day and needed to get some rest. I already knew what Sanaa was doing. She was trying her best to stay up until Soul made it back. Honestly, I thought he would have been back by now. I don't know what was holding him up.

The room door pushed open and Soul finally graced us with his presence. "Am I missing something here?" he quizzed after his eyes landed on me.

"You missed a lot while you were gone," Berlin spoke for all of us.

"Like what?" He went over and kissed Sanaa on the lips.

I raised my hand so they could see the new addition to it. "Oh. My. God! You guys didn't!" Sanaa yelled. I could tell she wanted to get out the bed and properly congratulate me, but I was certain she was in pain from the surgery she had not too long ago. "I'm so happy for you guys!"

"Thank you." I smiled gazing down at my ring. I couldn't believe I had actually done that. My mother was going to probably be angry about it because she was so excited about me getting married and I had done it without her or my father walking me down the aisle. She had to understand it was what I wanted to do.

I thought having a huge wedding was something I truly wanted but turned out, it wasn't. I was fine with just my man being there. It was me and him against the world. Well, now Junior was added to the equation weeks early. But doesn't matter. I was in love with my little family.

"Guessing you being with Berlin for the rest of your life finally hit you and you went into labor," Soul joked and everyone in the room laughed except Berlin.

"That shit ain't even funny, bruh."

"Calm down, bae, he was only joking." I already knew how he could get sometimes. I didn't need him tearing up these people hospital room over a silly joke. He promised me he was going to work on his anger and I could only hope he was going to keep that commitment.

"I don't know about y'all but I'm about to go to sleep." Soul kicked his shoes off and pulled his t-shirt over his head like he was at home or something. He pulled the curtain back between Sanaa's and my bed.

"You're not about to do anything until you tell me where you've been all this time," Sanaa said and I could tell she was serious from the tone of her voice.

"Babe, please don't start with me right now."

"Where you been at Soul? You left me while I was sleeping. Didn't even bother to wake me and tell me you were leaving. I had to find out from Naomi."

"Let's just say you don't have to worry about Sofia anymore. Can I go to sleep now?" It got quiet on the other side of the curtain so I assumed that they had laid down.

I shifted my eyes from the curtain to Berlin who was sitting in the chair beside my bed. If only he knew exactly how much I loved him.

"I love you," I softly spoke.

He peeled one of his eyes open and stared back at me. "You know I love you too, Mrs. Maserati. Now get some rest."

"I love you forever and ever," I lowly whispered and shut my eyes.

SANAA

I sat in the hospital room, holding Gabby in my arms as she slept. I still couldn't believe I just had a baby. All I could do was thank God she'd come out healthy. I was really nervous about her coming early especially after the fact Sofia had jumped on me the way she had. Lucky for her, Soul had gotten to her before I could because I promise she was going to pay for the bullshit she had done. Knowing him, he probably made her death quick and painless. Far from what I had planned for that ass.

Since they were finally going to let me out the hospital today after keeping me for a few days to observe Gabby, Soul was coming to pick me up. Naomi had left the day before and it really was lonely since she'd been gone. I totally understood she had to be at home with her own baby. I just wished that we would have left around the same time or day. I wasn't really stressing too much about it long as my baby was straight, that's all I was concerned about.

Buzz, Buzz

I grabbed my phone off the bed beside me and stared down at the message that just come through from Soul. He was letting me know he was outside and about to come up. I got up and gently placed Gabby into her car seat, making sure to securely strap her in. With it being my first child, I was afraid I was going to end up doing something wrong or something. I was extra cautious when it came to her.

After she was strapped into her car seat, the door pushed open and Soul appeared. I couldn't help the smile that graced my face after seeing his. He looked so happy to see us and he hadn't even been gone away that long.

"You look so handsome." I went over gripping him by the waist and swayed my hips. "I missed you."

"I missed you too, future Mrs. Maserati." He pecked me softly on the lips then went over and glanced down at Gabby in her car seat. "Daddy missed you too, princess." He grabbed her by her tiny foot and wiggled her leg. "Let's get y'all out of here."

"Yeeesssss, because I'm ready to go."

They had finally come back into the room with my discharge papers and let me out of the hospital. Everything with Gabby was fine so we both were expecting to go home but ended up going to Soul's place. I didn't really have the energy to argue with him about taking me home so I just kept my mouth shut and went where he took me. I was sure he wanted to be around Gabby anyway. He barely left our side since she came into the world. It was cute to me though. He was willing to cater to the both of us.

Soul grabbed Gabby's car seat and diaper bag then took them into the house, sitting them by the front door. He wouldn't let me get out of the car until he came back to help me. I was still kind of in pain from my surgery and the only thing I really wanted to do was lay down and sleep. With Soul being there, I was sure I'd be able to get at least a couple of hours of sleep in.

He helped me out the car and into the house. He grabbed Gabby when we stepped over the threshold and shut the door.

"Come with me I want to show you something."

"Can you just tell me what it is?" I asked him, not really feeling up for surprises at the moment.

"I'd rather just show you." With his free hand, he gripped mine and led me upstairs. He took me to a bedroom door and we halted. "I've been working on this ever since you told me that the baby was mine." He gave me a half-smile then pushed the door open.

My mouth fell agape and eyes grew misty as I stared at the beautiful pink and white nursery. I mean, it was shitting on the one I had at the house. It was just gorgeous.

I slowly walked over to the white trimmed in pink bed. I couldn't believe he actually done all that for me. Well, in a way, I could believe it. He had gone and bought me a new house and truck so I should have seen it coming.

I turned and brushed my fingertips across the stuffed animals that lined the white couch. Having a white sofa in a nursery wasn't ideal for me, but it's what he bought so I wasn't going to complain. "I love it." I turned to him with a smile spread across my face and tears still in my eyes.

"I'm glad that you do." He stepped into the nursery and kissed me softly on the lips then set Gabby's car seat down on the floor.

"There's something I wanted to ask you."

"What's that?" My eyes shifted from Gabby to his handsome face.

"Do you want to move in with me? I know you probably planned on it after we got married, but I want you to now. As in right this very moment."

He caught me off guard with that one. The thought had crossed my mind. I knew he was going to try and get me to sooner or later especially since I'd already had the baby and he'd just asked me to marry him. It probably would have been the logical thing to do so I said, "Of course I will, but what about the house you just bought me?"

"We can sell it, it's no big deal."

"Well, I guess we can do that." I closed the short gap between us and brushed my hands from his stomach up to his chest. I cupped his face and stared him deep into the eyes. "I love the hell out of you."

"I love you too." He gently kissed my lips, then took Gabby from her car seat. "You need to get you some rest. I got this in here," he made known.

SOUL

There wasn't a doubt in my mind that Sanaa wouldn't move in with me. I figured she was going to say yes that's why I went ahead and got the nursery done. Even if she wasn't going to move in, I still planned on doing one, just not that quickly. Things between us were moving great. I wouldn't change the things we've gone through for the world.

I grabbed Gabby from her car seat after Sanaa left out the nursery. She was sleeping but that didn't stop me from steady holding her. I sat in the white rocking chair and just gazed down into her face as I rocked. I couldn't believe this little girl was actually mine. She'd come from my nut sack. Her and Junior were going to one day carry on the family name and legacy. I wasn't too certain if that's what I wanted for her, but knowing her being my child, it's probably going to be the road she took.

"I promise you that I'll do everything in my power to protect you from the world." I leaned down kissing her on the center of her forehead. I sat there for a while longer just holding her in my arms. Finally, I got up placing her over into her bed then grabbed my baby monitor.

As I stepped out into the hallway, I heard a noise coming from downstairs. The closer I got to the staircase, I could tell it was the front door.

Boom! Boom! Boom!

Someone banged on my door like crazy. I wasn't certain who it was because I wasn't expecting company. When I got to the foyer, I opened my table drawer and grabbed my Nine from there.

Boom! Boom! Boom!

I pulled the front door open with my gun drawn. I eased my hand down when I saw it was Mr. Romano. "Where the hell is my daughter!" he roared, bursting straight past me into my house.

"I'm going to need you to tone your voice down. My daughter and wife are upstairs sleeping."

His eye twitched as he glared at me. I knew he was going to try something when I saw his hand ball up. He rushed me, gripping me by the collar of my shirt and pinned me up against the wall. "I don't give a damn about your daughter or your fucking wife. I want to know where the hell my daughter is and you're going to tell me. I know you did something to her!"

"First of all, you're going to get your muhfuckin' hands off me right now." I shoved him back away from me and he stumbled a little bit. I hated whenever people touched me when they weren't permitted to. "Secondly, don't come in my shit disrespecting my family. That's the quickest way for you to catch a hot one in your ass. And lastly, I don't know where the hell your daughter is at and quite frankly, I don't give a damn."

"You know where she is. I know that you know. I told her to leave your ass alone but she just wouldn't listen. I don't know what you were doing to her for her to be so stupid over you." I wanted to tell him *slanging this dick*, but I opted out of it.

I roughly grabbed him by the forearm and pulled him toward the front door. "Like I said, I don't know where your fucking daughter is. Don't come back to my house or else I won't have any other choice but to cause you to come up missing like her." I half-smirked and slammed the door in his face.

When I told him, I didn't know where his daughter was, I was speaking facts. I honestly didn't. The clean-up crew got rid of her body. What they did with her remains had nothing to fucking do with me. Truthfully, I didn't really want to know anyway.

Scrubbing my hand down my face, I exhaled. I put the safety back on the gun and placed it back in the drawer before heading upstairs. I peeped into the nursery to make sure Gabrielle was still sleeping then went into the bedroom. Sanaa was lying in the bed with her back facing me. I just stood there glaring at her. She was sleeping so peacefully because she didn't even know I was in the room.

I neared the bed and kicked my shoes off before sitting on the edge of it. She must have felt when I sat down because she turned over and her low eyes peered at me. "What took you so long to come in here?"

"Had to take care of something first." I palmed her face, brushing her hair back behind her ear. She slowly eased up in the bed. "What's wrong?" I asked her, feeling her uneasiness.

She shifted her eyes from me down to her lap. She rubbed her hands up and down her thighs. "Do you really think that we are going to work this time?" I don't know how I didn't see that coming.

"Are you still worrying about that?"

She got up on her knees. "Of course, I am, it's still bothering me because of what I did." I saw the tears forming in her eyes. I grabbed her by the wrist, pulling her into me.

"You don't have to worry about all that. I forgive you for that babe. I completely understand why you did it. I should have told you the truth in the first place. In a way, it's partly my fault. You're the one I want to be with. Stop stressing about it. I promise you that you don't have anything to worry about." I pecked her on the lips.

She laid down with her head in my lap and her eyes closed. "I can't believe that we're parents, Soul. It feels so surreal."

I brushed my fingertips up and down her forearm. I could see the goosebumps forming on her arms. "Well, believe it. And you're going to be the best mother."

"What makes you so sure of that?"

"I just know." I had no doubt that she wouldn't make a great mother. That's why I got excited when I found out that she was pregnant. The thought of having a child had never crossed my mind, but she definitely planted the seed there.

"I can't wait to marry you." She peeled her eyes open and grinned up into my face.

"Gone and start planning the wedding. You have plenty of downtime now since you're not working." Honestly, I couldn't wait to marry her either. See her walk down the aisle in her gorgeous dress. See her happy tears. For me to cry tears of joy knowing she was mine and only mine. Spend the rest of my life showing her exactly how she's supposed to be loved.

She's told me about her past. I knew some of the things that she's been through. I just wanted to make up for the last nigga's mistakes. I know it wasn't my obligation to, but it's what I wanted to do.

"I know nothing about what I want my wedding to be like. I wasn't like most girls who fantasized about her wedding day when they were younger. If I'm being completely honest, I never thought the day would come that I'd get married at all. I didn't think that type of happiness actually existed. But after I met you, and fell in love with you, I knew it did. I'd be happy just going down to the courthouse and getting married to you. I don't need no big fancy wedding. It could be just me, you, and Gabby as far as I care. Oh, and Naomi and them." She smiled. That was the one thing I loved about her. She was pure, well sort of.

"I love you," I said and kissed her lips.

NAOMI

Six weeks had gone by and I felt like I was going crazy being locked up in the condo. Out of all the time that I've known, Sanaa, I don't think I've ever been away from her that long. Sure, we called and FaceTimed each other but that's all we could do until the babies were old enough to leave the house. Sanaa tried to leave sooner than the six weeks, but Soul wasn't having that shit. She was angry about it but soon got over it.

Today marked the sixth week and I couldn't wait to get out the condo. I reached over and grabbed my phone off the nightstand before glancing at the baby monitor to ensure Junior was still sleeping. Once I saw he wasn't making any noise, my head crashed back into the pillow and I dialed Sanaa's number.

"Hello?" her voice cracked as she spoke. I could tell she had probably been sleeping before I interrupted her.

"Don't tell me you're still over there sleep. Thought you would have been up by now."

"Man, Gabby kept me up all night. Last night she didn't want to sleep for shit." She sighed heavily, then I heard ruffling noises in the background. It wasn't long before I heard water running. "I don't know what's wrong with her." She mumbled as she scrubbed the toothbrush across her teeth. Thank God I wasn't having those problems at the moment. Let me not speak too soon because it could still happen.

"I'm sorry, boo. I was calling to see if you wanted to go to lunch with me. Know it's the sixth week and I can't wait to get out of this house." I picked at my fingernails awaiting her answer. *I sure needed to get my nails done.*

"Where were you thinking about going? Shoot, I'd go to McDonald's right about now. Anywhere is better than these four walls." I knew exactly what she meant. I felt like the walls were slowly closing in on me.

"Uh, I don't know. What about Bogart's Smokehouse? I got a taste for some finger-licking barbeque." My mouth was already watering thinking about their ribs. The shits were off the chain.

"Oh my God, you don't even have to convince me. I'll meet you there in an hour." She paused for a moment then said, "Nah, make it two. Forgot I have to get Gabby dressed as well and that little girl doesn't like clothes." I snickered just imaging how her face looked at the moment when she said that.

"Poor tink, it'll be alright." I laughed and disconnected the call. Lucky for me, I had a son and not a girl. I could just throw him something on and be out the door.

I climbed out the bed and went into the bathroom to handle my hygiene. Once I was done, I just settled on a simple pair of denim looking joggers and a white t-shirt. I was not trying to look cute or anything. I already had my man and he loved me just the way I was.

After I got Junior dressed, I placed him in his car seat and we headed out the front door. When I got into the car, I texted Berlin to let him know I was about to meet Sanaa for lunch. I didn't want him to come home for whatever reason and be looking for me. That nigga would probably turn the entire city upside down just to find me.

It didn't take me long to make it to the restaurant. I didn't spot Sanaa's car or truck anywhere so I knew she hadn't made it there yet. Grabbing Junior connecting his car seat to his stroller, I pushed him inside the restaurant. I sat down at one of the first empty tables I saw and waited for Sanaa to arrive.

"Can I start you off with something to drink?" the waitress asked me when she made it to my table.

"Uh," I wanted to have something with liquor in it but knew I couldn't since I was breastfeeding. It was killing me being inside that condo for that long with all Berlin's liquor and couldn't touch any. "You can just bring me a water. That'll be fine for now," I told her then took my attention back to my phone.

"Sure thing," she responded and bounced off.

I snapped a picture of Junior sleeping and posted it on my Snapchat. It killed me how I saw so much of his father in him. "How come you couldn't look like mommy, huh?" I questioned him like he was going to be able to answer me.

"Because he wants to look like daddy. Ain't that right little man?" Sanaa smiled when I glanced up at her.

"You look good for someone who didn't get any sleep last night." I admired the black skirt two-piece she wore. Her body had damn near snapped back to its original size. Me on the other hand, I had a little bit more extra baby fat left. Berlin was loving it so I wasn't complaining.

"I tried." She sighed and plopped down in the chair across from me. I waved my hand for the waitress to come back over. Since Sanaa was here, we both could order. My stomach rumbled just thinking about the delicious food.

We both rambled off our order to the waitress. After she left I glanced Junior to make sure he was still sleeping. His big eyes were glaring back at me.

"Since I can leave the house now, Soul wants to get a nanny so I can start planning our wedding. I'm not sure how I feel about having someone I don't know taking care of my baby. Not with so much they have going on in the world today."

My eyes expanded as my head jerked in her direction. "Oooh, I got an idea. Instead of planning a wedding, how about you take the one that I planned? It'll be like a wedding present."

"No, I couldn't do that."

"Why not? It's already paid for Sanaa. The only thing you have to do is find the perfect wedding dress." She sat there in deep thought for a moment. "Just think about it, what use is it going to be for us? We're already married and I'm sure Berlin won't mind."

"Yeah, I don't know about that..."

I quickly whipped my phone out and dialed Berlin's number. "What's wrong!" he answered on the first ring.

"Does something have to be wrong for me to call you?" It was like ever since Junior came into the world, he was worried about me more. Maybe it was just the life he was living that had him so paranoid.

"No, just thought something was wrong, that's all."

"I was just calling you because I wanted to get your permission for something even though I don't think I need it in the first place."

"What's up?"

"Well, Sanaa is supposed to be planning a wedding for her and Soul, and I told her..."

"Yeah," he cut me off.

"What you mean, yeah? You don't even know what I was about to ask you."

"Doesn't matter." I rolled my eyes and exhaled.

"I told her that they can have the one we were planning."

"Okay..."

My eyes shifted from the table and met her gaze. "See, told you. Alright, babe, I'll see you when you get home." I hung the phone up and placed it on the table in front of me. "I told you that you could have it."

"Fine, if y'all insist." The waitress brought our food out to the table and placed it down in front of us. "I don't even know where to begin looking for a dress."

Junior started fussing so I grabbed one of his bottles out his diaper bag and shoved it into his mouth. "Don't even sweat all that. What you think you got me for?"

SANAA

I t's the night before Soul and I's wedding. It seemed like the day had snuck up on me out of nowhere. I was excited about it but nervous all at the same time.

We decided to stay in hotel rooms. Naomi kept saying something about it being a tradition or something where the groom doesn't see the bride until she walked down the aisle. I thought maybe she knew what she was talking about. She was the one who was all into the wedding mess, so I just agreed with it.

I couldn't lie and say I didn't want to go and be with Soul because I really did. He was the only thing I could think about. I was supposed to been listening to Naomi, Mia, Layla and some of the other girls that worked at the salon but I had long tuned them out. I wanted to be near Soul and couldn't believe I had foolishly agreed to this bullshit.

"Sanaa," Mia called out, bringing me back from my thoughts.

"Yeah?" My brows furrowed as I stared at her. She was trying to hand me a glass of wine. Since I had pumped my breasts for enough milk to hold Gabby over for a while, I accepted it. No way I was going to spend my last officially single night sober. This was like my fourth glass of wine along with the couple shots Naomi talked me into taking so the liquor was definitely taking its effect.

"You good girl? I had to call your name four times for you to answer."

"Yeah, sorry."

"She just sitting there thinking about Soul and that dick," Naomi teased.

"You can talk about me all you want to." I stuck my tongue out at her then turned my wine glass up.

"Girl, if you miss your man, then you better take your ass and find him," Mia encouraged.

I sat there debating for a while on what I really wanted to do. I was certain he wasn't even in his hotel room in the first place. He was probably out somewhere with Berlin having fun for his bachelor party. Or worse, someone could have been at his hotel room. That just made me want to go by there even more. I didn't think Soul would cheat on me, but there are things that happened before weddings to make people think differently.

"Fuck it, I'm leaving." I gulped down the last bit of my wine then dashed out of the hotel room.

"That's right girl, you better go find that man!" I heard Mia yell behind me just before the door shut. It's crazy because we were both staying in the same hotel just on different floors. I stopped at the elevator and pressed the up button. I stood there anxiously waiting for the doors to open.

"Please don't let nobody be in there with him," I prayed to myself as I stepped on and the doors shut.

I stopped in front of his suite door and exhaled before knocking on it. It took him a moment to answer it but when he did, I felt relieved. He stood before me with his shirt off and all his tattoos on display. My eyes couldn't help but dart to the scar I left in his chest where the bullet entered him. I immediately felt bad. I brushed my fingertips across the scar with glistening eyes.

"What are you doing here?" he quizzed, grabbing my hand pulling it up to his lips and kissing me softly.

"Couldn't stop thinking about you." He pulled me on into the suite and shut the door behind me. "Thought you would have been out partying or something."

"No..."

He cupped my face, staring deep into my eyes. It was then, I knew I didn't have anything to worry about. Soul was for me and only me. I was tripping and stressing myself for no apparent reason.

"I know I wanted to wait until our wedding night, but I want you to make love to me." Soul and I hadn't had sex in a couple of weeks. I watched this movie where the girl stopped having sex with her fiancé so it would be extra special on their wedding night. I told him I wanted to wait until our wedding night to make love. If he had known where I got the idea from, he'd think I was crazy. But the way I was feeling at the moment, I didn't think I'd be able to wait one more day. I needed him now. In the worst way.

"You sure?"

I pulled my shirt over my head, tossing it to the floor. His eyes gazed down at my breasts and I could see the lust evident in them.

"I've never been surer."

His fingertips tickled my skin as they roamed from my shoulders down my back. He pulled my frame into him with my lower back and his lips found mine, sucking my lower lip into his mouth. A moan escaped my lips and his tongue slithered into my mouth, intertwining with mine. In one swift motion, I was lifted up into the air and carried over to the bed.

He softly laid me down on it and hovered over my body. He pulled away long enough to slide his sweats down. As he pulled his pants down, I wiggled my way out of my tights. I couldn't wait to feel him inside me.

He rubbed his dick up and down my slit and I nibbled on my lower lip. I knew my pussy was drenched because it was always that way whenever I was around him. I leaned my head back just as he penetrated me and he quickly caught the hint. I could feel the tip of his tongue stroking against my neck, then his teeth sunk down just as I moaned out.

"Ungh!"

He was slowly but surely filled up my insides. He kept kissing, licking, and biting until he got down to my nipple. He tugged on it before tenderly sucking it.

"Mhm," I moaned, shutting my eyes. His thrusts sped up. I wrapped my arms around him and held onto him for dear life. "Fuck!"

My pussy was so tight, wrapped around his dick that it felt like I was having sex for the first time. He leaned back from me and his hand held my hip as he pounded deep off inside me. My gut balled into knots with every pump he gave me. I felt like he was rearranging my insides.

"Shit," he groaned. I peeled my eyes open to see that his was shut. His lower lip was tucked firmly between his teeth. My pussy gushed and a puddle formed underneath me. "This shit wet as fuck." He leaned back down, kissing me softly on the lips.

My mouth formed a huge "O" as I felt my climax coming on. I gripped his biceps tightly, digging my nails into his arms.

"Cum with me," I encouraged him. I wanted to feel the intensity of us cumming together like we did the first time. I grabbed him by the face, forcing him to stare at me. "Cum with me, Soul. I want you to cum with me."

He forcefully pounded into my pussy. The vein in his neck pulsated and I could tell he was about to reach his peak.

"Fuuuucccckkkk!" I screamed out, feeling my orgasm take over my body. He grunted and I felt his warm seeds emptying inside me.

Easing out, he fell down on the bed beside me. "Fuck," was all he could manage to get out. His chest heaved as I gazed at him out my peripheral.

"Just wait until I get that dick tomorrow night. It's going to be twice as good," I boasted, just imagining the things I was going to do to him.

He grabbed his phone off the nightstand and checked the time. "If we're even going to make it to our own wedding, then we need to get some sleep."

I laid my head on his chest and listened to him breathe as he slept. "I love you, Soul."

BERLIN

L ife couldn't be any greater. I had everything I could have hoped for, my girl, my seed, and the family hustle. Everything was sweet. I worked my ass off to get to this spot and I damn sure was going to reign supreme.

Soul and Sanaa tied the knot the day before and ran out of town for their honeymoon. I tried to take Naomi on one but she said that she'd just wait until they got back. It was understandable. I wasn't in no rush to leave the business behind. Unless I talked Soul into stepping back in to run things while I was away. He just might do it, it's not like he doesn't have a damn thing else to do with his time anyway.

I reached over putting the blunt out in the ashtray. I stared my cousin Bone in the face. "You ready?" I had been grooming this nigga to become my main-man. He was a soldier but since Soul left, I had to have someone out there in the streets to have my back. He was the best option I had so far.

"You know it." He lifted his Glock from his lap and slapped the clip into it.

I climbed out the car, placing my piece in my waistline then covered it with my shirt. My eyes roamed up the tall glass building.

"You sure he's in there?" Bone asked me when he got out of the car.

"Trust me, he in there. I had eyes on his ass for the last twenty-four hours." I was confident in that.

We both crossed the street and entered the building. The security glanced at me when we stepped in the door but I didn't stop, I kept on trekking.

"Can I help you?" he called out to me but I didn't utter a word. There wasn't shit he could do for me. Only one nigga in that building could help me and I wasn't stopping until I made it to his office.

We stepped on the elevator and went up to the twentieth floor. All eyes fell upon me as I strolled through the office up to the door. I knew which door it was because I had been there one time before. I hated whenever I had to come to niggas that didn't want to come correct when it came to my business. If I had to make my presence known to a muhfucka then I'd do it in a heartbeat.

"Stand guard at the door," I told Bone and pushed the door open, stepping over the threshold. I locked the door so no one could enter it behind me.

"Ber-Berlin, what are you doing here?"

I folded my arms across my chest and just gazed at Felix. This nigga was really trying me and I hated whenever niggas did that. "Had to come and find you since it seems like you forgot what my number was and shit. What's up with that?"

Felix and I were supposed to be going into business together. Well, I wouldn't really call it that. He had a location that would be beneficial to me, so I gave him an offer. At first, he told me he was going to sell it to me, then days later, he sent me a message saying he didn't want to anymore. No explanation. No nothing. I tried calling him back to see what his problem was but he couldn't seem to answer. I hated whenever people wasted my fucking time and he damn sure did that having me thinking I was about to make a purchase and putting in the work to upgrade the building.

"I told you I wasn't interested anymore," he nervously stated, then picked his phone up off his desk. I knew he was probably calling the security on me but I didn't give a damn.

I went over and snatched the phone from him, hanging it up. "You owe me an explanation."

"I don't owe you shit. If I'm not interested anymore then I'm just not." He relaxed back in his chair and I couldn't believe the shit that was flying from this nigga's mouth. He was acting like it was the end of the discussion when it was far from that.

I pulled my strap from my waistline and planted it on top of his desk. "Nah, see that's where you're wrong. You owe me an explanation. And I'm not leaving here until I fucking get one."

"I can't sell to you, Berlin. Most people already know what you're in to and it'll be bad for business on my end. Sorry, but I just can't do it."

"That's not a good enough explanation for me. I've already scheduled construction and more shit. Basically, what you're trying to tell me is that you wasting my time and money, right?" I eased the gun from the desk and scratched my temple with it. Obviously, he had me all the way fucked up.

"No, that's not—"

I zoomed over to him behind the desk, placing the gun at his dome. "Is that really what you're telling me, Felix?"

"No-no." His body trembled and eyes watered.

"Ain't no one allowed in there," I heard Bone's voice through the door. That was probably his bitch ass security.

"What are you trying to tell me then?" I leaned my face down by his ear so I could hear clearly whatever he was trying to say.

"I'll get the contract drawn up for you."

"Good boy." I pulled my gun from his head, placing it in my waistline. I strolled toward the door but stopped in my tracks. "I'll be expecting those papers delivered soon. I'd hate to have to come back here. Next time, I won't be so polite and a bullet will find its way into your skull. You would have wasted my time twice then. So, if you don't want these problems, then you better do what you fucking say you are."

I pulled the door open and Bone was standing there in front of this white lean security guard who looked like he wouldn't even bust a grape. I chuckled in his face and headed for the elevator with Bone directly behind me.

Felix might think that I'm playing with him but I better have that paperwork soon. He had wasted my time long enough.

"What did he say?" Bone asked me as we stepped off the elevator.

"He's supposed to cooperate this time. If he doesn't then I'll just put a bullet in his dome." I pulled the driver's side door open and climbed into the car. "Where you headed?"

I don't know where he was going but I was heading home to spend time with my woman. I had told her I was going to help out with Junior and Gabby while Soul and them were away. I had already been gone too long and she's probably going to be bitchy by the time I got there but I also had to take care of business.

"You can just drop me off at the warehouse. I have a few things to take care of before I head home."

I grabbed the blunt out the ashtray placing it between my lips. "Bet," I mumbled lighting the tip of it.

NAOMI

Trying to watch both kids was kind of a struggle for me. If one wasn't crying then the other was and vice versa. I had finally got them both down for a nap. Exhausted was an understatement for how I was feeling at the moment. I thought it would never happen.

Berlin told me he was going to help me out. That's the real reason why I agreed to this in the first place. He had been gone all morning doing only God knows what. I wanted to call and curse him out for lying to me about helping me out, but I opted out of it. I knew he was probably out handling business and didn't want to disturb him but baby, when he walked his ass through that front door, he was going to hear nothing but my mouth.

Sanaa had been calling me almost every other hour to check on Gabby. I should have known it wasn't going to work with her being away from her baby for a week. She had only been gone a day if it had been that long yet and she couldn't stop calling to save her life. I love my best friend, but she was killing me with the phone calls. She should know her baby was in good hands, so she didn't have to keep stressing about it.

My phone rang and I got up from the couch to grab it off the end table before it woke the babies up. I didn't feel like going through another hollering round with them. And if they were to wake, whoever was on the other end of that line was going to catch my backlash.

I sighed when I stared at Sanaa's name flashing on the screen. I should have known it was her. She had been calling like clockwork.

"What Sanaa?" I answered the phone and plopped back down on the couch. I glanced down at both of the babies that were sleeping peacefully in their bouncers.

"You have to answer the phone like that?"

"Yeah, when you've called me, uh I don't know five times already today." I rolled my eyes and picked with my fingernails.

"Have I really called you that much?"

"Yes..."

"Sorry, it's just I'm so bored right now. Soul is out handling business and has been gone most of the day."

"Ain't y'all supposed to be on your honeymoon? What type of business could he be handling that doesn't involve your pussy?" My brow arched when I asked her that. If Berlin was to try and pull some bullshit like that on me, he knew he wouldn't hear the end of my mouth.

"I said the same thing, but he claims that it's very important that's really why I haven't been bitching about it. I wanted to call him and see how much longer he was going to be. If I'm going to be sitting in a hotel room the entire trip by myself, then he could have just left me at home."

"You're not on a honeymoon, you're on a business trip." I laughed.

"Fuck you." I could tell I was ticking her off from the tone of her voice. "Where my baby at anyway? I miss her." I took the phone from my ear and FaceTimed her so she could see Gabby.

"Wish you would hurry back and get this monster. I think it's Yonnie in another life."

"Bitch are you really trying to come for my mother and daughter all in the same breath?"

"I'm just speaking facts. She is going to run me up a wall with all that fussing before you get back."

"She just misses her mama that's all."

"Well, you need to come get her ass if you ask me." I turned the phone back to me and got up heading into the kitchen to grab a bottle of water out the fridge. "Besides you being stuck in the hotel room by yourself right now, how is the rest of the trip going?"

"It's beautiful out here, Naomi. We definitely have to plan a girls trip one day and leave the babies at home with their fathers."

"Girl, Berlin would go fucking crazy if I did that. He's been ducking me now but was the one to volunteer to help me out in the first place." I rolled my eyes then leaned against the counter with an arch in my back.

"I'm sure he isn't ducking you."

"I'm pretty certain he is. It's all cool though because when he comes in and wants some pussy later, I'm going to be dodging him."

"Say what now?" I heard Berlin's voice coming from behind me.

Smack!

He slapped me hard on the ass and I felt it jiggle. I had been so caught up in talking shit about him that I didn't even hear him come in the house.

"Oooh, sounds like someone is in trou—" Berlin snatched my phone from me and disconnected the call before Sanaa could even finish her sentence.

"Uh, rude much?"

"So, you're in here talking shit about me now?" His brows furrowed.

"I wouldn't be talking shit about you if you would have had your ass at home helping me with those babies like you said you would."

"Had some business to take care of." He gripped me underneath my arms and lifted me up, sitting me on the countertop. He shoved my legs apart and stepped in between them. "But, I'm here now." He squeezed my ass and kissed me softly on the lips. "Shouldn't that be all that matters?"

I stroked my fingertips across the side of his face. When I fell for Berlin, I fell hard. The love I had for this man had come completely unexpected and I wouldn't have it any other way. I'd do anything for this man. I'll cut off my own hand and give it to him if he needed it. That's how much in love I was with him. He may do certain things that I don't agree with, but I wouldn't trade him for the world.

"Of course, that's all that matters."

He half-smirked and tugged at the waistline of my shorts. I already knew what was on his mind and also knew it wasn't going to work before he even got started.

"Stop Berlin." I giggled.

"Come on, you haven't given a nigga any pussy since yesterday."

"Wooow, you're acting like that's been forever."

"It has in dick years."

His plump, soft lips found the side of my neck. They immediately sucked on it and my pussy purred in my shorts. "Stop Berlin. You know we can't do this right now."

"Why not? Both of them sleep ain't it? And it's not like they are going to see anything." He kept kissing and sucking on my neck. I got to the point where I didn't have any other choice but to surrender to him.

"Okay, let's just make it quick." I lifted up some so he could pull my shorts down. He whipped his dick out his jeans so fast that it was a shame. I eased down off the counter and turned around, gripping the top of it, bracing myself for when he entered me. He glided his dick head up and down my slit getting it nice and wet. Just when he was about to enter me, Junior began screaming at the top of his lungs.

"Damn little man stop cock blocking," Berlin fussed while still trying to enter me.

"Told you it wasn't going to work." I shook my head and leaned down picking my shorts up off the floor.

"Man come on, just let me get a couple strokes in then I can just finish my shit in the bathroom."

"Guess you're just going to be beating that dick tonight." I laughed and went over, picking Junior up before he woke Gabby.

"Both of y'all just wrong." He stuffed his dick back down into his pants and left out the kitchen.

"I love you!" I shouted at him. "You're wrong for stopping me from getting some dick." I sighed and flopped down on the couch with him in my arms.

SOUL

I swished the Remy around in my glass. My eyes roamed around the restaurant waiting for my lunch date to arrive. It seemed like I had been there forever. I was close to getting up and leaving but had to realize that I was on their time and I needed them more than they needed me.

This was my second glass of Remy while waiting for them. I wanted to call and see what was keeping them but didn't want to seem anxious for our meeting even though I was nonetheless.

I felt bad as fuck for leaving Sanaa alone in the hotel room especially on our honeymoon but this meeting couldn't really seem to wait especially if things were going to get to moving before we make it back to the states. I had everything planned all out if things worked out in my favor today.

I stared down at my Rolex and saw it was going on two. If they took any longer, this lunch meeting would turn into dinner. *Ten more minutes, then I'm walking my ass out of here.* I finished off my glass and set it down on the table.

This woman walked through the entrance with nice long, black, flowing hair. She was tall for a woman, standing at maybe 5'9". She had nice long toned legs. She was a little overdressed in her white form-fitting knee-length dress. If anyone hadn't known any better, they probably would have thought this was a date and not a meeting. Guess now I could see what was taking her so long to get here. She must have taken all morning to get dressed. Then, all that makeup on her face was unnecessary as fuck.

"Mr. Maserati," she said when she stopped at the table.

"It's Soul."

"Soul." she smiled then sat down in her chair across from me. "Sorry that I'm late. I had a prior engagement that ran over."

"It's cool."

She raised her hand calling the waiter off. I sat there staring at her intently as she ordered something off the menu. Preferably, I would have liked to gone and get our meeting started. She was already late as hell then wanted to come in and order some bullshit.

"And for you, Sir?"

"Just bring me another round."

"How many of those have you had?" she questioned me.

"Enough," I dryly stated. I had been around enough women to know when one was flirting with me and she definitely was trying.

The waiter nodded his head then walked off. "Can we get this meeting started because I do have other things to attend to."

"Of course, sorry."

I grabbed my metal briefcase off the floor, sitting it on the table and unlocked it. Taking the papers from it, I handed them over to her.

"This was what you agreed to, right?" Her eyes roamed up and down the paper as if she was reading it word for word.

"And this is for all five buildings?" Her eyes lifted from the paperwork up to my eyes.

"Yes."

"Good, so you can sign the paperwork." I reached across the table attempting to hand her the pen but she just stared at it.

"Think I want to have my lunch first."

"You can't be serious."

"Oh, but I am." She put the papers off to the side and sat there with her hands planted in her lap. I didn't take her serious at first but when she didn't retrieve the pen, I had no other choice but to. "I don't like to make big decisions on an empty stomach. I mean, you are asking me to sign over all my hard work to you. I think I should simmer on it a little while longer."

When she said that, I wanted to jump across the table and whoop her ass. My blood began to boil which wasn't a good thing. If she kept playing games with me, someone was going to end up hurt, and that someone was her.

I shut the briefcase, placing it back on the floor where I got it from. I sat there in awe waiting for the waiter to bring her food out. The sooner they came, the quicker I could get back to my wife who I was sure would call me soon or later wondering where I'm at.

"Why do you keep staring at me like that?" I asked her finally getting enough of her gawking.

"You're just so handsome. Has anyone ever told you that before?" She giggled, displaying her perfect set of white teeth. "Sorry, that was a silly question. I'm sure they have."

"Yeah, my *wife* tells me that all the time," I spoke putting emphasis on wife so she would remember that I was married. That was the entire reason we were here in the first place. She knew I was already spoken for but that still didn't stop her flirting.

"Oh yeah, I forgot that you were married."

I tossed back the whole glass of Remy to help me get through the rest of this lunch. Keisha was really pushing it with me at the moment.

"How could you forget? I've said *my wife*, like a million times since we've been speaking."

"Are you happy with your wife, Soul?" she asked seductively. Suddenly, I felt her foot go between my legs and brush against my dick. I quickly slapped it down and had to restrain myself from going across her face with my fist.

Boom!

My fist pounded down on the table. "Sign the got damn paper Keisha so I can fucking go!" I barked. I hadn't realized I was that loud until I felt all the eyes on me. I rarely raised my voice but she had been pushing it ever since she strutted in here in that little ass dress. It was time for me to get the hell out of there.

"Okay, dang you don't have to be so mean about it." I shoved the pen back into her face and she snatched it from my grip. I watched as she signed her name on the dotted line. *What was so hard about that?* If she would have done that in the first place, then I could have been out of there.

"Thank you." I placed the papers back in the briefcase and rose from my chair. "Your money will be wired to your account. It wasn't a pleasure doing business with you and make sure you don't ever reach out to me again." I strolled out of there like I hadn't just hurt Keisha's feelings but she was begging for the shit. I was about to rush back to the hotel room to be with my wife and to give her the good news.

SANAA

itting in this hotel room was driving me completely insane. I had called Naomi a dozen times already just to take my mind off things and it didn't seem to be helping. I stood at the floor to ceiling glass windows and glared out at the ocean crashing against the beach. It was a beautiful beach right outside my window and all I wanted to do was sit in the hotel room and wait for Soul.

I didn't imagine my honeymoon being this way. When he first brought up the idea, I thought we were going to be making love every day all day. I'd get a little sand in places that it wasn't supposed to be. Everything was going to be all romantic and shit. But I got the complete opposite.

I sighed staring out at the people on the beach. I noticed a few couples out there hugged up and having fun. "That's supposed to be me and Soul," I huffed, getting even more irritated. "Was this really what our marriage was going to look like? Him putting other people before me..."

I heard the door open behind me. I turned around and saw Soul stepping in. He wore this navy-blue Armani suit and a metal briefcase hung in his hand.

"How did it go?" I asked him, giving him an uneasy grin. I'm sure it was evident that I was frustrated by being stuck in this room.

"I'm sorry that it took me so long. She showed up to the meeting late and—"

"She?" My forehead wrinkled. He told me he was going to a lunch meeting but said nothing to me about it being a *she* he was meeting with. It only made me wonder, but I quickly pushed the thought from my head. This was Soul I was talking about. He wouldn't dare cheat on me, so before I go ballistic, I needed to hear what else he had to say.

"Yes, she. I'm not sure if you know of her but I had a meeting with Keisha who owns *Glam Nails*."

"And, what were you meeting with her for?"

He set the briefcase down on the floor alongside his feet then tread over to where I was standing, stopping directly in front of me. I stared up into his eyes waiting for him to answer my question.

"As you may know, *Glam Nails* is a nail salon chain. She has two in St. Louis. One in Alabama and two in Atlanta."

"Okay, so can you just get to the point here because I'm not following."

"Well, she was offering to sell her locations." He rushed over grabbing his briefcase off the floor and popped it open. He took out some papers and brought them over to me. I stared down at a building with *Glitz* on the front of it but it wasn't mine.

"What's this Soul?"

He grinned at me and I couldn't help the smile that crept up on my face. I kind of had a feeling where this was going but I didn't want to jump for joy too soon.

"Soul..."

"I bought her chain. I'm getting every building remodeled as we speak and they're replacing *Glam Nails* with *Glitz*. Congrats babe, you own your very own chain of nail salons." Tears came to my eyes. I couldn't believe what he was telling me. All Soul has ever done was the unthinkable for me. Ever since day one, he's been looking out for me and I've been feeling undeserving of his love and affection.

"But babe, you shouldn't have," I sobbed. I hated when I cried because I cried ugly as hell.

"I wanted to. It's my wedding present to you." I draped my arms around his neck and just cried. I cried because I had found a man that actually loved me and would do anything for me even give me the world just to make me happy. I cried because all my sadness and revenge had been replaced with pure bliss. I also cried because I didn't expect my life to turn out this way. *What better man could I have asked for?*

"I just want to give you everything and more, babe." He eased back away from me and kissed my lips. "I love you more than life itself." He pecked me on the lips once more. "While you're with me, I promise you won't have to worry about anything else." He reached behind me untying my bikini top and it fell to the floor.

"I don't?" I already knew that but I was loving the rhythm he was in at the moment. He gently kissed me above my right breast. "Mhm, don't stop."

"Oh, trust me, I'm not going to stop." He roughly pulled his suit jacket off and tossed it to the floor. I yanked his shirt open and the buttons went flying everywhere. He snatched on my bikini bottoms and they ripped right off. They were expensive, but the way I was feeling at the moment, I didn't give a damn about that materialistic bullshit.

He spun me around and pressed my body firmly up against the glass. I heard his pants unzip, so I spread my legs and arched my back getting ready for him to enter me.

"Ungh!" I moaned out soon as he entered. My breasts were pressed firmly against the glass as well as my hands. Soul pounded inside my pussy mercilessly from behind. I threw my ass back on his dick trying to break his shit. My head flew back in ecstasy. The only thing I was thinking about was getting this orgasm out of me. The shit felt so strong and was intensifying with every thrust he gave me.

"Fuck!"

I tossed my ass back even harder. I felt my juices dripping down my inner thighs.

"Ooh, Soul!" I whimpered.

His large hand went around my throat squeezing it. I felt my climax nearing. My heart rate sped up in my chest. Right before I reached my peak, I felt something coming up my chest. I pushed back off the glass and Soul's dick slipped out of me. My hand went up covering my mouth as I ran toward the bathroom.

"Bae, you alright!" he called out behind me.

Just as soon as I made it to the toilet and pulled my hair back out my face, I instantly began throwing up. "Fuck, not aga—"

The End.

I'M ADDICTED TO HIS LOVE

PLEASE BE KIND ENOUGH TO LEAVE A REVIEW

Good or bad, I'd really love to hear from you.

Facebook: www.facebook.com/authortaniece
Personal Facebook: Taniece McDaniel
Join my reading group: Taniece's Reading Group
Instagram: www.instagram.com/taniece
Twitter: www.twitter.com/_taniece_
Email: Taniece91@gmail.com
Website: www.novelsbytaniece.weebly.com

Also, by Taniece
I Wanna Be Your Girl: A Love Story (Incomplete)
She Got A Hitta Catching Feelings 1-2
A Kiss Sealed With Fate: A Novella

CPSIA information can be obtained
at www.ICGtesting.com
Printed in the USA
LVHW110746130220
646719LV00011B/725

9 798600 980211